Cheers for
The Executrix

" . . . *The Executrix* is one of those books hard to put down, something like your eyeballs being attached to it with Gorilla Glue. You'll like this first of a planned trilogy and perhaps so much so you'll impatiently await the successive volumes."

—Pat Wilkins, *West Side Newspaper,* Salem, OR

"*The Executrix* arrived and I could not put it down. The story sucked me in and kept me hostage until finished. Courtney Pierce is an awesome story teller . . . "

—Reader Review, *The Executrix*

" . . . I loved it, and other items on my to-do list were totally ignored until I had finished reading the final chapter—twice!

—Reader Review, Jan's Paperback's, *The Executrix*

Cheers for
The Stitches Trilogy

"*Stitches* is a treasure of simple story telling at its best…Courtney's ability to describe her characters and the places they live and visit is second to none, in my book. I can think of many lauded authors who should have her ability…Courtney had touched a place in my heart with her characters.

—Reader Review, *Stitches*

"The way she describes the painting absolutely brings it to life in my mind's eye. I enjoy being transported into a life of magic, fun, and adventure with Courtney Pierce leading the way."

—Reader Review, *Brushes*

"I LOVED *RIFFS*! As the third volume, it was like visiting old friends and going on their adventures with them. It reminds me of *Hart to Hart* with a magical side. I would suggest this book to anyone who likes, adventure, romance, intrigue, and wonderful characters. I will miss them."

—Reader Review, *Riffs*

Indigo

Lake

Courtney Pierce

Windtree Press
Hillsboro, OR
http://windtreepress.com

Windtree Press
Hillsboro, OR
http://windreepress.com

Cover Illustration:

Jake Pierce

Autumn on Indigo Lake

Oil on canvas
Used by Permission

ISBN-10: 1-943601-19-4
ISBN-13: 978-1-943601-19-6

Dedication

To my Mom, Aunt Ann, Uncle Harry, and Aunt Martha.
Uncle Alph would've fixed everything to make my characters happy.
You're all heroes.

"Sisters don't need words. They have perfected a language of snarls and smiles and frowns and winks—expressions of shocked surprise and incredulity and disbelief. Sniffs and snorts and gasps and sighs—that can undermine any tale you're telling."

~ Pam Brown

Acknowledgements

My singular triumph in life is that I've been married to the same wonderful, rockin' man since 1979. Second to that, my ability to make my mom and my two sisters laugh out loud as they see themselves in my characters is pretty high on the fun meter. Books are a family affair, and my nephew, Jake Pierce, yet again, did me proud on creating the oil painting for the cover. The original will hang in a place of honor.

My editor, Kristin Thiel, wiggled her fingers to get her hands on this manuscript. That she looks forward to reading my books tickles me to no end. With her lovely cat, Izzy, on her lap, Kristin keeps me coloring inside the lines.

Every writer needs a Carole Florian, a dear friend, a grammarian, and a story scientist. She laughs at my jokes, not at my mistakes, and explains the reasoning for every change. I'm forever grateful for her expertise and friendship.

Endless thanks go to my critique group, the Sisters in Scene. Their valuable feedback every week and emotional investment in my story fueled me to the finish. Because of these amazing women, I had a love story on my hands.

Several early readers provided inspiration at every stage. Thank yous go to Helen Dupre, Christina Dupre, Debbie Gerber, Tina Jacobsen, and best-selling author Karen Karbo. Their thumbs up gave me pause to appreciate how lucky I am to have their support.

My literary family at Windtree Press keeps me on my toes in the real world of publishing. From social media and websites to distribution and trends, Maggie Lynch helps all the authors at Windtree to remain current in an ever-changing marketplace.

Finally, I owe a round of applause for the continued support of independent bookstores, especially Jan's Paperbacks in Aloha, Another Read Through in North Portland, Jacobsen's Books & More in Hillsboro, and the Reader's Guide Bookstore in Salem. They work tirelessly to turn readers into fans. Special hugs to Tina Jacobsen.

Chapter 1

The Spider's Invitation

The release of Olivia Novak's new novel, *The Executrix*, sent her into a cleaning frenzy of her three-bedroom, 1920s Tudor in Eastmoreland, a quiet suburb across the Willamette River from downtown Portland, Oregon. This book didn't fit into her normal genre of romance. This one showcased her two sisters . . . and her mother. Olivia's die-hard fans might never understand, but her mother's death had changed everything.

To burn off nervous energy, Olivia changed the sheets, buffed the glass stovetop, and polished the granite on the kitchen island to a brilliant shine. She moved to the front entryway with a Swiffer duster. A black spider in the corner of the ceiling caught her eye. Unacceptable. Dealing with hard-to-reach critters had been Adam's job.

Thirty-two years of marriage couldn't be erased with Adam's sudden loss from a hit-and-run accident. Even after five years, Olivia still expected him to pull into the garage from picking up that stupid lemon at the store. Hours had marched into days, into months, into years in her obsessive hunt for the white Suburban that had taken his life, their life together. When the culprits were finally found by Ryan, a Portland cop and her younger sister's husband, the distraction of pursuit had settled to quiet, the house even more so.

Olivia hauled the vacuum from the hall closet, the extension wand ready to suck up the eight-leg menace. When the phone rang, she eyed the ceiling.

"You wait right there. I'll be back." Olivia padded to the kitchen in stocking feet—never shoes in the house—and snatched up the receiver.

"How much do you worship me as your agent?" Karen Finnerelli said in her thick New York accent. Rhetorical questions from her literary agent were always followed with a zinger.

"All right, I'll bite," she said and tiptoed back to the front hall. The critter skittered along the ceiling to the stairwell. "I worship you more than my Miele vacuum. How's that?"

"Then suck up this. You, Lauren, Danny, and Pogo are going on the *Wake Up with Jo Show.*"

Olivia dropped the cord. "Are you kidding? My sisters and the dog too?"

"Joanna Josephson's going to interview you herself. Pack your bags. You're all in the air Sunday and on the air Monday morning."

"I'm not ready." Olivia raced back to the kitchen and rummaged through the junk drawer for a pen and the pad of sticky notes with the saying: *Smile while you still have teeth.*

"It's only Thursday. You've got three days to get ready. I'll email you all the details. And you might be asked about your mother's book. There's interest in a movie deal, so mention Ellen's book as many times as you can."

"A movie of *Mom's* book?"

"Separate conversation."

Olivia tossed the pen back in the drawer. Always her mother. After her death two years ago, Ellen Dushane had become a one-hit wonder by happenstance. When Olivia had found the manuscript for *Indigo to Black* in the safe and submitted it to her agent, her mother's book became celebrated beyond anything Olivia, herself, had written. It had even won the prestigious National Book Critics Circle Award.

"Some pretty famous names are being tossed around for the character of Becky."

"Like who?"

"Confidential—but Taylor Swift."

Olivia's jaw dropped. "She's a pop star, not an actress. Lauren and Danny might get squishy about that choice."

"Climb out of your writing cave, Liv, and board the marketing pain train."

"Lauren's never been on television."

"She'll be fine."

"Danny's going to insist Pogo sits in his own seat on the plane."

"Four in first class. Done. Gotta go."

Karen clicked off. *Lord.* Danny would be easy to convince; she loved attention. Her younger sister never went anywhere without Pogo, the stately standard poodle she'd turned into a therapy dog, but Lauren might be another matter. This development was best delivered in person.

Olivia raced back to the entryway and grabbed the vacuum hose. Her Himalayan cat, Freesia, stood at the top of the stairs, blinking her crystal blues as if the commotion had disturbed her afternoon nap. Freesia's mink-brown mask offered a permanent frown of disappointment in humans. The spider had disappeared.

With her hands on her hips, Olivia raised her eyes. "You're a big help."

An image of the invader sneaking upstairs to crawl into bed would be hard to erase. Olivia clattered the vacuum cleaner back into the closet.

"This is your *job*, Baby Girl. I don't ask you to do much, but I expect you to get bugs in the house." Olivia tied her sneakers. "The vet thinks you're adorable, but I've got your number."

Freesia didn't appreciate the dictation of chores. The cat's brown muzzle puffed in protest: *I don't do bugs.*

"Get that spider while I'm over at Lauren's."

Silence.

Olivia did one last scan of the ceiling before she pulled the front door shut.

~ · ~ · ~

Olivia's older sister lived right next door—sometimes too close; other times not close enough—in a Tudor a bit smaller than Olivia's. Lauren only wanted to garden, watch disaster movies, read, and wait for Olivia to cook for two. Convincing her to appear on television next week required some finesse, maybe a dose of guilt. Olivia would get "the jaw."

Lauren inherited Mom's stubborn jaw, the one that locked up with refusal to explain her outrageous claims. A newly retired sixty-two going on sixteen. And then there was Mom's book.

For the past two years, their mother continued to live everywhere: online in tweets, in comments on Facebook, in glowing reviews, and in speculative chatter at literary events. *Are you sure Ellen's book is fiction? Did Ellen's story really happen? Give us the scoop.* Mom popped up every day, somewhere. Whether Ellen Dushane had intended it or not, royalties from *Indigo to Black* had become the bulk of her and her sisters' inheritance.

On her trek across the driveway to Lauren's house, Olivia planned out the conversation. She'd made a habit of glancing at the faded oil stain on the cracked concrete, the discoloration left from Ardy Griffin's broken-down Datsun.

"Rest in peace, Ardy," she said.

The press of the doorbell released a long peal of carillon bells inside. Lauren kept the door locked—for good reason. The mob had believed Ardy Griffin lived in the house when they'd made an attempt on his life. After Lauren moved in, Olivia couldn't shake the possibility of her sister becoming a residual target. Olivia had learned in short order from writing Ardy's story that a fine line separated association and guilt.

"It's meeee," Olivia said and peered over the iron rail to assess the yard. Fresh mulch for fall crowned the garden bed under the front widow. Organized piles of crocus, tulip, and hyacinth bulbs sat next to an abandoned spade, ready to be planted before the first frost. Lauren took personal pride in owning the home after years in an apartment. Her husband's death from cancer right about the time Olivia lost Adam had left them both adrift in their own worlds. It took their mother's death to bring them together again.

Five stomps behind the front door preceded the clatter of the chain and turn of the deadbolt. Lauren opened the door dressed in overwashed navy-blue sweats, her chestnut hair frazzled. "C'mon. Help me figure out what to do with this damn chicken breast. I've been staring at the dead thing for fifteen minutes. Lunch is in it somewhere. Then I have to deal with those bulbs."

Lauren re-bolted the door after Olivia stepped inside and kicked off her sneakers. In quick step, she followed her sister down the short hall to the small kitchen. The French doors were wide open to a quaint patio, also known as Lauren's smoking area until she quit.

"Do you have a lemon, olive oil, and some fresh basil?" Olivia said. The white tiled counters with contrasting brown grout and the old avocado appliances needed an update. "You can broil it, slice off thin strips, and put them on greens. Drizzle apple cider vinegar over the whole thing for dressing." While Lauren had won the battle to kick the cigs, the battle to maintain her weight raged on, not quite as rancorous as the Hatfields and McCoys, but close. Maybe the issue had something to do with a box of white zinfandel in her refrigerator and the turn of its spigot.

"Sounds like too much work." Lauren scowled. "Fresh *basil?* What do you think I'm running here, a test kitchen for the Food Network?" She stared at the raw chicken breast like an *Iron Chef* contestant charged with turning it into cheesy potato skins.

"Put it back in the fridge for dinner. Fix something else." Olivia studied the ice crystals on the frost-bitten specimen. "How about a can of tuna?"

"Had fish yesterday. What I really want is a bowl of popcorn with butter and Parmesan."

Olivia pulled a baking pan from a drawer beneath the stove and plopped the sparkly road kill in the center. After a vigorous hand-washing, she rummaged through the cabinet for a bottle of olive oil and a jar of lemon pepper. The chicken got a drizzle and a sprinkle. With the press of a worn button that read *roil*, Olivia set the broiler on high and shoved the pan on the top rack.

"There. Lunch in twenty minutes. I need to tell you something."

Lauren sighed. "What? That I need clean my oven?"

"No—well, yes, you do—but we need to go to New York first." Olivia scrunched her eyes as the words landed.

"What do I want to go to that pit for?" With a fist on her hip, Lauren wrinkled her nose. "The streets stink and the people smell worse."

"Think of this as a vacation. We've been invited to be on the *Wake Up with Jo Show* on Monday—all of us: me, you, Danny, and Pogo. Joanna Josephsen is going to interview us. Danny doesn't know, yet."

"Ohhhh, no. TV makes people look fat. Even the skinny ones." Lauren snapped the elastic on her waistband.

"You've lost weight. You're fine." A boost of Lauren's ego might help move the conversation forward. No matter what she did, Lauren's weight remained the same. Medical tests all came up normal. The Fitbit step monitor had finally come off her wrist, a miserable failure blamed on bad software.

"Liv, I don't do PR. That's your thing."

"Well . . . it's *our* thing with the release of this book. Karen said we *all* have to be there. I guarantee Danny and Pogo will go." Seal the deal with the odd-sister-out argument.

"I'm still doing consulting work part-time. I'm only home because I took a sick day." Her dark-brown eyes rolled. "See this distended stomach? I'm starving to death."

Olivia pulled out the emergency talking stick of guilt. "Do this for Mom."

"That was a low blow, Liv."

"And Karen thinks there might be interest in Mom's book for a movie deal."

Lauren studied the ceiling and blew out a breath. "Do I need to talk?"

"Only if you want to. All you have to do is sit, keep your legs crossed, and smile."

"Ugh. Is your publisher buying the ticket?"

"Yep. We leave early Sunday morning."

Mom's voice lurked, giving advice to each of her children. Olivia could hear her mother assessing each of them:

Lauren had a loose tongue under the influence of wine and an amazing ability to catch a fly in mid-air. Mom would say, *get behind it; they take off backwards*. Olivia had inherited her mother's love of books and the obsession to clean to keep up appearances. *You never know who's going to show up at your front door. Stay one step ahead with a change of sheets.* Danny—Mom's favorite—had sucked up everything their mother had to give. *Leave her alone. She works so hard.*

"Let's call Danny." Olivia lunged for the phone, triumphant.

Old mobster Ardy had had a soft spot for Danny too, and left her and Ryan his enormous black standard poodle named Pogo. Danny trained and certified the dog for therapy and service—but Pogo became his own version of a spoiled crime boss. The poodle was in high demand and even had his own fan base.

Olivia called the number for the small downtown office suite where Danny managed the Pogo Charitable Trust. The three sisters funded the endeavor from half the royalties of their mother's book and went into partnership with the Oregon Humane Society to train shelter dogs as therapy companions.

Within two rings, Danny picked up.

"You're on speaker," Olivia said.

"I'm trying to finalize Pogo's schedule for next week," Danny said. "Ryan and I think he's overcommitted. Three hospitals, two assisted-living facilities, and training sessions at OHS are too much. Pogo's worn out." Papers rustled in the background. "What's up?"

Danny, the youngest at forty-seven, was never denied anything with those love-me-forever chocolate eyes of Mom's. Hard to believe Danny lacked confidence with all those enviable Mom parts: shapely legs, tiny waist, and shiny dark hair that didn't frizz in any type of weather. Danny got the whole spoiled package, including her childhood bedroom—since she had been Mom's live-in caregiver—and the freedom to sleep until noon before marrying Ryan.

"You and Pogo need to take a break." Olivia nodded and stuck out her tongue to Lauren. "The four of us are going to New York on Sunday to be on the *Wake Up with Jo Show*."

"Shut *up*." Danny's voice brightened as she turned from the phone. "Want to go on a trip, Pogo? Be on television? Show everybody you're a pretty boy?"

Olivia churned her hand at the dog's barked response in the background.

"Pogo's in. What should I wear?"

"Tasteful. Think grant presentation." Olivia pictured Danny packing three suitcases: two stuffed with designer wear for herself, one for Pogo filled with special food, toys, spa towel, blanket, and a back-up therapy-dog vest. She'd pat at the air, sporting black sunglasses and pretending to be blind so Pogo received special treatment. Either that, or Pogo would mush Danny like a sled dog as he rode the luggage dolly.

"Pogo gets his own seat on the plane, right?" Danny said. A condition of flight.

"Yes . . . Service dogs can go in the cabin. I'll request the bulkhead."

"He really should be in first class." Danny turned again from the phone. "Right, Pogs? Big boys need cushy leather seats?"

Ruh . . . Ruh . . . Ruh.

"Karen's taking care of it," Olivia said. "Check with Ryan. See if he can drop us off at the airport on Sunday morning—*early*, which means you have to get up early too."

Olivia hung up and shook her head at Lauren's rump. Bent over, her sister stared at the browning chicken breast through the clouded oven door. "Well . . . This is going to be a royal fiasco."

Lauren turned her head. "And this would be way better with mozzarella, noodles, and tomato sauce."

Chapter 2
Della

At ten o'clock on Friday morning, Della Rainey gummed the final spoonful of milk-soaked Shredded Wheat and set the bowl in the sink. She popped in her dentures in preparation for the ten-minute trip to Alten's Books on her three-wheeled bicycle. Her health-nut son hammered on her about the need to exercise. Today, the '77 Pinto could stay behind; this might be her last bike ride of the year. A September chill signaled that the recent Indian summer had made its exit from Tuftenboro, New Hampshire. The New England fall colors might peak in a week or so, Della's favorite fiery show of vivid red, burnt orange, and warm gold. Three wraps of a long knit scarf and the final button-up of her plaid wool coat and she was off. She gave the front door an extra tug to make sure it latched.

Today might be a good haul if Catherine Pratt wasn't in a foul mood. Pickings had been good because of those who wanted to purge their attics and basements before being cooped up for the winter.

Even at the age of eighty-seven, Della aimed for the leaf piles at the side of the road, triumphant at the crunch under her wheels. Small activities became a competition. Her one good foot did all the work for the skid-stop in front of the bookstore entrance. With a wince, she dismounted and hobbled to the rear wire basket filled with books, her latest estate sale finds. The gout in her foot slowed Della's trek. Her swollen big toe throbbed with pain, and the boot the doctor put on at Huggins Hospital in Wolfeboro crimped her style. Della took inventory and piled the titles on her portable luggage cart: three Stephen King's, two out-of-print Beverly Barton romances, one Ayn Rand, and three Steve Martini legal thrillers. Even though not a first edition, Diana Gabaldon's *Outlander* might get a spot on the shelf before going back out the door.

Fridays bustled at Alten's Books. A positive sign for negotiations to go her way. Locals paired hard work with new reads for the weekend. Della dragged her squeaky handcart to the door of the quaint shop, a brown two-story colonial converted from the old general store. Every step shot pain up her leg.

The bell tinkled as Della pushed open the front door of the bookshop. The aromas of both aging and fresh paper drew her forward, albeit with no small amount of effort. She needed a good book, and the latest haul might produce enough for a decent trade—with any luck, with some change to spare.

Della abandoned her cart at the counter and moved to the main display of hot sellers. One book titled *Indigo to Black* held a prominent place in the lineup. The sign read: *Now in Paperback.* How had she missed this? The vibrant watercolor image on the cover caught her attention: Indigo Lake, less than an hour away. She'd given a similar work to her cousin back in the forties. Or the exact same one? A different version sat in her own kitchen. The author's name took her off guard: *Ellen Dushane.* Della grazed her hand over the raised letters of the title. It couldn't be the same. A table tent extolled a handwritten endorsement: *Hang on to your hat. This thriller's local. Real? Or fiction?* Next to *Indigo to Black* sat the new release of *The Executrix* by Olivia Novak. The sign read, *Ellen Dushane's daughter releases a wild ride. Gotta love Novak. She keeps us guessing.*

With both titles under her arm, Della limped in her boot to the cash register, ready to do battle with the owner, Catherine Pratt.

"Do you have these used?" Della said.

"Sorry, Della," Catherine said. "I can't even beg for a used one. Folks read *Indigo to Black* over and over and give it to friends. You're lucky I got this new shipment. I've been out for a while now. Olivia Novak's book is a new release."

Della grimaced and jutted her chin toward her cart. "Will you take these in trade?" Paying full retail price for books was unthinkable, and the long wait at the library would never do. She turned over the book and read the back cover of *Indigo to Black*. The suction of her dentures clicked against her gums as she gave her lips a nervous lick.

Catherine stepped around the counter to assess Della's trade-ins, fiddling with the zipper on her fleece vest. Intelligent hazel eyes examined the titles like lasers scanning UPC codes on boxes of cereal. She pointed to the stack. "Your trade-ins plus ten dollars."

"*Ten* dollars?"

"Ten dollars. You didn't pay more than fifty cents apiece for those books, Della. I'll grant you the Diana Gabaldon is worth a few bucks. *The Executrix* is brand new. A bestseller. I'm being generous. Lucky for you *Indigo to Black* is now in softcover."

"Ellen Dushane's my cousin. And Olivia Novak is her daughter. I want a family discount."

Catherine sighed. "Must we get into a fracas, Della? You're making that up."

Della pinwheeled her arms. "I mean, call her, if you want!"

"Ellen Dushane died two years ago." Catherine's tone was that of a person speaking to a child. "You're lying about that."

Della widened her eyes at the news, and they became even wider behind the thick lenses of her glasses. No one had bothered to contact her about Ellen's death. "I'm not. I swear I'm not."

Della sensed a crack in Catherine's shell as the woman studied her.

"Well . . . I'll give those to you for five then."

Pawing through her coin purse, Della produced three curled one-dollar bills. Her plump fingers picked out four quarters, five dimes, eight nickels, and ten pennies. She scooted the coins into a pile.

The cash register drawer popped open, and Catherine did her own quick count. She separated the change and unfurled the bills. "Thanks, Della. You'll like these." Catherine pushed the drawer shut and handed over the two new books in a reusable cloth bag.

Della frowned. "I'd bettah for that much." She inspected the bag, thinking her groceries would fit.

Della hobbled out of the bookstore with the bag and her empty cart, sure the bell over the door laughed behind her back. A rip-off. The hooks of a bungee cord secured everything to her wire bike basket. Pity discount. A chilly breeze gusted through the birch trees, producing a flurry of gold leaves that had lost their fight to hang on. She gripped the handles of her bike and pushed off with her good foot. Ellen Dushane might be dead, but the story wasn't. And Ellen's daughters were to blame.

~ · ~ · ~

At six forty-five on Sunday morning, Olivia stood in her driveway, her laptop case stacked on her roller bag. She'd learned after years of book tours to travel with only a carry-on, no matter how long the trip. A frugal pack sped her right past the aggravation of baggage claim. Climbing Mount Hood was easier than conquering the airport; her survival gear included black slacks, black suit jacket, a pair of yoga pants, an oversize T-shirt, and four blouses in the same style but in different colors. The zipper on her case required extra finesse to accommodate her favorite loose-knit cardigan and a taupe turtleneck. A couple of necklaces and scarfs were tucked in for oomph. Her sisters were another matter. Lauren and Danny would have been racing around to assemble four options per day, with Pogo stuffing his own suitcase with toys.

The seven o'clock pickup time closed in. Thirteen more minutes. Her new stress centered on Danny's arrangement of the cat sitter for Freesia. As she waited, Olivia counted how long it took for the steam of her breath to dissipate in the frosty morning air.

Lauren's screen door hissed open next door. Her sister's gigantic, soft-sided Samsonite bumped through with Lauren behind it. The case clunked down her front steps as she wrestled with her equally huge purse. Olivia didn't worry about forgetting anything, because emergency supplies could be garnered from the depths of Lauren's handbag.

"Why did we get up so early, Liv?" Her sister's eyes drooped. The purple fleece jacket over her matching purple jogging suit made Lauren appear to be an eggplant hovering over grass.

Olivia scratched her nose. "You needed time to get ready . . . " Her voice trailed off, pretending she saw headlights approach.

"I'm sorry I'm not a light packer like you, but it's not all clothes." Lauren hesitated. "There's a gun in my suitcase."

Olivia stared at her older sister with an open mouth. "A what?" The outfit was one thing, but guns had no place in her life.

"I'm legal. I have a permit."

"Jesus, God." Olivia squinted her eyes as the first rays of sun poked through the trees. "I don't want to travel with you."

"Well, that's about to change. You'll thank me if somebody tries to mug us in New York."

Olivia had only herself to blame for her sister's paranoia. Two years ago, Olivia didn't know that her neighbor, R. D. Griffin—Ardy as he was affectionately called—had received a warning from a crime boss after she'd written his memoir. Ryan knew, though. At his suggestion, the manuscript for *Protection* remained locked away in a safe-deposit box, too explosive to publish without potential retaliation by the mob against her, Lauren, and Danny. Her lawyer, Ted Beal, held the only key. After being moved with the Witness Protection Program, Ardy passed away at the age of ninety-three. Lauren moved into Ardy's house, and Pogo was left in Danny and Ryan's care. One day, someday in the future when Ardy's colleagues mentioned in the book were dead, the story of *Protection* would be sent to Olivia's literary agency.

Headlights flashed twice as Ryan pulled the police cruiser into the driveway. Per regulation, Danny sat in the backseat with Pogo. The dog bobbed back and forth behind the grilled separator used to contain perpetrators. Danny stepped from the car to reveal her designer outfit: a brown leather jacket with a turquoise silk shell. Her matching leather pants and heels were stunning, but she resembled a runway biker chick, not the director of a charitable foundation. Pogo swaggered out of the cruiser in his yellow service-dog vest like a dignitary descending from Air Force One. He immediately trotted to Olivia's Japanese maple by the front door and lifted his leg.

"Good boy, Pogo," Danny said. "All empty." The poodle bounded back to the cruiser and hopped into the front passenger seat. Seating for five allowed a breaking of the rules.

"The boys get to chauffeur the girls," Ryan said and opened the trunk.

Danny clicked the shoulder belt over Pogo's chest. "Liv, Maria will be here at ten. Why do you need a live-in sitter when all Freesia does is sleep?"

Relief washed through Olivia as she wheeled her case to the trunk. "Freesia needs her box cleaned within five seconds of her using it."

Ryan shoved Olivia's carry-on inside and stood ready to do the heavy lifting of Lauren's monster. Danny, as predicted, had brought three suitcases, all lined neatly on the bottom. Olivia slid into the middle spot of the backseat with her laptop, and three doors closed in sequence. Ryan and Pogo turned in the front seat to study the sisters, coincidentally lined up by age behind the partition. Olivia pictured herself as lunchmeat stuffed between two slices of bread.

"All set?" Ryan said. The dog sniffed the perp screen. Everyone accounted for.

Olivia pursed her lips. "If *one* of us doesn't end up in jail before we get to New York."

"Why?" Danny said.

Lauren scratched her lip. "Liv's freaked out about my gun."

Olivia flexed her forefinger toward the front seat. "Shhhh . . . "

Ryan smirked as he pulled out of the driveway. "I got it for her."

"You did? When?" A conspiracy. Both sisters remained quiet.

"About a year ago. She asked me for one, and I trained her how to use it. After the threat to Ardy, and her now living in his house, Lauren needed protection. She's damn good too. I'll bet she can shoot the fuzz off a caterpillar and the critter wouldn't even break stride."

"I wish I didn't know about it."

"Me neither," Danny said and pulled a tin of Altoids from her purse. "I don't want anything to do with the things."

Lauren shrugged. She reached across Olivia and held out her hand. "Give me one of those."

Olivia stared at the partition and opened her palm.

Chapter 3
Della Reads the Book

After a quick lunch on Sunday, Della sucked on sour-lemon hard candies for the second read-through of *Indigo to Black*. The first pass had been too fast. Today, she took time to absorb the vivid details, as if she were reading about someone else. Her gout-ridden foot ached from lack of movement. She closed the cover and smoothed her hand over the image of the watercolor she had given to Ellen on her sixteenth birthday—long before things got ugly. Decades later, Della gave a similar one to her son, Woody, for his birthday. Her own hung on the wall by the kitchen sink.

The serene watercolors depicted Indigo Lake wrapped in autumn hues of ochre, spicy paprika, and shocks of scarlet that lined the blue-black water. Darkness beneath the light. Back in the forties, she'd traded the three pictures by a local artist for a box of apples at the Tuftenboro General Store, only a mile away. The general store had become Alten's Books. Now, gazing at the very image on the cover, it dawned on her that an ugly and painful past might turn into an opportunity.

Della sat frozen after finishing Ellen's book: the story of a young girl, Becky Haines, who sought revenge on her boyfriend for standing her up on the beach. Della pictured the scene as if the slight had happened only yesterday.

Ellen's words might have been easier to ignore by focusing on the picture had they not captured Della's anguish with such vivid clarity. She'd waited on the beach for Asher, as the character Becky Haines had waited for her beau, who also never came. As in the book, fireflies and sparkles from the moon's reflection really did trip across the water of Indigo Lake that first night of summer camp. They'd met the year before. The long twelve months of handwritten letters had stretched hope. He was waiting for her. They would be reunited. The promise of her future had ticked with the second hand to nine o'clock, the time they'd arranged in their last letters to meet. The call of a loon overlay the footfalls in the sand. A hand, too feminine to be Asher's, rested on her shoulder—her cousin, Ellen Dushane. The words Ellen spoke could never be erased:

"Asher won't leave his cabin, Della. He's not coming."

In silence—shock really—Della had turned to her cousin. For an entire year, Asher had wooed her with promises and a lavish family home in Boston on Beacon Hill, with even a summer home on Cohasset harbor. He'd guaranteed a life above her station. And she'd counted on it.

Ellen handed her a ripped note on ruled paper, heavy from absorbing the humidity. Its limp texture and Della's shaking hands made unfolding the note difficult. She'd mustered the courage. Two ghostly words in black ink emerged through the blue-gray reflection of moonlight:

I can't . . .

"What does he mean *he can't?*" Della said.

"He didn't go into details, Del. I'm only the messenger."

Della's gaze locked on her cousin's. Ellen's dark eyes flickered in the uncomfortable silence. Ellen was prettier, thinner, and had all that hair. She'd bet that Asher fell in love with the lyrical lilt of Ellen's voice. Della's own finally found a way out, a rumbling from deep in her throat.

"He's going to regret this, Ellen . . . Both of you will."

"Do you want me to talk with him? Maybe I can—"

"No. I'll deal with this myself."

Wrath churned inside her, as it still churned nearly seventy years later, becoming molten and noxious. The memory never faded. Della's angry toe peeked above the opening of her elevated boot. She saw only red.

Della pulled the lever to lower the footrest and hauled herself up from the Barcalounger. The rotary wall phone in the kitchen drew her gaze. This might change everything for the better, fate finally shifting to her side of the line. Della pictured a house with more space for her estate sale finds, with lawn maintenance people blowing her leaves, and neighbors like the ones in that new development, Baxter Fields, up the road.

With a grunt, she picked up the book and limped the ten steps to the receiver. The coils of the cord rippled around the fingers on one hand; with the other, she whirled the cloudy dial. Woody usually worked at his law office on Sundays, but he might be out on Lake Winnipesaukee kayaking with his pilot friend, Casey. Three rings. She breathed when he answered.

"Ma? Everything all right?" Woody's deep, smooth voice registered sincere concern, a quality she appreciated, but she prepared for an onslaught of probing questions. Della had to remind herself not to get flustered. Woody was known for his calm, controlled manner, which unnerved his legal adversaries.

"About to be all right," Della said. She attempted to straighten the soiled curlicue of the phone cord, then opened Ellen's book and studied the copyright page. "I want you to sue Sloane Publishing . . . and Olivia Novak."

"Who? For what?"

"Plagiarism. Copyright infringement. Defamation of character. Pain and suffering. I don't care what you threaten. I want half the royalties."

"Back up. What's going on? You never wrote a book."

"My cousin wrote one that her daughters published. It's my story, Woody."

"You have a cousin?"

"*Had* a cousin. Ellen Dushane. Apparently, she died two years ago. I found out today from Catherine at Alten's."

"I'm so sorry." His tone became sympathetic. "You've never mentioned her."

"I'm mentioning it now. Don't be sorry. Her daughters will be sorry."

"What's the title again?" A drawer in the eighteenth-century desk in Woody's office opened and closed. Computer keys clicked.

"I didn't say, but it's *Indigo to Black*, like Indigo Lake in Vermont." More clicking.

"When was the book originally written?"

"Early fifties. She was supposed to destroy the manuscript."

"Hmmm . . . A challenge. Timing's not on your side," Woody said. "While she didn't destroy it, she didn't publish it either."

"Her daughters are liable."

"That remains to be seen. What are Ellen's daughters' names?"

"Olivia Novak's the one you want. The other two are Lauren Lyndale and Danielle Dushane."

"Shouldn't you be connecting with her daughters instead of suing them?"

"Never met 'em. That Olivia Novak probably has gatekeepers so the public doesn't bug her." Della wished her brain worked as fast as Woody's. He'd learn more about the girls in the next few minutes than she had in the past fifty years. More clicking of keys on his new-fangled computer.

"Olivia Novak is everywhere," he said. "She'll be easy. Lauren Lyndale retired from a real estate firm. Danielle must go by a different last name. Nothing comes up about her on the Internet."

With the phone balanced in the crook of her neck, Della flipped to the back pages of the book. "Says in the notes that half the proceeds go to the Pogo Charitable Trust."

While she waited, Della stared at her cousin's photo: an older Ellen Dushane in her seventies, wide smile, with one hand on top of a wide-brimmed gardening hat. Damn her. Ellen hadn't changed much from when they were kids, but then again, her cousin was dead.

"Got it," Woody said. "She's Danielle Eason." He scratched more notes. "Have you read Novak's new book?"

"Not yet, but I hear it's selling at a good clip. Olivia's the deep pocket."

"Says that *Indigo to Black* is fiction. There's no justification for claiming a fictional novel is based on true events unless specifically stated, or real names are used in an inflammatory manner. The book has a clear disclaimer. Is this book based on fact?"

"A good bit tells real details."

"You didn't answer the question."

Della gummed her dentures. Her son's voice had changed from familial to all business, as if grilling her on the witness stand.

"Table that for now," Woody said. "Are you mentioned in the book by name?" His pen stopped scratching, waiting.

"No, but it's real. I know it is." Della's fingers tightened on the receiver.

"I'm not a literary attorney, Ma. Maybe you should—"

"No. I'll only work with you. You're my son. I'm not explaining myself to a stranger."

"Sounds like you don't want to explain yourself to me, either. But the fact that this book got published posthumously is interesting. Could work in your favor—or not. Two years is a long time before filing a grievance. The publisher will want to know why we didn't come forward sooner. I'll pick up a copy of the book, so I can read it."

"I don't want to wait. Can't you send a threatening letter tomorrow?" Della closed her eyes, hoping to see something from this effort. "At the very least, they'll get scared and settle."

Woody's breath filled the phone. She listened for an inhale.

"Mom . . . " Woody hesitated. "I need more information—factual information—before we do anything."

"Let's meet tomorrow early at Wolfe's Tavern." Della stared at the happy, marching gingerbread man logo on the bread wrapper from the Yum Yum Shop. If she was going to make the trip into Wolfeboro, a stop at the bakery was in order. "You're buying."

"Let me do some research on the sisters this afternoon." Woody sighed. "A busy schedule tomorrow. I'm wrapping up the lawsuit against Cleary's Funeral Home. Eldridge's property dispute is draining what's left."

"This needs to be a priority."

"We'll have breakfast at eight thirty, then we'll come back to the office and put something together. Need anything else?"

"Everything. And we're about to get it. I'm your number one client, Woody. Don't forget that." Della set the receiver on the cradle. Woody would do well to remember she'd picked out everything in his hoity-toity office, never mind that he'd shelled out the cash. What's cash without taste?

The urge to buy something, trade something, welled in her chest. Della tried to ignore the stabbing pain behind her eyes. Instead, she pulled two slices of homemade bread from the long bag and made a ham sandwich with a slice of Vermont sharp cheddar to satisfy the grumble. The next book waited: *The Executrix.*

~ · ~ · ~

With one hand still resting on the receiver, Woodrow Rainey took off his tortoiseshell glasses and tossed them on his desk. So much for getting work done while the office was quiet on Sunday. His mother had come up with some pretty wild schemes in her eighty-seven the-world-is-out-to-get-me years, but this topped the list.

Gathering the papers for the Cleary lawsuit, Woody tapped the thick folder to align the pages and set it aside. Class action lawsuits in Wolfeboro, New Hampshire weren't like those on Wall Street; they were rare, especially against a long-standing, trusted member of the community. Cleary's Funeral Home had broken that trust, and Walt

Cleary might become a broken man from the ordeal. This phase—the part where he could see the finish line—of any lawsuit was Woody's least favorite part of being a lawyer in a small town. One party always limped away, worse for the experience—but both parties would still find themselves standing together in line at the grocery store.

Cleary's lawyer couldn't deny that Walt had mixed the dead, both cremated and interred, to save costs. The trouble started when Walt attempted to expand his business to pets. Empty urns were resold. The DNA tests on bits of bone had proved old Fido, a beloved barn dog, was spending the hereafter with Aunt Mathilda. Maneuvering through the emotional case took patience and charisma to shepherd all parties to an acceptable conclusion. Woody's goal next week was to encourage the shaking of hands over the quavering of hearts. Now, the process might take a bit longer.

Woody's gaze drifted back to his computer screen. He leaned back in his antique chair, rescued by his mother from the asset liquidation of a hundred-year-old bank in Moultenborough, and rested his stocking feet on his desk. A relative by the name of Ellen Dushane had never been mentioned in all his sixty-two years. Not once. Woody not only recognized the name Olivia Novak, but could see her books clear as day: the raised, reflective-gold cursive letters of her name graced suggestive book covers spinning on paperback racks at the supermarket, the pharmacy, and even at the Qwik-Mart gas station.

Olivia Novak stared back at him from the photo on her website, as if she might reach out her hand to shake on a deal. Something else about her caught his eye. This woman didn't get frazzled. Keen intelligence in her deep-brown eyes drew him forward. Her smile expanded his ribs. Calm. Quiet. Open. This Olivia Novak would pose no problem at all.

Chapter 4

Welcome to New York

A ll Olivia wanted was a hot shower. As the wheels of the plane hit the tarmac at La Guardia Airport, Olivia felt frazzled with travel buzz. The screaming child back in coach still rung in her ears. Tired and wired. If someone asked her for an autograph, she might bite their head off. Olivia popped the top of her compact mirror for an inspection. Crossing three time zones and the dry air had been particularly unkind to her face: a crow had done the Bristol Stomp around her eyes. To avoid catching any more flaws, she snapped the compact shut and elbowed Lauren, who was sketching in a notebook.

"What are you drawing?"

"Nothing. Just doodles. What time is it?" Lauren said with a yawn, her hair roughed up on one side from leaning against the window.

"Wine o'clock." That got Lauren restuffing her carry-on.

Olivia turned to check on Danny and Pogo across the aisle. Having never taken off her black sunglasses, her younger sister leaned forward and searched the air for Pogo's head. Apparently, Pogo was in on the blind act. He stood from the bulkhead and tucked his curly topper under Danny's hand. She clutched the handle on his service vest, while Pogo picked up her purse in his teeth. Danny plucked her handbag from the dog's mouth.

As two flight attendants fawned over Pogo, Olivia pulled her carry-on and laptop case from the overhead, ready to deplane as soon as the door opened.

"Bye-bye, Pogo," the flight attendants cooed in unison, hands on knees. "We're not allowed to pet you." One turned to the other. "Such a sweetie pie. He's doing something so important."

Pogo tilted his head at Danny, as if saying, *How long do I have to keep this up?* Danny gave the handle an imperceptible tug, and Pogo led her to the doorway. Olivia caught the flight attendants' surprised expressions when her sister had no trouble navigating to the threshold in high heels.

Olivia turned to Lauren and cupped her hand around her mouth. "We need to have a serious discussion with her."

"I think this is only the warm-up band." Lauren took a sip of water and wedged behind Olivia in the aisle.

When the door opened, Olivia's scowl turned to one of shock. One of the flight attendants took Danny's picture with her cell phone. Olivia tried to slough off the innocent gesture, but her stomach tensed from her sister's deception.

Pogo led the procession to baggage claim. Olivia stepped off the escalator to at least ten dark-suited men holding handwritten signs, as if showing answers on *The Newlywed Game*. She stepped toward the one labeled *Novak*.

"Welcome to New York, Miss Novak," the driver said in a Spanish accent. "I am Eduardo. Three of you, yes?"

"Mrs." Olivia knew that a lot of people defaulted to *Miss* when they didn't know a person's marital status, but the label kept Adam close to her. "And it's four, really. We're travelling with a service dog."

Right on cue, Pogo's suitcase emerged on the belt, and Danny gestured to it. The dog jumped on and rode with his case to complete the loop with his food and toys. Lauren stood at the opposite end with her hand on her hip as Pogo entertained the passengers waiting for their luggage.

"A lot of bags?" Eduardo said, snickering at the dog.

"You could say that." Olivia smirked back. "I requested a van."

"I apologize. I did not get that message. I believe three lovely ladies require a town car." Eduardo's accent and chiseled features reminded Olivia of the character of Ricky Martinez in her last romance novel, *Tex-Mex Nights*. Getting squashed in a car with Eduardo had advantages. She could listen to him talk forever.

Danny pulled off her third suitcase from the carousel. Neon-green tags hung from the handle: *Special Handling*. Lauren threw up her hands, still waiting for hers. Olivia turned back to Eduardo. "I'll sit in the front. I hope you have a big trunk."

"A *veeerrry* big trunk." Eduardo winked. "Excuse me. I believe your sisters need my help."

Olivia fluffed her dark locks and caught Eduardo's rear view as she rolled her carry-on behind him. Not bad. He must work out. *Lord.* Adding cougar to her credentials wasn't part of her plan for the trip, but travelling with her sisters somehow brought out teenage antics. Eduardo requisitioned a luggage dolly as Lauren's Samsonite finally joined the party.

When Lauren spotted Eduardo, she tucked her hair behind her ears and adjusted her purple jacket. Danny took off her sunglasses and dug in her purse. She produced a lipstick tube and missiled it for a fresh shine. The four of them waited for Pogo to round the bend with his suitcase. As Eduardo stacked Pogo's bag, the dog hopped off the carousel and jumped on the cart.

"He likes to ride," Danny said and ruffled the dog's head. "Go for a ride, Pogo?"

"Can I get on?" Lauren said. "My feet are killing me."

Eduardo smiled, but Olivia caught a tinge of pink in his cheeks as he struggled to maneuver the dolly. Pogo sat on top like a figurehead leading a pirate ship out of the harbor.

~ · ~ · ~

As much as she griped about New York, Olivia had to admit the bustling fall energy of the city carried an intoxicating air of hipness. Life was an urban emergency. Animated signs pulsed with the urgent message beneath a veil of grit and soot. Steam wafted from manhole covers with a distinct odor of rotten eggs and subterranean decay. But surprises lay hidden to the casual eye. An occasional celebrity or two could be spotted in the stream of pedestrians rushing to the subway, the theater, or to a dinner reservation. Unlike the quiet pace of Portland, the constant rush reminded Olivia that the wheels of commerce in New York never decelerated to take a breath.

After awarding Eduardo with a fifty dollar aggravation-appreciation tip and wink, Olivia secured three keycards at the front desk of the Jewel Hotel, a modern and stylish boutique home base, one block from Rockefeller Center. The porter pushed their luggage toward the elevator. Olivia handed a card to Lauren. Danny held on to Pogo as the dog did a nervous dance in the lobby after a blast of a horn outside.

"We're in the same room?" Lauren said after comparing the room number on Olivia's folder. The plastic card turned in her hand like a bad draw in a game of poker.

"We all are. A suite," Olivia said. "A queen for you and me, and a pull-out couch for Danny and Pogo. We're lucky to get it on short notice. At least we've got a kitchenette."

"You snore."

The young porter smirked but didn't make a comment. Olivia figured he had heard worse from other guests. Either that, or he didn't want to compromise the size of his tip. The elevator doors parted, and he turned a key to prevent them from slamming shut.

"My dentist made me a mouth guard," Olivia said and chuckled. "You can tell me if it helps."

Danny stepped forward and took her key, a wad of baggies in hand. "Time to walk Pogo. Can you deal with our luggage?" She lowered her sunglasses from the top of her head, an instant shift of her status from blind to celebrity.

"Take care of mine too," Lauren said to Olivia and stepped out of the elevator. "I'm off to get a box of wine to keep in the refrigerator."

"Grab a decent bottle for Danny and me." Olivia raised her hand. "And pick up dinner for the three of us."

"What do you want?"

Olivia immediately craved Thai food. She turned to the porter. "Any good Thai restaurants nearby?"

"Bhong Ping," he said and nodded for emphasis. "Good Pad Thai. Two blocks. Take a right toward Eighth."

Olivia turned to Lauren. "Pad Thai. Bhong Ping. Two blocks. Did you get that?"

Lauren pulled up the collar on her fleece jacket and moved toward the glass front doors. "Right. A tad Thai. Ping Pong. Two blocks."

Her sister's attention to detail. Olivia prepared her taste buds for Thai-American mystery meatballs because who knew what Lauren ultimately would think she'd heard.

Olivia eyed Lauren's suitcase on the cart. To her, the gun was on display to the whole world. Even being in the elevator with Lauren's Samsonite gave her the creeps.

As the doors started to close, a siren's blare bounced through the lobby. Red and blue lights of a police cruiser raced by the front entrance. Olivia glanced at the porter.

He shrugged. "Welcome to New York."

~ · ~ · ~

Albeit small, the two-room suite easily accommodated the three of them and the dog. Its kitchenette offered the comfort of making a grab-and-go meal resemble a homemade sit-down dinner. Sleek and modern, the room's spare appointments and neutral decor offered a stylish hideaway from the bustling activity outside.

Olivia relished the break from playing Scout leader to peel away the travel layers, get into her nightshirt, check her email, and review the questions from Karen in preparation for tomorrow morning's interview. The respite lasted all of thirty-five minutes.

The first keycard slipped in the lock. Lauren bumped through the door with a plastic sack of three clamshell cartons in one hand; a box of white zinfandel in the other. Her purse slipped from her shoulder into the crook of her arm as she gave the door a shove with her orthopedic shoe.

"Where's Danny and Pogo?" Lauren said.

"Not back yet." Olivia tugged on her oversize night shirt to cover her thighs.

"I'm not waiting. I'm starving." Lauren headed for the kitchenette for a water glass and ice, and then she searched the cabinets for plates. "I had to dodge a guy yelling that I was a sinner, a messenger kid who almost ran me down with his bike, and three dogs nipping at the bag. God, I hate this city."

"Did you go to Bhong Ping?"

"Yeah. Couldn't understand a word they said, so I figured that was a good sign."

Olivia lifted the lid on one of the cartons and took a whiff. The savory aroma of grilled chicken and the sweet-and-salty combination of tamarind, fresh ginger, and crushed peanuts seemed right, but something was off. Fishy. She unwrapped two chopsticks and took a bite straight from the carton.

"Did you get to take a peek in their kitchen?"

"Oh stop," Lauren said. "The restaurant looked clean. Everyone was chowing down."

Olivia decided to forgo a plate entirely, repositioned herself to sit cross-legged on the couch, and dug in.

The last keycard clicked in the lock. Pogo bounded through the door and circled two laps around the bedroom and the living area, as if claiming dibs on the sleeping arrangements. Danny surveyed the suite with her hands on her hips.

"Well . . . It's small," Danny said and followed the aroma of Pad Thai. "Pogo got a lot of smiles at the park, especially when the joggers found out he's a service dog. Working dogs get so much respect." Lauren rolled her eyes in response. Danny set her container by the side chair. She dug through Pogo's suitcase for a can of his dinner and kibble. After feeding Pogo, Danny plopped on the chair and slid the carton onto her lap. "He loves the attention."

"You mean *you* love the attention." Lauren handed her a plastic fork.

Danny raised her eyes. "Are we having a fight now? Gang Up on Danny Day?"

"No . . . but you need to stop acting like you're blind," Olivia said. *No time like the present.*

"The practice keeps Pogo's skills sharp." Danny stabbed the air with her fork and took another bite.

"Did you ever think about the ethics of behaving that way? That flight attendant on the plane took your picture."

Danny shot a surprised look to Olivia as she sucked down a drooping noodle. "She did?"

"All it takes is one tweet with a nasty comment about you faking being blind. Social media can spin that little ditty out of control." Olivia hesitated. "Danny, you run a foundation for service dogs. Lauren's and my reputations are connected to that charity too."

"She's right on this one," Lauren said and turned the nozzle on her box of wine. "Liv might be preachy, but you're gonna get nailed."

"I'm not preachy." Olivia set her chopsticks in the container and closed the lid. She liked to watch her food intake the night before a TV appearance. "I'm practical."

Danny crossed her arms. "Have you two been discussing this behind my back?"

"Only because your behavior affects all three of us. You're one of the three of us." Olivia studied her younger sister. "We're going on national television in the morning. What if one of those flight attendants happens to catch the show?"

Danny went quiet. Her knee started a jig.

"I suppose I can only blame myself," Olivia continued. "I was the one who started the whole thing two years ago when we tried to sneak Pogo into the hospital to visit Ardy."

"No," Lauren said. "Danny's a grown woman and made a choice."

"I'm sitting right here," Danny said. "Don't talk like I'm not in the room."

"Enough. Don't pretend anymore."

Olivia set aside the container and picked up her list from the coffee table. She unscrewed the cap on the bottle of red and sniffed it—worthy of plastic cups. She poured one for herself and one for Danny. "Let's go over some possible questions from Joanna Josephsen."

"For you two." Lauren took a sip of her wine. "I'm going to sit there, but not say anything."

Olivia reviewed a printed list of questions about *The Executrix*. She'd written the book as a work of fiction, but she'd threaded a good amount of truth into her sisters' characters. Hitting the highlights, she unfolded their experience of losing their mother, the discovery of Mom's manuscript, and adopting Pogo from a former mobster when the Witness Protection Program moved him after a threat. She'd left out one detail from the book: writing the mobster's memoir.

"What if Joanna asks if Mom's book is real?" Lauren said.

"We say it's totally fiction." The question niggled at Olivia too, and had done so for the past two years.

"Because it is," Danny said. Her eyes started to shine, but her expression stiffened with conviction.

Olivia's insides softened. Their mother's death had been a multi-step process of letting go, with many more steps ahead of them, especially for Danny. Her having lived with Ellen until her death, the relationship of mutual caregiving had left Danny fiercely protective of their mother's memory.

Olivia headed to the bathroom. "Keep the focus on *The Executrix*, not Mom's book."

"We did a lot of crazy stuff after Mom died," Lauren said and shook her head. "We'll get a good laugh if we talk about the bacon, lettuce, and tomatoes we had etched on her urn."

"Good one." Olivia emerged with her toothbrush and squeezed paste over the bristles. "We should bring up that chapter where Mom changed the year on her birth certificate three times." Lauren laughed.

"I miss her every day," Danny said. She paused and then seemed to force her attention to Pogo, who was nosing his suitcase. Danny sniffed away tears. "Pogo needs his frog." Foraging through the bag, she produced a green rubber bullfrog with worn red lips.

Lauren took a long pull on her wine. "I miss her too. I haven't been racked with guilt in two years."

Danny glared at Lauren as she handed Pogo his toy.

Olivia returned to the bathroom to rinse her mouth and wash her face. Danny had been a pampered child and still expected to be protected. Anything Danny did had received a pass from their mother, and now, anything Pogo did received a pass from Danny. Even the old mobster, Ardy Griffin, had protected Danny. Olivia poked her head beyond the door frame. Lauren was finishing her Pad Thai in silence. The real truth, though, was that middle-age orphan status had left all three of them pining for Mom's advice.

Olivia folded the hand towel and hung it on the bar by the sink. "We need to get up at the crack and be a happy threesome. I'm going to bed."

"Foursome," Danny said. "Pogo needs to be included. I gotta call Ryan, so he knows we got here in one piece."

When Lauren opened her suitcase for her toiletries kit, Olivia caught her checking the small handgun tucked into one of her shoes.

"What kind of gun is that?" Olivia said and grimaced.

"A double-action twenty-five." Lauren held up the small weapon.

"What's that mean?"

"I don't need to cock it to fire. Point and shoot. The resistance of the trigger acts like a safety."

"Ugh." Olivia flapped her hands. "Put that thing away."

"It's a girly gun," Danny said. "That's what Ryan calls it." She pulled out the couch and fluffed the pillows. The television sprung to life as Danny surfed the channels on the remote, stopping on Animal Planet. "Pogo likes *Meerkat Manor.*" She patted the end of the pull-out bed for the dog to settle in for a good chew with his frog.

Wok-wok . . . Reeeebit . . . . Wok-wok . . . Reeeebit.

Danny sat next to him and fired up her phone.

Lauren narrowed her eyes. "My turn for the bathroom."

Olivia crawled into bed and took a breath to relax. To erase the image of the gun, she listened to the sounds of her sisters: Danny chatting away on her phone, water running, suitcases zipping, hangers dragging on the metal pole in the closet, lights clicking off.

The bed dipped as Lauren filled the space to her left. Toy sounds continued as Meerkats fought for survival.

Wok-wok . . . Reeeebit . . . Wok-wok . . . Reeeebit.

Olivia pulled back the covers and stomped to Pogo's suitcase. She rummaged for his knobby ball. Victorious, she marched to the pull-out couch.

"Give me that frog, Pogo. Chew on this." She shoved the ball at Pogo in exchange for the bullfrog. She tossed the rubber amphibian in the suitcase. *Reeebit.*

Olivia rechecked that the clock was set for a 3:00 a.m. wake-up. Lauren must have noticed the time because she said, "I thought we had to be there at 4:30—it's only a block away.

"Danny needs to walk Pogo, and we should eat something."

"I won't be hungry. That Pad Thai is lingering. Move over."

"I always sleep on the left side," Olivia said.

"So do I. Deal with it." Lauren opened her book and switched on her book light.

Feeling squashed between the book light and the sliver of red neon that squeezed between the split of the curtain, Olivia tossed and turned, unable to find a comfortable position.

"Your feet are cold. And you need your toenails clipped."

"I'm not getting a pedicure. My toes are ugly."

"Use Pogo's clippers."

"I can't see that far. Go to sleep, Liv."

Meerkat Manor flickered from the living area as Danny chatted with Ryan. Olivia popped in her mouth guard and closed her eyes, rehearsing articulate answers to possible interview questions: *How close are the three of you? Did everything in* The Executrix *really happen? Tell our viewers about finding Ellen Dushane's manuscript. Did Pogo tear up the bagpiper's instrument at your mother's funeral? Did Danny's husband really propose to her at the service? Do you think your mother's book is based on fact?*

The last question gave Olivia pause. Lauren wanted the truth too, but neither of them had dared to dig for fear of what they'd find. The two yellowed newspaper articles in the family picture box had provided nothing, only names she didn't recognize. Danny was right to say they were only circumstantial, convinced that the real crime only provided inspiration for their mother's fictional story. Over the past two years, the three of them had speculated about their authenticity ad nauseum.

Olivia clamped her teeth on the guard, as if it were her own knobby chew ball. The siren of an ambulance grew louder as it passed the hotel and faded. Horns honked in urban confrontation. She checked the clock again: 10:03 p.m. Only 7:03 p.m. in Portland. Her shoulders relaxed as she sank into the memory foam mattress.

Greeeee . . . brooooyep . . .

Olivia froze and grabbed Lauren's arm. "What wath that?"

Lauren snickered. "My stomach's doing the Ping-Pong-Bong."

"Thon't you thare, Lauren. I'm therious."

Chapter 5

Agendas

Lewisburg Penitentiary had lumpy mattresses. At six o'clock on Sunday night, Little Frankie, Jr.'s mattress bowed under his substantial weight, the stuffing crunching when he leaned over to pick up the Entertainment section of the *Philadelphia Enquirer*—the only section he was allowed—from the floor of his cell. He wanted to check the television listings, an activity he looked forward to twice a day: once in the morning; once in the evening after what passed as dinner. He missed the fried calamari at Enzo's, but he had to admit the inner tube around his belly wasn't as strained as it was when he entered the clink two years ago. His prison issues were now a bit loose.

Despite thick walls, the rustling newspaper caught the attention of the inmate in the next cell.

"Hey, Frankie. Anything good for tomorrow morning?" The voice echoed around the cinder-block walls.

"I don't care what you wanna watch," Frankie said. "We watch what I wanna watch. Got that?"

"Who died and made you TV czar?"

"You, if you don't shut up."

By year two of Little Frankie's five-year sentence in this dump, he'd learned plenty, mostly about television: what was worth watching and how to get it. He'd been able to bribe the prison guard for control of that small consideration. The next win at gin rummy would include his extra viewing choices. Officer Winton had promised. For now, though, he had to settle for threats to the other criminal fodder in order to claim dibs on his favorite shows in the common room.

Little Frankie gave the listings a once-over. Reruns of *Law and Order* were out, and so was *Gunsmoke*. He checked for guests on the Monday morning talk shows: *Today Show, Good Morning America, The View,* and the *Wake Up with Jo Show.*

The line-up for *Wake Up with Jo* caught his attention, although he really wanted to stare at Pamela Anderson on *The View.* Easier on the eyes. Joanna Josephsen would have three sisters from Portland about some book—with their dog. He straightened and stared at the vertical steel bars on the sliver of a window. The dim light triggered his memory of the scene: him in the Lincoln, staking out a Tudor in a Portland neighborhood and waiting with his gun cocked in his lap to blow old man Fazziano away, once and for all. Instead, three crazy dames and a dog came out of that house. He'd even told his father about them. Craziest thing he'd ever seen; the old one made three laps around her red Honda and jiggled her butt like a washed-up pole dancer. Pops had called off the hit. That plan had landed Frankie in prison for attempted premeditated murder. The Feds nabbed him at the car rental agency outside of Portland International.

Damn broads.

Frankie wasn't going to take any guff in the morning. Tomorrow, he'd satisfy his curiosity. If those women were the same ones he'd seen in Portland, then what did they write a book about?

Little Frankie nosed the air and said, "We're watching *Jo Show.*" That ought to piss off his neighbor but good.

"Dammit, Frankie."

Shoving his hand beneath his lumpy mattress, Frankie pulled out his specially marked deck of cards. Time for a game with the guard. He might need to earn a phone call to Allenwood Prison after the show.

~ · ~ · ~

At eight thirty on Monday morning, Della hobbled into the nearly empty Wolfe's Tavern in downtown Wolfeboro. The hash sounded good to eradicate the chill from last night's frost. While Wolfe's made a good breakfast, the place would be teeming at happy hour with locals swapping stories and tourists yapping about their New England fall foliage tour.

Della spotted Woody at a table facing the bar, taking notes on a yellow legal pad. She paused just to admire him. Della sometimes stared at Woodrow without saying a word, still in disbelief she had created him. His tweed suit appeared to be freshly pressed, unusual for a sixty-two-year-old confirmed bachelor, but not for a lawyer like Woodrow, fastidious and fit. The spitting image of his father, Woody was healthy and handsome—and eligible. Women all over town lusted after her son and circled his wagon to no avail. She'd talked him out of going back to Boston for a partnership with that fancy law firm to keep him close to home. Wolfeboro needed its own fancy lawyer and, with no daughter-in-law to get in the way, she always had her son at her service. Woody looked up then, placed his napkin on the table, and stood with a raised hand.

"Ma. Over here."

Della limped to the small table and chose the seat facing the expansive bar. The morning programs were in full force on two flat-screen televisions.

"How's the foot?" Woody said, but tapped the menu, eager to get to the real conversation. He asked about her health only because she'd raised him to be polite.

"Hurts like hell. I think my toe's infected." Della pushed her menu aside.

"Go ahead and get it checked again." Woody leaned in for a conspiratorial whisper. "I found out some things."

Della gazed into her son's bright blue eyes, framed with dark lashes and a kayaker's tan. Outside of his law practice, Woody could be found on the Lake Winnipesaukee in his kayak, paddles whirling to reach a dock, a buoy, or one of its hundreds of small islands. A waste of energy to go nowhere.

"The sisters are fairly well off," he said. "Ellen Dushane's book sold over a million copies. Olivia Novak sold that much and more of her own books. She cranks them out like Farmer's Almanacs." Woody straightened and smiled as the server approached with two mugs of coffee.

"Mawnin', Della," she said, no order pad in hand. In her early sixties and trim, the woman winked at Woody, like they'd dated in the past. "What can I get ya?"

"The prime rib hash skillet," Della said with no hesitation.

Woody grimaced with disapproval. Then he offered one of those knee-gelling smiles of his. "The Fittingly Fresh for me, Nan."

"You got it." The server gathered the menus and swished toward the kitchen, showing off the daylight between her thighs.

Woody leaned in again. "Mom, you really need to limit the red meat. Gout is exacerbated by diet."

Della ignored the comment as her gaze followed Nan to the kitchen. "Did you date her? She ogled you all funny."

"No, Ma. We never dated." Woody laughed, deep and long, the kind of laugh that meant the opposite. "We went to grade school together."

Still suspicious, Della reached for the sugar and flapped the packet like it was on fire. "Ellen's daughters are loaded, huh?"

"The amount I think you should be asking for wouldn't even be missed. The sisters divert money into a charitable foundation for service dogs. The youngest sister, Danielle, gets a hefty salary to run it. There's not much on the older one, Lauren, except that she's semi-retired from a real estate firm." Woody took a sip of his black coffee.

"How'd you get all that so fast?"

"From the foundation's website. The world can be at your fingertips if you'd let me buy you a computer. All three sisters are listed on the board of directors. As a non-profit, its tax filings are public information. Novak's website is fairly comprehensive about her background. You might even like her. She's family, albeit somewhat removed."

Woody rested back in his chair and twisted his fraternity ring from Yale, studying her.

Della snatched another sugar packet from the wire holder. "I want four hundred thousand. That's how much I need to move into a nice house with a real kitchen, like the ones they built in Baxter Fields." She worked her tongue over her lips.

"You should go for more, if that's the number you want. Sloane Publishing will probably negotiate the amount down. And if you'd let me help you fix up yours and get all the stuff out, you'd have a nice little house."

"You laugh at me now, but someday that stuff will pay off big."

As Woody jotted more notes on his notepad, Della switched her attention to the television over the bar. A bouncy jazz tune chased the *Wake Up with Jo Show* logo around the screen. A caricature of the host held out her arm to halt the words.

"And I want a TV," Della said.

Without raising his eyes, Woody circled a bullet point on his pad. "We should arrange a meeting with the sisters first to avoid getting Sloane's corporate lawyers involved. Sometimes working out disagreements is better one-on-one."

"No. I've never met Ellen's girls. They might ignore me, not take me seriously. Going through the publisher will get their full attention. Less waiting around to make nicey-nice."

"I want to go on record that proceeding that way is not my recommendation." Woody twisted his onyx pen. The point disappeared. "If that's what you want, we'll head over to the office after breakfast and put together an email to Sloane's legal department. Short and to the point. I want to sort out some facts with you first."

Applause and cheers accompanied the booming voice of the announcer rattling off the list of guests on the program. All noise to

Della, until one guest in the lineup caught her attention.

" . . . and best-selling author, Olivia Novak, with her real-life sisters, the inspirations for the characters from her new novel, *The Executrix* . . . "

The throbbing pain in Della's foot disappeared. She fluttered her hands, then pointed to the bar. "Woody . . . tell the bartender to turn up the sound. It's *them*."

Woody's chair scraped the planks as he jumped up and dashed to the bar. With no bartender in sight, he slipped behind the counter and pressed the volume control on the television.

~ · ~ · ~

"Ten minutes, ladies," the producer's assistant said as she stuck her head in the dressing room door. She pulled her microphone closer. "Jo's on her way in." All business, the woman covered her hand over the mouthpiece. "She likes a few words before the show starts. Then we'll move you onto the set."

Danny swiveled Pogo in the make-up chair, combing his long, curly ears. Lauren stepped from the bathroom, rubbing her abdomen and squinting her eyes.

"Mmmm . . . my stomach's not right," she said.

"Just nerves," Olivia said and lined her lower lids with more definition. She fluffed her dark hair in the bulb-rimmed mirror.

"I'm looking forward to it," Danny said and puffed the mound on Pogo's head with a long-toothed comb. "Pogo's a pro. We're always getting requests for interviews when we do events with the humane society."

"Goody, goody for both of you," Lauren said. "My royalties at work."

Joanna poked her head in the dressing room, her auburn pixie cut appearing more carrot-like than on the small screen. Her olive-green eyes twinkled with anticipation. Each new show might make or break her career. She stepped into the room and extended her hand to Olivia.

"Call me Jo. Loved your book. The three of you and the dog are quite the vivid characters." She shook Lauren's and Danny's hand in sequence. With his tail swinging like a metronome set on allegro, Pogo jumped from the chair and sniffed at Jo's fuzzy slippers. "Nice doggy," she said, her fingers splayed as if her nails were wet.

"Anything we need to know before the interview?" Olivia said. "Karen Finnerelli sent us your prep questions, but—"

"I always like to be spontaneous. You're first up after my intro of the Jo-Jo Jammin' Newsy Bits. See you on the set." Joanna's shiny, plump lips broke into a smile to reveal her veneered teeth.

"Six minutes," the assistant said. "Let's get you three in position."

"Showtime, ladies. Kiss. Kiss. See you out there." Joanna breezed out of the dressing room.

Chapter 6

The Wake Up with Jo Show

At the center of the *Wake Up with Jo Show* set was Joanna's interview chair, upholstered in neon orange and anchoring the spot between two lime-colored love seats, their retro style designed to be uncomfortable. The furniture reminded Olivia of the sixties variety show *Laugh In*—move fast to get to the punchline. Olivia and Lauren sat on one side; Danny sat on the other with Pogo leaning against her knees. Even with strangers behind the camera equipment, the dog appeared to be perfectly at ease, although his chest quivered in response to the overly chilled air in the studio.

Six flat screen monitors lined the set, each with a different close-up image, including one of Pogo shaking his head to fluff his ears. Olivia twisted her wedding band, a habit that summoned Adam's support.

Danny checked the lapels of her pantsuit, a sophisticated autumn shade of cinnamon, finished off with tan snakeskin heels. Lauren pulled on the elastic waistband of her navy-blue pleated skirt, as if suffering from oxygen deprivation. Olivia straightened her loose peach-colored scarf to make sure the ends were even against her melon-colored silk blouse. She tugged the back of her black silk jacket to prevent any gaps.

"It's freezing in here," Lauren said.

"It's to keep you alert under the hot lights," Olivia whispered. "Cross your ankles. Your knees look like they're stuck together with Gorilla Glue."

Lauren scowled at the monitor when she spotted the commercial for Nutrisystem, displaying before and after photos of Marie Osmond. "I'm so uncomfortable. That meal last night got me all bloated."

"Suck it in. We came three thousand miles for our fifteen-minute shot at selling a ton more books."

Danny put her forefinger to her lips, then pointed to the floor director moving toward them, whispering into a headset. A man with a mission and a clipboard. A female assistant rushed ahead of him with a handful of wireless microphones. She clipped one to Olivia's lapel.

"Joanna will do her intro and then come over to the set when we go to break," the director said. "Whatever you do, don't look into the camera. Just talk naturally. Act like we're not even here."

"Yes, Pogo, only you can look into the camera," Danny said and rubbed his chest. "Everybody wants to see Pogy Boy."

The director pointed to Olivia's jacket. "Those mics are powerful. When we turn them on, they'll pick up everything."

"Everything," the assistant echoed. Lauren grimaced as the woman clipped the mic to the lapel of her blazer. "So make sure you keep your gestures to a minimum. No swishing."

Olivia nodded. Danny smiled. Lauren rubbed her stomach, already creating a racket. Pogo swiveled his head to Danny as if to point out he'd been left out of the microphone distribution.

The floor director sighed and rejoined the gaggle of employees buzzing with last minute tasks. He stood next to one of two cameras and counted down. On an adjacent set, Joanna sat on a stool, humming to warm up her vocal chords.

Olivia glanced at the sequence of monitors as Joanna went live. Lauren looked miserable. Danny pressed her lips together to make sure her gloss shined evenly.

After the introduction, the program went to a commercial. A deep breath did nothing to calm Olivia's nerves. Lauren might freeze up; Danny might say too much or get defensive, especially if a question came up about Mom. At least Olivia could count on Pogo to be a complete angel.

Joanna moved to the set, eased into the interviewing chair, and crossed her legs. "This will be so much fun," she said and patted her lap. "You three have a wonderful story."

"Four of us," Danny said. "We can't forget Pogo."

"Right," Joanna stretched her jaw to prepare for a natural smile. She reviewed her three-by-five cards in silence.

Olivia eyed one of the monitors that ran a commercial for State Farm Insurance and shifted her gaze to one of the cameras, hoping for her own accident forgiveness. A make-up assistant dashed to the set, brushed foundation powder on Joanna's chin and forehead, and made a hasty exit. The floor director counted down with his fingers. A red dot illuminated on one of the cameras like a sniper scope on a high-tech rifle. Joanna straightened and smiled, gripping her cards. From Olivia's perspective on the set, the overly bright lights made her face appear cartoon-like.

"Welcome back. We're here with best-selling novelist Olivia Novak, her two sisters, Lauren Lyndale and Danielle Eason, and Pogo, the renowned service dog. Olivia's latest novel, *The Executrix,* will resonate with boomer siblings everywhere. Both humorous and poignant, the story tells of the sisters' discovery of their mother's manuscript for another book you may know. Their mother is the celebrated Ellen Dushane, author of the posthumous hit, *Indigo to Black.* Welcome to *Wake Up with Jo.*"

"Thank you for having us," Olivia said. "It's been quite the ride for the past two years."

"Let's talk about how your latest book, *The Executrix,* came about."

Olivia flexed her toes inside her high heels. She noticed Jo had replaced her slippers with heels too. "After the death of our mother, we found a manuscript in her safe. This is a fictionalized story of what we went through to get Mom's book published. But the three of us had our own issues at becoming orphans in middle-age. No matter how old you are, the relationship between siblings never changes."

Lauren shifted and winced.

"And you did something unique with your mother's book."

"Yes. We created a foundation with a portion of the royalties— the Pogo Charitable Trust."

Like a hungry hawk spotting roadkill, Joanna zeroed in on Danny. "Pogo is the mascot. I read that a portion of the royalties from both *The Executrix* and *Indigo to Black* fund your work to train service dogs. Danielle, tell us how you acquired this gorgeous animal."

The monitor showed a close-up of Pogo's face. On cue, he rested his head over Danny's knee. *Ham.*

Joanna's aversion to reaching out to Pogo wasn't missed by Olivia. She'd heard the woman had an agenda that lurked behind every seemingly innocent question. Danny needed a reminder to be careful. To catch her sister's attention, Olivia flicked the end of her scarf. The noise in the microphone prompted Joanna to lean closer to Danny, blocking Olivia's view.

"From Ardy Griffin, Olivia's next door neighbor," Danny said, beaming. "Ardy was in the Witness Protection Program at the ripe old age of ninety-three. The sweetest man you'd ever meet." She waved her hand. "He was supposed to give me away at my wedding, but the FBI had to move him because of a threat. Thank God that Olivia was able to document Ardy's story in a memoir before he passed away two years ago. He left us with Pogo. My husband and I adopted him."

Olivia froze and shot her gaze to the monitor. Lauren's eyes widened, as if someone had poked her from beneath the sofa cushion. Danny's became two headlights at the magnitude of her faux pas. Joanna smiled like a honey badger crawling out of a garbage can with a chicken leg.

"He's a beautiful dog." Joanna turned to Olivia. "This is quite the scoop . . . romantic fantasies to felonies." Pogo stepped forward to nose the hem of Jo's skirt, soliciting a head scratch. She kept her hand flat and barely touched the mound on his head, as if tamping down the air.

Waving away Danny's words like motes of dust, Olivia dove into the conversation. "Uh . . . quite the change for me." This wasn't going according to plan. Every word out of Danny's mouth had been strictly off limits.

From the sneaky expression on Jo's face, the woman was about to double-dip her chip. Olivia braced herself. Lauren's eyebrows disappeared beneath her bangs.

"Is this a peek of a new book in the pipeline?" Joanna leaned forward as if Olivia's face had become a cherry lollipop. "A mobster memoir would be quite the departure for you. About as far from romance and women's fiction as you can get."

Olivia clenched her jaw. She wanted to scream to the cameraman to cut to a commercial but offered only a warm smile. "I'm branching out, Joanna, but that doesn't mean it'll get published. I doubt the memoir will ever see the light of day. Danny's work with therapy dogs is so important to those who need assistance. In fact—"

Danny leaned forward. "Pogo's abilities shine when he's given a job to do."

Ruh . . .

At the mention of his name, the poodle added his own comment. Hopefully, none of the millions of viewers understood dog-speak.

Danny smoothed the top of Pogo's head to keep him quiet. "It costs about thirty-thousand to fund the training and certification of a therapy dog. It's quite intensive—"

"I'm sure it is." Joanna flipped to a new note card. "Now, Olivia, you switched your writing genre after you found the person who killed your husband in a hit-and-run accident. Tell us about that."

The question about Adam took Olivia off guard, yet another subject she considered to be taboo. "I couldn't have made it through that time without my sisters." She scratched her neck, as if the loose scarf was too tight. "Closure is transformative. Lauren and Danny fueled my courage to face the perpetrator, and what came out on the other side was a lot of writing."

"Like that mobster's memoir? Was that part of your courage to move forward?"

The woman wasn't going to leave it alone. Olivia swallowed. She studied her own expression on the monitor and eased the crease between her dark brows. "Inspiration can come from anywhere." *Lame response.*

Joanna switched gears. "So let's talk about your mother's book. *Indigo to Black* is an amazing read. A game changer where the killer is a teenage stalker. Gave me the chills, folks." Joanna's gaze drilled into the camera as she shuffled her notes. "No spoilers, but I'm sure anyone with a daughter in high school has read it by now. Who hasn't, right?"

"It's wonderful," Olivia said and leaned back on the love seat, relieved the subject of Ardy Griffin was behind her. "I was swept away by our mother's prose when I first read it. I knew the book had to be published. The manuscript was just too good to keep hidden from the world."

"But it's fiction," Danny said and pursed her lips.

Joanna's gaze skipped over Danny to Lauren. "What do you think, Lauren? Is your mother's story based on fact? Could the character of Becky Haines be your mother, Ellen Dushane? There's been some speculation in literary circles about that possibility."

Silence loomed as Lauren tried to squeeze out words. "No . . . no, I don't think so. The three of us went over it a million times and always came to the same conclusion. It's fiction."

"That you know of, right?" Joanna winked. "The possibility lurks? To this day, a similar crime that took place over sixty years ago at the University of Boston remains unsolved."

Olivia bit her lip. She needed to rescue Lauren. "Our mother had a vivid imagination. We're so proud of her." A can of Silly String would come in handy. If she had one, Olivia would point the nozzle at the woman's face.

"The apple didn't fall far from the tree, Olivia," Joanna said. "I want to read this mobster memoir of yours. Promise me you'll come back when that juicy one gets published."

"Oh, it would be a pleasure." Olivia narrowed her eyes at Danny until she saw the scowl on the monitor. Lauren, assuming they'd gone to a commercial, started to stand from the loveseat and froze. Her eyes saucered when she caught her image on the monitor. They were still on the air.

Burrrreeeep . . . rrrrruuuup.

Olivia's eyes widened in shock. She scraped her microphone with her finger, but a beat too late to mask Lauren's intestinal indiscretion. Danny gulped.

Joanna's lips parted, freezing the O that had formed on her lips. In a panic, she said:

"Well, this couldn't have been more revealing. Thank you all for coming on the show today. *The Executrix* is a read you can't put down. Available in bookstores everywhere." Joanna held up the wrong book, the one for the next guest. The camera zoomed in on the cartoon image of a professional man with sweat squirting from the top of his head.

Danny let out a snicker, then covered her mouth with both hands.

Joanna grabbed air until her fingers found *The Executrix* on the coffee table. The cover showed a painting of Pogo in a whirl of manuscript paper. Her smile froze as her eyes shifted left and right. "Up next after a quick break, Dr. Gerald Hozenheimer will talk about his new book, *Conquering Colitis.*"

All color had drained from Lauren's face as the camera continued to roll. In an attempt to redirect, she pointed at Pogo.

With his ears catching lift, Pogo whipped his mug to the camera, cocked his head to the left, and gazed straight into the lens.

"Cut!"

Chapter 7

Facing the Agent

The revolving door of Rockefeller Center became a slingshot as Lauren and Olivia whirled through and ejected to the sidewalk. Danny used the side door as Pogo strained against his leash to get outside, clearly picking up on the magnitude of the chaos. With shaking fingers, Olivia pulled her phone from her purse to call her agent.

"You guys go ahead to the hotel. I'll meet you there," Olivia said to Danny as the call connected to voicemail. "Karen, it's me. I'm on my way to your office right now."

Already halfway down the block toward the Jewel Hotel, Lauren scooted as if a bag of Skittles had broken open in her pantyhose.

Olivia turned in the opposite direction and bumped into a young man with a briefcase. He appeared to be annoyed before recognizing her. He snapped his fingers.

"Hey . . . Weren't you just on *Wake Up with Jo?*"

Denying the appearance wasn't an option. "You saw it?"

"Hilarious. You're all over the video screens in Times Square. Check it out."

"Thanks for the warning." Olivia brushed past the man as she pictured Karen gawking at the footage from her office window. She prepared for the scolding of her life.

With her heels clicking on the pavement like a countdown clock, she felt like Karen's office might have been three miles away instead of three blocks. Olivia rounded the corner of Forty-Sixth at Seventh and gazed up at the expansive animated billboard replaying Lauren's final moment of humiliation. Joanna's wide-eyed look of shock preceded Lauren's fingerpoint at the dog and a freeze-frame of Pogo turning to the camera. The video looped and started again—and again and again—high over Times Square. If the steaming manhole cover in the street could have been easily removed, Olivia would have dropped herself inside. Instead, she turned and raced through the door of Karen's office building, one of the historic brick structures saved from the wrecking ball. She stepped to the desk attendant in the cramped lobby.

"Olivia Novak for Karen Finnerelli." She tapped the counter. "C'mon. You know me. I've been here dozens of times."

The seams of the security guard's navy-blue jacket strained as he chuckled. "Not lately. Go on up. Third floor. Check in with the receptionist." He picked up yesterday's paper and resumed his study of the Sunday comic strips.

The brass-plated elevator doors, etched in a geometric deco pattern, opened to a four-by-four claustrophobic box, circa 1927. She'd learned to smack the cracked ivory button four times before it illuminated to a dull yellow. Olivia tried to slow her pulse without success. After a jolt and a bounce, the doors parted into the lobby of the Finnerelli Literary Agency. The space had been decorated to replicate a private library in a lavish home, with a generous inheritance stocking the maple shelves. Rick Morick, the fashionisto receptionist, straightened and offered his best devilish smile.

"Well, well," he said. "I expected you to waltz in here with a platinum wig and sunglasses."

This morning, Rick's highlighted blond hair had been spiked with copious amounts of hair gel. Mischief filled his eyes.

Olivia squinted. "She mad?"

Rick poked at the whipped cream on his tall mocha and ran his tongue down the length of the straw. "Let's put it this way . . . I almost went out and bought her a bag of grapes to make me a bottle of wine. She's been stomping around here in those clunky black boots of hers for the past half hour."

"What's she most pissed about?" Olivia braced herself. "Lauren?"

"Oh, hon, Karen's ecstatic about Lauren. When a fart can get you on the ton-a-tron outside, it's a beautiful thing to behold. No . . . her polished claws are out for *you*." Rick bared his professionally whitened teeth and raked the air. "Meeeeow."

"Why?"

"She wants that mobster manuscript like yesterday." Rick flicked the eraser on the end of a pencil and made an arc to press the intercom. "She's heeeeeeere."

"Send her back." Karen's I'm-not-happy voice. As she thought about it, Olivia had never heard the I'm-happy voice, even when she was happy.

Rick raised his eyes to Olivia, the pencil becoming a yellow number-two blur between his fingers. "Want a Valium?"

"No pill is strong enough. Got any spare antidote for snake venom?"

Rick's lingering cackle pushed Olivia down the hall. She stood in the open doorway of the corner office and surveyed the familiar scene, unchanged from her last visit. Floor-to-ceiling maple bookcases, jammed with hard-bound editions, lined the perimeter of the cramped office. Karen's chair had been turned to face two sparkling-clean windows over a long radiator coated with multiple layers of thick paint. The autumn sun reflected off the building across the street, illuminating the wild outline of Karen's black hair. Her unruly tendrils appeared to be reaching toward the glass for a chance to escape. The jeweled butterfly clip that glinted in her jet-black locks did nothing to tame the Medusa-like vision. Through a wedge of daylight between the buildings outside, Pogo's face flashed above a racing scroll of news.

Olivia knocked on the door frame, prompting Karen to swivel her chair and point to her headset. She motioned to one of two cushy guest chairs. Stacks of manuscripts lined the desk and continued to the floor—the authors who were lucky enough to graduate to the *uber* slush pile.

Taking a seat, Olivia studied her agent. Karen's signature style dictated that she always dress in black with a shock of color. Today's outfit was no different. The ends of her natural-silk scarf, a deep shade of cerulean, disappeared beneath the edge of the desk. *A forty-two-year-old literary goth chick*, she thought. Karen kept a trim figure from nervous energy, even with a diet of lattes and Saturday lasagna feasts with her extensive Italian family. There had been talk of getting a nose job, but obviously Karen had chickened out. The bump on its bridge still earned her the secret nickname Witchiepoo. Her dark-lined eyes brewed with strategy and competition.

"Right. You won't be sorry," Karen said into the stick of her headset. "Twitter's all a-twitter about this book. Move fast." She disconnected and rolled her eyes at Olivia. "Self-publishing pisses me off. I want to go back to the days when writers did the begging."

Olivia had perfected the deadpan as a response to opinionated statements from Karen. Verbal ones were a trap for a sparring session. "Did you see the interview?"

"You mean, did I *hear* your sister on national television? Loud and clear. Sounded like she quacked a wet armpit."

"Yeah . . ." Olivia rubbed her forehead. "Lauren's mortified. She ate bad Thai last night."

"Great Thai. That's what I say." Karen waved her hand. "Forget about it. Hilarious. We couldn't ask for better publicity." She leaned toward her computer screen. "Fourteen thousand hits on YouTube in the last forty-five minutes. Go Lauren. And I'll sign that dog right now for a children's series. He's friggin' adorable. The way he turned to the camera might get him his own talk show."

"He's a pistol."

"Now, let's talk about the mob memoir you've been holding back from me." Karen's eyes turned into two stealth bombers on a mission.

"I want it."

"No." Olivia sliced the air for emphasis. "Too dangerous. Some of the people I wrote about are still alive. The manuscript is in a safe-deposit box."

"Unlock it."

"No. You don't understand. We—including *you*—would be in danger."

"Life is dangerous. I'll hire you a security guard." Karen's phone buzzed. She held her gaze on Olivia before pressing the button. "What?"

Rick's sing-song voice trumpeted from the speaker. "It's Slooooane."

Karen pointed at her. "Don't move. Sit tight while I find out what this is about."

Olivia studied Karen's face for clues. Sloane Publishing managed her mother's book. Paranoia kicked in. Her agent's smile melted to disbelief, then to anger as she scribbled notes on a pad while mouthing four-letter words.

"Olivia's sitting in front of me. I'll discuss this with her." Karen disconnected and tapped her polished red nails on the receiver. They appeared to have grown longer since Olivia had taken a seat. "That was Sloane. You're going to be sued for royalties on *Indigo to Black*. Something about defamation of character. Complicates things, Liv." She stared as if Olivia had better pop out simple answer.

"What?" The only word Olivia could muster.

"An email landed in Sloane's legal department before Lauren gave her intestinal high-five to three million people. Now, I want to crap *my* pants."

Olivia straightened in her chair. "Who would do such a thing? And why?"

An image of that spider in the corner of her entryway in Portland flashed behind her eyes. Denial hadn't kept her from acknowledging the bug was there, lurking in the crack to make an appearance when she turned her back.

"Somebody named"—Karen glanced at her notes—"Della Rainey." She fingered the jeweled butterfly clip in her hair. "Do you know a Della Rainey?"

"Uh . . . " Olivia turned to the bookcase. Three copies of *Indigo to Black* sat on the shelf. "Her name was in Mom's address book. I think Della's her cousin."

"Older or younger?" Karen appeared to calculate the lifespan of the problem.

"I don't know. Frankly, I wasn't sure if she was even still alive. I reached out to Della after Mom died. The card came back as undeliverable."

"Well, she's deliverable now. Her lawyer, Woodrow Something-or-Other, is requesting a million dollars and 50 percent of the future royalties on *Indigo to Black*." Karen tapped her infamous red pencil on the desk and nodded. "That's a lotta money, sister."

Sister. Money. Olivia's stomach clenched at the words. The money had purpose. Everything she and her sisters had created to honor their mother's memory could evaporate: her book, Lauren's security for retirement, the Pogo Charitable Trust, Danny's position to run the foundation's valuable work, and Olivia's own quest to be taken seriously by the literary community.

"You better think hard about which character your mother defamed in that book. My guess is that it's the character of Becky Haines." Karen pursed her lips and studied Olivia. "Did you research that manuscript before you sent it to me?"

"Well, not exactly . . . You know how this came about. My mother was already dead when I found the manuscript in her safe. I didn't even know she'd written a book. Besides, if I hadn't sent the manuscript to you under my own name first, you never would've considered it." Olivia tamped down her defensiveness. "It's *fiction*."

"What makes you so sure?"

"Fairly sure. I can't exactly have a chat with Mom about it, can I?" Olivia broke Karen's stare and rummaged in her purse for a Listerine strip. Her mouth tasted of the car exhaust in Times Square. "I need to go back to the hotel and talk to Lauren and Danny and then make a couple of phone calls."

"One needs to be to your lawyer." Karen pulled out a tube of lip gloss from her top drawer and swept the wand over her lips.

Olivia stood and adjusted her purse on her shoulder. She drew in a breath. "I'll keep you posted."

"You do that—within the next hour." Karen ran her tongue over her shiny lips. "And I want that mobster memoir. I could use a hit man, myself, right about now."

Witchiepoo.

Chapter 8

The Hack Attack

Olivia hung up from the five-block conversation with her lawyer, Ted Beal. With a sense of dread, she grasped the handle of the glass door to the Jewel Hotel. Facing her sisters with Karen's news would be a calamity, and Ted's plan might spark a rebellion; not facing them would be a disaster. She took a breath and walked in a circle around the lobby. The action helped her to think. As she paced, the clerk at the front desk smiled.

"Where's Pogo, Mrs. Novak?" he said.

She stopped. "I think he's already in the room."

"I just came on duty. The guests last night loved Pogo. He's a gem."

"Pogo's a good boy," she said and resumed her pace.

Stopping short in front of a heavy-set, bearded man, who sat in a bucket chair and typed on his laptop, Olivia paused as if he'd appeared from nowhere. She hadn't noticed him when she stepped through the doors. The man raised his eyes to her and took a sip from a can of cherry Coke. She moved to the picture window for privacy, blinking as her gaze followed a bike messenger, who, no doubt, was delivering bad news to someone else.

As an estate lawyer, Ted dealt with family disputes every day. She trusted his opinion. What she didn't trust was the timeline. Why didn't this come up two years ago when *Indigo to Black* hit the market? To dodge the victim response welling inside her, Olivia created a mental checklist of immediate tasks: rent a car; change the return flight to Portland; call Karen; pull up directions to Wolfeboro; check out of the hotel. Ted's words rung in her head: *Go settle the score.* The only clues to the score sat in the pages of a fictional novel—at least she hoped it was fictional.

Olivia turned and glanced at the man tapping on his laptop. A cord snaked from his ear. He was deep into a conversation, but his gaze sent chills up her spine, like he knew secrets about her. She trudged from the window to the elevator and hit the UP button three times, rehearsing eloquent words to explain the ugly situation to her sisters. The *ding!* signaled round one. She stepped inside and took one last eyeful of the bearded man in the lobby. His mean eyes bored into hers as he talked. Maybe it was her mood, but the slight smile beneath his scrubby facial hair appeared to mock her. His face squeezed to nothing as the doors closed.

A cacophony of sounds hit Olivia as she opened the hotel room door. A blow dryer strained with a high-pitch squeal in the bathroom. Danny sat hunched over on the couch with her head in her hands, a full-on crying fit in progress. Pogo paced and whined.

Olivia chucked her keycard on the desk, like folding in a game of poker, and slung her purse over the chair. She tilted her head back and stared at the textured ceiling, trying to find hidden pictures in the pattern.

"Lauren, turn that damned thing off and come in here." Olivia punctuated the words with a heavy sigh. Her arms hung limp as she turned to Danny. "What's the matter now?"

"You were . . . right, Liv." Danny hiccupped as tears streamed down her cheeks. "The Humane Society is upset . . . with the Pogo Trust."

"Why?"

Danny took a calming breath. "Somebody posted a picture of me on Twitter with Pogo that said, 'Faker, Faker, Faker.'" Then she started up again. "They want to have a . . . meeting when I get back."

"Dammit, Danny. I told you that you were headed for trouble." Olivia marched into the bedroom and yanked off her scarf and jacket. She tossed them on the bed. Despite the cool fall weather, sweat had soaked the armpits of her silk blouse.

The hair dryer silenced in the bathroom, prompting Olivia's shoulders to drop by two inches. Lauren emerged in the bedroom wearing her house dress and holding her spandex reinforcement to the light. She grimaced. "It turned out to be more than a gas bubble on the way back to the hotel."

"Classic." Olivia's stretched emotions exploded into peals of laughter. She collapsed on the bed. Pogo jumped up with her and dragged his tongue over her face. She sighed. "I'm sorry, Lauren. How are you feeling?"

"Fine. Now."

Olivia's smile faded as she sat up. "Well, try to hold on to that feeling, 'cause we're checking out this afternoon."

Lauren sat next to her on the bed, twirling her Spanks on her forefinger to finish the drying. "But we have two more days. We got here less than twelve hours ago."

"I thought you hated New York."

Danny sat on the bed next to Lauren. The dog settled between them like a fourth sibling. "Are we going back to Portland?" she said and smoothed her hand over Pogo's ears.

Olivia smacked her knees and stood. "Nope." She swung her roller bag on the bed and yanked on the zipper. Hangers scraped the metal pole as she pulled her clothes from the closet. "Forget Twitter. Forget YouTube. Forget the fact that Lauren almost crapped her skirt on national television. We're renting a car and driving up to Wolfeboro, New Hampshire."

"Why?" Lauren said.

"To go see Della Rainey."

"Mom's cousin?" Danny said.

Olivia kicked off her heels. "Della's suing us for a million dollars and—get this—*half* the future royalties on Mom's book."

"On what grounds?" Lauren's Spanks drooped like a flag in the doldrums.

"Defamation of character." Olivia unbuttoned her blouse.

Danny's face went slack. Lauren's mouth opened in shock.

Throwing a tired look at her sisters, Olivia paused and said, "Yeah, that was my reaction too. An old biddy with a grudge." She pulled off her slacks to change into black yoga pants.

"I knew it," Danny said. "I've been waiting for that other shoe to drop."

Lauren jumped up, marched to the desk, and picked up the phone. "How can you be so calm about this, Liv? Put some fightin' pants on." She held out the receiver to Olivia, with her underwear dangling from her wrist. "Call Ted right now."

"Already talked to him," Olivia said. "Ted's advice is to go visit Della and talk to her ourselves. If we leave this to the lawyers to duke out, it'll drag on forever and cost a fortune. We can't afford the negative publicity, either. In fact, I need to check my email. I was copied on the letter from Della's lawyer that went to Sloane. I couldn't open the attachment on my phone." She slipped a turtleneck sweater over her head and folded her blouse in the case.

"Wolfeboro, New Hampshire?"

"That's where Della and her lawyer are. And it's Mom's turf."

Danny stood and moved to Olivia's laptop. She stared, stone-faced, at the screensaver. "But we could lose all the funding for the Pogo Charitable Trust."

"And our income," Lauren added.

"That's why we're going to solve this on our own," Olivia said. "We're not spending one *dime* of our royalties to pay legal fees to fight this Della bitch."

"Did Ted see the *Jo Show* this morning?" Lauren set her head in her hands.

"Uh . . . yeah."

"Liv, in retrospect, we should have investigated Mom's story."

"It's not true," Danny said and revved up for a replay of tears.

Olivia groaned. "I don't know what the truth is." She flipped her hair from beneath the collar of her sweater and sat at the desk. After a vigorous shake of the mouse, she scrolled through her messages. "The three of us are going to find out. Here it is."

Danny and Lauren stood behind Olivia and each placed a hand on her shoulder. They leaned into the screen to read the email:

To whom it may concern,

On behalf of my client, Della Rainey, relative of Ellen Dushane, I hereby inform Sloane Publishing that we are requesting $1,000,000 in back royalties and 50% of future royalties for the publication, Indigo to Black. *While we acknowledge that Ellen Dushane is the author of the book, the story is directly defaming to the character of my client, Della Rainey.*

We require a response by midnight, September 21st. If we do not receive a satisfactory reply from you by that date, formal papers will be filed for a lawsuit in the state of New Hampshire.

It is our preference to settle this matter quickly and without formal legal proceedings. However, we are prepared to pursue the matter through appropriate channels.

We look forward to hearing from you.

Woodrow Rainey
Partner
Rainey, Bonner & Braden, LLC
Wolfeboro. New Hampshire

Lauren squeezed Olivia's shoulder. "That's five days from now."

Danny squeezed her other. "We only have five days to figure this out?" She asked the question, almost to herself.

Never one to be left out, Pogo jumped from the bed and nosed

Olivia's lap. He set his head over her knees. She stroked his ears, then grasped her sisters' hands. "Five days. We need to be ready to leave in an hour."

~ · ~ · ~

The dispatch for Serge "Cheese Steak" Romov to bring his laptop to the Jewel Hotel had come two hours ago, after he'd followed Novak's credit card transactions. Thanks to Little Frankie Jr.'s keen eye, the chain of communication had been sparked within minutes of the sisters' appearance on the *Wake Up with Jo Show*. Frankie had recognized the women and the dog from his trip to Portland that landed him in the slammer.

Through the hotel's unsecured wireless network, Olivia's laptop had become open season. Cheese Steak had turned his head when a woman jerked open the lobby door. Instinct took over. He'd hunched down in the bucket chair to avoid her attention. Little Frankie's description identified the woman as Olivia Novak—an upset Olivia Novak. She'd even walked in a circle around the lobby, as if she didn't know what to do. Then the woman stopped in front of him, becoming aware of his presence.

Deep, dark eyes bored into him. Cheese Steak's breath caught in his throat, but he'd kept his cool. With his fingers paused over the keyboard, he'd held her gaze until she moved to the front window to make a call. A slow stream of air filtered through his beard, warming his chin. He'd quenched himself with a cherry Coke.

Cheese Steak's gaze followed Olivia Novak as she marched to the elevator and hit the button. The doors parted. She studied him a second time before the steel panels squeezed over her form.

"She's going upstairs," he said.

"Let's see what she does," Little Frankie said in his ear. "Call me back when she gets online. I got only so much time on the phone. I'll wait right here."

For ten minutes, Cheese Steak clicked through the files on the jump drive. Nothing of interest. Then activity showed on Olivia's laptop. He made the return call.

"What?" Little Frankie said. "Hurry up. I gotta get off the phone."

"She's on."

Cheese Steak followed Olivia's keystrokes as he relayed information to Frankie. As an online gamer growing up in Russia, Serge had won a worldwide X-box contest and caught the attention of Nicky Palermo, head of the Philadelphia crime family. Serge had named his price to come to the land of plenty to bring the organization into the twenty-first century. The payoff for Palermo was that he could still run the operation from prison. Cybercrime from the inside. Maybe some people would assume his name had something to do with chopped meat, but Cheese Steak killed with numbers and passwords—his nickname just meant he had an affinity for Philly Cheese Steaks.

"Pops wants that memoir," Frankie said into Cheese Steak's ear bud. "Check for *Crow* or *Fazziano*, maybe try *Griffin* or *R. D.*"

"Something interesting. Folder named *Ardy*."

"Don't open it. Just copy the whole damn thing on a flash drive. Palermo will want you to print it out in hard copy. Light reading, so to speak. What's she doing now?"

"Made a reservation for a car . . . Just received a confirmation from some hotel in Wolfeboro, New Hampshire. Where is that?"

"About five hours away. They're on the move. Change of plan."

"What plan?"

"We're making a plan. Keep copying. I'll call you back."

Cheese Steak stared at the document exchange icon as the folder loaded to the flash drive. His mind whirled with repeated key words and phrases, clues to open any password-protected files: *Ardy, R. D. Griffin, Executrix, Dushane, Tex-Mex Nights, Adam, Pogo*.

Pogo.

That word had potential. Novak had recited it a few times to the desk clerk. Cheese Steak's curiosity got the better of him. After opening the Ardy folder on the flash drive, he found a three-megabyte file titled *Protection*. The document lived up to its name. A window opened to request a password. He typed *P-O-G-O.*

Nyet.

He added *1-2-3* to the word, a common extension.

A sea of American text bloomed before Cheese Steak's eyes. He started to read:

Kill or be killed. No one is safe—not even a killer. R. D. Griffin enjoyed little comfort in his long career with the Philadelphia mob, but in all of his ninety-three years, one ally earned his trust: a dog. This is R. D.'s—and Pogo's—story.

Cheese Steak pulled out his cell phone and smiled as he dialed.

Chapter 9
Hitting the Road

With the phone to her ear, Olivia slapped her license and American Express card on the counter of the car rental agency. Karen continued to push for a copy of the mob memoir. The young clerk in front of her appeared to be fresh from a newbie training session, over-eager to please. Olivia turned away when she spotted the angry pimple erupting on his chin. Her priority was to deflect Karen's attention from the mob to the preservation of her mother's book.

"That's right," Olivia said to Karen. "Tell Sloane that they shouldn't respond. Radio silence. I talked with my lawyer. We're renting a car and driving to New Hampshire. Della Rainey lives near Wolfeboro." She flapped her hand at Lauren to finish the rental arrangements.

Lauren threw the young man an apologetic smile. "Just give us the biggest damn car on the lot," she said. "How about a big-ass SUV? We've got a dog." The clerk nodded and clicked the computer keys. Lauren tapped Olivia's arm and handed back her license and credit card.

With the phone cradled in her neck, Olivia retrieved her wallet. "We have five days to get this done. We're leaving in a few minutes."

"Wait," Karen said. "You're going to Wolfeboro?"

"You bet. We're going there to fix this—in person."

"I'll make a call. A nice bookstore's up that way—Alten's, I think it is. Only game in town, and both *Indigo to Black* and *The Executrix* are doing big numbers. I'll arrange a signing."

Olivia rolled her eyes. Even in a catastrophe, Karen kept her focus on the prize—book sales. At least Karen couldn't spring into an argument from her grimace. "We'll see. Call me." She hit END and turned to Lauren. "What kind of car did we get?"

"I told him big." Lauren tapped her fingertips on the counter. "Danny's outside de-whizzing Pogo."

The clerk broke out in a sweat from the blitz of mature estrogen in front of him. His only defense was to stare at the computer screen. "Uh . . . there's a white Suburban and a beige Cadillac Escalade available. Do you have a preference?"

Setting her other hand on her forehead, Olivia's shoulders slumped. "What are the odds of *that*?"

Chasing another phantom to right a wrong that could never be righted. The exact same color of Suburban—white—had killed Adam. Confronting the culprits, a young woman and her father, had been the most traumatic day of her life, second only to receiving the phone call that her husband of thirty-two years was dead. Three dark years of obsessive hunting for that white Suburban had nearly done Olivia in. Without the support of her sisters and Ryan, Olivia wouldn't have been able to count survival as an option.

"The Escalade," they said in unison.

Olivia took a cleansing breath and signed the rental agreement, like autographing a book had she not been pressing so hard.

"We'll bring the Escalade around front," the clerk said.

Lauren's eyes drooped as they met Olivia's. No additional comment about the car was necessary. "C'mon. Let's scoop up Danny and Pogo and get the hell outta here. Once we leave New York, you'll feel better."

Olivia eyed the front window. Beyond the luggage piled at the curb, Danny wandered around the grassy patch with Pogo, her head down and lost in thought. "First thing's first. On the drive up, we need to help Danny compose a message for her to post on the Pogo Trust website."

Lauren followed Olivia's gaze to Danny. "And come up with some counter-tweets."

~ · ~ · ~

At eleven thirty on Monday morning, Della sat across from her son at his law office. The birds outside made a heck of a noise in the maple tree. Must be a change in the weather. While Woody returned his messages, she read the letter he'd sent to Sloane Publishing one more time. The morning's prime rib hash did a dance in her stomach every time she ran into the words *one million*. The check would need to be mighty long to hold that many numbers.

Della tossed the printed email on the desk and gazed around the room. Her son had converted the first floor of the historic colonial foursquare home to offices that housed two partners and a paralegal. The expansive living room with a fireplace had become Woody's office, the most impressive room in the house. Early American antiques, most of which Della herself had found for him at estate sales, graced the room. The five rooms on the second floor were his private apartment. Behind Woody's desk, the rippled glass in the panes of the front window animated the falling leaves outside, so they looked as if they were floating underwater. Sun emerged and faded behind dark, puffy clouds. Winter might come early.

Woody hung up the phone. His hand lingered on the receiver. "Sorry about that. A land dispute case. I can't convince Fred Eldridge—up near you, Ma, in Tuftenboro—that his stone wall from the 1700s isn't a formal survey of the property."

"Good luck trying to convince Fred of anything. Head's harder than that stone wall," she said. "Drives a Mercedes and his roof leaks. He steals people's newspapers and puts them back in the dooryard after he's read them. And he asks *me* to buy butter for him when I go to the store. Stacks it in the damn freezer." Della tapped the printed page in front of her. "Now what?"

"We sit tight. Go about your business for the next five days."

"What if they don't respond?" Della leaned her elbows on the desk to shift her weight off her sore hip.

"Believe me—we'll hear from somebody." Woody peered at her above the frames of his tortoiseshell glasses. "It'll be a matter of *how much* they come back with, not whether they respond."

"We should-a asked for more." As soon as Della uttered the words, she regretted them when the look on her son's face frosted.

Woody studied her. "Is there something you haven't told me?"

"Did you read the book?" Della shifted her gaze to the window. A wind gust swirled the leaves on the sidewalk. Clouds raced in front of the sun, darkening the deep blue walls of Woody's office to gunmetal-gray.

"No . . . I read the synopsis online," Woody said and narrowed his eyes. He straightened his claret-striped silk tie. "And I'll tell you why. My job is to achieve a satisfactory outcome for my client. I work from facts, not fiction. I'm not judge and jury, either, but I do need to argue your case. How is this book related to you? Your words, not the book's."

Della hadn't banked on Woody digging at her about the book. Instead, he should be digging at the publisher of the book for some bank. From the clench of that jaw muscle, he wasn't going to let up.

"Does it have something to do with the poisoning crime in the book?" he said.

"Maybe."

"Is Ellen Dushane connected with a real crime?"

Della worked her dentures with a cluck of her tongue. "She started it."

Woody creaked back his chair and tossed his fancy pen on the desk. "What are you— twelve?"

"Ellen was malicious. Don't question me."

"If you say that your cousin twisted truth into fiction as some personal slight . . . well . . . what's your justification for the outcome you want? I need information for the next round of negotiations. You've told me nothing of substance. I'd never let a normal client get away with this."

"Are you saying I'm not normal?" Della studied her short fingernails, noticing a small splinter jammed under the tip of her thumb. She picked at it.

"No . . . I'm operating at a significant level of bias at your insistence. If you're holding back something important, this whole case could be an embarrassing waste of time."

"Don't read the book, Woody. It's poison."

Woody raised his eyes and froze as she said the words. He leaned forward and picked up that damned pen. He tapped it on the desk like a woodpecker knocking on the downspout. "Very well . . . but I need you to be prepared to do a deposition as this moves forward, no matter what the book says. We'll need to provide the evidence you say exists."

"It's my word against Ellen's, and she can't speak."

Woody's blue eyes softened, more like her son's than a lawyer's. "That book really chapped your hide, didn't it?"

"Sure did," Della said. "You don't know the half of it."

"Then tell me a quarter of it."

"Don't badger me. I'm still your mother."

Woody turned to the window when a gust of wind rattled the frame. He pulled out his top drawer and slid a Jitterbug phone in front of Della. "Don't fight me on this. It has big buttons."

"What am I supposed to do with that?"

"You don't have a mobile. Since you're out and about, I might need to reach you." Woody picked up the cell phone and pointed to the answer button. "I'll call you if I get word of any updates. When it rings, it'll be me—only me." He stood and rubbed the back of his neck. "It's not too late to walk away from this, Ma. Not at all."

Avoiding her son's gaze, Della rubbed her knuckles. "What can I lose? I'm eighty-seven years old."

"I told you I'd get you anything you want. *I'll* buy you a damn house in Baxter Fields."

Della shook her head. "I don't want your money. I want what I've *earned.*"

Woody sighed. "You'd better get yourself home before it starts raining. Want me to drive you? You can leave your car here."

"No. I'll drive myself. Your highfalutin car scares me." Della dropped the Jitterbug into her handbag. "Sure as hell. Something's blowing in."

Chapter 10
The Invasion

On Monday afternoon, Nicky Palermo raised his milky eyes at the rattle of keys and the grind of metal. His cell door opened with an annoying screech, even though the Oriental carpet deadened its echo off the cinder-block walls. When his eyesight had failed three years ago, he'd requested his favorite carpet from the library of his summer mansion in the Hamptons before Little Frankie had it sold, one of the last favors before his son got sent to his own prison cell in Lewisburg Penitentiary.

The carpet had done little to block out the prison noise. Now, even at eighty-six, he could identify anyone or anything by smell and sound.

A looming blurry image filled the doorway. The warden. Wing tips and *Old Spice*.

"Your son must have won a card game," the warden said and chuckled. "Frankie wants to talk to you." He guided the phone into Palermo's hand. "Five minutes. I'll be right here listening."

"You're good to an old man," Palermo said and tapped his spotted temple. "I never forget. Send the guard back in when I'm done. We left off on chapter fourteen."

"He's going to start charging you, Palermo. Narrators make big money." Keys jangled as the warden clipped a filled ring on his waist.

"Forget about it." Palermo waved his bony fingers and put the phone to his ear. "This my boy?"

Three steps. The shadow turned and stilled at the cell door.

"Pops. You holdin' the place down?" Frankie said.

"They're granting me more favors. I must be dying."

"Did you get it? I had Cheese Steak print out that manuscript."

"I did. The guard is reading it to me. I got enough to know what's in that book."

"I'm reading it too. Fazziano told it all to this Olivia Novak, Pops. She calls him R. D. Griffin, but I know it's him. Didn't hold back nothin'. Wait till you get to the part about you blowing away his wife in front of his dog. She wrote about all the people we had offed, and some we didn't but said we did. Sending him Salgado's old dog collar didn't make it in the book, but the story about him killing that shepherd did."

Palermo's smooth voice softened. "We all hold a story, Frankie."

"Should we do somethin'?"

Palermo hesitated, sensing the warden's gaze drilling into him. "No. Bring this Olivia Novak to me. I want to have a discussion with her."

"Cheese Steak said Novak and her sisters and the dog are on their way to New Hampshire. Don't know what for."

"Have Rig and Checkers go after them. Bring them all here."

"What are you going to do?"

"I'll deal with this myself." Palermo held out the phone to the warden. "We're moving forward, my friend. The tree we're planting will bear fruit. I need permission for a visitation."

"When?" the warden said.

"Soon." Palermo shook his crooked finger. "Send that guard in to read to me."

~ · ~ · ~

"Read me those directions," Olivia said to Lauren. "We just crossed the New Hampshire border."

Rain pelted the windshield as Olivia struggled to make out the highway signs. For a few minutes, a rage of pea-size hail scared Pogo. The sun emerged from the dark clouds near Newburyport, so Danny unbuckled the poodle's seat belt to let him stretch out across her lap.

"Stay on 95. We'll veer off at Portsmouth to 16." Lauren took off her glasses and squinted at the map. "I wish this car had navigation."

"Maps are better."

"Help me with this tweet," Danny said from the backseat. "Here's what I've got so far: 'Pogo trains every day as a therapy dog. He needs to stay sharp. Hashtag, Pogotherapydog'. It has to be under 140 characters."

Olivia glanced over her shoulder. Pogo's paws twitched, dreaming with his head on Danny's lap. "Sounds good. Would you please call Maria to check on Freesia while Lauren and I come up with something eloquent for your website? I don't want to be on the phone while driving."

Danny gabbed with Maria about everything but Freesia. Olivia turned her attention to Lauren. "How about this: 'As director of the Pogo Charitable Trust, I am dedicated to our mission to promote and support the critical work of therapy dogs. These animals are always ready to meet the needs of others. They make no judgments for race, gender, or social standing. It is my goal to uphold these standards.' Short and to the point."

"Good, but don't feed it to her," Lauren said. "She needs to come up with a statement on her own."

"The less we have to deal with the easier it'll be on all of us. I'll have her email it to Ted for the legal sniff test," Olivia said from the side of her mouth. "He can post the message on the site."

Danny ended the call and slipped her phone back into her purse. "I heard you guys."

Olivia smirked as Lauren rolled her eyes. "How's Freesia?"

"She's fine. Sleeping, eating, playing, and complaining. Maria said Freesia hangs out on the stairs and watches the ceiling. Crazy cat."

"There's a spider that hides in the corner crack of the entryway."

"Well, whatever it is, she's busy." Danny held out her hand between the seats, and Lauren handed her the notebook. "I'm ready for the website message." She flipped through the pages. "Lauren, these pictures of Pogo . . . are really good."

Olivia turned to Lauren. "Was that what you were drawing on the plane?"

Lauren avoided her eyes and thumbed through a *People* magazine. "I dabble."

Note to self. Check out that notebook.

"I'm ready, Liv." Danny poised her pen over a fresh page.

Olivia repeated the message, but her mind was elsewhere, relishing the opportunity to discover hidden nuggets about Lauren. The dangers and the joys of thinking she knew everything.

"Thanks. The magic of words."

"Forward it to Ted, so he can bless it."

"Will do." Danny whirred down her window. Pogo jumped up, ready for action. Soft curls on his ears rippled as he stood on her lap and stuck his head out of the window. "Smell that, Pogo." Danny breathed in. "Ahhh . . . New Hampshire air. All piney and fresh after the rain."

"Put some glass back in that hole," Lauren said. "My lips are slapping my eyebrows."

Zzzzhhhh.

"Party pooper," Danny muttered.

Olivia chuckled as she glanced in the rearview mirror. Her smile sobered to serious study. The silver Lincoln was still behind her, one that had been in her sights since they'd crossed into Massachusetts. Every time she changed lanes, the Lincoln appeared to follow her movements. A sign with food and gas options whooshed by.

"Let's get off at the next exit and take a bathroom break. I'm sure Pogo needs a stretch." She kept her eyes on the road.

Lauren closed her magazine. "Good. Me too. I know I'm getting old when I don't know any of the people in *People,* unless they're doing a memoriam." Lauren stuck her hand over her head. "Danny, give me back my notebook."

"But you watch a lot of TV," Olivia said, trying to keep her voice jovial. She glanced at the Dalmatian spots on the notebook's cover as it passed to the front seat.

"Only the British shows, the Syfy channel, and my disaster movies on DVD."

Danny's face appeared between the front seats. "Ryan loves Syfy. We watched that new movie, *Big Ass Spider!* It's On Demand."

Lauren turned in the seat. "No *way.*"

"Yep. A fifty-foot spider chases these women in thong bikinis and stabs them in the butts; then he eats them."

"I'm all over it."

Olivia blew out a breath as she guided the Escalade down the off-ramp. The Lincoln didn't follow. Paranoia quieted to edginess. Her heartbeat slowed as she pulled into a full-service bay at the gas station. "We'll gas up and find something quick to eat."

Lauren eyed her. "Are you thinking about what you're going to say to this Woodrow Rainey guy? You think he's related to Della?"

Olivia shut off the ignition. "I don't know, but we need to stick together for Mom. This Mr. Rainey is about to have a run in with three big-ass spiders."

~ · ~ · ~

At three thirty in the afternoon, Olivia slowed the car as they turned on Main Street in downtown Wolfeboro, the pavement still shining from an earlier downpour. The quaint New England town stood at the eastern edge of the largest lake in New Hampshire. Wolfeboro drew tourists in the summer for boating and camping on Lake Winnipesaukie and even more sightseers in the fall for the show of foliage and pancakes with maple syrup—amber gold. For Olivia, the town held her youth in its palm.

"Pull into a space, any space," Lauren said, practically bouncing in her seat. "Whoa. There's a spot in front of Black's Gift Shop. They might still have those candy dots on wax paper strips."

"I'll go in too," Danny said. "They might have some homemade jerky for Pogo."

Olivia pulled the car into a diagonal space, shut off the engine, and turned in the seat. She surveyed three blocks in each direction, the length of the entire downtown. No silver Lincoln. "I'll wait here with Pogo. You two go in."

Olivia whirred down the car windows. Pogo whined as Lauren and Danny disappeared behind the front door of Black's. "They'll be right back." Reaching over the seat, she retrieved Pogo's leash from the rear seat pocket. "C'mon Pogo. Let's take a stroll."

After walking the dog the length of Main Street, Olivia spotted the Yum Yum Shop on the corner and smiled. As a child bouncing in flip-flops, she'd waited in line to pull a ticket from the red dispenser, a ticket that led to something warm and sweet. The bakery had been moved from its original location to a larger, more elaborate, facade across the street, but the same mixed scent of baking cheesy bread and browning vanilla cake wafted toward her like a beacon. Years peeled away with the delectable aromas. They remained deliciously the same. This would need to be their next stop. As she waited for Pogo to finish lifting his leg on a planter box, Olivia's gaze swept the bakery's parking lot. Her chest tightened. A silver Lincoln sat in a space near the entrance.

Olivia tugged on Pogo's leash. "Let's get Danny and Lauren." The dog guided her back to Black's Gift Shop. She took one more glance at the Lincoln and quickened her stride. If she had to, she'd drag her sisters out of the shop.

The door swung open as she approached the store with Pogo. Out came Lauren and Danny, each with a hemp-handled bag.

"We scored, Liv. Check it out." Lauren stuck out her green tongue, on which sat the same color of candy dot.

"Why didn't you wait?" Olivia said. "How seriously is this Yankee hick lawyer going to take us if we each go in there with a different color tongue?"

"Oh, right. We're supposed to intimidate him with our illustrious literary pedigree."

Danny held up her bag. "Venison puppy chews. And I got some maple syrup for Ryan." She ripped open a stapled cellophane package and handed a wrinkled strip to Pogo. He held it in his mouth like a shriveled second tongue. After a few cursory chomps, he drooled, dropped it on the sidewalk, and stared at it.

Olivia laughed on the outside, but curiosity fueled an inner mission. "We have one more stop to make."

"Where?" Lauren said.

"The Yum Yum Shop." Olivia pointed down the street. "It's on the corner."

Lauren's eyes widened. "Pizza bread."

"Hazelnut squares," Danny said.

"Then we'll go ambush Mr. Rainey," Olivia said. "Remember, we came here for a reason."

"I know, I know." Lauren started down the sidewalk. "Ten minutes."

Pogo plucked up his chew like a new best friend and pulled on his leash to follow Lauren.

Hazelnut squares and pizza bread were the bait, but the real fish was that Lincoln. She needed a glimpse of its owner. The familiar obsession started to creep under her skin. Hunting down a car led to trouble.

Olivia's gaze swept the parking lot as she crossed the street. An odd combination of disappointment and fear rose in her throat.

The Lincoln was gone.

Chapter 11
Sparks

After his last meeting of the day, Woody Rainey waved off Margie's offer of a cookie from the Yum Yum Shop's pink box. In her sixties, Margie had spent twenty-two years as the firm's paralegal and administrative manager, running the office with a military efficiency that was fueled by an affinity for sweets after three. Instead of relenting to an afternoon sugar rush, Woody sat at his desk and crunched on a carrot stick as he read a PDF of *The Executrix* on his computer screen. When Margie didn't budge, he collapsed the document, returning his screen to the picture and bio on Olivia Novak's website.

"What are you up to, Woody?" Margie said and pawed through the box. "I know that look. Your mother got you all knotted up, didn't she? That little crease on your forehead showed up when she did."

"Della has something interesting this time."

"Do tell." She held up an oatmeal raisin in triumph and took a healthy bite.

"Not yet. I'm doing some research." Woody smirked. "You can go away now."

"I won't be far if you need me to sniff anything out."

"I'm doing my own sniffing. Go eat your cookie."

Margie snapped the pink box shut and glanced at his computer screen. "I recognize that cookie on your computer."

"Olivia Novak, the author. Writes romance."

"I've read all her books. Yummy."

"Margie . . ."

"I'm going." Margie turned and closed the pocket door with the rest of her cookie secured in her teeth.

Woody chuckled. His curiosity about Ellen Dushane's daughters had ignited a strategy: start with Novak's book and then work back to her mother's. Chapter ten held critical information about the discovery of Ellen Dushane's novel, more than the morning's meeting with Della had revealed. *The Executrix* became a character study of his adversaries, especially Olivia Novak. Understanding each sister's personality provided the keys to maneuvering through the negotiations ahead: Lauren, an open book of fiery emotions; Danielle, willing to cave to keep the peace. But that Olivia . . . her tenacity and obsessive behavior might be problematic.

Woody raised his eyes to the window when a beige Escalade pulled to the curb in front of his office. Three car doors slammed. He checked his watch: 4:05 p.m. A walk-in would be highly unusual at this hour. He did a double-take. Three dark-haired, middle-age women and a statuesque black dog jumped off the pages of the novel and marched up the walkway toward his front door.

"Margie?" he called out. "We've got visitors."

Woody shoved the bag of carrots into the top drawer of his desk, swished a gulp of water in his mouth, and checked his teeth in the blade of an antique letter opener. Margie poked her head in the doorway.

"You don't have any appointments scheduled, and neither does Bonner or Braden."

"I . . . think they're here to see me."

"I'll find out what they want."

"No, just point them my way."

The front door opened, followed by the quickening taps of

Margie's thick heels. Woody stood and smoothed his tie. He hadn't expected to see the sisters so soon, never mind walk into his office unannounced.

"Olivia Novak," Margie said and retreated, but not before launching a wide-eyed smirk. She mouthed, *Get her autograph.*

Woody shook his head. A shallow breath never made it to his lungs as two deep-brown eyes appeared from behind the white trim of his office doorway. Not too much makeup. Olivia didn't need any, really. Naturally dark lashes lined her lids. Her long mahogany hair hung like a wavy frame. Her professional website photo didn't do her justice.

"Mr. Rainey? Woodrow Rainey?" she said and moved to reveal her full self. Even in casual slacks, loafers, and a turtleneck sweater, she exuded sophistication. Her spicy citrus perfume hit him like a pheromone blast.

"The one and only. Call me Woody. Everybody does. Woodrow is so formal." He squared his shoulders. "This is a surprise, Mrs. Novak." The details of several articles and interviews raced through his mind. His gaze landed on the wedding band Olivia still wore, even though her husband, Adam, had been dead for over five years. The first few chapters of *The Executrix* had painted a fairly clear picture of her obsession to find his killer. Nerves were unusual for him, but at this moment, deer flies buzzed in his stomach. Della had pushed him to move too fast. Speed put him at a disadvantage, especially with this woman. Something about Olivia Novak teetered his boat. He had to remind himself they were related—well, maybe not too closely related.

"How did you know who I was?" she said.

"There's a picture of you on your website—on many websites, as a matter of fact."

"Call me Olivia." She started to close the gap between them but stopped halfway and extended her hand. Her fingers floated as if air had substance. "That letter you sent to Sloane Publishing was a surprise too."

Woody stared at her suspended hand—it seemed unreachable—before he moved from behind the desk and prepared for an overly firm grasp, but the warm softness of her skin loosened his fingers.

"Can my sisters and I have a chat with you? I believe there are a few things we need to discuss." Without waiting for an answer, Olivia turned to the hall and waved her sisters into the office. An enormous poodle trotted over the thick area rug and ticked his toenails on the polished hardwood floor.

Woody rushed to add a side chair to the two already in front of his desk.

"I hope you don't mind," the youngest sister said, "but we don't like to leave the dog in the car. He'll be good. I'm Danielle, by the way, but everybody calls me Danny." She took the first seat. The dog stationed himself next to her like a garden statue. "And this is Pogo."

"Fine, fine." Woody couldn't remember a time in his forty-year career that he'd been less prepared for a meeting. He raised a brow at the dog. He wouldn't be surprised if a recording device dangled with the tags on his red collar.

"Nice digs," the oldest sister said—Lauren. She strolled around the room like an appraiser, taking in the glass-shaded lamps, hand-woven carpets, and Federal-style furniture. The way she inspected the pieces made Woody paranoid that the price tags hadn't been removed. She ran her hand along the line of antique pewter tankards on the mantle over the fireplace. Her gaze settled on the painting centered above them: Paul Revere on his horse, racing through the dusty streets of Boston. She turned her head to the side. "I'm Lauren. This painting should be in a museum. Is it an original?"

"I believe it is," Woody said and returned to this desk. "Please, take a seat." Olivia sat, but her gaze never wavered from his face, pinning him like a bug under magnification. Woody checked his cuff links and sat, self-conscious. Lauren lowered herself into the chair next to Danielle—Danny.

Olivia crossed her legs, trying too hard to act relaxed. He knew body language, and this woman was wound tight. "Why on earth didn't you contact us before sending that threatening email to Sloane? We aren't difficult to find—obviously—since you appear to know all about us." She was good. The way she cocked her head to the side made her appear genuine, her lips genuine, hint of a cool smile genuine. At this moment, he viewed himself as a fraud.

"Going forward was at the insistence of my client." Woody spread his hands in surrender. "That course wouldn't have been my personal choice." The dog trotted to him and sniffed his suit jacket. Woody assumed Pogo had been dispatched for cross-examination. A team effort.

"Speaking of which, I couldn't help but notice you have the same last name as your client." Olivia picked up his name plate and turned it to face him. "How are you related?"

"She's my mother."

"Ah . . . " Olivia nodded. "No conflict of interest there."

"Did you put her up to it?" Lauren said and glanced at Pogo. "Sniff out a pot of money? I know how you lawyers work. This office wasn't cheap. *Antiques Roadshow* would love to shoot an episode from here."

Woody paused. A change in tactic was in order. "Not like that at all. I didn't even know who any of you were until my mother called me. Della read Ellen Dushane's book."

Lauren gave a lazy wave of her hand. "We all read our mother's book. It's—"

"Fiction," Danny said. "Pure fiction." She snapped her fingers. "Come, Pogo. Get away from him." Reluctant, the dog returned to her side and sat. Pogo's ears helicoptered as his gaze whipped from Woody to Danny. Woody had lost his opportunity to create an ally in the room.

Olivia smiled, a somewhat uppity version, and flicked something invisible from her knee. "There's a disclaimer at the front of the book, Mr. Rainey. I'm sure you're a fine lawyer, so you know what that means. I don't know why we have a problem here. It goes something like this: 'All characters, organizations, and events portrayed are a product of the author's imagination or used fictionally.' I'm paraphrasing, but I believe that's what it says."

"I know what it says, but Della still believes that the book is about her."

"Did you read it—not mine but *Indigo to Black*?"

"I chose to read *The Executrix* first." Woody centered his desk blotter to avoid her gaze.

"You didn't answer the question. If you had bothered to do your homework, I doubt you would've been so hot to be litigious. You're obviously too close to be objective."

"Even fiction can be defaming if the character can be recognized."

"Only if you can prove financial loss as a result."

Woody fingered his onyx pen. "You do your homework too."

"When a test is required. I've been in publishing longer than you."

Woody retracted his pen, its tip disappearing as if for a reload of ink. "I've been practicing law longer than you."

Olivia leaned back and rested her hands on the arms of the chair. "If Della is the fictional character of Becky Haines, and you continue to pursue this, then you'll have more to contend with than the three of us. There's no statute of limitations on murder. I know it, and so do you."

Woody's spine stiffened. "Who said anything about murder? This is simply an issue of defaming Della's reputation in this community. She's lived here all her life."

"Not long enough to prove financial hardship—" Olivia stopped when Lauren patted her knee.

The older sister leaned forward and gripped the edge of his desk, as if her fingers were lined with sticky tape. "Pick your poison, Woody," she said, "because if this is about money, you and your mother aren't getting one stinking nickel." Lauren narrowed her eyes and jabbed her thumb toward the painting over the fireplace. "But if you're up for the truth, we'll jump on that horse with you right now and take a ride."

"What?" Olivia turned to her sister. "Lauren, can you step outside with me, please?"

"No. We're going to deal with this—right here, right now."

Danny shook her head. "Please, Lauren. We really don't want to go there." The same brown eyes as Olivia's, but hers expressed more vulnerability.

Woody did catch the word *truth* but had been distracted by the peek out and retreat of Lauren's green tongue. "I specialize in getting to the truth, Mrs. Lyndale." He shifted his gaze to Olivia for a response. Adventure lit up her eyes, the delicate crow's feet around them like fans in an exotic dance.

"Lauren may be on to something here," Olivia said, never breaking her gaze from Woody's. She too leaned forward. "Let's solve this together. Something happened between Ellen and Della. Aren't you even curious as to what it was?" The curve of her eyebrows raised like a draw bridge, waving him through. "This is a family matter, not a diaper you want unwrapped for scrutiny by the legal department of a publishing house."

Danny wrinkled her nose. "Olivia. *Really.*"

At a loss for words, Woody's chair creaked as he added an extra cushion of air between Olivia and him. Any answer would be the wrong one, a quagmire. Della had been cryptic about her early life, and she made sure it stayed that way. Olivia was right; this was a family matter that involved all four of them. The impromptu meeting unnerved him, but Olivia stripped him bare of his resolve.

"Where are the three of you staying while you're in town?" he said.

Olivia rapped the desk with her knuckles. "We'll be at the Wolfeboro Inn for as long as it takes to clear this up."

"Have you checked in? It's getting late." He glanced at his watch to accentuate the point.

Olivia fingered Woody's business cards in a hand-forged pewter dish. She picked one from the stack and flicked the corner with her fingernail. "After we check in, do you want to meet us for a drink, maybe dinner, to continue our discussion?"

"Good idea," Lauren said. "Let's loosen our tongues." Paper crinkled when Lauren pulled a strip of candy dots from her purse. She plucked off a red one and popped it in her mouth.

Danny's eyes turned to brown saucers as she stood with Pogo's leash. "Oh, Lord. I don't like the sound of this."

Olivia stood and slipped his business card into her purse. She took two more and handed one each to Lauren and Danny. "Give us half an hour. Meet you in Wolfe's Tavern? That's the restaurant in the hotel."

"I'm familiar with it . . . " he said. The situation wasn't at all what Woody had envisioned when these women walked through his front door. He stood and rubbed his chin.

Lauren stabbed the air between the two of them with his business card. "You're buying. Consider it pain and suffering."

Woody did a double-take when Lauren offered him a pink-and-green smile.

Chapter 12

Wolfe's Tavern

"Your teeth look like a Christmas nightmare," Olivia said to Lauren as they queued up at the tavern's host podium. The host's name tag read *Nan*, and she appeared to be a pro. Olivia could tell by the eyes, having written about servers like this one. Years of experience revealed themselves in a split-second size-up of everyone who walked into the restaurant. She could separate the sap from the syrup.

"I did it on purpose to unnerve Woody," Lauren said. "I think it worked."

Danny leaned around her. "I think Liv was the one who unnerved him."

Olivia thought it was the other way around. She changed the subject as her cheeks flushed with heat. "And what was with your offer to get to the truth? Can 'o worms, Lauren. Not a good negotiating tactic when you don't know what the truth is." She stepped to the podium. Now, all she could think about was seeing Woody and digging beneath his veneer.

Happy hour at Wolfe's Tavern teemed with locals and tourists, most of whom were crowded around the bar, glued to the Red Sox game on the television monitors.

"We're staying here at the inn," Olivia said to Nan. "Does that get us moved up on the list?"

"Yes, and so will that gorgeous dog of yours."

Next to the entrance, a corkboard held nearly fifty photos of visiting dogs of every breed.

"Do you mind if we bring Pogo into the restaurant? It's been a long day, and I'd rather not leave him alone in the room," Danny said. "He's a trained service dog," Pogo's yellow vest drew admiring glances from the other customers in line. He sat straighter and perfectly still, as if saying, *That's right. I'm large and in charge.*

"We love dogs." The host pulled out her cell phone and snapped his picture. "He's a beauty. He's going on the board. Want me to get him a bowl of water?"

"Would you?" Danny stepped forward. "He's had his dinner."

"Of course." Nan pulled three menus. "Where ya from?"

"Portland," Lauren said. "And there'll be one more joining us."

She turned and pulled another menu from the stand. "Maine?"

"Oregon."

"What brings you to town?" Nan said over her shoulder.

"We have family here," Olivia said.

"Who's your family? I know just 'bout everybody." Nan stopped at a long table for six, reserved for guests of Wolfeboro Inn.

Olivia took a seat with a view of the front door. Without looking up, she said, "Do you know Della Rainey?"

Nan laughed. "Oh, yeah. I know Della."

Lauren and Danny sat with their backs to the door. Olivia smirked at her sisters' purposeful arrangement of the seating; they'd left the seat next to her open.

"She's our mother's cousin," Lauren said. "We're meeting her son, Woody, in a few minutes."

A dreamy expression crossed the woman's face. She reminded Olivia of an older heroine in a novel, one who imagined herself sipping Lillet in Paris—while she changed the oil in her pick-up. "I know

Woody," Nan said. "Woody and Della were in here for breakfast just this mawnin'. A sweetheart." She winked. "A gal's heart isn't safe around that man. I think I've had a crush on him for fifty years." Nan dealt out four menus, making a show of placing one in front of the empty space for Woody.

Olivia rearranged the silverware, moving the fork to the left side of the placemat. "What's Della like? We've never met her."

"Quite the character. And, boy, does she keep a tight rein on Woody. She's the reason he never married."

"Sounds like you've had personal experience."

Nan rolled her eyes. "I wish. He'd be quite the catch. We've known each other since grade school. Just friends."

"So he's unattached," Lauren said and smirked at Olivia.

Nan caught the gesture and grinned. "Like a helium balloon at the state fair. I'll send the server over with waters all around, including for the dog." She turned and walked away, and Olivia suspected a new rumor was about to be launched.

"He's never been married, Liv," Lauren said. "His bike still has training wheels."

Olivia pursed her lips. "Oh, stop. It's not like that."

"I'm just sayin', sista. Mr. Woodrow Rainey LLC made eyes at you. I say, not so limited a liability. The way you played with his business cards could have been a scene out of a Beverly Barton novel, or one of *your* novels."

"Nooooo." Olivia dismissed the comment, but she couldn't deny the attraction. "We're related."

"Our mother's cousin's son? It's not like you'd have a kid with three heads."

"I'm way beyond having kids . . . and so is Woody."

Danny's face lit up. "You'd be like British royalty, Liv, except that Woody doesn't have goofy ears and horsey teeth. Total luck of the draw."

Beads of sweat lined Olivia's hairline. She snapped her napkin and dabbed her forehead. "Will you two quit the yap? The man's going to sue us. There's nothing romantic about that." Olivia changed subjects and tapped her finger on the table. "See, Danny? You don't need to fake it. Just be up front about Pogo."

Danny perused the menu. "You're right. Depends on the establishment." Pogo sprawled in front of the table like an Egyptian sphinx.

"I brought a copy of Mom's book." Lauren rubbed her handbag on the back of the chair, like summoning a genie from inside. "I can't believe he hasn't read it."

"That's good. He's at a distinct disadvantage," Olivia said. At the squeak of the front door Danny turned around. "Here he comes."

Olivia feigned an inspection of the menu, but the flutter in her stomach signaled Woody was near. She raised her eyes in fake surprise and took note of how tall he was: over six feet. "Well. You really did come. I had my doubts."

"Ladies . . . " Woody said. He slipped off his tweed suit jacket and draped it over the back of the empty chair next to Olivia. "I'm not billing my mother for this, so I hope you don't mind if I get casual."

As far as Olivia was concerned, he could have taken everything off. Lauren and Danny faced her, eyes wide, their expressions saying just about the same. Guilt eclipsed the thought.

Olivia patted the chair and hoped her voice would come out confident and not girlish with nerves. "Not at all. Have a seat." Success.

Pogo scrambled to his feet and sniffed every inch of Woody's jacket. He ignored the server setting a bowl of water on the floor.

"Don't mind him, Woody," Danny said. "He's just checking you out to see if you're honest." She snickered, but then her face sobered. "Are you?"

"Is this a tribunal?" he said and gestured to the approaching server. "Aren't we going to order a drink?"

"Excellent idea," Lauren said and turned to the server. "A glass of white zinfandel. Make it a carafe."

"Danny and I'll split a bottle of cabernet," Olivia said.

"Maker's Mark on the rocks." Woody turned and smiled. His tanned face made his teeth appear whiter than they really were.

The server's departure left an uncomfortable silence that drew their attention to the two televisions above the bar. A promo for *Inside Edition* teased the sleaze. "Wait until you see what happened on the *Wake Up with Jo Show* this morning . . . A guest's worst nightmare."

Lauren squeezed the skin between her brows. "So . . . " She cleared her throat. "Olivia loves public television. The Brits have shows like *Downton Abby*, *Sherlock Holmes*, and *Mr. Selfridge*. What do we get over here? *Larry the Cable Guy*, *Swamp People*, and *Here Comes Honey Boo Boo*."

"And *Inside Edition*," Woody said and laughed.

Olivia nodded a silent thank you to Lauren for recalibrating the mood to neutral. Pogo bumped her knees in his effort to get settled. She glanced under the table. The dog rested his head on Woody's polished loafers, the ultimate acceptance of a new friend. That did it. Olivia trusted the dog's judgment.

~ · ~ · ~

After ordering dinner, Olivia took a sip of her wine and decided that small talk would loosen the stripes on Woody's tie. The smells from the kitchen required them to steam ahead past drinks. "Have you lived in Wolfeboro all your life?"

"Born and raised," Woody said. "I only left for school and to clock a few years at a big firm in Boston. I had to come back. I'm all Della has. Plus, I can't leave the lakes here. I'm a kayaker. I compete with a buddy of mine."

Olivia set her hand on Woody's shoulder and squeezed. Its rock-hard texture brought forth the image of him getting a massage. "I can tell."

The boldness of the gesture surprised even her. But she didn't remove her hand. The softness of his white cotton shirt redirected her thoughts. Heat radiated through the fabric. To protect herself, she summoned her writer's brain: how would she write this man's character in a novel? How would someone else, more emotionally available, be attracted to this man? Patterns emerged in the splashes of gray she saw woven in his expertly cut hair. Confidence danced in his clear blue eyes. A keen sense of humor lurked beneath his stoic demeanor.

A flush raced through her cheeks when Woody looked at her hand; then he shifted his gaze to Lauren and Danny. Smiles bloomed on their faces. Embarrassed, Olivia broke the pull of his magnetism and returned her hand in her lap.

"Don't you think we need to meet Della?" she said.

"Good idea." Woody swirled his scotch, the ice crackling. He took a sip. "Let's keep it simple, work things out. Otherwise . . . this could get complicated."

"Uh . . . yeah, I'd say." Lauren drained her wine glass and grasped the carafe. After pouring a refill, she added three ice cubes from her water glass.

When her cell phone rang, Olivia reached into her purse and checked the screen. *Karen.* Lauren grimaced, reminding her of her no-phones-at-the-table rule. "Hold that thought," Olivia said. "I need to take this . . . outside." She rushed from the restaurant to the gravel parking lot, the wooden door squealing shut behind her.

"Progress, Karen," she said. "We're having dinner with Della's lawyer. What's up?"

"Good. I've made progress too."

"You first." Olivia needed to recover from that Woody shoulder moment. She lifted her palm to her nose, hoping the aroma of his laundry detergent lingered on her skin. Gain—Mango Tango scent. Her favorite. She straightened when a large bald-headed man in a dark synthetic suit came out of the door and lit a cigarette.

"Alten's is thrilled that the three of you are in town," Karen said. "They want to do a signing at ten o'clock tomorrow morning. And bring the dog. He's more famous than you right now."

"We might be pretty tied up tomorrow."

"You can spare two hours. Ten to noon. Get there by nine thirty. The owner's name is Catherine Pratt, and she's scrambling to send out an email announcement and calling her best customers. I'm sure it'll be all over town by tonight, with a line at the door in the morning."

"We're arranging a meeting with Della." *And Woody.*

"This is important, and not just for sales. I'm covering all our backsides with this."

"*Okay.* Alten's tomorrow at nine thirty. Don't blow an O-ring. Lauren's not going to be thrilled when I tell her."

"Remember, you're on Della's turf—and your mother's," Karen said. "Public support for the integrity of Ellen's book is the strongest ally you have. Think of this as a defense strategy. The court of public opinion wins cases, Liv."

"Good point. We'll be there."

Olivia disconnected and turned. The flaps of the man's sport coat disappeared into the tavern, her intuition following him through the door before it closed. A thread of white cigarette smoke streamed from the pebbles where the man had been standing. Her senses went on full alert as she surveyed the parking lot. The trunk of a silver Lincoln stuck out beyond two white compacts, sandwiched like a steel hot dog too big for the bun. A plan formed to flesh out the Lincoln's owner.

The gravel crunched as she approached the car. She peered inside the darkened windows. A map, worn at the seams, sat on the leather front seat. Subway sandwich wrappers littered the floor of the passenger side, along with two balled-up napkins and several empty water bottles. The model was late nineties. No navigation. No identifying dents. She pulled out a pen and a wadded gas receipt from her purse and noted the license number, three letters and three numbers. *Pennsylvania.* She marched to the front door, loaded for bear.

Chapter 13
The Flesh Out

Rig crushed his cigarette in the gravel and lumbered back into the restaurant. Good call to follow that broad outside to listen to her phone conversation. From the sound of it, that woman could be a problem, unnecessarily complicating things with non-stop lip. What did dames know about O-rings, anyway?

His given name was Rigoberto, but no one had the patience to say the whole thing, not even his mother when she had yelled at him as a child. He'd been called Rig since he was ten. Like many things, Little Frankie took credit for giving Rig his nickname—sure, it was the first syllable of his name, but Little Frankie also said his block-like physique reminded him of a long-haul truck. After he'd started losing his hair at forty, Rig shaved his head to keep things simple, secretly perfecting the shine with Nair, a lady's hair remover. Deep grooves at the base of his bald head formed two constant smiles.

And having to do this job with Checkers was anything but simple. The little twerp got nervous, edgy. His real name was Chester, but it had morphed to Checkers because he had to double- and triple-check the details of every job. Rig figured Checkers wasn't capable of making even a simple decision without debate.

The television flashed the current score. Rig eased his considerable heft onto the bar stool next to Checkers. He kept his eyes on the Red Sox game and dipped his hand into a wooden bowl of party mix. Peanuts and pretzel sticks ejected from his fist to his mouth like candies from a PEZ dispenser.

"We might have this wrapped up by tomorrow," he said out the side of his mouth.

"Was that the writer lady out there?" Checkers said. He took a sip from his bottle of Heineken with a thin finger looped around the neck.

"Don't think so. I think the writer Palermo wants is the old one still sitting at the table over there. I think she's called Lauren." Rig gestured toward the long table across the restaurant. Checkers started to turn. "Don't look, you idiot."

"How do you know?"

"I heard that other one on the phone. Something about 'Lauren's not going to be happy' about having to do some event at a bookstore here in town. I think the one outside makes all the arrangements, stuff like that." Rig tapped his meaty forehead. "I listen and pick up things."

"You got ears over your peepers now?" Checkers grimaced and chewed on a dead sprout of skin on his thumb, a cuticle that had seen repeated harassment. "When?"

"When what?"

"When's the thing?"

"They'll all be at a store called Alten's at ten o'clock tomorrow morning."

"We should check with Frankie, just to be sure."

Rig squinted and swept his finger over his molars to rid them of pretzel goo. "I got this. We don't need to check with nobody."

"But—"

"I *said*, we *got* this. How hard can it be to force three broads and a dog in a car? They won't know what hit 'em. We done jobs a lot harder than this. You're like an old woman."

Checkers jutted his thumb toward the table. "You sure the one drinking that nasty pink stuff wrote the book Palermo's all agimitated about?"

"If we run into problems and don't get 'em all, then we need to make sure we get that old one over there and the dog. If I had my way, I'd leave the bird outside behind. She sounds like a real piece of work. Pushy, and too much hair."

"We need to be sure, Rig. We can't mess this up."

Rig swiveled to face Checkers. "Which one do *you* think looks like a writer? The one who's all dolled up or the one who looks like she sits at a computer all day?"

Checkers turned to stare at the table, then swiveled back to face the television. "Yeah . . . I see your point. Who's Mr. Fancy Pants?"

"Not sure, but that guy didn't drive up here with them."

"Is he a problem?"

"Probably hired from an escort service, so those gals can get some action." Rig chuckled.

"Kinda looks like James Bond, 'cept with a scotch. Not a cheap suit."

"Well, he better get a martini—you and me are about to do some shakin' and stirrin'."

Chances for Rig to prove himself to Palermo didn't come along often, and this could finally be his moment. He didn't know what the old man wanted to do with the sisters once he got them to Allenwood, but that wasn't his problem. Frankie's instructions were to use any means necessary, without killing them, to get the sisters and the dog in front of Palermo—as fast as possible. Pretty straightforward. Scaring them was fine, but the old man didn't want the sisters hurt, especially the dog and the writer.

"Now what?" Checkers said.

"We get something to eat, watch a little porn back in the room, and get some shut-eye. Tomorrow, we go to that book thing at ten." Rig raised his finger.

The bartender moved from the other end of the bar as he wiped a wine glass with a snow-white rag. He held the goblet to the light. "What can I getcha?"

"Where's a place called Alten Books?" Rig said.

"Up 109A." The bartender gestured to the main road in front of the restaurant. "Keep going up the road until you see the sign for Tuftenboro. Take that. Once you pass Mirror Lake, there'll be a big farm with a Victorian house, like the one in that movie *Psycho*. Then you see a new development called Baxter Fields. Keep going past that. The bookstore will be on your left, looks like an old house." The bartender resumed his inspection of the wine glass. "Was at one time. Still is, I suppose. Used to be the old general store." He pointed to Rig's beer. "Get you another?"

Rig drained the rest of the bottle. "Hit me up."

"Bring us two menus," Checkers said, his gaze following the bartender. "Did you get all that? Somethin' funny about the people up here. Talk funny too."

"Yankees. That's why we got a map."

Checkers turned and glanced at the long table. "I think we should check with Cheese Steak. He knows who's who."

"Shut up—the feisty one just came back in."

~ · ~ · ~

Olivia cut in line at the podium, apologizing to the couple waiting for a table. She leaned toward the host.

"You may want to make an announcement, Nan," she said. "There's a silver Lincoln in the parking lot with its lights on." Olivia showed her the crumpled receipt. The woman wrote down the license number. "I wouldn't want the owner to come out to a dead battery."

"That's so nice of you." Nan stuck the note in her pocket. "Let me get these people seated first."

"Take your time." As Olivia stepped past the bar, she spotted the same heavy-set man who had been outside smoking a cigarette. The man spun on his stool to follow her movement. She memorized his features: bald head, wide nose, rubbery lips, eyes that appeared to cave in on themselves. A human toad in his forties.

Next to him sat a skinny, weasely guy about the same age, his greasy hair combed straight back from his forehead. He appeared to be a fan of Dapper Dan or Brylcreem. Olivia's father had called it "greasy kid stuff" before he swished the sticky paste over his buzz cut. While she was used to being recognized, she found Hefty Man's expression strange when he looked at her, a low-IQ version of sinister. That, plus the Lincoln outside, zapped her nerves like crossed electrical wire. She stopped and turned. Olivia moved closer to the men. A whiff of stale cigarette smoke that permeated his polyester suit made her want to gag.

"Is there a problem here?" she said. Olivia's jaw tightened.

Hefty Man swiveled back toward the television and held up his beer, as if in a toast. "Just watching the game," he said.

Olivia marched to the table and slung her purse over the arm of the chair. She sat and tapped Woody's shoulder. "Do you know those two guys at the bar, the ones in the cheap suits?"

Woody leaned around the heads and followed her gaze. "Hmmm . . . never seen them. Not local."

"That's what I thought." Olivia nodded. The instant look of concern on Woody's face surprised her. He revealed a protective nature. "I think those guys followed us up here . . . all the way from New York."

"Why would you think that?" Lauren said. "Have you seen them before? You never said a word." Her sister hefted her purse from the back of the chair.

"No, Lauren. Wait."

Woody studied her, confused.

"Don't tell me you have a stalker, Liv," Danny said, "because we can't deal with—"

Olivia held up her hand to quiet her sister when the host walked through the restaurant and called out the announcement above the chatter.

"If anyone has a silver Lincoln, your lights are on." Nan held the receipt and recited the license number. "We don't want any dead batteries."

Olivia trained her eyes on the bar and squeezed Woody's arm. "Watch who gets up."

Woody's gaze started at Olivia's hand and raised to scan the restaurant. Lauren turned in her seat and stared at the front door. Danny checked under the table to make sure Pogo was still asleep at Woody's feet.

Hefty Man fished his keys from his jacket pocket and handed them to Skinny Guy, who stood and looked around before darting toward the door. The oaf who remained took a sip of his beer, appearing uncomfortable.

Olivia beamed. "Bingo. Those are the guys who've been following us. They're up to something, and that something has to do with the three of us."

"Huh?" Danny said. "*Those* guys?"

"They followed us on the freeway in a Lincoln. The same car was in the parking lot of the Yum Yum Shop this afternoon, too, and then I saw the big guy out in the parking lot here, snooping on my conversation with Karen." Olivia tapped the table. "I want to know why."

Woody inspected the tines of his fork, listening.

"Whatever it is, I'm glad I have my gun," Lauren said, "but I do think you're being a little obsessive about this, Liv." She turned to Woody. "She does that with cars. You'll see. And if your oven isn't clean, watch out."

"The racks *must* shine, Woody," Danny said. "And if you misbehave, she'll come after you with her extendable Swiffer duster."

Woody gazed first at Lauren, then Danny. He took another sip of his scotch and shook the melting ice.

"Don't pay any attention to them," Olivia said to Woody.

"Seriously, though, why would those two men want to follow you?" His gaze shifted to Lauren. "And why are you carrying a gun?"

"That mobster memoir is why." Lauren patted her purse on the back of the chair like giddyapping a horse.

Danny scratched her lip, self-conscious. "I opened my big mouth on television this morning about a memoir Liv wrote. I can be a little too honest."

Woody's eyes widened. "Is the book that dangerous?"

"Yes, indeed," Olivia said. "And it's not even published. I wrote the memoir of a ninety-three-old mobster in the Witness Protection Program. His name was Felix Fazziano before it was changed to R. D. Griffin. We called him Ardy. He died a couple of years ago, but not before he received a warning from the mob. Danny's husband, Ryan, is a Portland cop who helped to protect him. We all did. When Ardy was relocated, he left Pogo with Danny."

Woody ducked his head under the table and then raised his eyes. "Pogo's a mob dog?"

Danny nodded in silence.

"I've been packing ever since," Lauren said, "because I now live in Ardy's house. Nothing's happened, though."

"Where's the memoir now?" Woody's features tightened.

Olivia sighed. "In a safe-deposit box in Portland. The mob can't get their hands on it."

Woody turned to Olivia. "Danny has Ryan and Pogo. Lauren's gun takes care of her. What about you? This threat is concerning." He jutted his chin toward the bar.

His blue eyes were like two aquamarine gems, giving her the sensation of floating when she looked into them. Olivia's throat tightened, making words difficult. "I take care of myself."

"Not if you don't have to," he said and slapped his napkin on the table. He moved to stand, but Olivia stopped him.

"Don't make a scene. Here comes our dinner."

Woody refolded the napkin into thirds and smoothed it over his thighs, a gesture of perfect manners not missed by Olivia. She glanced at her sisters. Lauren smiled into her roasted chicken quarter. Danny nodded as she inspected her brook trout. Olivia trained her eyes on the front door, ignoring her chicken pot pie. Skinny Guy pushed inside and stomped back to his stool, shaking his head. He tossed the keys on the bar.

Suspicions confirmed. Now Olivia wanted to know why. For the moment, she felt safe at the table with Woody there, safe enough to change the subject.

"Oh, by the way," Olivia's said, her voice brightening, "all three of us and Pogo are expected at a signing Karen scheduled at Alten's, the bookstore in Tuftenboro. Ten o'clock tomorrow morning."

"Have fun by yourself, Liv," Lauren said.

"Karen wants us all there."

Woody eyed her from the side. "I'd like to come to see you in action."

Olivia turned to him in shock. "You'd do that?"

"Oh no," Lauren said. "I've had all the audience I can take."

Danny bobbed her fork. "If you see us selling a ton of books, then you might sue us for even more money."

Woody smirked at his chef's salad. "I think we should try to work this out. I'll arrange a meeting with Della for tomorrow afternoon, say three o'clock? Will you be done by then?"

Olivia poked at the crust of her pot pie. "Should be. Where does Della live, anyway?"

"Off 109A on the Number Nine Road. Less than a mile from the bookstore." Woody inspected his glass, as if a bug were floating in his scotch.

"Mom must have had her address wrong. I sent her a card when Ellen died. It came back." Olivia took a sip of her wine and tipped the glass again. The conversation with Woody had cast a spell over her, making her lose sight of the real reason they were all there. She shook herself back into the moment. "So, you haven't read *Indigo to Black*?"

"Not yet," Woody said. "I was planning on reading Della's copy after I read your book."

Olivia's gaze lingered on Woody's. She wiggled her hand at Lauren. "Book and a pen, please."

"With pleasure." Lauren hauled her purse to the table. The shoulder strap dragged across her green beans. "No waiting. You get your own copy. Should we make him pay for it, Liv?"

"Here we go . . . " Danny said. She put down her fork and held out both hands.

The impaled cherry tomato on Woody's fork suspended its advance to his mouth. Silence reigned over the table as Lauren disgorged objects from her purse: a wrinkled ribbon of multi-colored button candy, her notebook, an eyeglass case, a roll of small garbage bags, three B. B. King CDs, and a Ziplock baggie that contained something that looked suspiciously like pot.

"What's in the plastic bag?" Woody said. As the pile balanced on Danny's palms grew, he offered an uncomfortable glance at the other diners.

"Calm down, Legal Eagle." Lauren shook the bag. "It's my salt-free herb sprinkle. I'm trying to lose weight." She slid the book and a pen across the table.

Danny handed the booty back to Lauren and shook her head.

The book's spine protested Olivia's attempt to write a note inside. She pressed the cover flat and hesitated before she committed to an alliance in ink, subtle words she hoped she wouldn't regret. Olivia scratched out a note. After capping the felt-tipped pen with an exaggerated tap, she closed the cover and pushed *Indigo to Black* in front of Woody. "Complimentary. Keep your mother away from the signing at Alten's tomorrow. The last thing we need is more drama. We'd be happy to meet you at Della's when we're done."

"I'll confirm the location," he said. "I'd prefer to conduct this meeting at my office." Woody stared at the book. "I'm not sure I want to read this."

"You won't be able to put it down," Lauren said and took a pinch of the herbs from the baggie. She dispersed them over her chicken like grass seed. "Can you please pass the rolls and butter?"

Woody slid the basket to Lauren. He held up his empty scotch glass to get the server's attention.

Chapter 14

Unsettled Dreams

That fourth scotch had been a serious lapse in judgment. After leaving Wolfe's Tavern at nine, Woody climbed the steps to his colonial, his striped necktie hanging in two exhausted strands from his collar. The key fought with his fingers as he tried to match the notches in the lock, compromising his grip on the book. *Indigo to Black* slid to the welcome mat.

The sisters had worn him out, especially one of them: *Olivia.* Unable to stop himself, he'd kissed her on the cheek before he left. A second lapse in judgment. He knew better than to get emotionally involved, to waver his focus on the matter at hand. She'd returned the gesture with a tight embrace. *No conflict of interest there*, he recalled of Olivia's warning when he'd met her. Her citrusy fragrance lingered on his shirt, opening all his senses. He picked up the book with a tighter grip.

Not bothering to check his messages, Woody trudged past his office, with scrambled thoughts following him up the stairs to his second-floor apartment. He hung his suit jacket over the bedroom doorknob for a drop-off at the dry cleaners. Under fuzzy aim to the closet, his white shirt made the rim shot into the laundry basket. He turned down the comforter on the bed and placed Ellen Dushane's book on the soft stack of pillows. The safety of his private nighttime routine marked the only calm moment of his day: floss, brush, face wash. In a trance, he left the light off in the bathroom, preferring to avoid the glare of additional wattage. Compelled by a force he didn't understand, he pulled the white shirt from the laundry basket and wadded it into a tight ball. A *whoosh* of sweet lemon . . . with a hint of spice . . . ginger.

Olivia.

Less than twelve hours ago in the same restaurant where he'd just had dinner, he sat with his mother and plotted to corner a woman he didn't even know. This morning, Olivia had been only a pawn in a confusing but potentially lucrative case; tonight, she had sparred her way into his thoughts. A chigger under his skin. Woody never could have predicted his day would end this way.

Della.

Woody crawled under the comforter and reached to the night-stand for his reading glasses. The watercolor image on the book's cover drew his fingers. He knew those waters, the trees, the shores. His mother had taken him to Indigo Lake as a child. Even now, the secluded lake was his preferred kayaking destination to ruminate on complicated cases—and none was more complicated than this one.

A similar framed watercolor hung next to his bureau, the same scene with only slight differences: the shapes and hues in the trees, the direction of movement in the water, a canoe stranded on the small patch of beach. The watercolor had been a birthday gift from his mother, years ago. Della said she'd picked up the piece at the general store in Tuftenboro, long before it became Alten's. Now, he believed the serene image of autumn foliage at Indigo Lake had a deeper meaning, one his mother wanted him to discover on his own.

Woody's thoughts pulled back to Olivia as he opened the cover of Ellen's book. The handwritten note at the top of the title page guaranteed the night would hold no sleep:

Is it fiction? Only your mother knows the truth. Let's find out together.

The blue ink of Olivia's signature appeared to speak through the strength of the *O* and the curves of the *N*, like rolling waves. He traced the letters with his fingertip, the cursive slant of the script urging him forward with a personal invitation.

Woody started to read.

~ · ~ · ~

Wolfe's Tavern had emptied of diners, with only the wrap-up discussion of the game flickering on the television. After Woody left, the conversation became a three-way dish.

"You think he'll read it?" Lauren said and scooted her chair back from the table.

"I hope so," Olivia said.

"Woody sure was reading you," Danny said and pulled the leash from the back of her chair. Pogo scrambled to his feet from a sound sleep. He shook his head until his ears spanked his snout.

"He was kind of in the bag when he left," Lauren said. "He probably won't remember that chicken peck he gave you. Is your cheek still burning?"

Olivia sighed. After their parting embrace, the fresh scent of Woody's shirt lingered in the fibers of her sweater. Her euphoria quickly dissipated when thoughts of the Lincoln drew her attention outside. Time for one more check.

"Pogo needs a walk before turning in," Danny said. "There's a grassy area next to the parking lot."

"Lauren and I'll go with you. We need the fresh air."

Lauren narrowed her eyes and studied Olivia. "You're obsessing about that car. Like those two guys might be out there. If they are, Ethel's in my purse."

"Ethel?"

"My gun."

"Shhh . . . Keep your voice down," Olivia said. "They're probably long gone. They left the bar after you ordered that last round of drinks. And that's not a purse. It's luggage."

Olivia felt a bit wobbly herself after that last splash of wine but not enough to abandon her curiosity. As she stepped outside, the chill turned her breath to vapor.

Less than thirty feet from their SUV, the Lincoln sat like an abandoned hulk in the parking lot, covered with evening dew well on its way to a crust of frost. No sign of the two men who drove it. Olivia set her finger to her lips and waved Lauren and Danny to follow with Pogo. As a unit, they crunched and jingled closer to the car.

"They must be staying here at the inn," Olivia said, wiping the glass of the back window with her sleeve, "to keep an eye on us." She peered inside. Nothing had been moved.

Danny circled the car and urged Pogo to lift his leg on each wheel. He did, like they were on fire. "Take that, you jerks," she said. "Good boy."

"You think they want to kill us?" Lauren said.

"To what end?" Olivia said. "They've had plenty of opportunities, if that's their goal."

"Blackmail, then?"

"Possibly, but they didn't need to send two goons for that. A threatening phone call would have sufficed." Olivia shook her head. "Must be something else."

"Do you think I should call Ryan?" Danny said. "He can talk to the FBI guys that protected Ardy."

Olivia straightened. "Riojas and Skidmore?"

"Yeah," Lauren said. "Maybe they can find out what's going on."

"Ryan would flip out. No . . . Let's play this a little longer before we send up a flare. All I've got is a license number and not one shred of evidence. Technically, these guys haven't done anything wrong."

"Yet . . . "

Olivia deadpanned. "Okay, Dirty Harry."

"My personal preference was the *Rockford Files*. Jimbo broke the rules too."

Danny led Pogo to the grass for the dog's last important task for the night. Half expecting the gun to make an appearance, Olivia visibly relaxed when Lauren pulled out the roll of plastic bags from her purse and meandered toward Pogo's evening deposit.

"Show's over." Olivia started toward the hotel's front entrance. "Let's turn in."

Dips in the building's foundation made for a creaky trek to their suite on the third floor of the Wolfeboro Inn. Sepia photos of the hotel's history as a private home lined the walls. Built in 1812 by Nathaniel Rogers, son of William Rogers who owned the land starting in 1779, the three-story building offered a panoramic view of Lake Winnipesaukee. Olivia sensed the eyes in the photos tracking her as she passed. The inn had earned a reputation for more than historical significance. Rumors from her childhood had stuck: ghosts of the original family lurked in the rooms of the expansive colonial structure.

Olivia stared at the bottom of their door. "The light's on. *I* didn't leave it on."

"Not me," Lauren said.

Danny raised her hands. "Not me."

Pogo's gaze made a triple play. From the tilt of his head, he anticipated an accusing finger in his direction.

"Maybe those two guys are inside." Danny grasped Pogo's collar.

Olivia pulled out her keycard. "We'll send Pogo in first. Dogs can sense a presence, human or . . . non-human."

"For God's sake, Liv," Lauren said and pulled out the gun. "You're one card short of a full deck. Get out of the way."

Olivia unlocked and cracked open the door, then jumped back to stand with Danny in the hall. With Pogo at her side, Lauren pointed the gun, two-handed, and pushed one of her Hush Puppies against the door. She gave it a hard shove and SWAT-fanned the weapon left and right.

"Go, Pogo," she said.

Pogo bounced into the room with no idea what to look for. He stopped and turned his head back to Danny and Olivia in the doorway.

Just as they'd left the room, a warm Federal ambiance greeted them like a beauty shot for a travel magazine. High-back side chairs, upholstered in navy blue, flanked a bay window that reflected the room's interior. Two four-poster double beds were covered with spreads of green vines with red hibiscus, white peonies, and blue hydrangeas, an early American flower garden. The bedspreads had been folded back by the turn-down service. A truffle on a gold-foiled doily had been placed on each pillow. Modern conveniences remained hidden in the tall-boy armoire.

"All clear." Lauren blew across the muzzle of the gun. "Crisis avoided."

Olivia pushed past her. "Put Ethel away."

"Everybody go back to what you were doing. Enough drama for one day." Lauren set the gun next to the Bible on the nightstand. Her hand froze, poised over the embossed gold-leaf print, and then moved in one smooth stroke. With her hand in a fist, Lauren stomped to the sliding door and cracked open the glass, shook her fingers on the other side, releasing, Olivia guessed, a deer fly, and relocked the door. Lauren stomped back to the edge of the bed.

"Keep your purse in the trunk tomorrow," Olivia said and pulled off her sweater. "I don't want a gun within reach. People get killed by their own weapons."

In response, Lauren opened the gun's magazine to check the bullets.

"I'm serious. It makes me nervous." Olivia bunched her hair into the teeth of a clip and washed her face. She stepped from the bathroom with two dark eyes popping through a lather of white foam. "We'll get up super early, ditch those two guys, and check out Della's house before we go to the bookstore."

Lauren fiddled with the alarm clock. "You're hoping to catch Woody there."

Danny wound Pogo's leash into a tight coil. "Let's stop by Mirror Lake. It's on the way." The dog jumped on the bed, stretching out and rolling onto his back, all fours churning in an upside-down paddle. Danny plopped down next to him. "Yeah, Liv," she said and rubbed Pogo's belly. "You just want to see Woooody."

"You kissed him, Liv," Lauren said.

"He kissed *me*," Olivia said and darted back to the bathroom.

"Woody's sweet on you. And it wasn't the scotch lighting up his eyes."

Olivia emerged fresh-faced and dug through her suitcase. She unhooked her bra. "He's trying to sue the pants off us."

"Don't you mean he's trying to woo the pants off *you*?" Lauren said.

To cover her blush, Olivia slipped an oversize T-shirt over her head, her favorite, which said: *Careful, you'll end up as a character in my novel.* "Right now, I'm more concerned about those two guys who are following us and that you gave your gun a name."

Chapter 15
Reviewing the Evidence

What started as inebriated skepticism at ten o'clock Monday night turned to sober confusion by five on Tuesday morning. The spine crackled on *Indigo to Black* as Woody closed the cover. The down comforter radiated heat, holding him hostage like the book he'd just finished. He turned his gaze to the window. From this place of comfort, Woody stared until a hint of dawn's light etched a pattern of branches from the maple tree outside. The glass appeared to be fractured as patterns emerged in jagged lines. They reminded Woody of his childhood hunt for hidden pictures in a *Highlights* magazine. No comfort emerged from the shapes: his mother's bitter face, one he thought he knew.

Woody grew up with his mother's obsessive need to hoard, her acerbic attitude toward everyone, and the belief the world held secret plans to target her and only her. In a moment of weakness, she'd talked about his father only once. That was years ago. He'd never questioned the motives for her silence—until now.

An elaborate explanation for the death of his father had been accepted as truth: a soldier in the Army, shipped out to Korea after their wedding and killed without ever knowing Della carried his child—at least that's what she'd told Woody. She'd been a good witness too, never wavering with a shift of her eyes when questioned. He'd taken the story at face value, and Della considered the subject closed to further discussion. He needed to push her for more information.

The character of Becky Haines in the book could very well have been based on his mother. Same personality: obsessive, angry, and nothing got in the way of what she wanted. The story soared past defamation because this smacked of an exposition of a crime—a still prosecutable crime. Olivia was dead right; there was no statute of limitations on murder. But why would his mother incriminate herself? A need for attention before death? Go out with a bang to ensure her existence didn't fade to black?

Through Ellen Dushane's eloquent prose, a young woman of seventeen had been rejected and left on the desolate shore of Indigo Lake in Vermont, spurned by her boyfriend who, it turned out, had been offering nothing but empty promises. Becky went after him, plotting her revenge with a bottle of Lydia Pinkham's Elixir laced with rat poison. She got away with the crime. In the book, Becky married another man and raised three daughters as if the atrocity had never taken place. Never caught. Never exposed. With an ending like that, Ellen's story would have been quite controversial if it had been published in the fifties.

Maybe Ellen was the true source of Becky's story. Ellen grew up in New Hampshire. Ellen married and raised three daughters. Why had Della reared up in such vehement anger after reading the book? Truth lurked in the lines of text, and only one of these two women remained alive.

Woody pushed back the covers. Five hours from now, Olivia would be at a book signing with her sisters at Alten's. The future had a pulse. He eased from the warmth and sat on the edge of the mattress, rubbing the scratchy overnight growth on his face. He put on his tortoiseshell glasses to clarify the objects in the room. A hard row on the lake would prepare him for the torment of a call to his mother. Della would fight him on coming to the office, but regardless of the location, and no matter the attraction he had for Olivia, the meeting with the Dushane sisters might mean trouble.

Woody pulled on a freshly washed pair of sweatpants. As he did so, his own words bounced back at him: *this could get complicated.*

~ · ~ · ~

At seven o'clock on Tuesday morning, Olivia awoke to the sounds of crunching kibble and ringing dog tags against metal. So much for getting up early. No alarm. Lauren zipped and unzipped her suitcase. Pogo wolfed down his breakfast and immediately left with Danny for a walk by Lake Winnipesaukee. The door clicked shut. Olivia squeezed her eyes of sleep and pushed back the comforter. She zombie-walked to the bathroom.

After a shower, Olivia decided on casual Down East chic for the signing: cream cotton turtleneck, a thick hand-knit cardigan, her black slacks, and loafers. No expensive jewelry. No flash. Blending in with the locals sent a message of respect, and staying low-key for the meeting with Della lessened the chance of igniting a confrontation over money.

Twenty minutes later, Olivia was done and ready while Lauren still scrutinized her outfit.

"Danny brought up real coffee and some English muffins," Lauren said and gestured to a tray on the desk. She turned a circle in a bulky maroon cable-knit sweater and black knit pants. "Does this make me look fat?"

Any answer would be the wrong one. Olivia skulked to the coffee pot and chose her words with care. Tough as jerky on the outside, her sister disguised a soft, chewy center. "Congratulations. You're a local. Dress it up with a scarf."

"Give me one of yours." Lauren pawed through Olivia's bag. "Love the sweater. You're fairly casual today, Liv. You usually get fancy for signings."

"I need comfort." Olivia's turtleneck peeked above the thick wool cardigan in a deep shade of sage, with swirls of eggplant, ivory, and pumpkin. "Adam bought me this when we went to Scotland. It's like he's still snuggling me. It's hot, though. I'm going on the balcony."

No comment from Lauren. Olivia plucked a muffin from the tray and stepped outside. In the distance, Danny and Pogo romped at the water's edge. Olivia's gaze swept the grounds to make sure the two weren't followed. Nerves squeezed her stomach. She pulled her cardigan tighter around her waist, as if asking Adam for permission to see Woody again. The haunting, early-morning calls of the loons floated up to her, seeking an answer. After swallowing a bite of muffin, Olivia cupped her hands to her mouth.

"Ooooh . . . Ooooooh," she called out. She waited and listened. Then . . . a faint return call from an eager mate.

Maybe today would hold answers.

Puffs of a chilly breeze came off the lake as the sun gained strength. She chuckled as Pogo pranced on the empty beach with a long stick of driftwood in his mouth. He dropped it to bark at the water. Free of his leash, he didn't have a care in the world.

Olivia, too, dared herself to release the self-made tether of grief. Mourning Adam carried responsibility, like a debt owed to a loan shark, one never to be paid off. What had Ardy told her? *Gotta keep the juice runnin'.* The reminder came when Danny clipped the lead to Pogo's collar and strolled back up lawn to the inn, the dog carrying his stick like a new-found best friend. Olivia stepped inside and latched the sliding door. The hair dryer silenced in the bathroom.

"Danny's on her way up," she said. "Five-minute warning. Almost eight." Olivia checked her phone for messages. A new one had been left while she was outside. Her pulse quickened as she listened to Woody's voice mail. She disconnected and turned to Lauren.

"The meeting's at Della's, not at Woody's office. From the sound of his voice, Woody's not happy about it."

"Could be the hangover. I can't wait to check out Della's house." Lauren fluffed her freshly blown bangs.

"I'm curious too." Olivia raced to make the bed and hung the towels as a signal they'd be used a second time.

The hotel room door banged open as Danny ushered Pogo inside. "That damned stick." she said. "I made him leave the thing outside. We gotta go as soon as I change my shoes. Those two guys are downstairs in the restaurant having breakfast."

"Did they see you?" Olivia said, now on full alert.

"No, but let's get the hell out of here."

After a scramble of shoe changing and purse grabbing, Olivia pulled the door shut and jiggled the handle. Locked and secured.

As the group streamed from the elevator, Danny turned Pogo's collar around and held it to prevent his tags from announcing their departure. She led him out the front door, with Lauren racing behind her. Olivia slowed her steps past the registration desk and whispered to the clerk, "Have a nice day."

Olivia and Lauren fanned in a hustle to the car. Danny herded Pogo away from his abandoned stick in the flowerbed by the inn's entrance. "We'll get you another one," she said, "when we get to Mirror Lake."

The Lincoln sat in the hotel parking lot undisturbed, sparkling with a glaze of frost as the sun marched toward its surface. With a finger snap from Danny, Pogo hopped into the Escalade, ready for his appearance at Alten's.

"Hurry," Olivia said and cranked the ignition. "Let's go before they find out we've left." After a final glance over her shoulder, three doors slammed, followed by the clicking of four seat belts, the dog's last. She gunned the engine. A rooster tail of gravel propelled the SUV out of the parking lot. The tires squealed as she turned onto Main Street.

"Whoo-hoo . . . Go, Liv . . . " Danny held her arm across Pogo's chest.

"Made it." Lauren smacked the dash. "Now, let's stop at the Yum Yum."

~ · ~ · ~

Rig sat across from Checkers at a small table in Wolfe's Tavern with a loaded breakfast plate in front of him. Four slices of bacon and a mound of hash browns snuggled up next to two over-easies like side cars.

Checkers sat up straight, his gaze trained on the window that over-looked the parking lot. "Hey! There go the dames and the dog."

"Not a problem. Forget about it," Rig said and poked the golden crust on the potatoes. "They make good taters here. The eggs are running sunshine too." Rig bobbed his fork as the yoke bled over his plate. "That all you eating?"

Checkers stabbed a cube of honeydew melon. "Nervous stomach. You sure we didn't lose those dames and the dog? 'Cause if we did, Palermo's going to—"

Rig grimaced. "I got this. I told you, the broads are gonna be at a bookstore called Alten's at ten o'clock. With my own ears, I heard the bitchy one say it on the phone."

"If we let 'em get away, we'll be stuck in this Norman Rockwell painting with Little Frankie and Palermo all pissed off."

Rig squirted a blooming circle of ketchup over his plate. A bubble of air in the squeeze bottle launched a red dollop across the table. "Here's the plan. First, we're going over to the bakery place."

"The Yum Yum Shop." Checkers scowled and dunked his napkin in a water glass and wiped the lapel of his plaid polyester suit jacket.

"Right. We get ourselves a couple of them maple bars. Then we go to the bookstore." Rig eased a folded map from his coat pocket. His finger followed a penciled line along Route 109A. "Fifteen minutes, maybe twenty, is all it'll take."

"We should go now." Checkers tapped his watch.

Rig scrunched his beady eyes. "No, stupid. We don't want to get there too soon. They seen the car. We gotta wait till they're inside before we pull in."

"Then what?"

"They come out, we push them and the dog in the car, and off we go. Nobody will see nothing 'cause there's only woods and houses along that road. We tell the gals to shut up for five hours, then we go see Palermo. Done." Rig smacked his hands together.

"And if we don't get 'em all?"

"Make sure we snag the old one—the writer—and the looker with the dog. If we leave behind the mean one with all the hair, so be it." A strip of bacon disappeared into Rig's mouth like a two-by-four on a table saw.

"Shouldn't we check who's who? Get 'em all straight?"

Rig tapped a pattern of greasy polka dots on the varnished table. "The writer is the one that drinks that nasty pink wine. I pointed her out. Remember?" He leaned back in the chair. "What was the old one drinking last night, while the mean one was outside?"

"Pink juice."

"Right. Now, let's pay up and go get a goddamned doughnut."

Chapter 16

The Mirror of Mirror Lake

The Yum Yum Shop didn't disappoint. Danny plopped into the car and tugged on the waist of her slacks. "I shouldn't have eaten two, but their honey glazes are better than Krispy Kremes'."

"Oh, please." Lauren brushed sugary crumbs from the front of her sweater. "I've already blown my diet. I went all the way. When I was working, the company kept tabs on our body mass index to keep their insurance rates low. Can you believe the skank in human resources had liposuction to lower her BMI? I'd like to pump my fat back into her body."

Olivia glanced in the rearview mirror at Danny, who wrinkled her nose. "Think of the doughnuts as a tip of our hat to Mom," she said. "Today is a big day for her too. Maybe we'll put a rest to this mess. Speaking of—any word from the humane society?"

"Not a word," Danny said and thumped Pogo's side. "We'll start our own training program if we need to. Right, Pogs?"

"That's the spirit." Olivia veered off Main Street to 109A, a two-lane road ribboning through a canopy of old-growth deciduous forest. Colonial farmhouses and Cape Cods dotted the route, some difficult to discern until the leaves made their final descent. Continuous stone walls, blanketed in moss, defined early property lines. Their father had walked the boulders with a metal detector, so sure the country's forefathers had buried coins in the ground as the banking system of choice in the 1700s. All he'd ever found for the digging were old glass medicine bottles, and among them were hand-blown ones for Lydia Pinkham's Elixir.

Lauren had gone unusually quiet. Flickers of sunlight animated her sister's face as she stared out of the window. Something percolated in that mighty, underutilized brain.

"What are you thinking about?" Olivia glanced in the side mirror. *No one behind her.*

Lauren sighed, still taking in the autumn scenery. "Pogo . . . Della . . . the signing . . . Ardy . . . how beautiful the trees are here and what we did as kids . . . Mom"—she turned and smiled— "and how life might change if you and Woody got together."

Olivia didn't respond. The last statement had become an obsessive daydream for her too.

Lauren dug in her purse. "Well, there's only one solution for this." She pulled out a B. B. King CD and slid the disc in the player. Within seconds, "The Thrill is Gone" released a lifetime of B. B.'s troubles, with his beloved guitar, Lucille, echoing the message like a nagging wife.

"Love it," Danny said, bobbing her head.

"You think it is?" Olivia said to Lauren.

"What is?" Lauren fiddled with the jewel case and studied the playlist.

"The thrill."

"I'll tell you what's gone—my eyesight. What's that song, about halfway down?"

Olivia eyed her sister and took the CD. "'Ain't Nobody Here But Us Chickens'."

"Mom's everywhere here," Danny said from the backseat. "Her stomping grounds. You're right, Liv, this is the most beautiful time of year." She craned her neck and pointed. "I can see water sparkles through the branches."

Anticipating her first view of Mirror Lake in over forty years, Olivia reduced her speed. "The road should be coming up on the left. I remember it being a gravelly one with white sand."

"We don't need to stop here, Liv," Lauren shifted in the passenger seat. "I'm fully aware of what Mirror Lake looks like." The edge in her sister's voice gave Olivia pause. Lauren wrung her hands with lotion.

Olivia slowed the car. "Are you okay?"

"Fine. Go ahead, but let's not stay long."

Through an opening in the trees, Olivia turned on an unpaved road that after a quarter mile emerged into a sandy lot. In front of her stretched an expanse of intense blue shimmering with sunlight. The gentle waves glittered like tinsel. The cool color of the water against the red-hot hues of turning leaves made her appreciate an artist's compulsion to paint.

"Right where we swam as kids in the summer." Olivia wanted to squeal, as she used to do at nine years old when she came to this lake for hours of exploring, floating, and dreaming of what life had planned for her.

Danny opened the car door and Pogo took a leap. She scooted out after him. Lauren put her feet on the ground, but stayed seated in the car, staring at the door handle, her hand gripping it. "I'm not going near the water," she said.

"Well, I am. C'mon. Don't be a fuddy-duddy." Olivia's gaze followed Pogo's bound to the beach, where he stood barking at the splash of small waves over his paws. She turned up her pants legs in anticipation of sticking her toes in.

With a sigh, Lauren slid out of the car. Olivia tiptoed over the scratchy pebbles to the haven of soft sand. She inhaled as she moved closer the waves. The water lapped at Olivia's feet like a cold tongue. Minnows scattered as she wiggled her toes.

"Warmer in August," she said and folded up her cuffs an additional turn.

Swishing her fingers in the chilly water, Olivia recalled her favorite passage in her mother's book:

Becky's hand skimmed the water as the canoe glided over the still glass of the lake, creating a tension of ripples. Warmth at the water's surface turned cold as her fingertips penetrated the cool layer below, echoing how she felt in her own core—cold.

"I love this lake," Danny said, "but it's not as pretty as Indigo Lake. You guys need to see it. Ryan, Pogo, and I had a fabulous time up there on our honeymoon."

"No lake is prettier than this one," Olivia said.

"I think you have fonder memories of this lake than I do." Lauren stood back on dry sand.

Olivia retreated from the water and stood next to Lauren. "Out with it," she said. "What's bugging you about being here?"

Danny joined them but kept an eye on Pogo. "What's going on, Lauren?"

"Do you remember the time Mom and Dad brought us here, and I had *leeches* stuck all over my legs when I came out of the water? Dad just yelled at me, 'You need salt. You need salt.'" Lauren stared at the water as if it were only a disguise for a terrifying dip in the earth's crust. Olivia caught Danny's eye, whose face also registered concern. Lauren grimaced and turned. "Where the hell was I supposed to get *salt*?"

Olivia closed her eyes and took a deep breath. "I'd nearly forgotten about that day. Hadn't thought about it in years. I was pretending to dive for sunken treasure in the sand."

Salt. Leeches. Only words, but they had sucked the life out of Lauren with their still-potent sting. All her sister had wanted was attention. Olivia wanted to kick herself for being so clueless. As a child, Olivia had basked in a solitary world of made-up stories, a universe of introspection and pretend. Parental attentiveness had been an intrusion. And Danny, as the cute, sweet baby, had soaked up every drop of attention, even repurposing the ones Olivia had shrugged off. But Lauren had ached for more. Even Lauren's impressive accomplishments went unrecognized, maybe because she appeared gruffer, maybe because she was the oldest one. Olivia vowed to right the slight, some way, somehow.

"I'm sorry, Lauren." Olivia clapped her hands at the dog. "Danny, I hope you brought something to wipe Pogo's feet. We can't get the car dirty." Pogo picked up a small branch and bolted down the length of the beach, daring a chase.

Danny turned. "Yes, Liv. All contingencies accounted for. I put a towel in the trunk. Do you remember takings baths in this lake? Mom said the water at Gramp's house was too cold. Dad drove me down here with a bar of soap."

"Soap," Lauren said. "Shoulda brought salt."

Olivia kicked at the sand and shook her foot of the guilt. "Pumped right up from the brook, straight off the mountain. Mom fished in that stream and made trout for breakfast."

"I remember," Lauren said. "Somebody else lives in Gramp's house now. I don't even wanna know who they are."

Silence settled over the three of them. Now that she was back here, Olivia almost couldn't accept another family living in their grandparent's house. A trio of gazes followed the fiery color rimming the lake as decades of their individual memories swirled on the autumn breeze. Its nip made the birch leaves shiver. In free fall, yellow disks floated to the sand like miniature parachutes.

"I met my first boyfriend here," Olivia said, breaking the quiet. "The summer of '73."

Lauren turned to her. "You did?"

"Yeah. My first skinny dip too. Touching skin under warm water is an amazing sensation. That's what I think of when I write love scenes."

"Did you go all the way?" Danny said.

"Nooo . . . Too scary back then. We did have music playing on the beach, though."

"On that portable eight-track player you had?" Lauren said. "Wasn't it red?"

"Good memory."

"What did you have playing?"

"John Denver . . . 'Eagle and the Hawk'"

Lauren nodded. "Nice. What was his name?"

"Scott." Olivia hadn't uttered his name in decades, and in doing so she pictured a piece of herself breaking off and floating away.

"What happened to him?" Danny said.

Olivia shrugged. "I can still remember his cologne, though. He wore *Brut.*"

"*Brut?*" Lauren laughed. "Stuff's deer wiz."

"To me . . . heaven." Olivia inhaled. "Sometimes out of nowhere I catch a hint of it."

"Sounds kinda Becky-like, Liv. You didn't poison him, did you?"

"No. But a first crush has a place in the DNA, like the aroma itself is the memory. Every once in a while, the young girl inside me comes out of hiding, the one who thinks there's a whole life still ahead."

"There is, Liv," Danny said.

"That's why your romance books sell so well," Lauren said. "You're a romantic at heart."

"Pffftt." Olivia waved her hand. "Now you two have to tell me something salaciously delicious."

Lauren eyed Danny, who offered a slight wobble of her head. She turned back to Olivia and said, "Naaaah . . . It's much more fun when you confess."

Olivia laughed. Typical. "Then let's go find Della's house. That ought to wet our whistles."

Reluctant to leave their childhood behind on the beach, the three of them meandered back to the car. The hardest to convince, Pogo wouldn't come without his waterlogged stick. After serious negotiation, he dropped it in exchange for the hand towel, which got a vigorous shake. Danny tossed the branch in the trunk with a *thunk*.

Olivia pulled a package of antibacterial wipes from her purse and held three sheets over the seat to Danny. "Pogo's got to wow the crowd in twenty minutes." With three more, she cleaned her own feet of sand.

As the car bumped over the ruts back to 109A, Olivia found the similarities between her childhood love and her attraction to Woody difficult to deny. Maybe the infatuation had been sparked by proximity—not real, only nostalgia. Returning to New Hampshire had become a powerful drug, and an uneasiness lurked beneath the surface, as if mere thoughts of her first boyfriend, and even Woody, were a betrayal of Adam. An emotional violation. The car remained quiet for two miles.

"There it is." Danny pointed. "Stop!"

Pogo strained in his seat belt when Olivia jammed on the brakes and backed up ten feet to a dirt driveway on the left. She pulled to the shoulder across the street and shut off the engine.

"*That's* Della's house?" Olivia whirred down the window to avoid smashing her nose against the glass. A cool breeze circled the interior of the car.

Lauren let out a slow whistle. "Ho . . . ly *shit*."

The three of them stared in silence. Olivia's mouth fell as if wet glue had failed to hold her jaw.

The tiny white clapboard structure did indeed look like a rural schoolhouse. Expansive windows lined the perimeter; the frames had long ago lost their paint. Exposed wood had absorbed the elements and become dry rotted. Junk flanked the front steps: pots of dead houseplants, a rusted Radio Flyer wagon, a mop of gray cotton dreadlocks, along with a broom worn down to the nubs. Mildew crept up the side of the structure like a water-stained photograph.

"Well . . . this is interesting," Danny said.

The understatement prompted a grimace. Olivia took in more of the riot of details. The scene reminded her of a picture game, the goal being to find each hidden object.

Muddy puddles shimmered in tire ruts from yesterday's downpour. Discarded objects littered the overgrown grass choked with weeds: tires, car parts, abandoned birdhouses, tools, and even a hand-crank washing machine. A faded Sunoco sign leaned against the house under one of the three front windows. A cracked chunk of concrete teetered at the corner of the bottom step, yet another obstacle to maneuver around to get to the front door. The screen on the outer one had been torn in three places, the shreds slumped like thirsty leaves. A dented orange Pinto sat next to the house in inches of mud, its wheel wells corroded from road salt. Rust on a metal patio chair licked up the legs like a skin condition.

This time, Danny leaned forward and stuck her head between the front seats. "Looks like the town dump. You think it's haunted?"

Olivia narrowed her gaze. "No, but there sits justification for the old bat's claim of financial hardship."

"How come we never knew about this place?" Lauren said and scratched her brow as if trying to dislodge a tick.

"Yeah," Danny said. "Nobody ever said a word about Della when we used to spend summers up here—Mom, Dad, Gramp, Gram—no one."

"Doesn't exactly qualify for bragging rights. She'd better not show up at the signing."

"Doubtful," Olivia said. "Woody promised he'd keep her away." She drummed the steering wheel. "Woody couldn't have been raised in that house."

"At three we'll find out what's inside," Danny said. "You think it smells bad in there?"

Lauren poked Olivia's shoulder. "The one time you didn't pack a HAZMAT suit, Liv."

She took one last glance and shifted the SUV into drive.

Chapter 17
The Signing

Not one space remained in the parking lot of Alten's. Some cars had even parked illegally on the shoulder of 109A. A line of mostly women and some bored-looking men snaked from the front of the bookstore and disappeared around the side. Olivia pulled the SUV into a stand of trees across the street.

"Holy shamoly," Danny said. "Are we famous?"

Olivia assessed the crowd. "This is a surprise. Big cities, yeah, but we're in the middle of nowhere."

"Exactly," Lauren said. "Nothing to do up here, except read and eat pancakes. I bet they came from Conway, Meridith, and Sandwich. Mom's considered a local."

"We're not gonna sell a ton of books, though," Danny said. "Most of them have one in their hand."

Olivia cocked the rearview mirror. A tube of *Make My Day* red got a twist. "Face check. That includes you, Pogo. Danny, make sure he doesn't have any eye boogers." She pressed her lips. "Shake, sign, and smile."

Danny pulled a brush and a compact from her handbag. She licked the corner of a tissue and dabbed the inner rim of Pogo's eyes. His head curls got a fluff before Danny freshened her rose-colored lipstick.

Lauren flipped up the visor after a swipe of lip balm. "This is as good as I get," she said and opened the car door. "I don't care how long the line is, I'm stopping at noon. We need time to get lunch."

"Uh-uh. No way," Olivia said. "You don't leave a signing with fans still waiting." She nodded to Lauren's handbag. "In the trunk. No guns in the bookstore."

Lauren grabbed her purse from the floor. "You left your signing at Powell's when Mom died."

"An emergency. No choice." The reminder of the events surrounding Ellen's death stung, not only of Olivia's abandonment of the signing at Powell's Books back in Portland but of the extra time she'd taken to make apologies before she did leave. The added delay for Lauren to smoke a cigarette in the hospital parking lot only deepened the regret. They'd never get back those lost minutes with their mother. Lauren hadn't gotten over the guilt. Olivia tried to.

"Stop it, you two," Danny said and unbuckled Pogo's seat belt. "Take my purse, please, while I put on his leash."

Olivia tossed all three purses in the trunk and locked the back window. Her gaze met Lauren's when the chatter in front of the bookstore escalated. The eerie change prompted a slow turn. All eyes of the customers in line were trained in their direction.

Uncomfortable with the sudden attention, Lauren pulled on her sweater, stretching the knit. "Does this happen all the time? Are we on *Candid Camera* or something?"

Pogo had emerged from the car and waited for his signal. Danny lowered her sunglasses from her head, tugged the leash, and threw the crowd an exuberant wave. The graceful poodle looked both ways before leading her across the street.

Lauren sighed. "Give me a break."

"Oh, leave Danny alone. This is fun for her." Olivia chuckled at Danny's regal stride to meet her fans.

"You sound like Mom."

The closer Danny and Pogo got to the store, the more the blur of colors and patterns bounced: puffy knit hats, red down vests, bright purple fleece, and striped scarves.

Olivia turned to Lauren. "You and I should go get a coffee while those two do this signing."

Several fans broke from the queue with outstretched hands, hungry to touch. One voice from the crowd soared above the din.

"Pogo's here!"

~ · ~ · ~

At 9:50 a.m., Catherine Pratt, the owner of Alten's, rushed to hold open the door to usher Pogo and his entourage inside. Several customers tried to push through behind Olivia, who was bringing up the rear.

"Five minutes. Let the ladies get the dog settled." Catherine pushed the door closed. She flipped the lock, turned, and beamed. "Welcome. I'm thrilled you're here. Will ya look at the turnout?"

Catherine had jumped off the pages of an L. L. Bean catalog, expensively dressed for chopping wood: white cotton turtleneck under a hunter-green zip-up fleece vest, with soft suede loafers poking from the bottoms of her tan wool slacks.

Bookstores empty of customers held a special kind of quiet, an alive quiet vibrating with new and used flatfoots, killers, lovers, and wizards. Olivia took in the layout. Stories whispered an invitation to peruse without urgency. Lauren heeded the books' calls and walked the aisles of maple shelves, followed by the tick of Pogo's toenails and the swish of his service vest. Stuffed chairs of flowered chintz defined each section, like petite healing gardens to sit and become inspired. A fireplace crackled near the front counter in what used to be a living room. The paper of the books surely absorbed the warmth like a sponge.

A long table had been arranged near the front door. An easel held a large reproduction of the cover of *The Executrix*, mounted on foam core: an image of Pogo in a whirl of manuscript paper, resembling a turn-of-the-century advertising poster. A dish of maple-leaf-shaped candies sparkled with sugar flecks. Fresh pens and bottled water waited in front of three folding chairs, along with pump bottles of berry-scented hand sanitizer. At the end of the table sat an ink pad and a rubber stamp in the shape of a dog paw. On the floor sat a ceramic bowl of water on a plastic place mat.

"Wow," Olivia said. "Catherine, you've outdone yourself."

"Give me a day, and you wouldn't believe what I can pull off. Your agent called me with instructions."

Lauren emerged from around a shelf with two paperback books in her hand, followed by Pogo. The dog appeared to be as triumphant as Lauren. "Where on earth did you find two out-of-print Beverly Barton novels? I've been hunting everywhere for these."

"Just got those in the other day. One of my customers is a book hound. In fact, she claims to be a relative of your mother's."

"Who?" Olivia said.

"Della Rainey."

Lauren widened her eyes at Olivia.

Catherine nodded to the front window. "Time to unlock the door."

Lauren checked the price on the paperbacks and pulled a folded five-dollar bill from her knee-high nylons. She slapped it on the counter. The dog pivoted his head from Lauren to Olivia with a what-the-hell look. "What?" she said to Pogo. "It's my emergency money. My purse is in the car."

Olivia pointed to the end chair for Lauren. "Age first, then beauty."

"Crazy before sane." Lauren let Olivia scoot to the middle.

Danny had already taken her place in front of the ink pad at the far end. Pogo took a quick lap from the bowl and sat. She inked the rubber stamp to test the impression of a paw print. "Pogo's ready."

Catherine unlocked the door.

Like a receiving line at a wedding, fans worked their way down the long table to gather signatures from Lauren, Olivia, Danny, and finally from Pogo. The dog received copious head scrubs while Danny stamped each copy of *The Executrix* with a paw print. Even the inside cover of their mother's book, *Indigo to Black*, got a pawed notarization when presented.

Several elderly customers claimed to have known Ellen Dushane from her high school days. Apparently, after death, passing acquaintances ripened to close friendships. As tempting as the opportunity was, Olivia held back her urge to inquire about Della. In quaint New England communities, smiles disguised treacherous waters fraught with wagging tongues.

By eleven thirty, Lauren was sighing and flexing her fingers to loosen the joints. Endurance wasn't one of her strengths. Danny and Pogo, too, were losing steam.

"My hand hurts," Lauren said to Olivia.

"Pogo needs a pee," Danny said from the side of her mouth. She threw a woman a broad smile. The dog stepped forward to receive his pat, pat, pat.

The line continued to snake out the door, but Pogo's *Cha Cha* dance prompted Olivia to signal Catherine with a nod. She rushed to Olivia's side.

"About cleaned me out of my stock of *The Executrix*," Catherine said. "You kicked off Christmas buying early. Your mother's, not so much. Nearly everybody already had one."

Olivia smiled, signed, and passed the book for a woman in line. Catherine's words were a gift to any author, but for Olivia they were music. "My sisters are going to take Pogo outside for a little break. I could use one too."

"They'll be back in five," Catherine said to those in the shop.

Grateful for a respite, Lauren stood and followed Danny and Pogo. The bell of the door jingled, a sound that had gone from charming to annoying after the first hour.

Catherine beamed as her gaze followed Pogo out the front door. "He's a star. I might adopt a dog to be a greeter." She led Olivia to a back room with a coffee pot and assorted packets of tea.

With the store's owner all to herself, Olivia took a chance as she dunked a teabag in hot water. "So, you mentioned Della Rainey is one of your customers."

Catherine appeared to sort out words in her head. "Lives down the road, a mile or so. She comes in every so often. Last week was the first time I'd seen her in a long time. In fact, I'm a bit surprised we didn't get a visit from her today, especially since she claims Ellen was a relative." She winked. "Heard you all had dinner with her son, Woody, last night. Nice fella, although he's on the wrong side of that property line ruckus down the road." Catherine pursed her lips. "Suppose you heard about that funeral home mess too. Shame on Walt Cleary."

Olivia nodded as if she knew what Catherine was referring to, but didn't offer up any details of her own for the locals to chew on. "What kind of books does Della like?"

"Oh, everything. Della has an excellent eye. She beats me to estates sales and buys up classics on the cheap, then turns around and sells or trades most of them to me. I don't begrudge her. She brags about having quite the collection tucked away, though. Not sure I believe her. Have you seen her house?" She shook her head. "Della's marching toward ninety and struggling to make ends meet."

"She told you the truth, Catherine. Della is Mom's cousin, although none of us has ever met her."

"Well, what do you know . . . " Catherine toyed with the hinge of the zipper on her vest. *Zip, zip, zip.* Olivia tracked the sound like subtext. "I figured she was fibbing. She'll say anything to get her way." Catherine eyed Olivia from the side. "How she had a son like Woody, I'll never know. A saint."

To skip over the subject, Olivia pulled out the type of question she always asked herself before pitching a book. "How would you describe Della in one sentence?"

Catherine peeked around the doorway for any lingering ears. She leaned in for a conspiratorial whisper. "Well . . . might take more than one, but she's a bit of a nutter with a ruthless streak. I wouldn't cross her." She punctuated the statement with a nod. Her chin stayed down as her eyebrows rose.

Shouts and barking outside drew Olivia and Catherine from the back room. Car doors slammed in succession. Tires squealed and burned rubber on the pavement of 109A. A customer who had left the store burst back through the front door. The overhead jingle resonated behind her like a fire alarm in a fairy tale. With wild eyes trained on Olivia, the woman froze with her hand gripped on the knob. "I think you have a problem in the parking lot."

Olivia shot to the front window. "What happened?"

"Two men just snatched your sisters and the dog."

"What?"

"Forced them in a fancy car and took off like a bat outta hell."

Catherine darted to the counter. "I'll call the police."

"They'll take too long." Olivia dug in the pocket of her sweater for her keys. "I'm going after them."

Chapter 18

Philip Marlowe? Or is it Sam Spade?

Olivia jumped into the rental and slammed the door. She revved the engine, backed up, and fishtailed on the pine needles, not bothering to buckle her seat belt. Shorting the curves through the forested portion of 109A, her wild gaze swept the woods on either side for a glimpse of the silver Lincoln. She turned into Baxter Fields and made the doughnut loop around the cul-de-sac of luxurious homes. Nothing. Smacking the dashboard, she gunned the SUV back to the main road and squealed the tires on a right turn.

Her attention darted from the road to the trees. *Left—right—mirrors. Left—right—mirrors.*

Breath didn't come easily as she tried not to envision the danger Lauren, Danny, and Pogo might be in. The murderous stories Ardy Griffin had told her for his memoir could never be erased from her mind. The mob wasn't above torture to get what they wanted, not even killing a dog to make a point.

Think. Voices of her sisters mutinied rational thought. Olivia skidded to the shoulder and jammed the gear shift into park. The steering wheel became a forehead rest while the engine idled. Her sisters carried no ID, no weapons either, their purses behind her in the trunk. Pogo would assess everyone in the car to identify friend or foe. Olivia pictured the inside of the Lincoln: Lauren causing a scene if the goons didn't stop to explain themselves; Danny offering no information to avoid inciting a confrontation, her arms around the poodle. Her mother's voice filled her head. *Don't fight with your sisters. Mark my words, you'll need each other one day.* Ellen had been right—so right.

No doubt Lauren would be mad, hopping mad, and latching onto her anger like that call for salt. *Salt.* The last place to piss off Lauren—*Mirror Lake*. Her sister would convince those guys to go there as a way to communicate their location.

Olivia raised her head and threw the car into gear. After five minutes of what should have been a ten-minute drive, blurred sparkles flashed through the foliage. She blinked her wet eyelashes and dragged her hand over her cheek. Dust floated in stabs of sunlight on the sand and gravel road, the same road she'd turned on this morning. This time the lake wouldn't hold any childhood memories, but those stories had led her here, with her sisters held hostage.

The car bounced in the dips and vibrated over the stones. She slowed to a crawl, determined to keep her head. The woods swallowed her frantic gaze. She was back to the volatile place from which she'd hunted for the car of her husband's killer. Solitary hell.

A glint of silver metal. *Pay dirt.*

Through the trees, the Lincoln sat parked in the sandy lot in front of the expanse of Mirror Lake, a breeze snaking exhaust from the tailpipe. Anger fueled her rescue mission. To stay out of sight, Olivia inched the SUV into a tight opening between two pines. Branches scraped the sides as she crunched to a stop and shut off the engine. The trilled tap of a woodpecker perforated the quiet as the keys dangled, still swaying, from the ignition. Never taking her eyes off the sedan, she pressed a series of buttons—all the buttons—near her left knee. The gas tank cover opened; the hood popped; the steering wheel retreated into the dash. Finally the trunk unlatched. The quiet cue started a thumping race in her chest.

Olivia cracked open the driver's door in millimeters. She

shimmied out and pushed away the branches. The door panel clicked shut with the press of her hip. Tiptoeing to the back of the car, she raised the window and reached for Lauren's purse. With two fingers, she floated out an open package of panty liners, a banded stack of scratched lottery tickets, an overstuffed wallet, and a box of bullets with the ribbon of button candies stuck to the bottom. Olivia paused when she pulled out the notebook, her first glimpse. Momentarily distracted, she flipped through the pages. *These drawings are wonderful.* If they got out of this mess, she vowed to bring them into the light. She shook herself back to reality.

A shine of steel at the bottom—the gun. Olivia picked out the smooth, weighty pistol and shook the short barrel. No rattle of bullets. It was loaded when Lauren checked it last night. Full or empty, it didn't matter. A prop. She abandoned the effort to reassemble Lauren's purse when the panty liners cascaded from the plastic package and littered the floor of the trunk. "Jesus, Lauren," she said aloud. As an after-thought, she snatched Pogo's two-foot stick, tucked the branch under her arm, and eased down the back window until it latched.

Twigs cracked beneath her loafers as she moved in a crouch along the tree line. With the pistol pointed in her right hand, she held back the branches with Pogo's stick with her left to make a path. One snapped back and smacked her in the face. Dead leaves stuck in her hair and on her sweater. *Move forward. Camouflage.* Her scalp prickled. *Don't drop the gun. Don't drop the gun.* The internal chant urged her toward the Lincoln.

Olivia stooped and crept to the back wheel well of the car, her grip tight on both weapons, making her hands sweaty, knuckles white. Cigarette smoke streamed from the open windows, both from the back and from the front. The protest of Olivia's knees caused her legs to shake. Her sisters and Pogo sat in the rear seat, the dog in the center. Lauren hung her hand out of the window. *Is she smoking?*

Hefty Man in the front seat, the one with a thick neck, laughed and had a coughing fit. A wicked sound. Skinny Guy on the passenger side followed up with a whiny cackle. Pogo barked, making Olivia flinch. *He senses I'm here.* She squinted, not daring to move a muscle. Ardy Griffin's words rung; he'd been forced by his boss to kill a dog once, to scare a man into paying a debt. Anger surged in her gut. *They touch one hair on Pogo, I'll pull the trigger.*

With her legs tingling from lack of circulation, Olivia summoned the voices of Sam Spade in Dashielle Hammett's *The Maltese Falcon* and Philip Marlowe from Raymond Chandler's *The Big Sleep.* How would they confront these men? Her first words needed to sound menacing and in control. *Even a good excuse is going to land you in the cooler. Well, well, didn't think I'd find you, huh? I've drilled bigger holes in smaller men than you.* She wasn't sure about the last one, but fictional character dialogue boosted her confidence as she fought the urge to stand. She inched forward along the door panel, using the stick to lean on. Lauren's cigarette smoke streamed through her hair like an extermination treatment. The flick of an ash hit her forehead and ski-jumped off the end of her nose. Without thinking, she scratched it with the end of the gun to keep from sneezing.

Lauren's eyes widened when she turned toward the open window. Olivia gave a slight shake of her head. She put the gun to her lips like a deadly finger.

The pistol wavered as Olivia moved forward and straightened. She rested the muzzle against the spongy flesh of the driver's temple.

Hefty Man stiffened.

Through clenched teeth, Olivia lowered her voice to a growl. "You lay a hand on my sisters or hurt that dog, I'll see daylight through your head." *Yeah, good. Sounded good.* Skinny Guy in the passenger seat held up his hands; his face registered shock.

Hefty Man's eyes shifted toward the gun; his thick neck kept his head still. "You the writer lady?"

"What's that got to do with anything?" Olivia stared in disbelief at the barrel she'd pointed at the man's head.

Lauren launched her cigarette butt out of the open window. "Liv. This isn't what you—"

"Don't say one word—you or Danny," she said. "Not one word."

Olivia leaned toward Hefty Man's ear. "What do you two want? Why were you following us? Why did you kidnap my sisters?" She nudged the muzzle into his skin with each question. "Why?"

"Slow down, woman," Hefty Man said and brushed away the gun. "Can't stand noisy broads with a shooter. They make me nervous. Put the damn thing down, will ya? Let's talk."

Skinny Guy lowered his hands and ducked to address her. "Did you write that book 'bout Crow Fazziano?"

Olivia gasped, then narrowed her eyes to the meanest squint she could muster. The voice of Sam Spade came to her rescue: "Depends. I might say yes. I might say no."

"The boss wants to talk. We're here to take you to him."

"Who's your boss? I'd like to have a chat with him too."

"Nicky Palermo," Skinny Guy said.

Olivia froze. The name sent a shockwave of electricity through her body. Her sweaty hand made her grasp on the gun falter. *Palermo. Ruthless.* She'd learned quite a bit about the don from Ardy, more than even made it into the memoir.

"I'm Checkers," he said and pointed. "This here's Rigoberto. We call him Rig."

"I've got better names for you two." Olivia couldn't come up with what those two names might be, but she tightened her grip around the stick in her other hand, ready for a surprise swing.

Rig inched his head in her direction. "Put . . . down . . . the *gun*." His beady eyes widened beyond their capacity. He sucked in a breath and groped at the leather seat. His fingers found a folded map.

"Liv . . . Don't move." Lauren grabbed the back of Rig's headrest.

The hair on Olivia's scalp stood on end. She spotted something moving above her eyebrow.

A leaf. A trick. Focus.

Danny squealed like a piglet and covered her mouth. She turned away in the rear seat. Pogo stared, stock still.

In one sweeping motion, Rig made an arc with the map and swatted the top of Olivia's head. A hairy-legged black spider raced down her arm and disappeared into the loose knit of her sweater. Every cell of her body squeezed with rejection, her reflexes uncontrollable. The gun fired over her head as Olivia fell backward to the ground, sailing Pogo's stick like a javelin toward the trees. The blast ignited a flock of birds to flight as the echo filtered through the woods.

Lauren burst from the rear car door. "Oh my god, Liv. Are you all right?"

"Get it off me. Ahh . . . ah . . . ah . . . get it *off*." Still gripping the gun, Olivia flipped four turns on the gravel in an attempt to squash the spider. Pogo leaped out of the car, barking as he charged to her side.

Lauren stood over Olivia and held out her hand. "Give me Ethel."

Danny knelt and pried the gun from Olivia's fingers, which were stiff, as if rigor mortis had set in. With her forefinger hooked through the trigger loop, Danny floated the pistol to Lauren. "Everything's fine, Liv. These guys didn't come here to hurt us."

Jagged chunks of rock embedded into Olivia's palms when she rolled over and raised to her knees. Pogo barked as the spider ejected from her sleeve and raced across the pebbles to make his getaway. The dog reared up, pounced with his front paws, and gobbled down the arachnid. In triumph, he trotted to a birch tree, lifted his leg for a quick shot, and bolted to retrieve his stick.

Leaves rained from Olivia's hair as she spit sand from her tongue. She turned her head to Danny. "What the hell do they want?"

Danny held out her hand. "You asked for it. They're taking us to meet with Palermo."

Chapter 19
The Deal

Rig held the flame of his lighter to a cigarette. "You broads are crazy." He straightened his jacket and paced around the Lincoln to open the back door.

Olivia glared as she collapsed into the backseat.

For the third time, Checkers threw the stick for Pogo. "Hurry up," he shouted from the beach.

"Give us a minute," she said and slammed the door. With the windows down and the engine turned off, privacy wasn't a possibility.

Lauren entered from the other side, sandwiching Danny on the hump.

"Are you guys okay?" Olivia rested her head back on the seat. Even in her humiliation, she thanked the stars for her sisters sitting next to her.

"We're fine," Danny said. "I wasn't prepared for being shoved in this car, though. I thought we were goners."

"You can't even use a gun." Lauren shook her head.

Olivia grimaced and brushed the sleeves of her sweater. A crisp leaf got a flick outside. "I wasn't exactly thinking of that, was I? You both could have been killed, and Pogo too. I called Catherine to apologize and nix the police dogs. I'm sure we'll be a juicy item in the *Granite State News.*"

Rig leaned into the window. "Hate spiders. I'd-a shot the thing." He took a drag on his cigarette.

Olivia pushed his meaty forehead away and turned. "So you two were all buddy-buddy with mobsters while I was frantic to find you?"

"They don't know why," Lauren said, "but Palermo summoned them to bring us to Allenwood Prison in Pennsylvania. He wants to talk to us in person—you, to be exact."

"They thought Lauren was you," Danny said and chuckled.

"God forbid."

"This is about the memoir." Olivia sighed and stuck her thumb toward the window. "Einstein over there pretty much said so."

Lauren shifted in the seat. "No way. The manuscript is in a safe-deposit box. All the other copies were shredded. Besides the bank, Ted's the only one with the key."

Remaining quiet, Olivia turned her face to the open window. Checkers wrestled the stick away from Pogo.

"Right?" Lauren pressed.

"Not exactly." Olivia closed her eyes, dreading full disclosure. "The hardest thing a writer can do is to hit the delete button on an entire manuscript . . . and empty the trash."

Danny set her hand on her forehead. "You left the manuscript for *Protection* on your laptop?"

"Why didn't you just put a bow around it and overnight the book to Palermo?" Lauren said. "The mob must have hacked into your computer at the Jewel."

"I had it protected." Olivia's stomach dropped.

"What's the password?"

Olivia wrinkled her nose. "Pogo123."

"Duh, Liv. Took them two seconds to figure that out," Danny said.

"Well, Bonehead, I'm glad I cut a deal." Lauren rubbed her eyes. "I've found your new mob name—Bonehead."

Olivia straightened. "What do you mean, you *cut a deal?*"

"I had to. You had Ethel." Lauren leaned her head out of the window. "Hey, Rig? Give me one of those cigarettes."

Rig swaggered around the car and smacked the pack. Lauren pulled out one and let him set the tip aglow.

"You quit," Olivia said.

"Not today." Lauren dangled her arm outside after taking a deep drag. She blew out the smoke like a shot of bug spray. "I told these guys we'd go talk to Palermo if they went with us to meet Della."

"You *what?*" Olivia pictured their feet ending up in cement, left to die of starvation or chew their own legs off at the knees.

"I was buying time. Tit for tat. They agreed. Plus, we might need some extra intimidation if things get ugly with Della."

"But Palermo's in Pennsylvania." The fresh image of five people and a dog smashed in the Lincoln for five hours held even less attraction. She had to convince them of an alternate plan.

Danny rubbed Olivia's knee. "We're alive, and if we go with them, we might fast-track this Della mess."

The bookstore owner's words about Della fast-tracked around Olivia's head. *She's a bit of a nutter with a ruthless streak. I wouldn't cross her.* To avoid borrowing trouble, she changed the subject.

"By the way, Lauren, your panty liners spilled all over the trunk." She gave a lazy wave toward the woods.

"You went through my purse?"

"Who hasn't been through your purse? We witness the parade every time you dig for treasure." Olivia smirked. "The notebook sketches are spectacular."

"Thanks." Lauren took a puff on her cigarette and made a smoke ring. It spread out like a lasso and fell apart over the front seat. She grimaced and tossed the unfinished butt out the window, trailed by smoky threads. "Let's go to Della's. Woody might be waiting for you."

Danny fanned away the smoke. She climbed over Olivia's knees and eased from the car. Flipping down her sunglasses, she addressed Rig and Checkers. "Guys? Follow us to the rental car."

"Lauren stays," Rig said. "She rides with me, so you three don't get slippery. Checkers rides in the rental."

Olivia elbowed Lauren. "Before you leave, go pick up that butt—both of them."

Her sister grimaced and opened the car door.

Danny clapped her hands. "C'mon, Pogo. Go for a ride?"

~ · ~ · ~

Olivia waited for Rig and Lauren to pull next to the SUV in Della's driveway, more like a mudway. Scraping the bottoms of her loafers wasn't what she had in mind for an afternoon activity. She turned off the ignition. Checkers surveyed the debris in the yard. "I don't think Mr. Fancy Pants is here yet. I doubt he drives a junked-out Pinto."

"Go get Lauren," Olivia said. "We need to talk before this meeting, just the three of us. Sit in the Lincoln with Rig."

Checkers studied her. Then he eyed the ignition. "Gimme the keys."

She dropped them in his hand. "Don't worry. We won't peel out of here on you."

After an exchange of door slamming, Lauren climbed into the passenger seat of the SUV. She held up the keys. "I'd better keep these since you're so keen to give them away." She dug in her purse and picked a red button candy off the wax paper. "We're early. It's only two. What do we do? Sit here?"

Pogo's gaze made the rounds as if waiting for an answer. Danny's head jutted between the front seats. "No. Let's go in. The element of surprise might work in our favor. We might get Della to talk if she's on her own."

"I think we should wait for Woody," Olivia said.

"Danny's right. Let's go in," Lauren said.

Pogo pawed the back of her seat. Three against one.

Lauren stuck her thumb toward the Lincoln. "What about Dee Dee and Kiki over there?"

Olivia smirked. "Rig and Checkers?"

"Yeah."

"They should wait in the car. Danny, go tell them to stay put. We'll wave them in if we need some muscle."

"You go." Danny opened the back door. "Pogo needs another piddle before we start this party." She scooted the dog outside. He bolted to an overgrown bush and gave the leaves a thorough watering.

"Something took a pee on this house," Lauren said.

Olivia pictured their suite at the Wolfeboro Inn, with its pristine view of Lake Winnipesauke and petite guest soaps, the fragrance of lavender. "I can't imagine what it's like inside."

"What if Della's insane?" Danny said, keeping an eye on Pogo while he investigated an old tire with weeds growing through the center. Expressing an opinion, the poodle squirted the offending treads. "I mean, literally."

"Don't forget, this woman's DNA is pumping in our veins," Lauren said. "Maybe that's why you're a clean freak, Liv. At odds with your inner slob. But even you'd be over your head with this place."

Olivia threw her sister her best deadpan look.

Tongue flapping, Pogo trotted back to the car. Danny poured water from a gallon jug into his travel bowl. "I don't trust anything coming out of Della's pipes."

"Give me a hit off that." Lauren held out her hand through the opening between the seats. She took a healthy swig and handed the jug to Olivia. "Should I get my gun?"

"Lord help me." Olivia sipped and sighed. "All weapons stay in the trunk; I'll arm us with hand sanitizer. Danny, put on Pogo's service vest so Della doesn't freak out. Not everyone likes dogs."

"Woody's the one who's going to freak out," Lauren said.

"That's what I'm afraid of."

As Lauren went to review the plan with Rig and Checkers, Olivia opened the center console. She pulled out a bottle of antibacterial gel and gave the nozzle three generous pumps. The sound of ripping Velcro, from Pogo's vest, started the next leg of what had already been a long day.

"Pogo's ready," Danny said. "Let's go in."

Lauren marched back to the SUV. "The boys are on board. They'll intercept Woody when he gets here."

With Pogo straining to sniff out cooties, the four of them stepped to the front door. Lauren raised her knuckles to knock, but a squeal behind the screen made her jump back.

"Thought I heard *thomething* in the dooryard," the woman said, scrimmed in a flowered terry-cloth house dress. "Well, well, Ellen's girlths." Della unlatched the ripped outer door. She offered a rubbery smile that caved in on itself. "Didn't think you'd show."

Lauren glanced at Olivia, her eyes wide. A thick New England accent without the benefit of teeth could be categorized as a foreign language.

Della turned and limped from the door in a navy-blue orthopedic boot. "Thuppose you'd betta come on in. Have a thit. We'll thalk," she said and squeaked the hardwoods in one Wallabee shoe, the other in a medical boot. "Lemme get my theeth,"

Lauren turned and whispered, "I'm never missing another teeth cleaning—*ever*."

Tentative, Danny clenched Olivia's arm with one hand, Pogo's collar with the other. She nodded for Lauren to step inside first.

The screen door banged shut behind Lauren, the house devouring her. Olivia gripped the handle and squealed it open for Pogo and Danny.

Olivia followed and sized up the cluttered space. Living room? Dining room? A bedroom? No place to sit, not that she would anyway. Stacks of newspapers, paperbacks, hardbacks, and magazines—waist high—dotted the room; shelves stuffed with old books lined the perimeter. One display case had been stacked with glassware, the only hint of something once shiny. The stale air in the house reeked of clothes in need of a wash, like the back room of a thrift store. Her gaze settled on a set of golf clubs in a cracked-leather, wheeled bag. A tag dangled from the strap: $8.00.

Della shuffled from a doorway, presumably a bathroom, with a mouth too big for her head. She resembled one of those creepy kibble commercials where a dog smiles with people teeth. Her wiry hair appeared to have been zapped by electrical current. "Used to be a one-room schoolhouse back in the thirties. I bought it for a song."

"I'm sure," Lauren said.

Olivia attempted to focus on one thing among the piles of stuff. A makeshift kitchen had been cobbled together in the far corner. A microwave oven sat on a wooden table with its plug stuck into a dangling extension cord. For lack of a landing spot, she leaned against the wall by the front window with her arms crossed. Lauren joined the united front. Danny trailed Pogo, trying to corral him. The dog's overloaded olfactory glands led him in multiple directions at once. He disappeared behind a rack of winter coats rimmed with record albums. Don Ho smiled through dust from the top of one stack.

"About the letter," Olivia said. "Can we talk about it?"

"I saw the three of you on *Wake Up with Jo*," Della said. "You each inherited some of Ellen's features, especially you, Lauren. You got that wicked jaw of hers." She brushed a pile of clothes to the floor, revealing a burnt-orange stuffed recliner in the center of the room. After plopping down in the dipped cushion, Della pulled the lever. Her legs shot up as if the chair might launch her into a half pike into the kitchen. "I read the book."

"Obviously," Lauren said.

"One of you could've at least called me when Ellen died."

"We wrote to you, but the card came back as undeliverable," Olivia said.

Della's face took on the cast of an insolent child. "Didn't try too hard, did ya? Been right here. You're lookin' at me."

In her mind, Olivia counted off the steps required to slap the sarcasm off the old woman's face. "We found you through your son, Woody. His name graced that oh-so-pleasant email he sent to Sloane Publishing."

The oh-so-unpleasant memory of the spider still itched Olivia's neck, her back, her arms. In no mood to appear polite after the trauma of the previous two hours, she pulled out the bottle of hand sanitizer, pumped a generous dollop, and pushed the gel under her fingernails. "Mom would be appalled at what you've done. Threaten your own family? There's no justification for a stunt like that."

Della grasped the soiled arms of her recliner, then raised her eyes with such malice that Olivia sucked in a breath. "*You* . . . you don't know what you're talking about."

"Mom wouldn't do anything to hurt anybody. She just wrote a good story."

"Ellen promised me."

"Promised you *what?*"

Della worked her inherited stubborn jaw. "Greedy bitches are making a fortune off your mother. Ellen's death is going to be quite the blessing for me too."

Danny straightened. Abandoning Pogo with Don Ho, she marched toward Della and gripped her gnarled hands, pinning them to the stuffed chair. "Don't dare say *anything* bad about my mother. You hear me?"

Like champagne, Danny lost the pretense of refinement when shaken. She was about to fizz and spill over. Lauren's mouth popped open. Olivia fought her instinct to intervene.

"*You're* the greedy bitch," Danny continued, her face flushed. "All Ellen did was help everybody else. *Everybody.* Now, you want to profit because she's famous?"

Della stared daggers. Her pressed lips held back poisonous words.

Keeping her momentum, Danny pointed to Olivia. "Without my sister, this book wouldn't have made a damned dime. You've done nothing. You've written nothing. You didn't even write a damned card. And when Mom died, the three of us were by her side—not you."

"That's the truth, Della," Lauren said.

Olivia winced inside. She turned and squinted through the smudged panes of the front window. No Woody.

"*Truth.*" Della spat the word. "I told Ellen not to write that story.

But—oh, no—she had to do it. I even pleaded with your father. He tried to talk sense into her." Della yanked *Indigo to Black* from the seat cushion and shook it. "*Trash.* Your mother wrote trash."

Olivia studied her adversary: wide forehead, cornflower-blue eyes alert for prey, keen wits for her age, white dandelion hair that might sail away with a good blow. "Why do you care? If the book's trash, why threaten us for money?"

Della rubbed her leg and winced. "This damn foot."

The elephant in the room begged for a prod, and Lauren held the stick of words. "Are you the character of Becky Haines?"

The thrum of an engine vibrated Olivia's chest. Then silence. Then the *phoomph* of a car door.

Chapter 20

Truth

The tires of Woody's red 911 Porsche kicked up a whirl of leaves along the two-lane road to Della's house. With his grip on the steering wheel, Woody hugged the asphalt with talking points on his mind. The digital clock on the dash clicked over to two forty-five. He'd timed his arrival at Della's with precision: five minutes to clear a place for the sisters to sit; seven minutes to attempt a productive conversation with his mother; three minutes of wiggle room, which would probably amount to finger-tapping in anticipation of seeing Olivia and her sisters—and their reaction to the state of his mother's house.

Woody had insisted the meeting take place in his office, but his mother wouldn't hear of it. She wanted to control the turf. Coaching Della about what to say—or not to say—was also out of the question. A lawyer's nightmare.

As he approached Della's house, Woody downshifted and slowed to a crawl. The sisters' SUV sat in the dooryard, a Lincoln parked next to it. Two men sat in the sedan.

Bewilderment turned to aggravation, but he kept his composure. Woody pulled into the least muddy spot and hesitated, gathering his thoughts before pulling the keys from the ignition. After getting out of the car, he pushed the door shut—harder than he intended to—and counted his steps to the Lincoln. When he got to seven, he waved away a stream of cigarette smoke.

"Can I help you?" he snapped but then recognized both men from the bar at Wolfe's Tavern. Olivia believed they were a threat. A protective instinct took over.

The heavy-set man behind the wheel turned to Woody with a bored expression. "Nope. Just waiting for Novak and the others." He took a deep drag on his cigarette and blew the smoke in Woody's direction.

Woody blinked but didn't flinch. "Why?"

"We got an appointment, so to speak. You can't go in that house. The girls got some business, maybe givin' the business." The man laughed, inflating the rolls of skin on the back of his neck.

"This is my mother's house. I have every reason to be here. I'm fairly sure you don't."

The large man unlatched the car door, stepped out, and ducked to address the scrawny one in the passenger seat. "C'mon, Checks. We're going in."

"How do you know Olivia Novak?" Woody said.

The man took a step to block Woody's path to the door. "We go way back."

Woody pushed past him and rushed up the front steps.

~ · ~ · ~

Pogo scrambled to the door. All heads turned.

Rrrr . . . ruh, ruh, ruh.

Olivia jumped when Woody burst inside and pointed at Della.

"Stop!" His long finger shifted from his mother to her. "Don't say one more word—either of you."

The fire in Woody's eyes took Olivia aback. Rig and Checkers eased in behind him.

"Sorry, Mrs. Novak," Rig said. "He barged in before I could stop him."

"It's fine," Olivia said. *Our kidnapper is apologizing?*

The ball on the end of Pogo's tail wagged like a cocktail shaker. Checkers crouched and ruffled the dog's head.

Rig hitched up the waist of his pants and gazed around the room. "What a *dump*."

Della set her jaw at the smart remark. "Woodrow? Who is that horrible man?"

"I'd like to know myself." Woody pulled off his glasses and zeroed in on Olivia. "I'm shocked that you came here early to talk with Della and didn't wait for me." He pointed to Rig and Checkers. "Are they reinforcements to keep me away?"

Olivia stepped to Woody's side. She stood closer to him than she meant to, close enough to sense his heat. "It's not like that."

"And what was that damsel-in-distress act at Wolfe's last night? Will you stop at nothing to get what you want?"

Della narrowed her eyes.

The vice grip of his words made Olivia square her shoulders. "No. When the situation warrants." She cleared her throat. "Something . . . unrelated happened this afternoon after the signing at Alten's. We left early." She shifted her eyes to Rig and Checkers. The instant concern on Woody's face registered the unspoken message had hit home.

"What happened? Are you all right?"

"Fine. I'll tell you later"—she glanced at Della—"but it didn't involve your mother."

Della scrutinized the undeniable chemistry between Woody and Olivia. "Are you two in cahoots together? Have a roll in the hay to laugh at me?"

Woody studied the tassels of his shiny loafers. Olivia scratched her lip at his discomfort. She had no reason to feel guilty, but she did.

After tripping over a pair of water skis, Lauren marched to the center of the group. Her forefinger made the rounds. "Enough, Della. Don't insult my sister. Woody, nobody's undermining you. Rig and Checkers, find a place to sit—if you can. Danny, get Pogo. Let's not turn this into a damn fiasco."

"Too late," Rig said and pulled out his cigarette pack. He put it away when Checkers swept a finger across his throat.

Reclaiming her spot at the front window, Olivia focused on Della. Dust motes from the commotion floated in the sunlight behind Della's wiry hair. "Where were we," she said and sharpened her gaze on Woody, "before we were interrupted?"

Woody paced. The panels of his suit jacket flapped with every step. "I want to go on record that the purpose of this meeting is to—"

"Becky," Lauren said. Her gaze darted to Della. "Are you the character of Becky Haines?" The authority in her sister's voice slowed Woody's pace, and Olivia pictured a microphone in front of her own face on the witness stand. She'd crumble.

Woody pointed to his mother in midstride. "Don't answer that question."

Olivia studied Della's face for clues. Her eyelids drooped in deep thought, as if released by a pulley. She gasped for breath. Olivia held hers. The future might change if Della exhaled.

"I need to answer," Della said.

Catching Woody's eye, Olivia placed a forefinger to her lips. In response, he offered an imperceptible shake of his head, a warning not to push.

Danny moved toward a low wooden chair piled with hardback books, one that appeared to be left from the original schoolhouse. She placed the books on the floor and hugged her knees when she took a seat. Pogo trotted to her side.

"Ellen knew the truth," Della continued.

Lauren stared out the cloudy front window, as if locked in detention while the kids played tag outside. "I remember Mom's fight with Dad." She turned. "Mom never typed another word. I still have the typewriter."

"I don't remember that." Olivia eased her jaw when she realized she, too, might eventually resemble her mother—or Della.

Della chomped on her dentures, thinking. "That book was Ellen's way of betraying my confidence. I begged her to destroy that manuscript. She promised me she would."

Olivia glanced at Rig and Checkers. They both leaned against the wall by the front door, fascinated by the family drama. The only thing they were missing was Jiffy Pop.

"Well, she didn't," Lauren said, folding her arms. "I hear it's impossible for *some* authors to dispose of their work."

"Duly noted," Olivia said and turned back to Della. "What's the story—the *real* story?"

Della hesitated and rubbed her knuckles. "I loved him." Her face went soft when her gaze settled on Woody. "More than you'll ever know."

On the cusp of hearing the truth, Olivia reached into her purse for another squirt of hand sanitizer.

"What was his name?" Woody said in almost a whisper.

Della remained quiet and turned her gaze away.

"What happened?" Olivia said.

"He made a promise. We made plans in a year of letters. We were supposed to meet that summer to talk about getting married. Then your mother delivered that wicked note."

"What did it say?" Olivia didn't need a verbal answer. The two words were in her mother's book, but she wanted to hear them from the old woman's lips.

Della closed her eyes. "'I *can't.*' Those words changed my life."

Olivia waited for a flood of tears, but none came. Della's arresting blue eyes, like Woody's, remained icy and clear.

Woody shifted on his feet, then swept a stack of newspapers from a hassock next to Danny and took a seat. His fingers steepled against his lips. Pogo abandoned Danny to sit between his knees. "Ma, you don't have to—"

"You need to know before I die." Della's demeanor changed in an instant. Now, she appeared to be relishing her command of the room's attention.

Rig squinted his eyes. "My Nonna did the same damn thing on

her deathbed. Said Nonno never did nothin' but chase skirts for fifty years."

Checkers thwacked Rig's arm. "Shut up. This isn't about *you*."

"Will you two be quiet?" Olivia said. "Let her talk."

"The worst summer of my life." Della's arms hung limp. "I blamed Ellen. If she had convinced him to show up that night, everything would've been different."

A crease formed between Woody's brows like a bolt of lightning. "What was his name?"

"Asher Woodard," Della said. "Came from a snooty family on Beacon Hill."

Olivia gasped. The name had been changed in the book, but this one sounded familiar. Her gaze circled to meet Lauren's and Danny's. They, too, recognized the name from the yellowed newspaper articles they'd found at the bottom of the family picture box after Ellen had died. In vivid clarity, the details of a student's death—from poisoning—at Boston University in 1947 came back to her. That student's name was Asher Woodard. The scenes of her mother's book clicked behind her eyes like 3-D images on a View-Master.

The faraway gaze in Della's eyes turned to spite. "Nobody snubs me. He was mine. Asher wouldn't come to *me*, so I went to Boston to find *him*."

Danny rubbed her knees as though they itched. "To accomplish what?"

"To get what I was owed."

"What was that?" Lauren said.

"An apology—and sex." Della tipped her head for emphasis. "The least he could do. I didn't want to get past eighteen and still be a virgin."

With wide eyes, Woody shook his head. "Ma . . . This is completely—inappropriate."

Olivia blinked, still processing the frankness of Della's words. No apologies. No embarrassment. She dreaded where the conversation was headed. Della would be painfully honest, because of her age, at least. No fear for the consequences.

Lauren grimaced. "Get what you wanted with your booty call to Boston?"

Danny's face registered shock. She ran her hand through her hair, but the locks flopped back over her eyes.

Della dug in the cushion of her recliner, as if the springs poked through the stuffing. She pulled out a cell phone and pushed buttons in random succession. Her eyes appeared dreamy. "I followed him from the campus to his apartment. When he opened the door, I was prepared to stay forever."

Woody's pocket rang out a dancing chirp. He reached into his jacket and silenced the call. He pressed his hands over his face. Pogo licked his fingers.

"Sounds like a chick flick," Rig said.

"More like *Play Misty for Me.*" Checkers bobbed his bony finger. "Scary, those clingy broads."

Olivia recoiled. In the process of finding Adam's killer, she could have easily been labeled a "clingy broad."

"We made love," Della said. "Our bodies tangled together . . . exceeded my wildest fantasies. His warm skin. I floated on air afterword." Della's expression darkened. "But he wanted sex, not *me.*" She raised her eyes at no one. "Do you know what Asher did?"

Everyone in the room leaned forward. Woody's hands slid from his face. Olivia swallowed hard. "What?" she said.

"That bastard threw back the sheet and bored his eyes into mine. Cold. Hateful." Della narrowed hers and, with a voice that came from another world, mimicked the words: "'Della, you're not good enough for me. Take a shower, get dressed, and go.'"

Olivia's mouth popped open, and so did Lauren's and Danny's. Woody's clamped shut, unable to even utter an objection. Rig and Checkers turned to each other.

"Harsh," Checkers said.

Lauren turned to look out the window. "Then what'd he do?"

Della churned the Jitterbug in her hand like a deck of cards. "He marched to the kitchen to make a pot of coffee and left me laying there in our sweaty sheets. So I got up, had a shower, and got dressed. We passed each other in the hallway, and he wouldn't even acknowledge me. Didn't say a word. When I heard the bathroom door close and the shower running, I went into the kitchen and—"

"Ma . . . Stop," Woody said.

Della's face reflected no emotion. Blank. She continued with vacant words. "I poured rat poison in the coffee pot and walked out the door."

"From a Lydia Pinkham bottle?" Olivia said.

"Your grandfather had so many on his sill. He never missed it."

In the wake of Della's confession, a chill settled over the room. Even Pogo didn't move a muscle. Rig was the first to speak.

"Nice," he said. "I gotta remember that trick."

Checkers nodded. "Get in, get out. Long gone by the time any-body finds the stuff."

Woody raised his eyes, wide with shock. "What did you do with that bottle?"

Della didn't answer, but she pointed to the window in her make-shift kitchen. Ten or fifteen empty antique bottles lined the sill, a shaft of light filtering through the bubbled glass in hazy shades of aqua and violet.

Olivia stepped over a pile of mismatched winter boots to get to the window. Her gaze settled on the eight-inch one of the collection—a smooth-shouldered bottle with raised letters. She knew it well. The aqua vessel matched one that had sat in her grandparents' kitchen window over the sink. She picked the specimen from the sill as though it were a guilty perpetrator in a police lineup and grazed the name with her fingertip: *Lydia Pinkham's Elixir*. "This one, Della?"

"Don't answer that," Woody said. "Olivia . . . this whole con-versation is off the record."

"Need I remind you that Della is trying to extort money from *us* because she said Mom's book was about *her*?" Olivia rocked the bottle in her fingers. "The truth?"

"Della started it, Woody," Lauren said. She motioned for Della to proceed.

Olivia glanced at Danny. Her eyes shone. Checkers unwrapped a stick of Juicy Fruit and folded the pliable ribbon into his mouth. Rig held out his hand for one too.

"Go on, Della," Olivia said. "Then what happened?"

The old woman's gaze skimmed each face in the room. "A month after I came home, Ellen had been cutting out the articles from the Boston paper about Asher's death. I never told her what I'd done, but somehow she figured it out. She knew. Ellen threatened to go to the police, but I was able to stop her."

"How?"

"I was pregnant."

All color drained from Woody's face. "You told me my father was killed in the war."

"Having a child out of wedlock was different." Della rubbed her forehead. "In this town, it's always a subject of dinner talk. So I told everyone . . . I'd eloped before my husband was shipped out . . . that I kept my name." Della's speech had become somewhat slurred. A confused furrow crossed her brows. "Ellen got back at me . . . She wrote . . . that . . . book a few years later." Disbelief washed over her face. "She wrote . . . that book."

"Della?" Olivia said. "Are you all right?"

"I'll be fine . . . Headache." Pogo released himself from Woody's side and trotted to Della. The dog rested his head over her knees. She stroked his curly black fur. "He's beautiful. What's . . . his name?"

"Pogo," Danny said. "He's a therapy dog. Signed, sealed, and certified."

"He's a good . . . boy." Della's hand tremored, but her voice filled with wonderment. "Like a child."

Woody's mouth tightened. He closed his eyes and said, "Am I Asher Woodard's son?"

"You were such a beautiful baby . . . I was . . . sooo . . . proud." Della's hand slowed. The right side of her face went slack. Her vacant gaze floated to Woody. "*Asher?* When did . . . you get here?"

"Call an ambulance!" Lauren lunged for her purse. "She's having a stroke."

Olivia scrambled to Della and grabbed the Jitterbug from her hand. She punched in 9-1-1. Rig and Checkers made for the front door.

Woody sat frozen.

Chapter 21
Melted Defenses

After the paramedic shut the back doors, the ambulance tore out of the driveway. The siren blared in a fading *whoop-whoop* for the fifteen-minute drive to Huggins Hospital. Lauren raced to the SUV with Danny and Pogo. Rig and Checkers slammed the doors of the Lincoln and fired up its engine.

"C'mon, Olivia." Lauren tossed the keys to Olivia and gripped the handle on the passenger door.

Immovable, Olivia stood on the steps. She leaned to peer inside the house. Woody remained on the hassock with his head in his hands. She tossed the keys back to Lauren. "You go. Woody and I'll meet you there." Olivia tipped her head toward the open front door and pressed her lips together.

Lauren fingered the keys and stepped to the driver's side of the SUV. "You've got to write a book about this, Liv. I can't believe what happened in there."

"Mom already did."

"Write the sequel."

"I don't know how it ends."

Lauren pointed at the front door. "Here's an ending—go in there and get Woody to drop his plans for a lawsuit."

Danny leaned her head out the car window. "Hurry up!"

Lauren nodded, climbed into the seat, and started the engine.

After the car pulled out, Olivia stared into the brisk twilight through the trees. The setting autumn sun illuminated the leaves into a warm pumpkin and gold glow. A fresh pine scent blended with the organic aroma of decay as a long, throaty call from a native bird announced an invader of its nest. With a vigorous brush of her arms, Olivia turned back into the house.

"Woody? Do you want to talk?" she said and closed the front door. The infusion of cool air tensed the mood as Olivia crept toward him.

"Technically, I should talk to the authorities," he said without moving. "You're the last person I should discuss this with."

The sunlight shifted, darkening the room to a spooky gray. The chill in the house made Olivia search for a thermostat instead of a reply. An old-style one was set into the wall by the front door. She rolled the notched dial. A rumble under the floor signaled the heater still had life, and the air began to fill with an acrid stench of burning dust.

"Better?"

"Ma rarely turns on the heat," Woody said.

Olivia didn't want to voice the possibility that Della may never be shivering through another winter in this house. Instead, she sneezed before she could retrieve a tissue from her purse. Like a thumbprint or a laugh, a sneeze was unique to the individual, and hers came out loud and long. She waited for a "gesundheit" but it didn't come. Instead, Woody flinched and straightened.

"I should change that filter," he said, his words hollow. The dullness in his eyes portrayed a calm demeanor, but she sensed he wasn't far from unraveling. "I need to find her a good lawyer, more experienced in criminal law than me. 'Conflict of interest', as you so astutely suggested. And I doubt they'd send my mother to prison for murder at her age. There'll be leniency. It's been decades since the crime—"

"Could be a non-issue." Olivia crossed her arms and dabbed at her runny nose.

Woody raised his eyes, halted by her words. Then he understood their meaning. "She has no end-of-life directive. She wouldn't even discuss it when I pushed her."

"Stop with the lawyer stuff." Her shoulders dropped. "What I'm trying to say is that Della knew this was going to happen. What transpired in here was a desperate woman confessing a crime to her son. I doubt she was even aware the rest of us were here in those last fifteen minutes."

Woody's eyes glassed, which only made him more fascinating and vulnerable. "I didn't know any of this. Where was I?"

"Doing what normal people do. Building a career. Trying to do the right thing. You believed what your mother told you." Olivia scrutinized the junk in the house. "People hoard for reasons. Something is missing in life. Obsession. Anger. Or maybe there's too much of something . . . guilt. Della wanted attention, otherwise she would've remained silent."

"Well, she's got it now." Woody rubbed his face as if he could erase an equation on a chalkboard.

"You need to get to the hospital and talk to her if she's cognizant."

"Give me a minute."

Without comment, Olivia reached for the switch on a glass-shaded lamp next to Della's stuffed Barcalounger. Hand-painted roses and peonies popped with 3-D color. The warm light drew her attention to a stack of old books on the floor next to Woody. Unable to help herself, she knelt on the dusty pine floor and inspected the pile that Danny had moved from the schoolhouse chair.

"Woody?" With a reverent touch, she smoothed her fingers over the cover of *Rebecca* by Daphne du Maurier and checked the spines on the others. "I'll bet these are all first editions. Sitting in this stack alone is Agatha Christie, F. Scott Fitzgerald, and Daphne du Maurier."

"Look around." He gave a lazy wave toward the stuffed shelves.

"She has hundreds of old books."

Olivia flipped to the copyright page of *Rebecca*. "Says it's a first printing . . . 1938. I'm getting that twinge, like the tingles I got when I found my mother's manuscript . . . and confronted the girl who killed my husband. Bittersweet. The process could never bring them back, but the truth changed everything." She held out the book to Woody, being careful to not disturb the delicate, brittle dust jacket.

With an expression similar to when he gazed at her for the first time, Woody took the book and fanned the pages. "I read this as a child. Scared the bejesus outta me. Did you know that Maxim de Winter didn't call his new wife by her name? The reader never knows what it is. I rooted for Maxim because I knew he didn't kill Rebecca. I wanted to be the lawyer who defended him."

"And you are . . . in a way," Olivia said. "Books inspire us to overcome the impossible. But I'll tell you one thing . . . Della didn't hoard indiscriminately."

"You think? She'd find these books and bring them home every day, all kinds, one or two at time. She'd find out who had died and swoop in to pick through their books. We'd read after I finished my homework." He let out a worn-out chuckle. "We didn't have a TV, or even a radio. I remember the house being so quiet."

"I read every night too. Both Adam and I did."

"Looking back now, I think I learned to jump out of my world to bask in somebody else's."

Olivia placed her hands over Woody's to close the cover. "Careful. Don't crack the spine."

Woody met her gaze. "I need to figure this out."

Taking a seat next to him on the hassock, she gestured to the book in Woody's hands. "When my husband was killed, I didn't know who I was. We shared an identity. Through my books, I could reinvent myself and fix what happened. Kind of like what Maxim did when he jumped into a new marriage on the rebound. He couldn't reconcile how damaged he was. Worse for me, though, since, unlike Rebecca, Adam didn't have a spiteful bone in his body. We had a very loving marriage."

"That's why you wrote all those romances?"

She nodded. "That's the juicy inside scoop, and not for public consumption. I've never told that to anyone before, not even my sisters."

Olivia backpedaled inside. Flirting had been fun, like oiling a rusty bike, but this reveal had crossed into a serious race she hadn't trained for. She gripped her knees to steady her pulse.

"I think we need to unravel this in steps," she finally said.

"Continue," Woody said and studied the floorboards. She'd underestimated his skill of extracting information.

"First, you need to drop this potential suit about my mother's book."

"Consider it done. I'll send a retraction to the publisher."

"Second, we're going to see how fast your fancy sports car can traverse the curves of 109A to Huggins Hospital. Lauren and I missed being with Ellen before she died because we were too busy bitching about life and our own problems."

"I should stop by the office to pick up the power of attorney."

"If this is the end for Della, you won't regret being by her side, no matter what she's said and done. I'm no fan of hers at the moment, but if your mother lives, then don't make the time she has left more miserable than the past seventy years have been for her. Bypass the office. Forget the paperwork."

Woody turned to her. His features softened as he took her hand and squeezed. "Thank you for not being ugly about all this."

"I'm a nice person when you get to know me."

"C'mere." Woody wrapped his arm around her shoulder. Not an official hug, but in the neighborhood of one. He rested his chin on the crown of her head, his breath breezing through her hair like warm netting. "Do you smoke? Your hair smells like—"

"Uh . . . no. A story for another time." Olivia tried to raise her head, mortified, but his pull kept her close. "Don't listen to me, Woody. I'm making a mess of everything these days." The cotton pinpoint of his shirt absorbed her words. "We should go. I don't want to keep you from Della."

"You already are."

"Not true." She smiled inside.

"Uh . . . Yeah, it is. My cuff link is stuck in your hair."

~ · ~ · ~

Through the tangle of curves of 109A, Olivia explained the presence of Rig and Checkers. With his foot heavy on the pedal, Woody pressed for more information about every detail with intensity: her chase to save her sisters with the gun, the hidden mob memoir of R. D. Griffin, his history with the Witness Protection Program, the attempt on his life by Nicky Palermo, and even how Danny had come to adopt Pogo. The last nugget was the summons to meet with the don himself.

"I don't know what to expect when we go to Allenwood," she said, "but right now your mother's life is on the line."

"I know, but your life—and your sisters' lives—could be on the line," Woody said. He pulled the car into a parking space at Huggins Hospital. The engine silenced. "What does Palermo want?"

"Don't know. But we agreed to meet. If we refuse, it'll be worse. I think he's got my manuscript for Ardy's memoir."

"If you exposed crimes, some of them could still be prosecuted. Aren't you worried about retaliation?"

Olivia tilted her head and gawked at him. "Damn straight I'm worried. And being sued about my mother's book worried me too. Just another case for you, but it could've unraveled two years' worth of getting my life back and restoring a family with my sisters." Her shoulders slumped. "I'm sorry, Woody. I didn't mean to sound so harsh. Like you, I don't know what we're going to do, but Lauren and Danny have a stake in this too."

Woody's tanned face cooled in the halogen lights of the parking lot. "You three have a lot to lose."

"So do you. Let's go in."

As the doors at Emergency parted, Olivia allowed Woody his space to approach the information desk on his own. But she couldn't help eavesdropping on the conversation.

"Mrs. Rainey has been admitted," the volunteer said and recited the room number. She pointed to the sign marked ICU. "The doctor has been waiting to talk with you." The purse of her lips sent out an invisible guilt message to Woody that he should have arrived sooner. Olivia, herself, had thrown that look to Lauren when they'd arrived too late for their mother. She regretted having done it now.

The volunteer pushed a button under the desk to part the automatic doors. Woody, being polite, waved for Olivia to go ahead of him. Danny rushed to her from the other side, having been waiting in the sterile hall. Her sister's eyes weren't hopeful. Woody's eyes were all business as he broke off to meet with the doctor standing at the nurses' station.

Danny grasped Olivia's arm and pulled her close. "Della's talking, mostly gibberish, and she's been asking for *Asher*." She glanced at the nurses' station. "How's Woody holding up?"

"I'm glad I stayed with him," Olivia said.

"Do afternoons get any more bizarre than this one? A book signing? Getting kidnapped by mobsters? A murder confession? And now doing time in a hospital, like I did with Mom? Help, help me Rhonda."

Olivia had no credible response. "You remember that song?"

"The Beach Boys."

"Where are Lauren and Pogo?"

"In the room with Della. Lauren made a fuss. Surprise, surprise. She told the nurses that Pogo was Della's dog. They relented because he's certified."

"And Rig and Checkers?"

"In the cafe." Danny rolled her eyes. "They were hungry."

Olivia gazed back at Woody deciphering the assault of medical terminology. The doctor's furrowed brows didn't reflect reassurance. She followed Danny to Della's room, half expecting the police to be waiting inside. When she pulled back the curtain, all was quiet, except for the beeps of machines and the buzz of a blood pressure cuff squeezing for a reading. Three pillows elevated Della's bare foot, her toes swollen with a bluish cast. Lauren sat at Della's bedside.

"She's asleep," Lauren said. "Pretty doped up."

Pogo sat on the other side of the bed with his head resting on the mattress. A curly head with no body.

"She's a fighter," Olivia said. "Ornery enough to survive. I don't know how I feel about that option, given the things she said about us."

"And Mom." Danny nodded. "She was nice to Pogo, though. He's doing some good, I think."

Strapped in his yellow service vest, only the dog's pouty brown eyes shifted as Danny spoke.

Olivia studied Della. She appeared lifeless: eyes closed, muscles on the right side of her face slack, and skin pallid. Her halo of gray hair could have passed for puffy rice noodles. Danny nodded toward the computer. Her younger sister had been through this type of drill with their mother. After years of interpreting doctor-speak, Danny had a trusted ability to weave through patronization and conflicting assessments. Her sister tiptoed to the computer screen to snoop into the medical record.

"No password. The record's open," Danny whispered.

The tapping of keys sparked a sudden realization in Olivia as she gazed at Della: she'd never actually touched the woman. An odd circumstance given her status as family. Della's chest rose and descended with lazy breath. Beyond the machines and slow drip lay a woman whose pain could never be eased. Olivia gripped the bed rail, certain of Woody's fate, like hers, to become a grown orphan. More out of respect for Woody than unconditional family loyalty, she leaned down and kissed Della on the forehead. Cool. Fragile.

"I hope you and Mom will work it out, Della," she said. "*Indigo to Black* is not a weapon. We were never going to allow you to turn it into one."

In the absence of any response, Olivia pulled a chair next to the bed and stared at the rhythmic lines on the heart monitor, cresting and falling, much like her own life.

"We couldn't have predicted this in a million years," Lauren said. "A damn rollercoaster."

Peaks and valleys. Fate had been both a joyous and cruel partner: thirty-two years with Adam before the accident took him away; finding *Indigo to Black* after her mother's death; Pogo and Ryan giving a new life to Danny because of R. D. Griffin's painful memoir. Her manuscript of Ardy's life sat unresolved, and her gut said a conclusion waited with Nicky Palermo. Balance. The yin and yang. Woody held spark and danger too, but she wouldn't know what fate had planned until the woman in front of her was gone.

Without turning, Olivia said, "What are they saying, Danny?"

"Not good. Della has diabetes and unchecked high blood pressure that's damaged her kidneys and a pretty serious infection in her foot. Considered little stuff compared to the stroke."

"Are they sure she had a stroke?"

"They've done a brain scan. Could be caused by an aneurysm. Either way . . . not good. Surgery is an iffy option at her age. Woody needs to get in here."

Della moaned as her eyes fluttered open. "Cold . . . " she said and licked her lips.

Lauren stood and stepped into the hallway. "Where's the damn orderly? I told him to bring a warm blanket for her. He should have been here by now." Her sister disappeared from view.

Danny lowered her voice. "Lauren's acting weird."

"I think I know what that's about," Olivia said.

"What?" Danny moved to Lauren's vacated chair. Her eyes snapped to attention.

"Lauren and I weren't with Mom when she died. Only you were there. We were in the parking garage, on our way up. Then you called with the news."

"I thought she'd gotten over that."

"Took me a while, but I finally accepted I couldn't change how the whole thing went down." Olivia gestured toward the hall. "But Lauren? She's still working something out."

"What about Woody?"

"He's got stuff to work out too. What Della did . . . in his eyes is unforgivable."

"Which part? The poisoning part or the lying part?"

"All of it. We may need to stick close. I'm worried about his reaction . . . or lack of one. Still waters and all."

Danny studied Olivia's eyes for more details. "Did you talk to him about the lawsuit?"

"It's fine. We're good."

"That's a relief. But Rig and Checkers . . . We need to go, Liv."

Olivia rubbed her neck. "I know. I *know*. Let me think."

No one had uttered words of blame, but Olivia's inner voice berated her plenty. Publishing Ellen's book had been her idea. Writing Ardy's memoir, *Protection*, had been her idea. Convincing her sisters to go on that damn talk show to sell her book, *The Executrix*, might as well had been her idea. Even eating the Thai food that had embarrassed Lauren had been at her request.

Lauren rushed into the room with a white blanket in her arms. She unfolded it over Della, being careful to not disturb her angry foot. Pogo lifted his head as she tucked in the blanket and rested his nose back down. His eyes drooped from the warmth.

Olivia rubbed the stinging spot on her head. Woody's cuff link probably still held a couple strands of her plucked hair. She had time to stop this nonsense. She picked the keys to the SUV from Lauren's purse. "When Woody comes in, tell him I went to the cafe to find Rig and Checkers."

Chapter 22

Pulling Strings

"Where's Olivia?" Woody said as he stepped into Della's room. Danny glanced at Lauren, sending a message encrypted with secret sibling code. Woody recognized the look as one of conspiracy or guilt.

"She went to the cafe," Danny said. "Liv specifically told us to tell you where she'd be. Sounds like you two had a good talk."

No secrets with these sisters. He'd do well to remember the power of three, the sum stronger than each individual. Noted and filed.

"You and Lauren should make sure Olivia's okay," he said, "and take the dog with you. Thanks for staying with Della, but I need some time with her. I'm sure you understand."

Lauren stood and clipped the leash to the Pogo's collar. The dog pulled toward Woody. "Take all the time you need."

He thumped Pogo's side. "I'll join you in a bit."

Lauren's shoes squeaked as she made a hasty exit with Pogo. Danny followed in her wake and closed the door.

Woody turned and studied his mother. The skin on Della's face, translucent and sunken, revealed the physical manifestation of unhappiness, nothing he hadn't witnessed for the past forty years. Aging only accentuated what was there all along. Her mouth bore the lines of a permanent frown without her teeth. Less pronounced with them.

"Ma? Can you hear me?"

Beep. Beep. Beep.

"You shouldn't have said anything," he continued, as if she'd responded. "Look how many people are affected by this admission of yours."

Della's finger twitched.

"What am I supposed to do with this information? Keep my mouth shut? You know I can't do that. A line's been crossed—with witnesses. But I think any criminal attorney worth their salt will be able to impose sufficient reasonable doubt."

The white blanket stirred as Della attempted to move her elevated foot. Her lips worked to form a word. "Family . . . "

Woody leaned over her and gripped the bedrail. "What family? My father's?" He glanced at the monitor as the jagged lines tightened. "A little late for that now, Ma."

Della offered a slight shake of her head. "Find them . . . "

The doctor had warned Woody that Della may have moments of clarity, but he had advised him not to get his hopes up. In Woody's mind, survival posed the bigger challenge, a thought he'd never voice. He took off his glasses and pulled a suede polishing cloth from his pocket. He took a seat in a side chair.

"And solve what?" he said as he cleaned the lenses. "Turn that family upside down for a second time, maybe a third, when you're charged with premeditated murder? This closure stunt of yours is selfish and serves only you. Look what you've done to Olivia and her sisters . . . to me." He held his glasses to the light. "Frankly, Ma, I'm not sure what to believe, but I can't defend you. Conflict of interest. And I told Olivia we're dropping this whole issue with Sloane for the royalties on Ellen's—"

"Books . . . "

Woody tilted his head with inquisition. "Books? What books? Ellen's?"

"Your . . . books . . . " Della's head drifted to the side.

The alarm on the monitor started to blare. Della's moment of clarity clouded his thoughts. Erratic lines on the monitor stretched and settled. Woody stood and searched the equipment for the cause. He leaned over the bedrail, his mouth close to Della's ear.

"Ma?"

~ · ~ · ~

"Scoot over," Olivia said to Checkers. She plopped her purse on the vinyl seat next to him and slid into the booth. She snatched a french fry from Checkers's plate and dragged it through a pool of ketchup.

"She doing okay?" Rig said. He took a bite of his hamburger and gave Olivia the eye, acting overly protective of the sandwich.

"Woody's still talking with the doctor, but Danny's opinion is good enough for me."

"Curtains?" Checkers pushed his plate in her direction and gave her a weak smile over another stolen french fry.

"My guess is that Della doesn't have long," Olivia said. "Round-the-clock care in hospice is the best we can hope for." She pointed to the untouched cheeseburger on Checkers's plate. He waved for her to take it.

"Then let's rev the engines tonight," Rig said with a full mouth. "Palermo's waiting."

"Can we take an extra day? We might need to help Woody. We'll know more about Della's condition in the morning. If she's holding her own, then we'll go."

Checkers turned sideways in the booth and rested his head against the wall. With a smack of the lever on a dispenser, he plucked out a toothpick, peeled off the plastic covering, and stuck it in his mouth. "I feel for the guy, you know? Bum rap. Della's a piece of work." He lolled his head to the side. "C'mon, Rig. One day won't mean nothing. Palermo ain't going nowhere."

"We got a long drive, and my hemorrhoids are killing me." The vinyl groaned as Rig shifted on the seat.

Olivia swallowed and wiped her mouth when Lauren stepped into the cafe, followed by Danny and Pogo. She waved them over. Lauren slipped into the booth next to Rig, while Danny commissioned a chair from a neighboring table.

"Woody's with Della," Danny said and reached across the table to snatch the secondhand burger from Olivia. She took a bite and held out the remainder to Lauren. After Lauren downed two chunks, she slipped the last piece to Pogo.

"Glad to oblige," Checkers said and churned the toothpick over his lips. "You three want to pass around my napkin too? How about my first-born child?"

Rig picked up the pace to reduce the size of his burger. "You ain't got a kid, and with that ugly mug, you won't even get a wife." He swallowed. "So . . . Della's a Veg-o-matic, huh?"

Olivia cringed. "It's a waiting game. She's not a candidate for surgery because of her age . . . and other serious health issues."

"Better than prison," Rig said.

Lauren reached for a fry on Rig's plate, but he moved it away. "Not really."

"Speaking of prison," Olivia said, "I asked these boys if we can wait a day to leave for Allenwood. I want to make sure Woody's all right."

Danny's eyes widened. "Did you tell Woody about that?"

"Everything."

"And now we have to go to a prison to defend the next book," Lauren said. "Just gets better and better. Right, Liv?"

There it was. Blame. Her obsession to write had become the source of their plight.

"Ouch," Olivia said. "Wicked jaw is right."

"I ain't gettin' in the middle of skirt talk." Rig sighed and pulled out his phone. "Move, Ethel. I gotta go outside and call Palermo. Can't get a signal in here. This ain't gonna be no fun."

"Phone call, Palermo." A buzz preceded the warden's turn of keys in the lock. Nicky extended his hand the exact distance to the button on the cassette player. The tape squealed, scattering Maria Callas's smooth voice singing Puccini's "O Mio Babbino Caro" like shards of shattered crystal. He finally found the STOP button.

"You interrupted *Gianni Schicchi*," Palermo said. "Maria Callas must *never* be interrupted." He closed his eyes to listen for the warden's movements, the shadow drawing close enough for touch. "Disrespectful." He groped for the phone. "Who is it?"

"Rigoberto. He wants to give you an update on the sisters' arrival."

Warden Franklin's massive shape retreated after he released the mobile. Palermo set the device to his ear. On the other end, wind distorted Rig's microphone. His henchman must be outside. The heels of Rig's wingtips clicked against asphalt, not cement. The subtle difference—softer—indicated a parking lot, not a sidewalk.

"We got a complication, Boss," Rig said.

"I'm not interested in complications." Palermo followed the looming form shifting in front of the bars. "Bring the women and the dog to me."

"I'm working on it. We'll be there tomorrow. A relative's in the mix. She's dying."

"I'm dying. I won't tell you again. I need those sisters and the dog."

"I'll get 'em there."

"When? I don't want details or tiresome excuses. I want to know *when*."

"Tomorrow. Late-ish."

"I expected you tonight." Palermo paused for effect. A vase of deep rust-colored chrysanthemum clusters drew his cloudy gaze, their richness only imagined through the fog. He fingered the feathery petals, like a woman's skin. The curves of the plastic vessel drew his caress. "You disappoint me, Rigoberto."

"Checkers got soft, especially with the dog."

"You have until the end of visiting hours tomorrow."

"What time is that again?"

Palermo sighed. "Four o'clock. You know this."

"Right. We gotta a long drive. They got a rental to drop off in Boston. We might be late."

Without responding, Palermo held out the phone to the warden.

"Change of plans?" Warden Franklin said.

"The last. Permission to extend visiting hours for tomorrow." Palermo grunted, distracted. "Requisition the recording equipment. I'm an optimist."

The warden lowered his voice. "You got it. And they're bringing the dog?"

"Hopefully, Ben. Hopefully."

Palermo reached to the cassette player until his finger found the first button to rewind the tape. His eyelids lowered for eight seconds as the curtain prepared to rise, then he pressed the third button. Like the delicate tap of the conductor's baton, the aria started again. Maria Callas's soaring voice reverberated off the cinder-block walls like a lonely bird taking flight.

Chapter 23

The Loons Aren't So Lonely

"It's been an hour. I'm going to find Woody," Olivia said and slid from the booth in the cafe. "If I'm not back in fifteen minutes, go on to the hotel without me."

Checkers straightened. "Oh no—"

"Relax. I only want to make sure he's okay."

Lauren eyed Checkers and commandeered the crunchy pickle from Rig's abandoned plate. "Liv's got a thing going on with Woody."

A flush rose up Olivia's neck. The turtleneck hid the evidence, but the collar turned into a ring of heat.

Danny held out her hand. "Give me the car keys . . . just in case."

"In case-a what?" Rig said and eyed the pickle, like he wanted to grab it back from Lauren.

Danny and Lauren pressed their lips together. Olivia rolled her eyes and dug in her purse.

With a quick whine and a lick of his lips, Pogo's gaze trailed the keys to Danny and returned to her. The dog's assessment rushed Olivia out of the cafe.

Olivia followed the signs back to the ICU, trying to compartmentalize her anger toward Della, fear of what might transpire with

Palermo, and her inexplicable attraction to Woody. The pull and push between them was undeniable. As she rounded the corner to the waiting area, she spotted Woody sitting alone and staring out the window. In the seven o'clock hour, there was nothing to see outside except for Woody's reflection. She contemplated going back to the cafe, but there was that damn pull again.

Approaching Woody from behind, she set her hand on his shoulder. He didn't move. "Woody?"

"I knew you'd be the one to find me," he said and patted the seat of the empty chair next to him. "Sit."

Woody didn't turn to see her wrinkling her nose at what sounded like a command for Pogo. She obeyed against her better judgment. "Did something happen? I mean—something new?"

"She's gone."

"I'm so sorry, Woody." Conflict percolated about the sentiment, but she only sighed. "When?"

"About half an hour ago. I had to deal with the paperwork."

"Did you get to talk with her?"

"I wouldn't describe it quite that way, but some, yes." Woody studied the weave on his wool slacks, then raised his eyes to her. "That I should find my father's family. I think that's what she meant. Ridiculous. Nonsense, really."

"Whoa. Talk about opening Pandora's Box."

"Wasn't exactly at the top of my to-do list. Then she said something about the books. After what she dumped on me—on all of us—her last words were about damn books." Woody shook his head.

Summoning an instinct to comfort, Olivia rested her hand on his leg and quickly attempted to pull back. Woody grasped her fingers, then twisted her wedding band around and around. If he'd had one of his own, it might have been a nervous habit. The intimacy of the gesture took her off guard. To cover, she kept going with more good advice he probably didn't want to hear.

"Call Catherine Pratt at Alten's," she said. "Your mother has hundreds of books, and I think we only touched the surface of what's in her house. As Della's executor, you'll need to tackle a complete inventory of everything in there. That alone is quite a to-do list."

"Don't remind me. I've had power of attorney, but power over nothing. God knows where her papers are—birth certificate, bills, whatever. I don't even know if she has a damned social security card."

Olivia shifted and pulled back her hand. "Do *you* have a birth certificate?"

Woody rubbed his forehead. "It's in my safe at the office. I haven't looked at it since I got my law license."

"Does it indicate your father's name?"

"Woodward Rainey." Distracted, Woody gazed beyond her. "I never questioned it."

Olivia tapped the arm of the chair, as if connecting cognitive dots. "There is no Woodward Rainey, but Della reworked Asher Woodard's last name, then called you Woodrow. Call this hack psychology, but don't some people who deceive leave a trail to thumb their nose at the world, to prove they're smarter than everyone else?"

Woody shifted his eyes back to her. "Premeditated murder, Olivia, not a deception."

"I'm not a lawyer, either, to know if this changes anything, but hers was a crime of passion."

"You know a lot for not being a lawyer or a psychologist. Not sure I completely buy all that, but let's hear your theory."

"Okay. Misdirected passion, then. I stand corrected." Olivia thought of her own misdirected passion of hunting white Suburbans. The compulsion had been a survival tool, but it only made her angrier. "When I looked into the faces of the two people who were responsible for Adam's accident, I understood that. It scared me to realize that I was capable of harming someone with my bare hands—with no remorse, and no concern for the consequences. I was sure I wouldn't have any. I didn't do it, of course, because I have a conscience."

"My mother didn't appear to have a conscience about what she did."

"Key word here is *appear*. She wouldn't have mentioned Asher's family if she didn't."

"Maybe you're secretly with the Behavioral Science Unit of the FBI."

"Nothing that sexy. I'm just a writer who makes this stuff up."

"Who said that wasn't sexy?" Woody didn't turn, but a hint of a smile crossed his lips and quickly disappeared.

Unable to stop herself, Olivia took his hand. A clicking sound emanated from behind them in the waiting area, the only sound as Woody's fingers entwined with her own. She memorized the ridges of his nails, the tiny tears of his cuticles, and the distinct shape of the rough calluses on his palms from rowing. His lifeline stretched long and unbroken to his wrist, met with a road map of blue veins. Their fingers fit together like puzzle pieces. Line up the edges; match the soft curves. Woody flinched when she finally found her voice.

"If you pursue this," she said, "be prepared to be more miserable than you can possibly imagine."

"You? Or my father's family?" His voice came out barely audible.

"We have to leave in the morning. Palermo, and all."

"I'm not happy about it." He swept a lock of Olivia's hair from her shoulder. She glanced at his cuff link. As predicted, it still held a strand of her hair hostage. "You shouldn't go. It's too dangerous." The way he gazed at her, Olivia didn't believe the danger waited in Allenwood but right here in Wolfeboro.

"What's the worst thing the old bugger can do? Threaten to kill us if I publish Ardy's memoir?" She shrugged. "So I won't. I'll keep it in the safe-deposit box. Not an issue."

"I don't know. People's actions continue to surprise me. That's why I didn't go into criminal law. Sometimes I wish I'd had, to really understand that level of desperation. I never thought that insight would hit so close to home, though."

Olivia tightened her sweater around her. "It's getting late. I should get back to the hotel." She glanced over her shoulder, hoping, but not hoping, to catch a glimpse of her sisters. The waiting area had been vacated, except for an elderly woman on a couch giving life to a new afghan. The rhythmic click of knitting needles agitated the ball of Christmas-red yarn next to her. "I gave Danny my keys. She and Lauren probably left with Rig and Checkers. It's nearly eight o'clock." Olivia opened her purse to retrieve her phone. Woody held her wrist to stop her.

"I'll drive you to my place. You must be hungry. Then I'll take you back to the inn."

"Woody . . . our dispute was about Mom's book. It's irrelevant now and—"

He held up his hands. "Just a salad. And I could sure use a scotch."

"I *can't* . . ."

Woody's face slackened. In that instant Olivia recognized the power of her words, two murderous written words on a ruled-paper note that Della had described.

"Yes, Liv. You *can.*"

Chapter 24

The Mistake

A buzz jolted Olivia awake. Her phone. Woody's bedroom. She gently lifted Woody's arm from around her waist and eased from beneath the warm comforter. Stepping over the tangle of clothes, Olivia reached for her purse on the bureau. The small, illuminated screen indicated three in the morning. The middle of the night. Wednesday. She extended her arm to make out the caller ID and pressed the answer button.

"Lauren?" she said, keeping her voice low. She glanced at Woody's dark form. Still asleep.

The emotional barrier had been easy to cross with the distraction of senses: white-hot touch, whispers and sighs in the dark, pulse and sweat. The other side, though, became fraught with unknown dangers.

"Where are you?" Lauren said, like she'd already known the answer.

"I'm at Woody's."

At the mention of his name, Woody turned on the bedside light. He propped himself on one elbow to gaze at her. His grin radiated Cheshire cat; hers must have screamed guilt. Olivia pulled on the front of the borrowed T-shirt to stretch away the clingy details. She tugged the hem to cover her backside. She turned away. The first sneak attack came from the mirror. She inspected her sorry form in horror: hair a pile of exploded insulation, mascara smudged to make her look like the loser in a prize fight. Under Woody's shirt—*Indigo Lake Kayaking Championships, 1995*—too tight on her, every lump and bump showed like braille spelling out the word *pathetic*.

You're beautiful, Woody mouthed behind her in the mirror's reflection.

Olivia swished her hand.

"Is everything okay? You didn't call," Lauren said. "I didn't want to bug you, but Danny got worried. I left you three voicemails."

"I wasn't worried," Danny said in the background. "Lauren was. I knew what you were doing."

Olivia shook her head at Woody. "We were talking. Della died after you guys left." Woody's smile collapsed. She mouthed, *Lauren.* "We lost track of time."

Basking in the afterglow was not to be. The night held an image of the two of them sitting in bathrobes and snacking on cantaloupe for breakfast while the trees shed their leaves. Fantasy. Of course that was fantasy. The morning held different plans.

"What were you thinking?" Lauren sighed into the phone. "You're scooting around Woody's sheets right after his mother died? Danny and I were at the hotel trying to convince Rig and Checkers that you didn't take an out-of-state breeze."

"Slow down."

"No. You slow down." Lauren paused. "Did he wear protection?"

Olivia rolled her eyes. "Lauren . . . "

"Well, did he?"

"I'm on my way." She jabbed the END button and turned to Woody. "I need to go." Olivia pulled on the shirt to cover her thighs, embarrassed. "Last night was so wrong . . . for me and for you."

Woody threw back the comforter with no modesty concerning his nakedness. In the lamplight, his fit body created a shadowed replica on the wall, as if two men were coming toward her. The shadow was surely

Adam trying to get to her first. She inhaled as Woody grasped her shoulders. The taut muscles of his arms made the printed words *Indigo Lake* stretch beyond their capacity. Her switch flipped to high-beams.

"This is so right," he said.

"It was a mistake."

"My mother made the mistake—a serious one. Compared to mine, your mother was a flipping saint."

"That's a big leap. If I hadn't had my mother's book published, none of this would've happened."

"*Exactly.* Don't you see? The only good thing my mother did was to have me threaten to sue you for Ellen's book—that amazing, beautiful, deadly book."

Olivia thawed as she took in the details of his face: the bits of the silver shine in his stubble, and the flicker of thoughts in his sky-blue eyes forming some conclusion. She ran her fingers through his soft chest hair. His words sailed by like a tailed comet.

"Huh?"

Woody lifted her chin. "It brought you here . . . to me."

Olivia's eyes widened. "No—" She struggled against his grip. "You don't understand. This is wrong . . . so wrong . . . "

He grasped her arms, begging her to look him. "I'm the one who's alive. I'm standing right here. Let go of Adam. He's *dead.*"

"Don't . . . "

Woody lowered his voice and drew her to his chest. "You're the one who said it last night, Liv. We all deserve a second chance. Maybe we both can be part of the lucky few."

At the boomerang of her own words, Olivia collapsed to her knees on the antique rug and groped for the hand-knit cardigan that Adam had given to her, tossed on the floor like last night's rag. Woody's strong arms lifted her. He searched her face.

"What the hell are you so afraid of?"

A thousand words had described this moment in her own novels, words uttered in the complete safety of fictional pages, articulate and elegant. With Woody's desperate fingers digging into her shoulders,

Olivia could only stumble out one:

"You."

"Why?"

"I haven't made room for someone like you."

Olivia held his desperate stare until, in defeat, his fingers eased. Woody started to move away. "Forget it. Let's take a shower, get dressed, and go."

Olivia stiffened and gripped his arm. She yanked him back. Confusion gave way to clarity with the arrangement of words, and those particular ones had set a lifetime of pain with cement mortar. "What did you say?"

Dumfounded, Woody's eyes widened. He, too, recognized the last murderous words his father had uttered to Della.

Chapter 25

Skunk—or Skank?

Olivia remained quiet on the way to the Wolfeboro Inn. Time slowed to an excruciating crawl after she and Woody had dressed in a rush, foregoing a shower. Woody had thrown on his jeans and a yellow sweatshirt before shoving his bare feet into deck shoes. Olivia felt like yesterday's bad news in her same clothes. No other headlights shone on the road to interrogate her about her indiscretion. Woody didn't even reach for her hand. He apologized more times than she could count, but his remorseful words only served as a reminder that this relationship was a test. Lauren had said as much on the phone: *What were you thinking?*

Woody pulled into the parking lot and cut the engine. The keys dangled from the ignition under the glow of the inn's floodlight. "You're never going to forgive me for something my mother did, are you?"

"It's not that, Woody." Olivia pawed through her purse—breath mints, lipstick, room key—anything to distract herself, but she came up with only gas receipts.

"What then?"

"We're both too raw to talk about this, and me in more ways than one."

"We can have breakfast when the restaurant opens."

Olivia let out a bitter laugh. "Oh, right. With my sisters and Rig and Checkers in the jury box on one side, and you grilling me on the other? Pogo can be the judge on the dais."

"Point taken." He offered a weak smile that turned serious. "I apologize for what I said about Adam. That was uncalled for."

Turning in the seat to face him, the translucence of his eyes reflected the cool light. She dug deeper. "Have you ever been in a serious long-term relationship?"

Woody shifted his gaze to the windshield. "About four years ago, a lawyer I consulted with on a case in Boston. I spent two years with her. I got this Porsche to speed back and forth. But I made the mistake of introducing her to Della. End of that relationship." He returned his gaze to her. "How about you? No one since Adam?"

"Which time do you mean, ten o'clock last night? Or midnight?"

"The first was need . . . The second was want."

"Now you sound like Dickens' *A Christmas Carol*. The ghost of the present. As I recall, the boy was ignorance . . . the girl was want." Olivia squeezed his knee in the wrong place. He jumped and recovered. "This will never work, Woody. I'm three thousand miles away, and I can't—won't—leave Portland. Plus, Lauren lives next door, and Danny needs help with the Pogo Trust. We're kind of a package deal since Mom died."

Woody sighed. "It'll take a year to sort out Della's string of misdeeds, never mind all the crap in her house. Then I'll be ready to do something else, maybe go someplace different and sell out my practice to my partners. Nothing to keep me in Wolfeboro after that. I doubt I'll ever retire. Maybe consult. Who knows?"

"What will you do about Della? Hold a service?"

Woody's expression changed behind the reflection of his glasses, reverting to one of a lawyer who unraveled emotional details into a tactical plan. "First, I'll meet with the business office at the hospital. Review the damage. Then I'll make arrangements at a funeral home for cremation. No service. I'll take her ashes up to Indigo Lake. Seems appropriate given the circumstances."

"You should take the day and go row on the lake. It'll clear your head."

Woody set his arm on the back of her seat. "The past fourteen hours have been quite a ride. You were the high point, by the way."

"If I'm the best thrill ride you've ever had, then you haven't met the right woman."

"You were last night, Liv." A slight smile evened the mood as he rearranged the gray in his hair, then ran his fingers through hers. "Quite the doo you have going on there."

"Gives a whole new meaning to your mother's accusation of a 'roll in the hay'."

When Woody called her by her nickname, Olivia's pulse became electrical current. He leaned in and kissed her as though her lips were the last gasp of a hopeful moment, one that didn't include emotional complications or death decisions. She lingered until her eyes stung. No way would she cry, but under his scrutiny on the witness stand she'd blurt out a confession. The door handle became a safety shut-off valve. She pulled it and stepped out of the car, their collective family baggage sucking out behind her.

She leaned down for one last look at him. "I'm sorry about Della."

"Thanks," he said. "Will you call me after you meet with Palermo, so I don't worry?"

Olivia nodded and closed the door. His final words were stuck to her sweater.

~ · ~ · ~

When Olivia stepped into the lobby of the hotel, she wasn't expecting to be met by a greeting party. Rig and Checkers sat in two leather chairs playing games on their cell phones. No one manned the front desk to hear the random growls of profanity that accompanied an electronic shuffle of cards and cartoon-like beeps.

"What are you two doing down here at this hour?" she said. "It's four o'clock in the morning."

"Waitin' on you," Rig said. He raised his eyes and started to laugh. "Check it out Checks."

Checkers paused the *bee-boop* of his game. "Geez. He worked her over but good. Della's not the only one who made a booty call."

Olivia narrowed her eyes. She and Woody had only completed the "get dressed and go" part of the exit plan.

Rig's belly jiggled. "With those gray roots and smudgy peepers, she looks like a mean 'ole skunk that got her sniffer caught in the zipper." He elbowed Checkers and laughed again, only louder. He transitioned into a coughing fit. "Don't get her riled up."

"Yeah . . . riled up . . . like that hair." Checkers wheezed and doubled over. "Bet she hissed at him."

Olivia attempted to smooth down her tangled locks, but they had other plans. "Give me half an hour."

The leather groaned as Rig leaned to the side and pulled a handkerchief from his pocket. "Dolly Cakes, you need more time than that." He wiped his eyes and blew his nose. "Let's take a bet for how long it'll take her to clean up. A buck a minute. I say forty-five."

Checkers tapped his upper lip as he sized her up. "Hmmm . . . least an hour. Might as well gimme sixty bucks right now."

Wrapping her cardigan tighter around her waist, Olivia stomped past the two of them. Their residual snorts of laughter quickened her steps to the staircase. She about-faced and marched back to the lobby.

"Stop laughing. Della died," she said. "You two are completely insensitive."

Their faces sobered as she turned and rushed back to the stairs.

At the landing on the top floor, she leaned against the wall to catch her breath. The stern expressions in the spooky photos appeared to be judging her behavior. She hadn't even had anything to drink to use as an excuse. The memory of Woody's grip made her arms pulse. His delicious grip. *What are you so afraid of?* She inhaled. Small gestures injected magic into courtship: graze of fingers, sweep of hair from the forehead, help with the clasp of a necklace. She'd taken those moments for granted in thirty-two years of marriage and starved for them in her five years of widowhood. With Woody, the clock spun back to the burn of a teenage crush with the newness of those gestures. She fished her keycard from her purse.

The floor under the carpet creaked as she proceeded down the hall, with her mother's voice ringing in her head. *You didn't call. Let me see your eyes. You're grounded.* Olivia slipped the card into the lock. The little green light urged her to go in, but a shadow of a nose sniffed at the bottom of the door. Pogo. She pictured herself as that skunk.

"Back. Back," she said and stepped into the room. Pogo commenced an olfactory inspection of her shoes, pants, and sweater.

Danny turned off the television and stared. Lauren looked up from her suitcase in mid-zip. The shocked expressions on their faces at her appearance might as well have been a dress-down with a string of profanity. She wasn't a skunk—she was a skank.

Olivia planted her hand on her hip. "Do my roots look gray? Tell me the truth."

Lauren shifted her eyes to Danny. "A little."

"Bastards."

"Who?" Danny said.

"Rig and Checkers."

Olivia marched into the bathroom and slammed the door.

~ · ~ · ~

Like a police lineup, Lauren, Danny, Pogo, Rig, and Checkers waited for her outside at seven o'clock in bright morning sunshine. Their bags were already loaded in the car. Rig smoked a cigarette with Lauren; Danny stood with Checkers and watched Pogo prance around the parking lot with a new stick in his mouth. He wasn't going to let this one get away. Sunglasses were in order to hide her blushing face as Olivia wheeled her bag through the front door.

"I checked us out," she said and pointed her finger at Rig, then

Checkers. "Neither one of you goons wins any money."

She'd lingered under the hot water for twenty minutes and dragged her feet to dress in simple black pants and an electric-blue blouse. Another ten minutes slipped by to apply only minimal makeup, but it took at least fifteen minutes to inspect her roots and crow's feet in the mirror. She'd locked herself in the bathroom until her sisters' luggage wheels squeaked and the hotel room door shut. After she'd packed, Olivia stood on the balcony and tried to sort out her confused thoughts about Woody, Della, and Adam without success. She couldn't change what had happened with any of them. By the time she'd looked at her watch, three hours had gone by.

"Nothing to see here people," Lauren said and shooed her arms.

"Yeah. Leave Liv alone," Danny said and turned to Rig. "She had to console a man last night who lost his mother."

"Give me your trash. I'll throw it away." Lauren gathered their water bottles, gum wrappers, and gooey muffin papers like a disinterested politician seeking baby kisses and leaned in to Olivia's side. "Gotta go. We need to drop off the car and get to the prison by the end of visitor's hours."

"Lauren . . . " Olivia gripped her sister's arm. "I screwed up."

"Forget about it. But quit walking funny. You've got a Jackie-O knee-squeeze going on."

Olivia tightened her thighs and followed Lauren and Danny to the car. "We have plenty of time."

"I'm just sayin'." Lauren tossed the debris in a nearby bin and climbed into the passenger side of the SUV. "And we still need to return this sweet ride to the rental place."

As Olivia stored her bag and laptop in the trunk, Danny coaxed Pogo into the backseat of the SUV with his wet stick.

"We shoulda been outta here by now," Rig said and glared at Checkers. He plunked into driver's seat of the Lincoln and slammed the door.

Checkers waved at Lauren. "We gotta arrive at Allenwood in the same car. Looks better, like we're not going soft or nothing. I should ride with you guys."

"Girls only," Lauren said. "You two follow us to Boston. Then we'll go with you from there." Checkers grimaced and ducked into the passenger side of the Lincoln. She tossed Olivia the keys. "Get in, Liv."

Pogo nosed the five-inch gap in the back window to get one last whiff of Wolfeboro before Danny buckled him in. Olivia had an urge to do the same.

A pause of silence filled the SUV with all the doors closed. Danny broke it.

"Sooo . . . how was it, Liv?"

Lauren clicked her seat belt. "Yeah . . . Inquiring minds need to know."

Olivia lowered her sunglasses to the end of her nose and glanced at Danny in the rearview mirror. "Let's just say he lived up to his name."

Propelled by peals of laughter, she tugged the gearshift and hit the gas. The Lincoln ate her dust.

Chapter 26

Facing the Music

After dropping off the Escalade at a rental agency in Boston—and getting dinged an extra fee for the remote courtesy—Olivia, Lauren, Danny, and Pogo crammed into the Lincoln with Rig and Checkers for the rest of the drive to Allenwood Prison. With all their luggage in the trunk, Olivia feared they'd get stopped as low riders. For the last two hours of the trip, Pogo sat in the front seat with his head over Checkers's lap. Lauren had insisted on a climbing-over-knees rotation schedule every hour to avoid any of them getting stuck with the middle spot of the backseat. Olivia's stomach filled with nerves.

Rig nosed the dusty sedan to the gates of Allenwood Prison at four thirty. He lowered the window and waved over the guard. "We got an appointment, a specially arranged appointment."

After confirming this with his clipboard, the guard leaned out of the booth to inspect each person in the car. His square chin jutted toward Pogo. "Can't take the dog in."

"Yes, we can," Danny said, leaning over the front seat. "He's a service dog. Certified. We have permission."

Olivia tapped the headrest and shook her finger at the sunglasses looped over Checkers's breast pocket. He got the message and slipped them over his thin nose.

Checkers threw the guard a grin of crooked teeth. "I'm blind."

The guard squinted his already squinty eyes. "You ain't blind, Chuckles. You been here before."

"If he says he's blind, he's blind," Rig said. "Make a call. Warden Franklin's waiting for us. We're already late."

The guard retreated into the booth and picked up the phone. His stony expression became decidedly Dick Tracy-like from beneath the visor of his official-looking cap.

"You shouldn't have asked Checkers to do that, Liv," Danny said. "I believe your exact words were, 'did you ever think about the ethics of behaving that way?'"

"Yeah, O . . . *liv* . . . ia," Lauren said. "You're the one who needs an ethics lesson." She jabbed Olivia's shoulder. "We're firing you from the behavior-lecture circuit."

She had deserved that dig, but right now Olivia was desperate to get inside the prison. Joking around might lighten the mood, but she knew better. She checked for messages on her phone: four from Karen, none from Woody. She sighed. "What's taking so damn long?"

"Probably calling Big Ben," Rig said.

"Who's Big Ben?

Checkers held up his hand. "Shhh . . . Twinkle Toes just hung up,"

The guard stepped from the booth and pointed. "Go down to the sign marked security entrance. No weapons. No drugs. Phones and purses stay in the lockers."

Rig turned his meaty head. "Leave me and Checks any snacks you got. You could be in there a while."

A clatter rose from the backseat as Rig rolled the car forward. One by one, a bag of mixed nuts, two bags of airline-issue pretzels, a handful of sugarless Jolly Ranchers, and a chewy granola bar cascaded over the front seat and landed on Pogo. The final item was a cellophane bag of venison chews. Lauren refused to part with the strip of button candies.

"Be ready to take us to the airport as soon as we come out," Olivia said. "We have reservations on a red eye at eleven o'clock tonight out of Philly."

"Got it," Rig said. "We'll be waitin' in the car."

Checkers raised his arm over the headrest to Lauren. "Gimme the gun, Miss Pinky Juice."

"Dammit," she said. "It's at the bottom of my purse."

Olivia closed her eyes and sighed. "If we ever really needed you to use that gun, we'll all be dead."

~ · ~ · ~

At four thirty on Wednesday afternoon, Woody tapped the end of his pen on Della's death certificate as he sat in the business office of Huggins Hospital. With a glance at him every few seconds, the administrator clearly found the annoyance difficult to ignore. The nameplate on her desk read *Elma Richards*.

Elma turned and waited for the laser printer to spit out more paper. Woody's mind wandered, since the woman's office held few items of interest. Must be on purpose. Happy, peppy personal pictures only nicked the open wounds of those steeped in grief and sticker shock. A folded *Granite State News* sat on the desk. He turned it around. The heading on a small article read, *Ruckus at Bookstore in Tuftenboro*. If they only knew the real story. He'd need make a phone call to the reporter to squash any future articles.

Only the hum of his car's engine had accompanied Woody on the drive back to the hospital. His mother gone. Olivia gone. The sisters gone. He even missed the dog. Rig and Checkers he could have done without, but they'd added the ridiculous to the sublime. For a few short hours last night, life held promise.

Olivia stormed into his life and gusted out, leaving devastation behind. He considered claiming himself as a total loss on his life insurance. To avoid going home to the reminder of an unmade bed, he'd taken that suggested long row on the lake, grabbed a sandwich at the Dockside Restaurant, then come to the hospital to deal with the unsettled details of his mother's death, one of them being an estimate of the bill.

The printer finished belching. "We're so sorry for your loss, Mr. Rainey," Elma said and handed him a stack of hot paper.

Woody gazed at her as if she were joking. *Did she see Olivia leave this morning?* He recovered. "Thanks for your patience while I took care of a few things."

"I understand." The woman had clearly done this before. In her fifties, Elma had probably held her first job at this hospital and worked her way up. Papers lined her desk blotter in perfect order, including copies of the hefty bill. *Hefty.* Olivia had put her life in the hands of Hefty Man behind the wheel of that Lincoln.

Pushing up the sleeves of his yellow sweatshirt, Woody breathed in Olivia's citrus scent that lingered on his skin. Images of Olivia appeared like camera pictures: her face gazing at him last evening, in the middle of the night, and before dawn this morning.

"Do you want to go over the estimate, Mr. Rainey?"

The unusual pattern of bird's-eye notches in the maple desktop drew his fascination. When he tried not to blink, they appeared to move.

"Mr. Rainey?" Elma pressed.

Woody netted a professional demeanor like he might a struggling trout. "I'm sorry, what did you ask me?"

"Your bill. Do you want to review the estimate now, or call me later if you have questions?"

He stared at the six pages of the statement, jammed with words that looked like they'd been thrown there in a toss of jacks: names of drugs, procedures, equipment, hospital billing codes, and a list of doctors he'd never spoken to. Woody flipped through the pages, wanting to question every item but offering nothing that would prompt an exchange. The number, in bold, at the bottom of last page told all: *Balance due: $37,262.41*

Woody raised his eyes to the woman. "Separate needle charges for Della's IV?" He sighed, picturing the balance in his retirement account draining through a clear tube. "I don't make anything when I lose a contingency case."

Elma's tight lips appeared to soften. "Unfortunately, health care doesn't work on contingency. Sounds awful, I know, but your mother had no insurance. Now, if you want to go down the Medicaid route, we might be able—"

"No. That won't be necessary."

"What are your instructions for transferring the body?" Head down, Elma reviewed the death certificate. Woody had employed that trick too. Focus on the details to not humanize the task with emotion. *The plaintiff. The defendant.* His mother was now considered *the body.*

"Send Della to Walt Cleary. I'll give him a call." Woody pulled out his phone, but he really wanted to check his messages. He stared at the screen. Nothing from Olivia. Still on her way to Pennsylvania.

"*Cleary's* Funeral Home?" In surprise, Elma's forehead accordioned. "Didn't he mix up all those ashes not too long ago? Terrible mess. Nearly put Walt out of business. Didn't you handle the—?"

"Yes." Woody stood and gathered his copies of the papers. He tapped them on the desk several times to line up the edges. "I was the one who filed the lawsuit on behalf of the families."

Chapter 27

The Meeting

Olivia brushed her purse of residual dust after it emerged from the x-ray machine—with her heart in her throat. Her bare feet got a swipe too, before she shoved them back into her loafers. She found it difficult to take in a full breath. Along with the criminals, the gray walls had imprisoned a pungent stew of sweat, bleach, and body odor. She'd tossed off the prospect of coming to this prison when talking with Woody in the hospital. No big deal. And it hadn't been. Until their arrival at the prison, Palermo had only been a character in Ardy's memoir, a deadly phantom. Now, he was real.

The warden waited at security for Olivia, her sisters, and the dog to endure the guard's scrutiny. The first one through, Olivia stepped toward him to introduce herself. The biggest, meatiest hand she'd ever encountered awaited a shake. When compared to his, her fingers resembled those of Tinker Bell's. Olivia sensed that the warden's six-foot-five frame disguised a keen intellect that didn't need muscle to command a room. His fifty-inch shoulders didn't even strain the arms of his business suit, and she wasn't going to give him any guff—no way, no how.

"Mrs. Novak. I've been looking forward to having all of you here, especially the dog. I love dogs. Forget the warden title. Call me Ben—" he pumped her hand—"Franklin."

"Ben Franklin? Seriously?"

"My mother wanted a son who tried new things. Don't think for a minute that I escaped a ribbin'. *The* black Ben Franklin. Nobody forgets my name. And I make the rules." He pointed to a row of lockers near security. "Purses stay here. Sorry, one rule I'm not willing to cave on."

Before Olivia locked away her purse, she turned and tucked a package of wet wipes into the front of her bra. She stepped back to Big Ben.

Pogo got a pat-down and a thorough inspection of his service vest. Danny waited at his side to monitor every touch of the dog before sliding her purse next to Olivia's.

"Bag check," the screener called out. "Is that BB ammo?"

"Candy." Lauren stood in her bare feet and snatched her sneakers from the belt.

"Hurry up," Danny said.

Pogo swiveled his head from Danny to Lauren, unwilling to go forward without their fourth sibling. The screener snapped on a pair of rubber gloves and dumped out Lauren's purse. When the last item fell to the pile—the package of disheveled panty liners—Pogo turned to the screener and whipped his head back to Lauren.

"Go without me, Pogo." Lauren spread her arms. "What am I supposed to do? You don't need to worry about being fresh."

"In the locker," Ben said and pointed. "You'll pick up your possessions on the way out."

Lauren jammed her feet into her sneakers, the Velcro straps flailing to grab on to something. She pointed to the screener. "Don't even think about eating one of those candies. I have them counted." Lauren secured her shoes and hopped to the group on one foot as she adjusted her heel.

Warden Franklin offered a hint of a grin as he buzzed the door. After it opened, all three sisters and the dog were escorted to the visitor's room. That door was embedded with wire mesh.

"Mrs. Novak? May I have a word—in private—before you go in?"

Olivia waved her sisters forward and shrugged when Lauren threw her a quizzical look. "Of course." She hung back in the hall with Ben.

"Don't let anything Palermo says upset you," Ben said.

"What does he want?"

"He's been reading your book—or should I say, your book is being read to him."

"Which one?"

"Mr. Griffin's—Fazziano. We'll talk as a group after your meeting, but Palermo has a proposition for you. We both do. I'll get Nicky. Wait inside."

"Pogo waits in the hall." Olivia steeled her gaze at the warden. "The dog needs a guard."

The warden signaled to a man in a blue uniform by the visitor room door. Ben pointed at Pogo and made a hasty exit. The man adjusted his weapon and stepped to the dog's side. The expression on Pogo's face turned anxious, as if he'd been given a time out.

"Stay here, Pogo," Olivia said. "You're a good boy. Nothing's wrong." She turned and stared at the door. As she grabbed the handle, Olivia became convinced that she was way over her head. Her mind raced with the details of what she'd revealed about Palermo in the book. She'd never intended to face the don with the truth of her written words, but that's what this meeting was—accountability. Palermo was supposed to be dead—and so were she and her sisters—before *Protection* could be published.

Three molded-plastic chairs waited in front of a Plexiglas screen. The one on the end, next to Danny, had been left empty for her. A line of round metal grills dotted the thick barrier and appeared to sneer at the prospect of carrying voices to the other side.

Olivia studied her lap to avoid taking in the details of the soulless room. All other visitors had long since vacated. She'd never voiced the story of Salgado and, at this moment, it haunted her.

"This is fun." Lauren grimaced. "What did Ben want to talk to you about?"

"Palermo has my manuscript for Ardy's book. Palermo and the warden have a proposition."

"Huh . . . Whatever that means. Not sure it'll be honorable."

"Maybe," Danny said. "People can change."

Olivia wasn't so sure.

Surrounded by cement, linoleum, and plastic surfaces, Olivia reminded herself to not touch anything. Nothing appeared to have been sprayed with anything labeled antibacterial. Fingerprints smudged the thick Plexiglas, which shielded the ability to touch but collected evidence of the attempts. She rubbed her fingers in disgust and pulled the packet of moistened towelettes from her bra. Keeping four, she dispensed the remaining contents to her sisters.

"This is gross," Danny said and wiped the counter in front of her.

"Germs keep you healthy, Liv," Lauren said. "I should run my tongue over that divider to strengthen my immune system."

Olivia's stomach lurched, prompting her to swish the wet tissue over the divider in tight circles, more out of fear than disgust.

A muffled buzz opened a door on the other side. Through the wet swirls, Olivia couldn't miss the massive warden leading a frail, elderly man in prison-issue linens. From his appearance, Olivia figured the man was in his late eighties. Like a deflated pumpkin, the seams of his bright orange shirt and pants hung from their charge like loose ribbons. As the screen dried, his image sharpened. She followed the man's guided shuffle to a plastic chair bolted to the floor. Time had carved ridges on Palermo's cheeks; his skin took on a quality similar to dried fruit.

Danny leaned back to check on Pogo through the meshed window of the door. Olivia followed her sister's gaze, catching the guard's confirming nod. She turned to see that Palermo had lowered himself to the chair only a foot away. Determined to not let the don sense her fear, Olivia leaned forward, with her mouth dangerously close to the grilled opening.

"What do you want, Palermo?"

The old man's face broke into a grin of yellowed teeth. "It *is* you, Miss Novak. I know the voice from your colorful interview." He swirled his bony hand like an orchestra conductor. For his age, Palermo's voice was surprisingly smooth. "Much like your prose, no? Lilting . . . enunciating every syllable with precision and grace."

"It's *Mrs.* Novak." Olivia held up her left hand and wiggled her ring finger.

The warden sat in the open chair next to Palermo. "He's blind, Mrs. Novak. Nicky, here, has been with us a long time. Won't see the light of day again."

Lauren crossed her arms and blew out a breath. "Yeah, well, he's in here for a reason—probably a thousand reasons—but that's not our problem."

With nothing for him to see, Palermo closed his eyes. "Not a *problem* . . . exactly," he said. "Think of this visit as . . . an oppor*tun*ity."

The old don was listening for nuances in each of their voices, a reminder to Olivia that she'd need to choose her words with care, and also to watch how she said them. In Palermo's world, respect followed the one who had control—of assets. "How did you get Ardy's manuscript?"

"I enjoyed what I heard very much."

"You had my computer hacked."

Palermo shrugged. "What are they going to do? Throw me in prison?"

"That's enough, Nicky," Ben said.

Olivia stared at the warden, incredulous. Control be damned. "Are you going to let him get away that? He's just admitted to another crime. Is this being taped?" She rapped on the plastic screen. "I want this taped."

"Cool it, Liv," Lauren said. "You left the damn thing on your computer. Let's hear what Nicky wants, so we can get outta here."

Olivia folded her arms across her chest and set her chin. "Thank you for yet another refresh of that message."

"Go on, Mr. Palermo," Danny said and shifted her eyes from the warden to Palermo. "You want something."

"I want. I want. I want." Palermo bounced his fingers in pizzicato. "That sounds so selfish, Danielle. But yes, I do. And so do you."

"I can hear it now," Olivia said. "You want me to edit out your crimes from the book, don't you?"

"Where did the Feds ever come up with the name *R. D. Griffin?* I do love the word *memoir*, however. Rolls off the lips like communion wine." Palermo paused. "No . . . I want you, *Mrs.* Novak, to write *my* memoir. I believe mine will make an excellent second entry after Fazziano's."

Olivia's jaw dropped. "Are you giving me permission to publish Ardy's story? As is? No changes?" She couldn't have hoped for better news. A second book would be explosive.

Palermo nodded. "I think Fazziano's story will be an appetizer to the wonderful meal to come. A series is in order. At my insistence, others are willing to record their stories for a noble cause. Lionetti . . . Rizzo . . . Tullio, the list goes on. All have agreed, as long as they're the first to benefit from our plan."

"*Our* plan? Who's plan?"

Palermo shook his finger. "Patience, Mrs. Novak. I'm enjoying this. I'm willing to share but not to compromise. Ben and I have had lengthy and spirited discussions about a prison program to supply dogs to inmates who are suffering, physically, from the cruelest sentence of all—old age." Palermo clawed the air until his fingers found the warden's shoulder. "You see, Ben and I believe that dogs would be quite beneficial inside the prison system . . . quite beneficial. I'll let you work out the details together, but give Mr. Franklin here—and me, of course—credit in the acknowledgments of each book in the series."

"He's right, Mrs. Novak," Warden Franklin said. "Lots a good talks. The Pogo Charitable Trust does this kind of work. We want to talk about it."

Danny audibly inhaled and covered her mouth. Lauren rubbed circles into Danny's back.

Still suspicious, Olivia summoned her best *Godfather* imitation. "I get something. Danny gets something. Warden Franklin gets something. You get something," Olivia said. "That's it?"

Lauren's expression elongated. "What do I get?"

"Shh . . . We'll think of something."

Palermo nodded. "A good negotiation, I believe."

Olivia studied the old man's relaxed hands, so relaxed that they appeared to dangle like a mobile of bones, and with blood on them from the crimes he'd ordered but never, himself, committed. A hidden demand lurked beneath Palermo's veil of benevolence.

Olivia leaned forward. "And if I don't write your book?"

Palermo rolled his fingers in a rhythmic wave. "If you do, the endeavor will support an important cause—your family's cause. To walk away from the offer, you wouldn't be hurting me, Mrs. Novak. You'd be hurting your sisters."

Blood churned hot in Olivia's veins. "Are you blackmailing me with my own family?"

"Call it what you will, but don't deprive your eager audience of a series that stands to make you and your sisters a fortune. The publicity from the series will shine quite a bright light on the Pogo Trust."

Lauren tapped the counter to get his attention. "Except for a massaged ego, what do you get from this, Palermo?"

Palermo's head followed the sound. He spread his skeletal hands. "I'm just an old man with a story. But without my agreement, Olivia can't publish Fazziano's book. And she'll want that. All three of you will."

Olivia played her bluff. "Then Fazziano's manuscript stays right where it is."

"Ah . . . That's where you're wrong, Olivia. You see, now I know about it." Palermo pointed to his temple. She couldn't quite distinguish whether the gesture was a memory reference or a death threat.

"Who's going to pay for this so-called 'program' until Fazziano's book is released?"

The warden nodded. "A grant from the Pogo Charitable Trust. But when you publish these books you'll replenish the funds."

"So this is a mobster charity pitch session?"

Ben's face brightened. "Somewhat. Okay, yes. Therapy dogs will be rehabilitative, especially for lifers who develop disabilities. Touch is a mighty powerful remedy."

Danny turned, openmouthed. "It's a great idea, Liv. An incredible opportunity, especially if you use the Pogo Trust to market the books." Danny squirmed in her seat. "We could hire the best trainers and place dozens of service dogs, maybe hundreds, in prisons all over the country."

"Makes for a good news story to blab about, Liv," Lauren said. "Danny needs a boost."

The words of Ellen Dushane swirled around Olivia like wispy sprites of wisdom. *When you buy fish at the grocery store, smell the package before you cook it.* Palermo's dead eyes, long past their sell date, held the promise of a stomach ache.

Olivia leaned back in the chair and bit the inside of her lip, working the flesh until she tasted metal. The rusty taste of blood. At that moment, she knew Palermo wanted some of it.

The etched crags on Palermo's cheeks appeared to deepen. Like a wet sheet, the papery skin on his long neck revealed the details of each tendon. Olivia wiped her lip with her forefinger and studied the red tinge.

"No conditions?" she said.

The old man tipped his head in deference and worked over his own lip. Something intangible but distinct oozed from behind his milky eyes. "Only one."

Olivia struggled for a breath.

"Here it comes," Lauren said and hung her head.

A hint of amusement crossed Palermo's face. In an instant, the coating of warmth dissolved to ruthless determination. "Grant a wish for a dying man."

"We're all dying. From the moment we're born," Olivia said. She stared at him. "Depends. I doubt you want a ticket to Disneyland. And I certainly don't think—"

Danny gripped Olivia's arm to stop her. "Of course. Anything. Whatever you want."

Palermo leaned toward Danny's voice still lingering in the metal grill.

"I want Pogo."

Chapter 28

Pact with the Devil

For a brief moment, silent shock reigned over the visitor room. Panic overcame Danny, not in stages but with a single primal scream.

"Nooooo!" Danny bolted to the hallway. The door slammed with an echo.

Chairs scraped the linoleum and overturned as Olivia and Lauren launched into emergency response and raced to the door. Lauren pushed through first; Olivia paused, grasping the handle. Her stomach dropped as she caught the warden's perplexed expression; Ben hadn't known about Palermo's final demand.

In the corridor, Olivia found Lauren alone as the guard at the far end of the hall buzzed open the security door. Danny and Pogo streaked through it.

Lauren threw up her hands. "She told me to wait here. Then she took off with Pogo."

"I'm going after her." Olivia started to turn, but Lauren grabbed her arm.

"Don't. Let her spin down. You won't be able to discuss this rationally."

Her own hand shaking, Olivia pried away Lauren's fingers. "Where was she going?"

"Hell if I know. There's nothing outside except pavement and barbed wire."

"He's the *devil* for saying that to her."

"She invited that devil's bargain, Liv. *'Anything. Whatever you want.'* There endeth the lesson . . . like a ton of bricks."

"Unqualified offers shouldn't be made to people like Palermo. He took advantage." Olivia searched her sister's eyes. "No way can he have Pogo."

"Look at it this way, Danny should be proud of Pogo," Lauren said. "He's obviously made quite an impression."

Olivia gawked. "You're okay with this? What the hell? This isn't about Pogo."

"What then?"

"Pogo was important to Ardy, so Palermo wants him. Palermo's making a statement."

Lauren's shoes squeaked as she started to pace. "Pogo could keep us all from getting killed. I live in Ardy's house. They know where we all live. I could be a dead woman, and so could all of us." She stopped and imitated Palermo's gesture. "Didn't you catch that finger to his temple?"

"You have Ethel to protect you, remember?"

Lauren stilled. Her lip started to quiver. "A gun's the only thing I'm walking away with in this deal. Just like always." She turned her head toward the closed security door. "Queen Olivia gets another book, and Princess Danny got a job handed to her when Mom's book got published. Why don't you guys just leave *me* here, and *I'll* snuggle up with Palermo. Mom would've volunteered my services."

"If you want credit, then stick up for yourself and bring something to the table. You just bitch about everything and act like a victim."

Lauren wiped her cheek. "Danny's spoiled rotten. Mom spoiled her, and we picked up the baton."

"I should be balls-to-the-wall with marketing my book, but where am I? Here. Doing this for you guys."

"And for yourself," Lauren added.

Olivia glared. "Of course for me. I have to support myself. There's no cop at home to protect my life. There's no gun in my nightstand. And there sure as hell isn't a husband waiting to wrap his arms around me."

"What about me? I'm alone too."

Olivia held up her hands. "Stop it. We have to pick this *deal* apart, not each other. Mom handed the three of us a pretty good thing with her book. What Danny does with the Pogo Trust is important. We can't blow it."

"Kills me to admit this, but I know you're right. What would Mom do in this situation?" Lauren whispered the words, more to herself.

"Loaded question," Olivia said, softening her tone. "Don't forget, she changed the date on her birth certificate to get discounts."

"Mom was sneaky. Passive-aggressive." Lauren's crocodile tears had miraculously dried. The words popped out with no hesitation.

Olivia nodded. "Her whole book was a roundabout way to expose Della without having a direct confrontation. It worked."

"A weapon that ended up killing Della."

"Woody could make that argument, and it would hold water. That's why Mom locked it in the safe. She didn't want to go that far."

"But we went that far, Liv," Lauren said.

"Not intentionally. We need to talk with Warden Franklin."

"Shouldn't we wait for Danny? Call her phone."

Olivia bit her already sore lip. She winced. "Our purses are in the lockers. Let's go get 'em."

"What do we say to the warden?"

"I think Palermo's last request was a surprise to Ben too. You should have seen the look on his face after you both left the room." Olivia squared her shoulders. "Everything Palermo proposed works, except his demand for Pogo. I don't approve of Palermo's methods, but the man obviously needs help. Didn't you see how Pogo connected with Della? And she was a murderer."

"Yeah. Pogo's a mob dog. He's a criminal sympathizer."

"That dog has experienced some pretty tough stuff in the last twenty-four hours"—Olivia hesitated—"but this could be *Danny's* most important assignment yet—not Pogo's."

~ · ~ · ~

After Olivia and Lauren retrieved their purses from the lockers, their calls to Danny's phone went unanswered and had flipped to voice mail. A cursory check of the parking lot produced no sighting of Danny, either. They did see Rig and Checkers snacking in the car and focused on their own phones. As the guard escorted her and Lauren to Ben Franklin's office, he mentioned that he hadn't seen Danny or the dog since they'd left the building.

"Do you think she just left with Pogo and went to the airport in a cab?" Lauren whispered, her shoes squeaking like dueling pacifiers.

"No. I think she's having a time out," Olivia said from the side of her mouth. "We'll just have to tap dance and vamp with Ben."

"Right. Act normal."

Three empty government-issue chairs had already been positioned in front of Ben Franklin's expansive desk, spanking clean with not a paperclip out of place. Hoping to catch a glimpse of her sister, Olivia couldn't pry her gaze from the bulky monitor on the warden's credenza that rotated video images of various areas of the prison: guards walking the cell blocks, workers prepping the next meal in the kitchen, an empty visitor room, security personnel at the front entrance, and every closed door to the outside world. When she shifted her eyes back to Ben, his focus was trained on her. A mission lurked behind his dark, intelligent eyes.

"Where's Danielle and Pogo?" Ben said and gestured to the vacant chair.

Lauren shot a glance at Olivia.

Olivia paused and sniffed. "She had to make a phone call. Palermo's last request upset her. It upset all of us."

Ben turned to his credenza and grabbed a square box of tissues in anticipation of tears. Apparently a normal occurrence. As he slid the box across his desk, Olivia followed the images of colorful butterflies on each side. Definitely not government-issue tissues. She pulled out one and set the cube in front of the middle chair left empty for Danny. Her sister had moved up a spot in the line-up. If Danny showed, sandwiching her between two siblings might keep her calm.

Ben refolded his thick fingers. "I apologize for Palermo's insensitive request. I didn't know that's what he wanted."

Olivia pursed her lips. "Let's table that subject until Danny gets here. How well do you know Palermo?"

"I'm a warden, Mrs. Novak, not a goombah. I have Leonetti, Tullio, and Rizzo in here too. While at times they can be endearing—recipes, music requests, colorful stories, and such—I never forget what they've done."

"Why didn't you come directly to us with a proposal?" Lauren said. "We didn't need all this drama."

Ben shifted his gaze. "Mrs. Lyndale . . . Funding the programs I want to create is no easy task, and I don't like begging for money. I don't have patience for bureaucracy either."

"I hear *that*."

Ben waved his hand in dismissal. "We would have gone back and forth with conference calls and messages. Or more likely, my letter would've been buried under all the other letters begging the Pogo Charitable Trust for money. Palermo urged me to get things done in person, so I played along to get you here."

"Danny gets a lot of requests," Olivia said, "but I doubt yours would have been ignored." Even to her, the statement came off as defensive.

"The three of us decide how the money in the trust is spent," Lauren said. "The program has to be a win-win."

"Which mine is. Admittedly, with a twist," Ben said. "You wouldn't be sitting in front of me now if it weren't for Palermo, or his wish to have a book written about his life."

Lauren leaned forward. "Are you doing his bidding?"

Ben threw his head back and laughed, showing a wide row of even white teeth. "Hell no. He's doing mine. Palermo wants a dog and to document his life story; I want to create a dog program that will allow lifers to die with dignity. Palermo talked to me about a way to make us both happy, and that involved the three of you and Pogo. He asked specifically for Pogo." Ben pulled a thick folder from his drawer and fanned the pages. The typed label read, *Therapy Dog Program.* "I've learned a thing or two by working with serious offenders."

The candid sincerity in Ben's deep voice lured Olivia's trust. He could sell flood insurance in the Himalayas. "What's that?"

"Partnership. Speed. Getting things done and *mea culpa* later. Palermo's dying. I've been trying to get an animal program in here for two years." Ben shoved the folder back in the drawer.

Olivia had an image of Danny pacing the parking lot. It had been nearly half an hour since she had taken Pogo outside. She glanced at Lauren, who tapped her watch.

"Prisons are like self-contained ecosystems," Ben continued. "I work with the toughest oil spills in here. When a criminal gets life, he still *has* a life, albeit not the one he planned for. At some point—maybe after decades—these guys finally realize they're going to die right inside these cinder-block walls. Some get it. Some don't. But when they do, they change. No one wants to fade away without making a mark. It's up to me to make sure that mark is a good one. Feeds the ecosystem in a positive way."

Olivia scrutinized a row of photographs on a shelf above the credenza: Ben with three different presidents, Clinton and both Bushes; Ben with a group of teenagers in front of an inner-city high school; Ben making Oprah appear small in a bear hug. The real Ben had been waiting for her gaze to come back around to him.

"If you read up on me, Mrs. Novak, you'll see that my programs work," he said. "My goal is to have empty cells at the inn, but if they're not, I want the inmates calm."

Olivia whipped her head around when Ben's office door groaned open. Relief washed over Lauren's face, too, as Danny stepped inside and hand-signaled for Pogo to remain in the hall with the guard. Without offering a word or a revealing expression as to where she'd been, Danny sat in the empty chair. She betrayed no evidence that she had been crying, either.

To communicate her worry, Olivia showed her sister the tattered tissue she'd balled in her fist. Danny snatched three fresh ones in rapid succession and winked. "Here, Liv."

Lingering doubt in her younger sister evaporated, reminding Olivia that she needed to trust. Lauren's shoulders rose with an intake of breath. Olivia let hers out.

Danny slung her purse over the back of the chair. "You and I, Mr. Franklin, have a meeting tomorrow with the director of Sore Paws and the Humane Society in Philadelphia. We're going to discuss a partnership for your program."

"What's Sore Paws?" Lauren said.

"They train service dogs for vets with PTS—post-traumatic stress—and physical disabilities. Amazing dogs. They have training programs in prisons too."

Ben's shoulders dropped. "With all due respect, Mrs. Eason, I've talked with both organizations. Their programs don't directly benefit inmates. The dogs interact for training, but then they go into real service on the outside."

"A checkbook has a way of convincing dogs to stay." Danny glanced at Olivia and smirked. She dreaded to find out what the statement meant. "And so does a pen—with fresh ink."

"Well, I'm happy to go with you, but those two groups are tough to crack, especially for new programs." The arms of Ben's expansive suit jacket bunched as he laced his fingers behind his head. "I'm listening."

"The details have yet to be worked through, but we're going to create a partnership to keep dogs here for the inmates. We'll start small . . . with *one* dog. To get things rolling, I'll stay here for a week. Do you have space here to care for the dog when he's not working, including a residence for a full-time handler?"

"Depends," Ben said. "How much are you prepared to put on the table?"

Olivia widened her eyes at Danny. "Can the three of us step outside for a moment to discuss this?"

Danny held out her hand. "In a minute. I want to know that Palermo isn't a threat to any dog."

"Pogo?" Ben said. "He's perfectly safe here."

Olivia stiffened and leaned forward to catch Lauren's eye. "We don't think—"

"I've found another dog," Danny said, interrupting. "He's chocolate-brown and just completed training. A big Labradoodle."

Ben tapped the desk with his forefinger. "Palermo specifically asked for Pogo. He was quite adamant. Why?"

As soon as Ben asked the question, Olivia knew exactly why Palermo wanted Pogo. The story had been the most heartrending of her career as a writer. Listening to Ardy relay the details had resulted in her driving home in tears.

"Salgado," Olivia said. "The story's in the memoir I wrote. Palermo ordered Fazziano—Ardy—to kill an Australian shepherd named Salgado, back in 1938, to force its owner to pay a debt. Danny's husband, Ryan, told me the dog's collar had been sent to Fazziano as a warning before he died. Intimidation. That's why the FBI moved him to Iowa."

"Ryan never told me that, Liv," Danny said.

"Me neither," Lauren added.

Olivia toyed with her wedding band, tighter on her finger since the morning's embarrassing antics with Woody. "When Ardy was moved, having to leave Pogo behind—and fear—ultimately killed him." She raised her eyes to the warden.

Ben nodded with new-found understanding. "Now, Palermo doesn't just want the dog; he *needs* the dog. Ben spun his chair to the computer monitor on the credenza. He punched in four numbers. "He's no threat. Take a look."

Olivia, Lauren, and Danny rushed to stand behind the warden's desk. The monitor showed a live video of a jail cell decorated with a vase of rust-colored flowers, a cassette player, and an Oriental rug with an elaborate design. Nicky Palermo lay on his cot, the outline of his thin legs visible under a dark blanket. One of Palermo's hands swung in a rhythm of wide loops. A faint shine pooled in Palermo's sightless eyes.

"Nicky loves opera. Blubbers like a baby." Ben chuckled and switched on the sound. Two sparkling soprano voices ebbed and flowed in the famous duet of "The Flower Song" from Leo Delibes's opera *Lakme*. One of Olivia's favorites. She recalled the aria being used in a television commercial for British Airways.

"How long does Palermo have?" Lauren said.

Ben shrugged. "A few weeks, a month—maybe two. He's failing fast."

Danny pulled out her cell phone and held it up. "His name's Beauregard. The director sent me this picture. We'll bring him back from Sore Paws tomorrow. Not a purebred standard poodle, but he's the best I could do on short notice."

Olivia, Ben, and Lauren leaned toward the small screen. Beauregard's dark, inquisitive eyes made Olivia's chest swell. With his long, wavy-haired paws splayed, the dog appeared eager to jump into an adventure. His chocolate-brown curly fur did indeed invite touch, like a giant, soft Teddy bear in a display window. Olivia immediately wanted to take him home—a Pogo of her own.

Catching Lauren's eye, Olivia nodded toward the door. She stood and tugged on Danny's leather jacket. "Ben, can you excuse us for a few minutes?"

~ · ~ · ~

In the hall, Olivia waved away the guard for the conversation with Lauren and Danny to remain private. A sibling huddle wreathed around Pogo, with the ball at the end of his tail sticking out beyond three pairs of legs.

"You want to pull a switcheroo on Palermo?" Olivia said to Danny.

"Yeah. He's never met Pogo."

Lauren squinted. "What if Palermo finds out?"

"He won't," Danny said. "The old coot's blind."

Olivia grimaced. "Can the Pogo Trust afford to get a dog for Palermo *and* pay for a handler?"

"We'll have to. We don't have a lot of choices here, Liv,"

"How much is in the account now?"

"Hundred and fifty thousand . . . give or take."

"Which? Give? . . . Or take? It was double that six months ago."

"Take. You both approved new therapy vests with the Pogo logo and a redesign of the website."

Lauren stinky-cheesed her nose. "We did, Liv."

Olivia blew out a breath, picturing Pogo's custom-embroidered face, like a giant Girl Scout badge, gracing piles of yellow vests in boxes. So much for a volume discount. "The royalties from Mom's book are slowing. A movie deal is years away, if it ever happens. I need to get *Protection* into Karen's hands—*pronto*—and start on Palermo's book."

Lauren brightened. "I'll help you. I organized all the research for Ardy's."

Olivia raked Pogo's head with her fingers. "Thanks. But if we do anything here, then the trust needs more funding."

"Waiting for money from the book will take too long," Danny said. "Pogo's in the hot seat *now*."

In sequence, all three sisters stared down at Pogo. In poodle-like fashion, he raised his eyes and cocked his head, appearing to assess his responsibility as a poster child for criminals.

"Make double sure Bauregard's a male, Danny," Lauren said. "Palermo will know."

Pogo sat and wrapped his tail around his back paws, as if to protect his dog parts from the conversation.

"For God's sake, Lauren." Olivia rolled her eyes and turned to Danny. "Shave Beauregard's tail so it has a ball on the *end*."

"I'm pretty sure he's neutered," Danny said, without missing a beat.

"That's not what I meant," Lauren said. She narrowed her eyes at Olivia. "You can't even tell Woody about this."

Olivia considered it, but dismissed the idea. Then she considered it again. "I won't."

"I'll have to fill in Ryan"—Danny karate-chopped the air—"but that's all. You two swear this is only between us and Ben before we go back in?"

Olivia held up three fingers. "Girl Scout's honor." Technically, Danny's wording made it legal for her to tell Woody after her first step into Ben's office.

"I got kicked out of Girl Scouts." Danny pushed Olivia's hand away. "I didn't earn any badges."

"I didn't even cut it in Brownies," Lauren said.

Olivia set her jaw, just like her mother's. This time she didn't fight it. "We make our own badges—custom ones."

Lauren grasped Danny's arm. "If you can't get Beauregard, what's our Plan B?"

Danny straightened. "That I sit my sorry ass in a cell and watch Palermo pet Pogo—until Palermo's sorry ass dies." She broke from the huddle and gripped the door handle to Ben's office. She paused and turned. "And Liv? If I can get this dog for Palermo, then I'll need one for each of those other goons you're going to write a book for. You'll need to subsidize them. After my salary, there won't be enough in the trust account."

Olivia stood openmouthed and watched Danny lead Pogo into Ben's office. As her sister's form diminished beyond the doorway, the jamb appeared to widen to accommodate the wake of her determined spirit. And to punctuate the moment, Pogo's tail resembled an upside-down exclamation point.

Lauren bumped Olivia's elbow. "She pulled a *Columbo* on you, Liv.

The ole' zinger of an exit line."

"Just like Mom."

"Exactly like Mom."

~ · ~ · ~

When Olivia slipped back into her chair, Danny and Lauren were already in full getting-down-to-business mode with Ben. Pogo paced a continuous circle around the desk, forming an invisible lasso around all four of them. To keep powered up, the poodle paused for a head scratch from Ben.

"I'll get my facilities manager right on it," Ben said to Danny and reached for his desk phone, his other hand petting Pogo. "Before we were turned down for funding, we'd commandeered some rooms near our Transitional Unit."

"Wait, Ben. Hang up the phone," Olivia said. "There's an important caveat." As the warden replaced the receiver, the tally of expenses spun in Olivia's head, adding a whole new meaning to name *Sore Paws*.

Lauren nodded. "A non-negotiable one. Right, Danny?"

Showing her first hint of nervousness, Danny scratched her upper lip. "Palermo can't know that Beauregard isn't Pogo."

"He'll know," Ben said. "The dog's name, if nothing else."

"He answers to Bo. I'll work with him to change the command 'Bo—Go for a ride' to 'Bo—Go'."

"Let's hope Palermo's hearing's not so good," Lauren muttered.

Ben's expression blanched. "You're serious about this?"

"You bet I am," Danny said. "Nobody messes with Pogo or tries to split his loyalty. Palermo would like nothing better."

"It could work, Ben," Olivia said and rested her arms on the chair, attempting her most mobster-like pose, "but you have to help Danny convince Palermo that Beauregard is Pogo. He can't find out."

Summoning her own inner mobster, Lauren mirrored the stance to flank Danny with sibling weaponry. "Otherwise, everything else we agreed to—the books, the program, the funding—all evaporates. The three of us and Pogo will go home and call it a day."

Unprepared to go that far, Olivia gawked at Lauren. Her sister wavered her hand below the edge of the desk, a signal to remain quiet.

"How will I get access to write Palermo's story?" Olivia said to Ben.

"I've already requisitioned the recording equipment for him to use," he said. "Periodic video interviews can be conducted over the Internet through our Virtual Visitation program."

"Fine. But I have one last request, or there's no deal."

The room went silent for a few seconds, then Ben squinted, waiting for her words to land.

"I want Beauregard when Palermo dies."

Ben gazed at Olivia, then offered a slow nod of understanding. "*Quid pro quo*, Mrs. Novak?"

"You got it."

Danny broke into a wide smile. "I'll introduce you to him on the screen, Liv."

Olivia's stomach tingled in triumph; she nearly let out a squeal. To recover, she glanced at her watch. With time closing in to leave for the airport, Woody's voice in her head whispered lawyer-like advice. "Shouldn't we put something in writing?"

Lauren hefted her purse from the floor, pulled out her notebook, and ripped a fresh page from the back. "Danny, get out your stamp pad."

"What for?"

"We're gonna hold Ben's finger to the fire to ink this deal. We don't have time for paperwork, and Ben doesn't have patience for it anyway. We'll all sign our names and add a thumbprint. If we did it in blood, Liv would freak about germs."

Ben's eyes widened, showing a frame of white around his dark irises.

In sequence, the sisters signed their names, inked their thumbs, and pressed a print to the paper. Danny slid the black pad to the warden.

After Ben signed, he pressed the largest thumbprint Olivia had ever seen above his name. She handed him a fresh tissue.

"I like the way you do business," he said and scrubbed his thumb. Pogo bounded from his side to Danny's. "You get the last say, Big Fella."

Danny beamed. "Pogo gets a proxy vote for Beauregard." She inked the wooden block with the raised impression of a paw print and stamped the paper.

Chapter 29
Hidden Treasures

At six thirty on Wednesday evening, Woody wound his way back to Della's house. Around each bend and twist of 109A, his headlights caught the reflective glow of eyes tucked in the trees: deer, bears, raccoons, maybe bobcats. He'd planned to tackle Della's house in the morning, but Walt Cleary at the funeral home needed his mother's birth certificate. Walt had been shocked to hear from Woody, but in the end he welcomed the business. Death was a job with a lot of paperwork, and Walt vowed to play by the book. Woody had also scored a win with the *Granite State News*. The reporter agreed to not publish any more stories about the bookstore ruckus, satisfied that no juicy follow-up was warranted now that Olivia had left town.

A coiled cord snaked from the lighter outlet to Woody's phone on the passenger seat, pumping juice into the device like life support. Olivia remained unresponsive. His stomach churned for what might have transpired in the sisters' meeting with Palermo, and he didn't take the lack of response as a good sign. Truth carried a catch or a price. He'd been through that drill with more case settlements than he cared to remember. She must still be with Palermo, her phone in a locker. Or the silence may be from Olivia running, running away as fast as she could. He'd left three messages on her cell since leaving the hospital.

Woody pulled into Della's dooryard and shut off the engine. The headlights would stay on for thirty seconds, enough time to illuminate his path to the front door. With the toe of his shoe, he tapped the piece of broken concrete on the bottom step. A chunk fell to the ground with a *thunk*. The screen door squealed in protest. He turned the small key in the lock of the inner door. The headlights faded to black.

"I should've left the door open to save myself the trouble," Woody muttered and stepped into Della's dark, cluttered world. He turned the switch on the domed lamp next to the orange recliner, its stuffed arms dark amber from wear. Warm light filled the frosted glass shade to reveal a perfect mound of golden roses and blooming pink peonies in relief. The flowers were so realistic that they might release fragrance.

Woody returned to his comfort zone: papers. He flipped through a stack of envelopes next to the old Frigidaire: his mother's current bills for electricity, phone, and water. Okay, maybe he wasn't quite ready for papers. He pulled the fridge's long handle to check for spoiled food. The inside held nothing but a pint of creamer, a package of ham, some Cabot's extra-sharp cheddar, and three spotted apples, picked from the tree out back. A long, waxy bread bag sat next to the sink with a picture of a gingerbread man in happy stride, the logo of the Yum Yum Shop. He raised his eyes from the cutting board to the wall. A small watercolor similar to his own, and to the one on the cover of Ellen Dushane's book, faced him, a not-so-gentle reminder of what started this mess. He leaned closer to inspect the title: *Indigo Lake*. The same.

Turning away, his gaze landed on a glass-fronted hutch. The wooden edges scraped as he opened the door. The shelves were jammed full of glass bowls, wine glasses with etched flowers, plates with scrolled vines, and several vases embellished with nests of painted birds. Tucked in the back were two pieces of folded paper yellowed with age. The first was his mother's birth certificate. Della was born in 1927 at Huggins Hospital and died only the roll of a gurney away. His grandparents were phantoms. He did recall flashes of Vernon and Dolly living on the farm down the road. The second piece of paper, wrinkled and torn around the edges, held only two words: *I can't.* The block letters were in all caps: his father's handwriting. He stared at the letters and compared the strokes to his own. His leaned right; his father's did too. The paper appeared to have been balled in a fist and smoothed with second thoughts. He stuck the papers in his jacket pocket. The damn story was true.

Before he shut the glass door, one piece in the cabinet drew his eye: a crystal apple, the clearest glass he'd ever seen, even covered in dust. Smooth. Flawless. He hefted it in his palm; must have weighed three pounds. With the apple in his hand, he wandered the few short steps to the living area. The door of the hutch hung open like a yawn.

Low bookcases lined the perimeter of the walls. Until his early teens, the room had doubled as his bedroom. For as long as he could remember those books had graced the shelves, some of which now sagged in the middle. His fold-out cot had backed up to Walt Whitman, Jules Verne, and Kurt Vonnegut. His goal had been to change the bed's position until he'd worked through the alphabet to *A.* He'd stopped at Agatha Christie when he got a full scholarship to Phillips Exeter Academy in the ninth grade. He missed these books, the aroma of their thick paper. Once he'd left for school, his childhood remained here in pages read with a flashlight.

Woody set the apple on the top of the first bookcase and rippled the tip of his finger over the spines of all colors and sizes, like a stick on a picket fence. Two, three, maybe four hundred books, too close to render an objective opinion. He'd only hinted about his childhood with Olivia, and he needed a consult with her now, the one person to hold his trust. He pulled his phone from his breast pocket to try one more time. She answered on the first ring.

"Woody," Olivia said. "I was just getting ready to call you."

"How did the meeting go?" he said and pulled out *A Tale of Two Cities,* drawn to it by Olivia's earlier mention of Dickens. "I've been worried sick."

"Good—I mean, not that you were worried, but that the meeting ended well. It was a strange way for us to get there, but it wasn't anything horrible, in the end. Danny did a deal to get Palermo a therapy dog, and Palermo wants me to write a book—a series, in fact."

"So that's how book deals get done?" Woody slid *A Tale of Two Cities* back into its dusty opening. He spotted a twist of a knot between the next set of titles. Several small envelopes had been tied with kitchen twine. He pulled them out and stared. All were addressed to Della. *Don't say a word.*

"It turns out Palermo's blind. Long story, but we've worked through it. The paperwork trail will be even longer, but for now we signed with a thumbprint."

"Sounds like you need a lawyer." The same handwriting as the note. His father's. Justification. He fingered the knot and slipped the packet in his pocket with the papers.

"I do, in the worst way—but not only for paperwork."

Woody closed his eyes, the seductive turn in her voice washing over him. After a beat, he cleared his throat and tried to regroup by changing the subject. "I'm at Della's, going through her things. I need help."

"What did you find?" A hint of humor in her voice.

"How much battery power do you have left in your phone?"

Olivia laughed. The trill lifted his spirits. "Not a lot. Lauren and I are leaving to catch a red-eye back to Portland. We won't get home until after dawn. And I'm starving."

Woody picked up the crystal fruit. "I'm holding a glass apple." He returned to the hutch, still balancing the weighty lump in his palm like a baseball, with a sudden urge to toss the orb in the air and catch it.

A slight hesitation. "Is it clear and smooth, about four inches tall?"

"How the hell did you know that?"

"Mom had one, Woody. It's sitting on a shelf in my den. It's Steuben. Della must have one too."

"Whoa, Nellie." Woody carefully returned the piece to its original spot and patted the stem. "There's a ton of books, so many more than you saw, Liv, and painted lamps, china, and wineglasses. Della didn't even drink."

"Don't do anything until you get a professional opinion."

"You sound like me."

"We went through this process after Ellen died. If Della has Steuben, then those lamps might be Pierpoint or Tiffany. I wouldn't be surprised. The one with the flowers next to her chair is beautiful. Don't you watch those picker shows? People collect for all kinds of reasons. There might be Limoges and Lalique in all that junk."

Woody stepped back to the bookcases. "And the books?"

"The copyright page tells all. Do they have the original covers?"

Woody leaned down to inspect the spines. "Most do. At least what I'm looking at." He chuckled. "As a writer, you must have favorite words."

"I like onomatopoeia, words that are alive and sound like their meaning . . . *rip, swish, zip, thump, fizz, bark,* and *purr.*" Her voice took on a different quality when she talked about writing. "Don't you want to keep those books? They'd be beautiful in your office."

Woody flashed on the hospital bill sitting on his desk. He thought of selling the books to Olivia, but that negotiation could prove awkward. "No. Best to make a clean break."

"Box up the ones you want to sell and take them to Catherine Pratt at Alten's. She's a good egg. She'll know what they are. Do a commission deal for her to sell them. Then call an antiques dealer or an estate sale company for the other stuff."

"Can I give you a consulting fee to handle this for me?"

"It might end up being the other way around." A distinct pause. "Woody . . . Palermo gave me permission to publish Ardy's memoir."

"What's he get out of the deal?"

"A dog. He wanted Pogo. I'm not supposed to tell you this part, but Danny's staying behind with the warden to get Palermo a different dog."

"And?" Woody pulled out James Herriot's *All Creatures Great and Small.* His chest warmed. Olivia probably had this one in her collection.

"His name's Beauregard. I've only seen a picture, but he's fantastic."

"Maybe you should've stayed behind instead of Danny."

"Too much to do. Palermo wants me to write his story. He's got others who want their stories published. My agent's going to flip when I tell her."

"You're going to be busy." Woody fingered the envelopes in his pocket, wanting to tell her about them. He resisted.

"For at least a few years, anyway."

"Will you call me when you get home? I don't care how early or late."

Olivia paused. "Rig and Checkers are waiting to take Lauren and me to the airport."

"You didn't answer the question."

"Always the lawyer. If I don't, will you hunt me down with a subpoena to appear?"

"Something like that."

"That actually sounds more fun than a simple phone call."

"You have a lot to learn about me. I'm quite determined."

"We need to go."

Woody ended the call, with Olivia's voice still reverberating like a tiny bell. He sized up the books, the lamp, the china, and the glassware. His gaze came full circle to the apple. It had a twin. He rinsed the life-size piece in the farmhouse sink, keeping a tight grip under the stream. With one hand, he snatched a potato-sack towel and dried the piece like a wet baby. Magnified golden light flashed through the flawless crystal like a beacon through the fog. The glow from the overhead kitchen light refracted through the glass and threw an undulating rainbow of reflection over the wall: red, orange, yellow, green, blue, and violet. If held it to the light long enough, the piece would start a fire.

"Olivia Novak," he whispered. "Who the hell are you?" He wrapped the apple in the towel to quell the blaze. This memento he'd take home—and one other for a different reason. He didn't want anyone's hands on it but his.

Stepping to the kitchen windowsill, Woody seized the cloudy Lydia Pinkham's Elixir bottle—without a rinse—and slipped it into his jacket pocket, already heavy with a story. The inciting incident, the motive, and the evidence were now united.

Chapter 30

Home With No Danny and Pogo

Before six o'clock in the morning, airline terminals take on an otherworldly atmosphere. Bustling, jostling, and rushing throngs of people are replaced with the sleep deprived, shuffling past shuttered stores and darkened counters.

The gate area echoed with emptiness as Olivia emerged from the Jetway with Lauren, new emotional baggage in tow. Without Danny and Pogo, their homecoming was dampened. Steps slower. Smiles few and far between. Physical exhaustion aside, Olivia couldn't believe what she and her sisters had endured in less than a week. She actually missed Rig and Checkers. They'd gotten soft about Danny and Pogo on the ride to the airport. The drop-off ended with hugs, an exchange of contact information, and the return of Lauren's gun, but not the snacks.

As she trudged through the terminal, Olivia had finally called Karen. Before she got in a word, her agent foamed about her not returning her calls. Anger had blossomed to elation once Olivia relayed the news: potential lawsuit thwarted with Della's death; mob memoir of R. D. Griffin would be on its way after a nap and a trip to Cascade bank, and a forthcoming memoir series with the addition of Palermo's story and its charity angle. A romantic liaison didn't make it into the conversation before disconnecting.

"You all right, Lauren?" Olivia said and slipped her phone into her purse.

"I'll be fine when I get out of here and into my bed. I couldn't sleep on the plane."

"Ryan will be waiting. I'll get the bags."

Lauren slowed her steps. "Would you?"

"Go," Olivia said. "Get the car with Ryan. I'll meet you outside of baggage claim."

Beyond security, Ryan's badge flashed before she saw his smile. A round Band-Aid on his chin signaled a nick in a rush-job shave routine. Olivia wished Woody had been waiting for her on the other side of the cordoned barrier, with Beauregard in tow. Hearing Woody's voice before they had left the prison rekindled the attraction. Then she took a longer look at Ryan's face. She recognized that smile, the one that held a combination of sadness, anxiety, and Irish pride. He had presented it to her when he'd broken the news about finding Adam's killer. Now, it held a different meaning: sadness for Danny's and Pogo's absence, and the complete trust that his wife would succeed.

When Ryan spotted the two of them, he waved like the winning bidder at an auction. Olivia waved back.

"His face has Danny all over it," Lauren said, "even though he knew she wasn't coming."

Olivia turned to her. "And Pogo. He's their most loyal fan club member. We're loved by association."

As if weighted down with two pails of water, Lauren's shoulders dropped. "I really need to go to bed, Liv. It's nine in New Hampshire. You dare to call me before four this afternoon, I'll pull out my gun."

Without responding, Olivia stacked her laptop on top of her carry-on and snaked through the exit barrier. She wrapped her arms around Ryan—with an extra squeeze from her little sister.

"You take Lauren and get the cruiser," she said. "I'll pick up the other bag and meet you downstairs."

~ · ~ · ~

The thirty-minute ride home precipitated a two-way information dump on Ryan. The rehash of the week's antics amazed even Olivia upon recounting them.

"Danny's doing something important," Ryan said. "On the phone, she sounded like a woman on a mission. She and Ben are in their meeting right now. She stepped out to call me."

"She's saving our butts," Olivia said.

"Maybe. But the house is too quiet." Even though off duty, his eyes still scanned beyond the highway. He switched off the crackling radio on the dash of the cruiser. To the hum of the souped-up engine, Olivia stared at the grill separating her and Lauren from the front seat. Danny would be behind bars, quietly becoming a hero while her hero attempted to quiet his ability to put criminals there. Yet another book someday. She glanced at Lauren, sketching the rear-aspect scene of Danny and Pogo walking into Ben's office. She'd gotten Pogo's tail just right.

The four of them had been a tight unit for a week. But Freesia needed company too. Olivia pictured introducing Beauregard to her cat, but quickly dismissed the blurred image of claws and paws. Then there was Woody—all arms and legs.

"Liv's in *looove*," Lauren said, her pencil a blur. "It's so romantic."

The comment prompted a smile from Ryan in the rearview mirror. "Thrill me. I'm lonely. Do tell."

"Don't tell," Olivia muttered. She turned and stared at the hills along highway 205. "Just for bringing it up, Lauren, I'm going to make you get a pedicure. I swear I will."

"I think I need to meet this guy to make sure he's good enough for you."

Olivia tried to hold back a smirk. "Yes, Dad."

"Danny told me all about it." Ryan chuckled. "I wanted to see which one of you would spill first."

"Leave it to Lauren to take the first shot."

"Actually, Liv," Lauren said, "you made the first one. Tell Ryan about that."

"He probably already knows."

Ryan nodded. "I only wish I could have been there to see it. I haven't had a hairy-spider call in years. Rig and Checkers sound like quite a pair."

"You have no idea. I can name those tunes in one word—'Veg-O-Matic'."

"And Della?"

"Don't get me started."

Lauren laughed. "I wouldn't know where to begin to draw *that*."

After Ryan had dropped her and Lauren off, the lingering guilt followed Olivia into the house. The anticipation of Danny's return with Pogo floated on air without words.

As she parked her bag in the entryway, Olivia swore she could hear the tick of Beauregard's toenails on the hardwood floor, and her mother's voice in the once-expected phone call asking, *How was your trip?* Olivia flipped the switch next to the front door, Adam reminding her to turn off the porch light. *Don't forget to lock up.* The spectral tingle of phantom limbs. And then Woody's voice brought up the rear. *Call me. I don't care how early or late.*

Olivia greeted Freesia with copious kisses, checked the kitchen appliances, ignored the flashing messages on the phone, and made sure everything was locked up, per Adam's cerebral instructions. Freesia led her up the stairs to commence a nap without worry.

The cat curled on the left side of the bed as Olivia slipped on a fresh oversize T-shirt and brushed her teeth. She pulled the drapes to block out the morning light and glanced at the alarm clock. Danny, Ben, and Pogo were in the thick of negotiations for Beauregard. Woody was probably deep into the day's tasks with Della's affairs. She wanted to help him, share what she'd learned from working through the process of death beyond the law. Calling him now would only give her fitful sleep. In the comfort of her familiar surroundings, she felt their brief time together could have been a dream. So far away.

Olivia eyed Freesia. "That's my side. You're a space invader." She didn't seek a response. Instead, she retreated, spit, and rinsed. She left her mouth guard on the edge of the sink, since no one but Freesia would hear here snore.

The cat curled upside down and purred as Olivia wrapped her arms around her seemingly boneless body.

"You'll keep me warm." Olivia kissed Freesia's whiskers. "You deserve to sleep on the left because I left you for a week. You might need to learn to share."

At Woody's, she had slept on the right side. Woody was a lefty. Uncomfortable, Olivia vowed to sleep on the right side, to try it out in earnest. The left had been hers for nearly thirty-seven years. The space still filled with Adam's presence, beyond Freesia, beyond her, beyond life itself.

Olivia sank into the pillows. Lauren would be alone in her own bed. Tonight, Ryan would retire to his without Pogo and Danny. Woody might be reading one of the Della's books. Beds were empty, one way or another, but they all wrapped themselves in sheets. Woody's soft sheets would get a wash, washing away the evidence that she had been there at all. She'd have to find soft Italian sheets in Portland. Hers were good but not like the thread count of Woody's.

The alarm clock was set for 2:30 p.m. Then she'd head to Ted's Beal's office for the key. She'd walk into Cascade Bank and pull Ardy's manuscript from the safe-deposit box. At least she could make one person in the world happy . . . Karen.

As sleep threatened to roll over her, Olivia checked her cell phone for messages. None. She reached for the home phone on her night-stand and called Woody's cell number. She'd promised. Four rings tossed her into his voice mail. She left a quick message:

"I'm home. I'm tired. I'm going to bed now—on the right side."

Chapter 31

Reconnection

Olivia's home phone jolted her awake before the alarm went off. With the drapes pulled, she squinted one eye at the digital clock: 2:15 p.m. Then she remembered it must be Thursday afternoon. She'd been asleep for five hours under a blanket of jet lag. Her fingers found the phone as its lime-green buttons shivered with every ring.

"Did I wake you?" Woody said.

"Uh-huh." Still in a somnolent state, Olivia ran her tongue over her teeth, actually missing the sensation of her mouth guard. She rolled on her back, which released a mew of protest from Freesia.

"What was that noise?"

"My cat. I'm trying out the other side of the bed. Apparently, the experiment wasn't successful."

"Practice makes perfect. I got your message. Thank you for letting me know that you made it home safe." The purr of his car engine filled the receiver.

"Nice having someone to call. Where are you?"

"Traveling up 109A. The leaves lost their color after you left town." He chuckled. "I'm on my way back to Della's to deal with all the books."

"I need to get up and deal with a book of my own." Olivia swung her bare legs to the edge of the bed. She teetered as she organized her thoughts. "I'm sending Ardy's manuscript to my agent tomorrow. I need to go to my lawyer's office to pick up the key to the safe-deposit box and get to the bank before it closes."

"I thought I was your lawyer."

"Conflict of interest, Counselor."

"If the manuscript is still on your computer, why not print it out to save the time?"

"I don't know. Save the toner in my printer?" One other, un-spoken, reason for going to that bank lurked behind the conversation. Olivia couldn't tell Woody, or they'd move dangerously close to the subject of Adam. "I just want to hold it in my hands again . . . the original. A new one wouldn't be the same."

"Then you'd better get moving. Are you wearing a T-shirt?"

"Uh-huh."

"You didn't take one of mine, did you?"

"Nooo . . . " Olivia inspected the skin parts in need of a wax. "Mine covers everything."

"Covering nothing is better."

Olivia pressed her knees together, slamming them like the covers on a vintage classic. "Take care of those books, Woody. I'm jealous that Catherine gets to go through them with you and not me. Let me know what she says."

He hesitated. "I promise."

"I'll hold you to that. Spend some time with them. Once they're gone . . . they're gone."

"Speaking of being gone, did Danny get Beauregard?"

At the mention of the dog's name, Olivia straightened, now wide awake. "I've been asleep. She didn't call. Not on my cell, either." Olivia eyed her dark mobile phone. It wouldn't illuminate. Drained.

"Dogs know good guys from bad guys, Liv. I'd like to meet Beauregard."

"Me too. Can I call you later?"

"I'll hold you to that."

The alarm started to buzz when she hung up. Olivia smacked the button and raced down the stairs with her cell phone. As she pulled the charger from her purse, the home line rang again.

"Danny left me a message," Lauren said, out of breath. "Two hours ago. I was asleep."

"I just woke up. What'd she say?"

"She got him, Liv. She and Ben got everything."

Olivia's chest swelled. "Beauregard?"

"By now she's introducing him to Palermo. You'd better stop by your own bank on the way to get that manuscript. Sounds like Danny's ready to catch a fast money ball."

"I'm going."

Olivia set the phone in its base on the kitchen counter. She had to get to her lawyer's office and then rush to the bank—two banks. A jumble of thoughts raced ahead of her up the stairs, but one image slowed her steps to the bedroom window. She pulled open the black-out curtains, exposing herself to her garden. Gray light washed over the rumpled sheets. Outside, a steady downpour stabbed at her hunched chrysanthemums, the color of rich cinnamon, almost like the ones in Palermo's cell. With every ounce of faith she could muster, she had to believe the declining don couldn't tell what color those flowers were.

~ · ~ · ~

After Woody hit the END button on his phone, he stared at the front of his mother's house. Olivia might as well have been a million miles away, but next to his ear she remained close.

Her voice spurred him forward. Without Olivia's support, he might not be able to do this. Flattened book boxes filled the back and front seats of his sports car. A dispenser of packing tape sat on the floor of the passenger side.

After hauling the boxes inside, Woody got to work. Olivia's favorite words came back to him as he assembled the boxes: *swish* of cardboard, *zip* and *rip* of tape. A sudden wash of mixed emotions took him off guard as he stared at the bookcases. Start with *A*, the opposite as he'd done as a child. He picked out Louisa May Alcott's *Hospital Sketches* from 1863. He'd finally read this one in the college library, about the character of Tribulation Periwinkle coming of age during the ravages of the Civil War. He set it in the box. Woody never did read *Little Women*. Too sappy. He picked up the 1868 edition and put it aside for Olivia. Just the kind of book she'd admonish him for selling. He picked out two more he thought she might like: Raymond Chandler's 1939 edition of *The Big Sleep* and Arthur Conan Doyle's *A Study in Scarlet* from 1887, the first Sherlock Holmes in novel form. Cloak, dagger, and sap, much like the contrasting sides of Olivia's personality.

It took an hour to assemble the rest of the books into eighteen boxes. Near the end of the alphabet, Woody took some time to revisit a few pages of Jules Verne's 1869 English translation of *Five Weeks in a Balloon*. He sat cross-legged on the floor to flip through the illustrations. Unable to let it go, he set the book with Olivia's pile to take home. The story deserved a fresh read with mature eyes.

The first six boxes required stacking like a puzzle to fit into the Porsche for trip number one to Alten's. The bookstore closed in half an hour.

With the first load in his arms, Woody announced his arrival with a toe rap on the front door's brass kickplate. He nodded as Catherine Pratt rushed to help him inside. The bell jingled, a sound he hoped signaled good luck.

"What on earth?" Catherine said. "Get yourself in here, Woodrow Rainey."

Woody set the box on the front counter and wiped sweat from his forehead. Colorful words buzzed around him like bees—on the bookshelves, in the box, and in his head.

"I'm so glad you stopped in—I've been meaning to call you." Catherine's eyes were kind. "My sister's a nurse down at Huggins. I'm so sorry about Della."

"Thank you," Woody said. He almost said, *She had a good life*, but he stopped short. He wasn't sure she had. "Catherine," he continued, "I need your help. I have to dispose of her books. Olivia Novak thinks they're valuable. Here's the first batch. I've got five others in the car and twelve more back at the house."

Catherine pulled an X-Acto knife from a drawer. "Let's take a look." After swiping the blade in two short strokes and one long score, she pulled back the flaps and stared into the box.

Woody drummed the counter. "Can you do anything? I need as much as I can get. There's an outrageous hospital bill with Ma's name on it."

"Della had all these?"

"Eighteen boxes altogether. Two more trips to make."

"But—" Catherine raised her eyes like the messiah had walked into her shop. The bell above the door appeared to hold a whole new meaning beyond good luck. "Woody, you have no idea—*I* had no idea Della had these."

"Heartache. That's what's in there. Olivia Novak said I could trust you to get the best price—auctions and such—if you deem them worthy."

Catherine smacked her palms together and raised her eyes to the ceiling. "God bless the Dushane sisters for making my year." She pointed to the door. "Now, bring in the others. Then get yourself in that car, burn some rubber, and bring me the rest of those boxes at Della's house. A consignment contract will be waiting for you when you come back."

Woody fished keys from his pocket. "Really? It's not too late?"

"Really."

Chapter 32
The Key

Olivia breezed into Ted Beal's office in downtown Portland at three o'clock, dressed in jeans and a red sweatshirt that said, *Eat, Sleep, Read*. She hadn't bothered with too much makeup. Ted had witnessed her in every emotional state, the best and the worst. He was not only her parents' former lawyer; Ted had handheld her through the estate details of Adam's death, managed the legal affairs of the Pogo Charitable Trust, and held the title of Keeper of the Key to Ardy's memoir. He also gave her publishing contracts a final once-over.

Olivia hadn't told Ted why she'd made the appointment. She had given him only a thumbnail of Della's demise on the phone but left out the real reason for the visit, except that it was off the clock.

"Thanks for seeing me on such short notice, Ted." Olivia turned to the bookcase. "Want me to sign those?" Her gaze floated to the line of familiar book spines on Ted's mahogany bookcase. Below the shelf of law books, six fresh hardback editions of *The Executrix* had been added to her romance series and her mother's book, *Indigo to Black*.

"Fair exchange for being a freebie." Ted's golf tan had deepened since her last visit. He, too, was casual for a Thursday. She dreaded the day he retired. He'd hinted at the possibility on her last visit.

After stacking the books next to Olivia, Ted sat on the corner of his desk and held out a pen. "I take it the drama with Ellen's book is now a non-issue. Killing your accuser is one way of dealing with the situation. Not recommended, of course."

"Della had a stroke. If anything, guilt killed her." Olivia flipped to the cover page and signed her name under the printed one. "Something else happened . . . quite unexpected."

Ted crossed his arms. "Let's have it. If anyone can complicate a situation, it's you."

"I had a . . . liaison, you might say." Saying the words aloud filled her with exhilaration—and made it real.

"In less than a week? You never mentioned that development when we talked this morning. How on earth did *that* happen?"

"The lawyer. He's Della's son, Woody—Woodrow Rainey."

Ted was a pro at hiding emotion, but his face lit up. He laughed. "You knocked off the perp and bedded the attorney? Who is this woman sitting in front of me?"

Olivia waved off the dig and picked up another book. "It might fizzle, but I can't deny the sizzle."

"You deserve a good time. But I can tell you're cooking up something in that mighty brain of yours. Another book?"

Pausing the pen, Olivia raised her eyes. "I need the key, Ted."

"*Protection*? That wasn't the deal, Liv. You asked the firm to hold access to that manuscript until you and your sisters—"

"Died. I know." Olivia jabbed the air with the pen. "I'm about to be billable. We need about twenty minutes, and then I'm off to Cascade Bank before they close."

Ted studied her like a disapproving father. He sighed and pushed the button on the clock. "Are you going to publish R. D.'s memoir?"

Olivia nodded. "And a few more. We cut a deal with Palermo and the warden of Allenwood Prison to write a series. The proceeds will create a therapy dog program for elderly inmates. You'll need to put together a grant program with the Pogo Trust. I don't believe the current paw print on a piece of paper will pass the legal sniff."

"Yeah . . . an auditor would have a heart attack."

"When Danny gets home, she'll arrange a separate meeting with you about the details. It'll be her gig."

"More mobsters? You're getting in deep. What's the catch?"

Olivia slapped the last signed book on the stack. "I have to spring a dog out of prison when Palermo dies."

Ted dragged both hands over his face. "The key's in the company safe. I'll be right back."

~ · ~ · ~

A clank in the lock preceded the jingle of a dog collar. Identification tags were more lightweight and delicate than keys. A happier sound. Pogo had arrived. The hinges of the cell door needed an oiling, but maybe the guards used the squeal as a reminder, a little torment that he, Nicolas Palermo, a once-important man, had been demoted. Ben would explain away the lack of maintenance as the favor of an advance warning system. Palermo's legs ached, forcing him to remain prone on his cot. He didn't even try to sit up.

The scrape of a chair stirred a fruity scent of pricey shampoo around a shapely form. A familiar floral scent wafted over him . . . a European perfume.

"Good evening, Danielle," he said. "I trust your meeting with Ben was satisfactory?"

"Quite. Mr. Palermo, I'd like to introduce you to Pogo." A snap of Danielle's fingers. "Bo. Go up?"

After a jostle of his cot, soft warmth beneath the curls eased the sharp pain in Palermo's hip joints. Puffs of breath streamed across his cheek. He encircled his arms around the dog. A lazy tongue licked his chilled fingers. "Thank you, Danielle."

"He's special, Mr. Palermo."

Danielle's voice came off as a little nervous, but he enjoyed her watching him, basked in it like an aria. It had been so long since he'd been fussed over, where someone waited to hear his opinion or was eager to please him. His fingers grazed the dog's loose loops of fur. "Not Pogo," Palermo finally said. "This dog has been freshly washed."

An intake of breath. A sigh. His words would extract truth.

"Yes, he's had a bath. Just for you, Mr. Palermo."

"You attempt to deceive."

A pause. "How?"

"You see, Danielle, if this dog were Pogo, he'd carry *your* scent. You would have hugged him before letting me touch. It would have pained you to release the real Pogo to me."

An uncomfortable silence, a void he enjoyed.

"Mr. Palermo, there's a slightly more crass version of this saying, but you shouldn't foul the plate on which you eat. I'm sure you get the gist."

Palermo chuckled. "'Look a gift horse in the mouth' is somewhat more elegant, my dear."

A hesitation. "You're right. That's better. Ben and I spent the whole day cutting a deal to find this dog for you. In fact, the Pogo Charitable Trust—Olivia, really—is going to provide dogs to your cronies too." Another hesitation. "*Quid pro quo*, Mr. Palermo. Olivia wants what you have in your arms. She wants this dog."

"Does she now? Is she afraid I'll find out he's not Pogo?"

"You bet she is. Forget Ardy. He's dead. Olivia's alive, and she has the ability to make you famous. Isn't that what you really want?"

"Hmmm . . . yes. Excellent point. I would like for Olivia to be at a disadvantage while she writes my story. She'll work faster." Palermo fingered the soft curls of fur, and as he did so a tail thumped the mattress. "He's a good dog. What is his real name?"

A pause to ponder the truth. "Beauregard."

"Beau . . . regard. As in the great Confederate leader, General Beauregard? A handsome man as I recall of his image in daguerreotypes. Self-assured, smart."

"He's a lover, not a fighter."

"You have done well, Danielle. Honesty will be rewarded." Palermo tightened his bony fingers around the dog's front paw as a spasm of pain racked his legs and receded. A comforting weight relaxed his feet as Beauregard rested his head across Palermo's chest. "You and I have a secret to keep from Olivia. Where is Pogo now?"

"He's with the handler, helping her to acclimate the other dogs."

"Will you bring Pogo to me?"

Her shape shifted on the chair. "Mr. Palermo, I don't think . . . "

"Just a touch, Danielle. Then you can take Pogo home. The General here will do fine."

~ · ~ · ~

By four thirty, nerves made Olivia jittery as she opened the glass door of Cascade Bank in Sellwood, a southeast suburb near her home in Eastmoreland. She hadn't stepped inside this bank for two years. Ryan had escorted her in the cruiser the day she'd placed the manuscript for Ardy Griffin's memoir in the safe-deposit box. To protect her identity at the time, the pen name she'd chosen for the manuscript was Della Pinkham. The combination had been an inside joke from two of her mother's books: a name in her address book, and the lethal weapon from *Indigo to Black*. Now, the prophetic words held a different meaning after she'd learned the truth. A new cover page would bear Olivia's real name when she sent Ardy's memoir to Karen.

The draw for using this particular bank was the fact that Jeff Rovinski, the father of the teen who killed Adam in the hit-and-run accident, worked as a loan officer here before receiving a one-year sentence for tampering with evidence. He'd been out for a year. In some twisted way, Olivia couldn't clip the last connecting thread to closure. Surely the bank hadn't rehired the bastard.

A hushed *thank you* crossed her lips at the sight of someone new sitting in Jeff Rovinski's old office. The bank manager, however, recognized her. He crossed the small lobby to shake Olivia's hand. Some expressions were reserved for known victims of a crime, and he displayed one of those now: a bit of embarrassment with the placating smile, a little nervous.

"Mrs. Novak. It's been a while."

"Yes . . . a while." Olivia held up the key. "I'd like to get something from my safe-deposit box."

"Of course. Let me get our copy of the key."

As she waited, Olivia checked the faces of the three tellers behind the counter. She recognized one from the shock of fuchsia in her white-blond hair and matching lipstick. The girl glanced up at her every few seconds from counting out bills, as if Olivia might go postal at any moment. Olivia smiled and moved toward the vault.

The manager unlocked the gate and waved her forward. Within seconds, the closeness of the steel walls triggered a claustrophobic reaction. Olivia's fingers tremored as she extended the key to box 304. A mere quarter turn would launch a new chapter for a familiar book.

With butterflies in her stomach, Olivia slid out the thick manila envelope, along with the two binders of newspaper articles holding documentation of sixty years' worth of bombings, bribes, corruption, and cold-blooded murder carried out by the Philadelphia mob. Lauren had compiled the clippings after poring through the boxes in Ardy's house. Over the decades, the old mobster had diligently tracked the very people Olivia and her sisters were now trying to help. And an innocent request by Ardy to babysit Pogo had come full circle with that same dog helping the criminal who pursued Ardy. Life was full of irony. She had to believe that Ardy would have accepted the devil's bargain she and her sisters had made. Even in death, Ardy couldn't shed the mob's hold on his life, but at least now Olivia could honor her promise to publish it.

Her arms full, Olivia nodded to the bank manager waiting for her outside the vault. She stopped in front of him.

"I . . . I have to ask. Do you know if Jeff Rovinski is still around?"

The manager's face softened. "No, Mrs. Novak. The last I heard, Jeff moved back East to reconcile with his wife. He's been gone for about six months now."

"What about his daughter, Melissa?"

"I believe she went with him."

"Thank you."

The words clipped the stitches of a wound that finally might heal. She'd still carry a scar, but at least the bleeding had stopped. Her fear of spotting the Rovinskis in a store, driving over a bridge, or waiting at a stoplight were over. All over.

An inner smile filled her with light. It gave her the courage to sneak one more submission into the envelope to Karen Finnerelli.

Chapter 33
Sibling Blood

After making a second stop at her personal bank to transfer funds into the Pogo Trust account, Olivia pulled into her driveway at five thirty. She didn't go inside the house. Instead, she stepped past Lauren's cherry-red Honda with her arms full of the two three-ring binders and the manuscript for *Protection*. She leaned her elbow on her sister's doorbell. The long chime erupted inside like a carillon concert.

The front door opened with Lauren holding her right hand wrapped in a towel, saturated with crimson red.

"What happened?" Olivia said and pushed back the screen door with her foot.

"I tried to cut a frozen steak in half to make it thaw faster. The knife slipped. Come in and help me." Lauren turned and scooted down the hall to the kitchen. "Is that the manuscript? Those binders look familiar."

"Yep. We're all set with Ted. He's calling Danny for a meeting about the grant program." Olivia plunked the pile on the kitchen table. "Let me see your hand."

Olivia unwrapped the towel and gasped. A diagonal gash cut through the meaty part of Lauren's palm below her thumb.

"Do I need stitches?"

"It's not that bad. Looks worse than it really is," Olivia said. "A little Neosporin and a tight bandage should do the trick. Where are they?"

"In my purse." Lauren dipped her head in the direction of the kitchen table. "On the chair."

"Jesus, Lauren. We can go to the emergency room and be home before I find Band-Aids in your purse."

"Dump it out. I'm bleeding like a hemophiliac here."

"Run your hand under cold water and hold it closed. Constricts the vessels, so it'll clot." Olivia rushed to the sink and turned on the tap. "Five minutes."

"It'll be sore as hell," Lauren said and stuck her hand under the cold stream.

Olivia overturned the leather handbag. Lauren's Dalmatian-spotted notebook landed on top of the pile. After a glance at Lauren bent over the sink, a plan of opportunity flashed. She slipped it under the manila envelope and pretended to dig through the array of junk. "I don't see any Neosporin, just Band-Aids. I have some at my house. I'll go get it."

"Hurry."

"Keep your hand under the water. I'll be right back."

No pain, no gain. Olivia scooped up the envelope containing Ardy's manuscript with Lauren's notebook and grabbed her keys. She sprinted down the hall with both clutched to her chest. The screen door banged behind her as she broke into a full run to her house.

Olivia turned the lock and burst into the entryway to find Freesia at the bottom of the stairs, waiting like a scolding parent. Olivia raced by straight to the den. After a frantic flip of the notebook's pages to get to the sketches, she lifted the top on the scanner. One after another, the images transferred to her computer: Pogo on the plane, Pogo with his nose out the car window, Pogo at the beach, in a canoe, and at the prison. Freesia scowled at her from the doorway.

"Don't look at me like that. Lauren needs this. She'd never agree to send these on her own.''

Olivia scooped up her keys, the notebook, and the manuscript and dashed up the stairs to her bathroom. With one hand, she pawed through the cabinet until she found a curled tube of Neosporin next to a brand new one. She grabbed both. Missing a step on the stairs, she tumbled down the last four and landed on her tailbone. Keys clattered behind her. The manuscript, notebook, and tubes of ointment slid to a halt in front of Freesia, who sat in front of her with a that's-what-you-get look on her face.

Wincing and rubbing her lower back, she tried to ignore the pain. The bruise would be wicked. She gathered all four items and limped out the front door. Olivia forced her legs to run before a spasm caught up with her. She skidded into Lauren's kitchen to find sister still hunched over the sink.

''Where the hell have you been?'' Lauren said. ''I'm dying here.''

''You're not dying. The tube of antibiotic ointment was almost empty. I had to find my new one.'' Olivia returned the notebook to the assorted contents of Lauren's purse and opened the crushed box of Band-Aids. She pointed. ''Dry your hand and come over here.''

''Don't you have a first-aid kit in every room? What'd you do, go buy the stuff?'' Lauren sat in a kitchen chair, holding the cut closed. ''Can you make dinner? Mine has blood on it.''

Olivia smirked. ''Don't worry. I got you covered.''

After squeezing out the last blop of goo from one tube and adding to it with the other, Olivia pulled two sticky bandages in a tight cross pattern over the cut. ''Now we wait. Don't mess with my handiwork.''

~ · ~ · ~

With a steaming cup of coffee, Olivia sat at her computer on Friday morning to print out a letter to her agent. She shifted in her desk chair, unable to find a comfortable position. She regretted not calling Woody last night, but fear factored into the decision to keep him at arm's length. Plus, living in dual worlds wobbled her focus on the business at hand. The thick envelope in front of her held two important ones: the manuscript for *Protection,* with her real name as the author, and the printouts of Lauren's sketches of Pogo. Too bad she didn't have sketches of Beauregard to add to the mix.

Last night's impromptu spaghetti dinner with Lauren became a rehash of her afternoon with Ted, the trip to the bank, and the information she'd received from the bank manager about Jeff Rovinski and his daughter, Melissa. Her sister had nodded, listened, and repeatedly lifted the Band-Aid to check her angry cut.

"No call from Danny about Palermo meeting Beauregard," Lauren had said.

"I haven't gotten one, either. I have to trust she has it under control."

"I'll let you do that worrying for me." Lauren had thrown Olivia a mischievous smile. "Karen's going to flip out when she gets that manuscript."

"In more ways than one." Olivia had peered over the rim of her wine glass and bobbed a wooden spoon. "The Pogo Trust is going to get quite the boost too." The tomato sauce enjoyed a slow stir. "The grant program needs a name. Any ideas?"

"'Pogo's Good Deeds'? Or 'Pogo Goes to Prison'? I don't know." Lauren held out her hand. "How's this look?"

"It'll heal if you stop messing with it."

"So will you, if you stop picking for information about the Rovinskis."

Now, Olivia shook her focus back to the computer screen. *I have to trust. I have to trust.* A flutter of excitement rippled through her chest at doing something sneaky for the right reasons. She wouldn't give Lauren the chance to slam shut a window of opportunity. Olivia's mind raced faster than her fingers to compose the letter to her agent:

Karen,

Enclosed is the manuscript for Protection, *R. D. Griffin's memoir. This will be the first of a series. In the near future, I'm going to be given access to a number of elderly members of the Philadelphia mob who are serving life sentences. They've agreed to share their stories. Through an arrangement with the warden of Allenwood Prison, a portion of the royalties from this memoir, and also the subsequent ones in the series, will fund a therapy-dog program within the prison system for inmates with disabilities.*

To further support this important effort, I've also included a series of sketches with accompanying narrative from my sister, Lauren Lyndale. I think you'll agree she's an excellent illustrator. With Pogo currently being the dog of the hour, a children's book series titled Pogo's Good Deeds *may boost publicity for Danielle's efforts to broaden her training programs sponsored by the Pogo Charitable Trust.*

It's a family affair. Get a tall latte and lock your door. Call me with your thoughts.

Olivia signed the letter with her scrolling script and slipped the paper into the thick envelope.

Chapter 34
Sinking on Both Coasts

A week had passed since Woody wrapped his arms around Olivia. Their routine of talking every other night gave him hope for the future, if only day by day. They'd only talked about small stuff: progress on Palermo's manuscript, legal opinions on news of the day, books they were reading, and, of course, the weather. Showers and gray skies in Portland; the first flurries and nearly bare trees in Wolfeboro.

At ten o'clock on Thursday night, Woody spent the final hour of his day doing laundry as he waited—hoped—for a return call from Olivia before turning in. It was one of their talk days. He'd left a message at six. No return call. Something might have come up. She'd become a working author again. Maybe the three-hour time difference made her think it too late to call. Or her life had resumed its normal course without him in the picture. He carried the phone with him to the laundry room and set it on the dryer as he pulled out the whites and stuffed the wet darks into the drum. He folded his white T-shirts into a symmetrical stack.

No call came from Catherine Pratt at Alten's, either. The estimate of the bill from Huggins Hospital loomed like a judgment. The clock ticked for him to call his accountant to write a fat check. Waiting wasn't one of his better qualities. He tucked the phone into the clean clothes and drifted back to his bedroom to gather anything else that needed washing, but not the sheets. They'd earned a reprieve for one more day.

Woody had spent the afternoon piling his mother's possessions into sections. The potentially valuable objects—crystal, china, lamps—had been gathered in their own corner for scrutiny by an appraiser from a local auction house. The rest could be donated or thrown out. Not hearing from Olivia was unsettling. Running into her voicemail—worse.

The watercolor on his bedroom wall drew Woody's gaze. He'd never be able to look at it again without thinking about his time with Olivia. Gossipy glances about him "with that famous author, Olivia Novak" met him everywhere around town. The speculation served as a reminder of how much he missed her. He'd led his life through books: classics, suspense, adventure, and law. Books had changed his life, might still change his life, and that insight had come from a woman who wrote them—three thousand miles away.

Woody took a deep breath, grasping for words that hadn't yet been written. An exhale couldn't hold back the flow of emotion for the lonely years that might extend beyond pages. Woody sat on the bed and placed his hands over his face. He pulled a tissue from the box on his nightstand and wiped his wet fingers of his situation . . . and Olivia.

~ · ~ · ~

By Thursday afternoon, a week had passed with no response from Karen about Ardy's manuscript and only superficial conversations with Woody. Olivia's nerves were stripped raw, so much so that she didn't even return Woody's last message. She didn't want to be a downer. The first video call with Palermo had been short, relaying only an introduction of the interview process. Danny's ruse had worked. Nicky Palermo had spent most of the session extolling the virtues of a brown version of Pogo and complaining about his own ailments. The conversation stabbed at her sister's and Pogo's absence. Danny had been unable to join the Internet call, but Olivia reached out to the screen. Beauregard's wet nose had steamed the camera lens several times, sniffing as if frustrated he couldn't pick up Olivia's scent. The session had been further complicated by Freesia walking across her keyboard to get to the dog's image. The cat was interested.

To prepare for her second video call with Palermo, Olivia pulled the pocket door shut in the den and rushed to the desk. The session had already connected, with a view of the interior of a bland room on her computer screen. The man of the hour faced her in a chair, with a sign behind him that read, *No Eating, No Drinking, No Smoking, No Cell Phones.* She winced as she scooted her own chair to the desk, a not-so-gentle reminder of her tumble down the stairs.

"Are we recording? Olivia's there?" Palermo said. Behind him, Beauregard barked twice. Warden Franklin ducked to fill the remainder of the screen.

Ben waved at Olivia over Palermo's shoulder. "Yes, she's there. Say whatever you want."

"I'm here, Palermo," Olivia added, a little too loud, "Hi Bo Go." She opened her legal notepad to a fresh page. "Since Fazziano's memoir ends with the courtroom scene before he goes into Witness Protection, let's pick up there with your reaction. That's a key part of the story and will provide a transition to your book."

"No." Palermo's forefinger jerked with a video delay of its shake to the camera. "I want to begin with Salgado. Fazziano's story starts with that dog . . . I want my side of the story to start there too."

Olivia couldn't deny the logic. Struggling to keep her mouth shut, she let Palermo talk. Gaps could be filled with off-line audio files. Ben Franklin had assured her that Palermo was allowed hours of recording time by himself, beyond the fifty-five minutes they'd been allotted for each video session.

Palermo stroked Beauregard's head. "Fazziano loved dogs. Find a man's love; you find his weakness. I used it to my advantage to toughen him up."

"You love dogs too, Palermo," she said, raising her voice to make sure he could hear her. "Why—how—could you have made Fazziano sacrifice that man's shepherd? Salgado didn't do anything wrong. He was an innocent dog."

"To get what I wanted," Palermo said. She spotted a slight ruthless smirk when the deep fissures in his cheeks shifted. "Debts must be paid."

"Did you have any idea what you did to Fazziano? He probably wouldn't have minded killing that man who owed you money over killing the man's dog. The order you gave to kill Salgado devastated Fazziano for decades." Olivia had promised herself to keep her anger in check for this interview, but the effort proved more difficult than she anticipated. The old don was testing her.

Palermo didn't quite nod, but his head dipped. He poked the air with his forefinger. "The true character of a man comes out when he's pushed. Makes him stronger." He shrugged. "Besides, I can't get my money if the one who owes me is dead."

"That moment became your undoing. Fazziano turned out to be stronger than you."

"Will and patience. I misjudged their power. I continue to believe I held the upper hand."

"How do you figure that? You failed in your attempt to kill Fazziano."

"Ah . . . You make an incorrect assumption, Olivia. Outcomes are best managed with fear, not bullets. On that, I believe I was a raging success. Still a success."

Thankful to be shielded by the screen, the pen in Olivia's hand started to shake. She didn't raise her eyes, only pressed the tip harder on her notepad. She underlined the word *fear*.

A spark of inspiration for the book's title became a momentary distraction. *Fear*. A chuckle released from the computer's microphone. She flinched.

"I got what I . . . wanted . . . needed . . . "

Olivia lifted her pen and paused, waiting in suspense for Palermo to finish the statement. She stared at the screen for an answer, but Palermo's head floated to his chest like a deflating balloon. The old man had fallen asleep.

A downpour outside rumbled Olivia's roof and ticked at the window, coming down so hard it might have been hail.

Warden Franklin leaned into view of the camera. "Nicky needs to rest. We'll pick it up again next week, depending on how he feels. Stay connected. Danny wants to talk with you."

Palermo's unfinished answer came from Beauregard. His tongue swept across the lens as Palermo was lifted from the chair. The end of the dog's tail swept in front of the screen like a puffy cotton ball dipped in espresso. The chair sat empty for over a minute.

Danny's beaming face suddenly filled the screen. She looked left and right, then leaned into the lens. "We're coming home tomorrow, Liv."

"It worked?"

Danny nodded but didn't speak.

"Did you get my wire transfer?"

"Thank you. It was more than enough. Ben's off and running."

"And Bo Go?"

"Worked like a charm."

~ · ~ · ~

After three hours of writing, Olivia clicked off her desk lamp and sat in the dark. Her sister and Pogo were coming home without Beauregard. A growl released from her stomach as Freesia rubbed the stubble on her legs. The rain never let up once it let loose, scrambling her sense of time. Five o'clock could have been seven with the sky so dark. A long, hungry *meow* prompted her to stand and stretch. She shuffled to the kitchen and flipped on the lights.

Like an automaton, Olivia popped the top on a can of cat food and plopped a chunk in Freesia's bowl. She dropped a fistful of kibble in a separate dish. Standing in front of the open refrigerator door,

Olivia stared at the glass shelves in need of a cleaning. Pickles, wasabi, and champagne vinegar didn't ignite her appetite. She tried to open the jar of pickles, but the lid wouldn't budge. Not a problem for Woody. Nothing frozen sounded good, either, and she didn't have the strength to cook. Settling for the no-energy option, she rolled a slice of Swiss cheese into a tube, hip-pushed the door shut, and stood at the kitchen island.

The sting of Palermo's ruthless words were salved by generous prose, but she had a long way to go. The fact that Palermo remained alive during this process filled her with consolation and dread: alive, Olivia could coax out the truth without having to interpret its meaning, but he held Beauregard hostage; dead, the onus would be on her to fill the bullet holes in Palermo's story, but at a safe emotional distance and with Beauregard at her side. Facing the man, even on a computer screen, gave her chills. She vacillated about whether Palermo truly had a heart. He had to. He had the dog—her dog.

Olivia took a bite of the cheese and unfurled the rubbery ribbon in her mouth. At least no animals were harmed in the making of cheese.

Ardy's memoir should have prepared Olivia for writing this second book. Not even close. Wide-eyed naiveté had been an asset the first time around. Now, she'd marched into Palermo's project from a place of fear and desire, but the don got under her skin with his wise-old-man superior attitude. Compared to Palermo, Ardy had been a mere worker bee who defected from a deadly nest.

She swallowed. Smooth. Satisfying. Her head started to clear. Where would she put Beauregard's dish? No way would Freesia share her space.

Fear. A good title. So was *Desire.* According to Palermo, a fine line separated the definition of the two words as weapons. The don desired Pogo to quell his fear of guilt. Olivia had caught the fear in Woody's eyes, too, when Della unfolded her story, along with his desire to punish his mother for the deception. In turn, Della used her fear of Woody finding a mate to undermine his desire for one. Olivia herself had used the distance of a continent to push him away because of her own fear of desire. *Find a man's love; you find his weakness.* Palermo was probably celebrating in his cell that she had become such an accomplished student of the master.

A sigh escaped her lips as she chewed. She tore off a piece of the cheese for Freesia. She turned at what she thought was scratching at the patio door. It was only the wind . . . and a wish.

Chapter 35

A Break in the Weather

At six o'clock on Friday evening, Woody sat at his desk and scratched out checks for the remainder of Della's outstanding bills, one of them a payment to Huggins Hospital. He raised his eyes when Margie pulled back the pocket doors of his office. Her two most valuable skills: researching and reading minds.

"You're on your own, Woody. You need anything before I go?" Margie said, buttoning her long wool coat. With its dark shade of dove-gray and open gap at the hem, Margie resembled the Liberty Bell.

"Everyone else gone?" Woody retracted the tip of his pen.

"Took off about half an hour ago." She paused. "Plans for the weekend? Weather's supposed to turn sunny by tomorrow, but chilly."

Woody followed Margie's gaze to the urn above the fireplace. She'd placed Della ashes on the mantle after picking them up from Walt Cleary that afternoon.

"Is it?"

Margie gave him a motherly smile as she wound a wool scarf around her neck. She fingered her car keys. "Somebody needs a hot toddy and a healthy dose of Olivia Novak."

Woody managed a smile and a quick wave. The floor creaked as

Margie stepped to the entryway. He waited for the final latch of the front door and raised his eyes to the mantle. His mother's urn held the center spot in the collection of antique pewter tankards, like a jailer guarding its charges. He'd chosen a simple aluminum vessel in the hope that it would fall seamlessly in line with the others. Woody didn't want the display to be obvious, but the urn's placement served two other purposes: a reminder of a family that may, or may not, accept his existence, and that Della's crime against his father remained an open case with the authorities.

Receiving Della's ashes from Walt Cleary was a bittersweet ending to the funeral home lawsuit. The business gesture had gone a long way toward healing the scandal that rocked the town. Between Walt's and Margie's efforts, gaps in his mother's dubious documentation had been filled. Walt, himself, questioned the legitimacy of the scrawled papers Woody had scrounged from Della's house. But in the end, Walt believed her birth certificate to be real. A niggle of question lingered, though, about whether Della had company in her urn.

No response, yet, from Catherine at Alten's about the books. And with the size of the checks he just wrote, his timeline for retirement probably needed a recalculation.

Woody hadn't spoken with Olivia since last night. Their conversation ended with talking about Danny's and Pogo's return today. He burned to be there to share in the excitement, but he had a practice to run; Olivia had a book to write. The empty tree outside drew his gaze. Beyond it, the sky was shrouded in clouds with no discernible shape. Halloween could be a crap-shoot for a dump of snow, and although the lake wasn't frozen, it was too cold for kayaking.

Restless, he stood and paced around his office. His fingers dragged the length of the library table. Margie had polished. A buzz shot his attention to the phone. A green blinking light. The digital display identified the caller: Alten's Books.

Reaching over the front of desk, Woody snatched up the phone and spun the receiver to his ear. "Catherine. What's the word?"

"Well, you have a decision to make, Woody—a big decision,"

Catherine said, her voice full of tease.

"Ready to make one." A ripple of anticipation shot through his body, the same feeling as when he waited for a judge's gavel to bang out a ruling.

"Do you want to keep the books together and sell them as a collection or parse them out for individual sale? Both options are lined up with hands itchin'."

"What are the variables?" Woody grabbed his pen and stepped around the desk to take a seat.

"Timeline or money," she said. "It'll take longer to sell them off one by one, but we could get a bit more than if we sell them immediately as a single lot at auction."

"What's the estimate?" Woody's arm muscles clenched, pulling a number home: the amount of his mother's hospital bill.

Catherine lowered her voice. "I told you Della had a good eye. The whole kit and kaboodle has a catalog estimate of $625,000."

A jolt of electricity stunned him. He tried to maintain his focus on Catherine's words.

"It could go much higher if the lot whips up a bidding war with rabid collectors and dealers. About thirty of those books are so rare that they make up the bulk of the estimate. I can't believe she had first editions of the two-volume set of *Frankenstein* and an 1897 version of *Dracula*. In their condition, those two titles alone are worth about seventy thousand."

Woody had read both works. He'd flipped the pages to get to the stories, with no thought about the physical books. His gaze circled the office, nearly everything in it picked out by Della: the desk, side tables, chairs, lamps, tankards on the mantle, and the painting above the fireplace. He lived with these objects every day, only purchasing them for a song at his mother's insistence. Lauren's words had provided a clue, which at the time he'd thought as sarcasm: Antiques Roadshow *would love to shoot an episode from here . . .*

"Woody? Are you there?" Catherine said. "If you want them in the next auction in New York, I need to get hopping."

"I—I'm here." He ran his fingers through his hair, picturing the gray patches in it disappearing from an hour ago. He tried to keep his voice professional. "Let's not drag this out, Catherine. I think the auction route is an excellent option."

"Righto. Auction it is. In thirty days, they'll be gracing the shelves of someone else's library. If I could afford it, I'd convince you to let me cherry-pick. I won't because I get a commission."

"Twenty percent, right?"

Catherine paused. "For Della . . . I'll do ten."

Woody fanned the tabs on a stack of file folders. Among humanity's thieves, cheats, and scoundrels, lurked quiet heroes. "Take a favorite, Catherine, and tuck it in your nightstand. A gift from Mom. That's what I did."

"Which one did you choose?"

"Jules Verne. *Five Weeks in a Balloon.* I set aside three for Olivia Novak too."

"Excellent choice, Woody. I have my eye on James Herriot's *All Creatures Great and Small.* It's only worth a couple hundred, so it won't make a dent. A favorite, though."

He smiled at the way Olivia had talked about Beauregard. "It's yours, Catherine."

"Now, I've got to fly. Thank you for trusting me with these books. I doubt I'll ever hold some of these again in my lifetime."

"Thank Olivia," Woody said.

Catherine giggled. "Thank you, Olivia Novak."

Exhilarated but with a heavy heart, Woody set the phone in the cradle. He now regretted his anger toward Della. Money had a way of changing minds. Yet again, Olivia had been right. The proceeds would certainly satisfy the debt, but he'd misjudged his mother, aside from her alleged crime. In fact, he *had* judged and sentenced her without a trial. Della had lived the best she could without an education, a partner, or a damn break. He needed to do something important with the remainder of the money after replenishing his funds.

Woody burned to share this news with Olivia. Her voice would have to suffice. He dashed up the stairs to the small kitchen in his apartment. He tossed three ice cubes in a tumbler and poured himself a scotch. As an afterthought, he grasped the bottle by the neck and carried it and the glass into the bedroom.

Easing to the edge of the mattress, Woody picked up *Indigo to Black* from the nightstand. Beneath it sat the 1869 edition of Jules Verne's *Five Weeks in a Balloon*. A handsome book, with its green clothbound cover and embossed gilt illustration of a balloon tethered to an elephant, still brilliant after 145 years. This particular one, his favorite for over fifty years, still held his own wishes as a young boy, trapped in poverty, then sent away. He'd let Daphne Du Maurier's *Rebecca* go. Another life. Old dreams realized.

He picked up the phone and pressed Olivia's home number. After three rings, he expected voice mail, but a clatter made him pull the receiver away from his ear.

"Woody?"

"Olivia?"

"Pffftt. It's Danny." She started laughing. "Sorry. I dropped Liv's phone. Ryan and I are here with Lauren."

"Congratulations, by the way. Liv told me that you did a bang-up job at Allenwood."

"Ben's the man. Me and Palermo—tight as goombahs now."

Woody chuckled. She even sounded like a mobster. "Can you put Liv on?"

Danny paused and took a sip of her drink. "Mmm . . . went to the store. We needed cilantro for the enchiladas. We're celebrating with Tex-Mex."

"It's only four thirty out there."

"Ryan got off early." The difficulty of Danny getting out the slurred words made Woody take a sip of his scotch.

"How long will she be?"

"Not too long. Ryan's sneaking a cigar outside while Liv's not here, and Lauren and I are having a little wine."

"A little?" Woody swirled the cubes in his glass with his finger to chill the liquor. "Should I call back?"

"No, no. We'll keep you on the phone. She'll be here any minute. Let me put you on speaker." After a fumbling clatter, the reception switched to an echo.

"Hey, Woody," Lauren said in the background. Ice rattled in a glass. "I'm glad we have you all to ourselves, so we can talk about Liv. She misses you like crazy. She sent the manuscript to her agent. No word yet. She's all nerves. Talk about grumpy."

"I received some news that I want to share with her . . . big news."

The phone clicked, interrupting the connection. "Hold that thought, Woody. Another call's coming in."

Woody topped off his scotch in the silence, willing Olivia to walk through her door. He liked Olivia's sisters but didn't care for the public scrutiny of speakerphone. His excitement waned the longer he waited on hold. When the orange minute number changed on his alarm clock, he hung up.

Fanning the pages of *Five Weeks in a Balloon,* Woody caught a musty whiff of aged paper. He closed his eyes and ran his finger over the raised edges of the gold-embossed illustration. Like reading braille, touching the cover allowed the lines and curves to become safety ropes, the upturned elephant's trunk an invitation to take a risk, and the smooth oval of the balloon a lure to a seductive adventure.

Fly. Undo the ropes and fly into the unknown.

A spectacular rescue mission began to form—*his* rescue mission—Olivia's and Beauregard's rescue mission.

Woody snatched up the Jules Verne book and nearly stumbled down the stairs to his office. He missed a step and winced, grabbing hold of the banister. Silence in the office greeted the riot in his head. He sat at his desk, pulled up the search engine, and entered first edition, Jules Verne, *Five Weeks in a Balloon*. He waited. A site came up offering the book for five thousand dollars. Catherine's words fueled a new search: the number for Allenwood Prison.

The negotiation of his life waited—with Palermo. He called Ben Franklin, ignoring the blinking light on line two.

Chapter 36
The Offers

Olivia didn't really need the cilantro, but it had provided an excuse to prove that going to the store for something simple could result in a safe return—alive, with her family waiting for her. She had been compelled to have a one-way conversation with Adam about Woody. The relationship with Woody had reached a critical point: dive in all the way, or break it off to minimize hurt feelings. She didn't want to be one of those crazy ladies who walked around the house talking with ghosts. Instead, she talked to Adam in the car.

"He's never been married, but Woody's got some baggage about his mother." She waved her hand. "Don't ask. Long story."

Silence.

"It's not like I'm a cougar or anything . . . not even close." Olivia made a left turn to her street. "He's older than me. And he's responsible . . . and has a career." She slowed and passed her house. "He loves animals. They're a good judge of character. Pogo's opinion is paws up."

Silence.

"Now that Danny's home, do you think I should go see him? I can write from anywhere on my laptop. And I should go to Allenwood, anyway, to sit down with the other subjects."

After driving around the block, Olivia pulled her car into the garage and shut off the engine. The rolling door faded the light behind her until the space darkened. The tick of the cooling engine counted down to the end of their conversation.

"If I had been the first to die, I want you to know that I'd have no problem with your pursuing a relationship."

Tick. Tick. Tick.

"Forget I said anything. I'll be fine if I get Beauregard. Unconditional loyalty wins. Not that you weren't loyal, Adam, but you know what I mean."

Olivia pulled the keys from the ignition, prompting the steering wheel to retreat back into its comfortable place in the dash. She held the bunch of cilantro to her nose and sighed.

"Why take the chance, right? New tricks are for kids."

The Tex-Mex party was in full swing when Olivia came through the mudroom door. As she stepped into the kitchen, Ryan waved at her from the patio and released a plume of cigar smoke above his head. He smashed the stub on the flagstone. From the looks of it, he'd puffed the stogie down to the wet chomp. Had she been gone that long?

A guilty smile crossed Ryan's face as he stepped inside. Then he pointed at Lauren. "She said I could do it."

Olivia stink-eyed her sister.

Lauren picked up her iced glass of white zinfandel. "I sent him outside. Don't start."

"Oh, like I couldn't smell it? The door's open." She pulled out a cutting board. "I wish the supermarket had self-checkout. A little brat had a temper tantrum about a stupid Sponge Bob birthday balloon." She shook the herb bundle under a too-hard stream of water in the sink. "I need a knife." Her chin pointed to the wooden block.

"The enchiladas are in the oven," Lauren said and stepped toward her, tumbler in hand. She took a healthy sip and held out the handle of a chopping weapon. "Danny made them, and I shoved them in."

Her younger sister smirked. "Lauren can rip tin foil."

Ryan slid onto a counter chair. "So . . . tell me about this Woody guy. He called while you were out, but he hung up."

"A telemarketer interrupted the call, and he couldn't wait," Danny said. "Your phone's goofy."

"I'll call him back," Olivia said and rolled a cilantro leaf between her fingers. A complex aroma of coriander, parsley, and a touch of licorice awakened her senses. "He's so far away."

"Go see him then. What's stopping you?" Ryan fiddled with the cigar label on his little finger.

"The book . . . Not hearing from Karen . . . " Olivia counted off the reasons as she plucked the leaves one by one. "I can't go any-where." She stopped plucking and started chopping. "There aren't enough hours in the day." Olivia chopped faster, turning the cilantro into near paste. "Maybe I'll go see him in the spring, after I've finished the first draft."

The phone rang. In synchronization, all eyes stared toward the trill. Lauren lunged before Olivia could reach for it. Her sister studied the screen and widened her eyes. "Witchiepoo," she said and held out the phone.

Olivia breathed in and set the knife on the cutting board. She let it ring one more time.

"Hi Karen." Olivia tried to keep her voice bright. "I've been meaning to call, but I've been so busy." A mechanical whir and back-ground chatter on Karen's cell phone fuzzed the reception. "Where are you?"

"On the train from the airport," Karen said. "I left early from a writer's conference in Atlanta. My ears are bleeding from back-to-back pitches. I've had nothing but a bag of friggin' peanuts in the past four hours. And if I listen to one more author utter the words *zombie*, *werewolf*, *vampire*, or *undead*, I'm personally going to fly out to Portland and throttle the cast of *Grimm*."

Olivia glanced at Lauren and moved her fingers like a yapping shadow puppet. "Speaking of gore, did you read the manuscript?"

"And you're a problem too. I couldn't sleep because of that damn manuscript. I'm exhausted."

"You said you wanted it. And do I recall begging in there somewhere?"

"I want the whole *Protection* series."

"I'm drafting Palermo's now. The working title is *Fear*." Olivia winced inside, having added another layer of deadline pressure to deliver.

"Love the one-word titles . . . How about *Cornered, Crooked, Trouble, Murder* . . . "

Olivia traced her finger over the long handle of the stainless steel refrigerator. *Adam, are you hearing this?* "I haven't even finished interviewing Palermo, yet. My sisters and Ryan are here. Can we deem our impromptu party a celebration dinner?"

"How the hell did you pull this off?"

"Let's give the credit to Danny and Pogo." Olivia turned and stuck up her thumb. Danny leaned into Ryan and wrapped her arms around him. Lauren mouthed, *What?*

"We'll talk more tomorrow," Karen said. "Sloane wants first dibs. We'll need to draft a new contract for this series. Now, if Lauren's there, I need to talk to her."

Olivia's stomach queased. Lauren knew nothing about the sketches she'd sent to Karen. She'd lost her nerve to admit the deception. Like it was a magical artifact full of promise, Olivia held out the phone to Lauren. "Karen wants to talk to you."

Danny's cell phone rang. Olivia motioned for her to step into the den to take the call. The pocket door closed.

Lauren's eyebrows disappeared beneath her bangs. She took a too-big sip of her wine with wide eyes. "Am I in trouble? The *Jo Show* crapfest?"

"Not at all. She won't bite." An invisible wish trailed as Olivia released the phone to Lauren's custody. *Please say yes.*

As her sister listened, a character sketch of emotions crossed Lauren's face: anxiety softened to confusion. Her eyebrows made a reappearance. Cheek muscles gave way, elongating her face with shock. Lauren's mouth popped open as her eyes slammed shut. She pulled off her glasses and rubbed her eyes. Stumbled responses escaped her lips, with only one word ending the conversation.

"Okay . . . " Lauren blinked in rapid succession as she handed the phone back to Olivia.

"Good news about the special addition I slipped into the envelope?" Olivia said to Karen, her gaze lingering on her sister.

"Your sister is an oasis of hidden talent," Karen said. "As soon as Lauren finishes the narrative and does color variations of those sketches, I'm shopping them for a children's book series. I know three houses that are looking for something like this. We need to start a marketing platform for both her and Pogo. And get more dogs. The more the better."

"There's a fabulous one named Beauregard."

"Where is he?"

"Allenwood Prison with Palermo."

"Then bust him out. You'll need to get a new author photo with that dog to promote Palermo's book. Pogo needs to do some events with Lauren. Danny needs to create a new page on the Pogo Trust website. Those dogs are going to be freaking stars. I gotta go. My stop's coming up." After a racket, the line silenced.

Olivia replaced the hot phone on the charger. She turned to see Danny whispering to Ryan, and then to Lauren.

"Do I get an invitation to your book launch, Lauren?" Olivia said.

Lauren smiled and sniffed away tears. "I hate you for being sneaky, but I love you for it. I'll get you back."

"A challenge I fully accept." Olivia turned and snatched up the still-hot phone. "I'm calling Woody with the good news. Ryan only has two arms."

"Wait!" Danny said. "Have a glass of wine first. Let's talk."

Olivia waved away the suggestion and turned her back.

Four long rings on Woody's cell phone tossed her into his voice mail. Olivia hung up and called his office number, figuring he might be working late. Again, Woody's recorded voice kicked in, deflating her good-news buzz.

"Where the hell could he be?" When Olivia turned, three faces stared at her from the other side of the kitchen island.

"He's a busy guy," Ryan said and spread his hands.

Danny shrugged. "Yeah. Really busy."

Lauren dragged her arm over her eyes. "I'm hungry. Let's eat."

~ · ~ · ~

After talking with Palermo, Woody believed himself to be a darned good negotiator. Either that, or he'd had just enough scotch to smooth-talk some redemption into the old don. Ben had been on board with his plan too.

Woody called his kayaking buddy, Casey Carter, a retired military helicopter pilot in Boston, now running a charter excursion business. A hero with a purple heart, Casey still hungered for the excitement of a mission, whether whitewater rapids or white-knuckled flight. He lived to make the impossible possible. At least Woody hoped so at eight o'clock on a Friday night.

"You've got to get me to Allenwood Prison in Pennsylvania," Woody said when Casey picked up.

"You in criminal law now? Or just checking in for a quick holiday?"

"It's a rescue mission. I've got to bust a dog out."

"A dog?" Casey chuckled. "When?"

"Tomorrow. I need a helicopter to help me pick up the dog, and then you have to get me on a charter jet to Portland."

"Maine?" Paper ripped and a pen scratched.

"Oregon."

Casey let out a whistle. "Well, Money Bags, you're lookin' at about five Gs an hour for the jet"—keys tapped on a calculator—"plus another fifteen hundred for the chopper. About seventy grand total with cush. You gotta pay for the jet to come back whether you're on the bird or not."

Now, it was Woody's turn to whistle. He turned and stared out the window, leaving a stretch of silence in the phone cord. He figured the cost in books. *Frankenstein* and *Dracula*. An eerie howl filled his head. The orange glow of a harvest moon beckoned him to stand and gawk. He left his practical side in his chair.

"A nice jet? I want all the amenities . . . for the dog." Woody grabbed the half bottle of lukewarm water that sat on his desk.

"On second thought," Casey said. "I'll only charge you for the fuel to Allenwood because I want in on this. Must be some dog. We'll refuel in New York. If you drive to Norwood Airport in Boston tonight, I can meet you there in the morning. It's about ten miles from Logan. Does the prison have a helipad?"

"On the roof." Woody took a sip of tepid water and paced the length of the carpet, the cord knocking files to the floor.

"Get yourself to Norwood Municipal Airport."

Woody rubbed the back of his neck. "Meet you at seven in the morning?"

"Coffee will be hot. With refueling, we'll need about three hours to get to Allenwood once we lift off. A top-line jet will be waiting for you at Williamsport Airport near the prison after we pick up the dog. Then you're off on the Oregon Trail in the sky. Give me the warden's number, so I don't get shot at when we come in."

Woody recited Ben's number and Casey clicked off. He dashed back to his desk, swiveled his chair to the phone, and called Ben. The warden picked up immediately, having been waiting for Woody's return call.

"We'll be there at ten tomorrow morning. Coming in by helicopter. Casey Carter, the pilot, will call you for final arrangements."

"Fine. I know a driver who can pick you up at that airport out in Portland," Ben said. "I'll coordinate with Casey when he calls. Beauregard will get a good walk in the morning."

"I promised Palermo that he could have the dog in his cell tonight.

Sort of a deal sealer, Ben. After Bo leaves, give Palermo the retriever."

"Not a problem." Ben hesitated. "By agreeing to this, I think our Nicky's making good on that mark he wants to leave behind."

"We all want to leave a mark, Ben. And you're helping me make mine. If I were there right now, I'd shake your hand."

"Not as hard as I'm gonna shake yours, Rainey." Ben's laugh faded as he hung up.

Woody contemplated not sharing his plan, but he thought better of it when he had an image of Olivia not being home when he arrived with Beauregard. Plus, women were funny about surprises. Someone needed to know to prevent any mishaps. Woody called Danny's cell phone.

"Can you keep a secret?" he said when Danny picked up.

"Let me go to Liv's den, so she won't hear," she said. Woody waited at the slide of a door. "Okay. Talk fast."

"I'm flying in tomorrow afternoon with Beauregard, but Liv can't know anything about it."

"Are you serious? You're swooping in like Spiderman? Does Ben know?"

"All on board, and a buddy of mine made all the travel arrangements."

"Who's your friend? Give me his number in case of emergency."

"Got a pen?"

"Go."

Woody recited the number and chuckled. It had been a long time since he'd wanted someone to worry about him, if ever. "With any luck, I'll be at the door by four Pacific. Remember, not a word, but you and Lauren make sure this doesn't put Liv's into an embarrassing situation, if you know what I mean."

"Leave it to me, Lauren, and Ryan. We'll make sure she's all fixed up. I'm so excited I could bust. Travel safe."

"I will." Woody hesitated. "Palermo's behind this too. He's actually a decent guy."

"I know."

The office rested in silence as Woody set the receiver in the cradle. His gaze lingered on the crystal apple under his desk lamp. A flash of refracted rainbow light made him bolt out of his chair.

Woody dashed up the stairs, two at a time. He threw his leather duffel on the bed. A pair of jeans, three white T-shirts, underwear, and a tweed suit jacket launched into the bag. He scrambled for toiletries on the shelves in the bathroom. Screw it. He'd buy the rest in Portland. At the last second, Woody stacked the three books for Olivia and *Five Weeks in a Balloon* on top on his clothes. The zip of the duffel made him pause to appreciate the sound. Then he raced down the stairs to scribble a message to Margie:

You were right. I'm going to Oregon to see Olivia. Have Bonner or Braden take my appointments. Hold down the fort. Wish me luck. I'll call you.

Woody placed the note on Margie's desk, smack in the center, and pulled his black cashmere overcoat from a peg in the front hall. He slung it over his shoulder. Before he locked the front door, he patted his back pocket for the lump of his wallet. A phantom voice gave him permission to load up his credit cards. He stepped back inside and flipped on the porch light. The lock on the front door got a double-check.

The car engine thrummed to life, eager to start the two-hour trek to Boston—less if he had his way. At this moment, he regretted not springing for a convertible. Freedom. A shout to the stars with a frigid wind through his hair. Yes, too cold. Yes, impractical. And no, he didn't give a damn.

As the car hugged the curves of Highway 28 on his way to 95 south, adrenalin coursed through his veins. The role of cool hero had its rewards. Danny had sounded exhilarated. Now he was in on the sisters' ruse with the dog, with an added twist of his own. With a hard shift into overdrive, it was time to see what the car could do. He laughed and thumped the steering wheel.

"Mr. Bo is goin' for a ride!"

Chapter 37

The Rescue Mission

At 9:59 a.m. on Saturday morning, the outline of Allenwood Prison became a geometric puzzle of squares and rectangles connected by a robin's-egg-blue roof. Right on time. The rotors growled as Casey lowered the helicopter and aimed for the red circle on top of the main building. By Woody's calculation, his buddy was going to stick the landing.

A thick metal door swung open from a projection on the roof. Two dark figures emerged, one with blowing chocolate curly fur under a bright yellow vest, the other towering and solid and holding a duffel bag bearing the logo of the Pogo Charitable Trust. Beauregard and Ben Franklin. The warden's suit jacket whipped like sails from the force, but the rest of him remained immovable. The chopper touched down with the precision of a mosquito on a baby's skin.

Woody slipped on his black sunglasses and jumped out, his black overcoat billowing behind him. He ducked to clear the rotors' velocity. The warden's expansive hand pumped Woody's before the exchange of words.

"Ben Franklin," the warden shouted. "You don't look like a lawyer."

"Woodrow Rainey. I don't feel like one," he shouted back. "And you don't look like any picture of Ben Franklin I've ever seen."

The warden's imposing physique couldn't disguise the slight sadness in his broad smile as he passed the leash to Woody. Head down, Ben carried Beauregard's duffel to the chopper. Woody urged the Labradoodle closer to his side to soothe him from the roar of the blades.

Ben stepped back to Beauregard and squatted, his face inches from the dog's. With a light touch, he placed his strong hands on each side of Beauregard's muzzle. "Time well served, big fella. You're going to your new home. Don't forget to give Pogo back his stick." Ben raised his dark eyes to Woody. "It's in his bag."

Beauregard dragged his tongue in long strokes over Ben's spongy cheeks.

"I'll bet you don't get that level of gratitude very often," Woody said over the whirling din.

"You got that right. I'll miss him." Ben's ebony face shined with the dog's saliva as he fished a lumpy, letter-size envelope from his pocket. The corners caught lift as he handed it to Woody. "Palermo wants Olivia to have this."

"I'll get it to her."

Woody tucked the envelope in the breast pocket of his overcoat and trotted Beauregard to the helicopter. The dog hopped inside. Woody turned to Ben and put two fingers to the rim of his sunglasses and jumped into the passenger seat.

The helicopter lifted off and paused to hover twenty feet above the concrete. Casey dipped the nose of the chopper twice, threw the warden his own two-fingered salute, and ascended for the five-minute flight to Williamsport Regional Airport.

Ben returned the gesture by raising his long arm in a slow wave. From the air, Woody followed the warden's diminishing form until it disappeared through the roof's metal door. He hoped one day to sit down for a real conversation with the man over a scotch.

Beauregard stuck his head between the seats, barked, and climbed onto Woody's lap. With his arms around the dog, Woody turned to Casey. "Thanks, man. I owe you one."

Casey chuckled behind his mirrored aviator sunglasses. "Don't thank me yet. Wait till you get a load of the jet."

~ · ~ · ~

At 10:30 a.m., right on time, the door of the Gulfstream G280 sealed the cabin, with only a faint whine of the engines vibrating Woody's seat, the same rumble of anticipation as the day he drove the Porsche off the dealer's lot. A reward for services rendered with no billing statement. He glanced across the aisle to Beauregard, deserving of his own reward for services rendered. From the satisfied expression on the dog's face, nothing less than a charter flight would do.

The modern jet seated ten, but the configuration resembled a sleek living room of cream-colored oversize seats and couches outlined in black piping. The aroma of freshly brewed coffee and unblemished new leather permeated the air of the cabin, warmed to a comfortable seventy-five degrees.

"May I hang your coat, Mr. Rainey?" the flight attendant said. Gold wings on the breast pocket of the young man's navy-blue suit flashed in the late-morning sunlight. Below them, his name badge read, *Vince*. With near-military deportment, precision-cut dark hair framed alert brown eyes. He appeared ready to pick out wine or pick up passengers from a water landing.

"Yes, please."

"Call me Vinny. Anything you need, just say the word."

"Thank you." Woody handed over his cashmere coat and nodded to Beauregard, whose nose busily imprinted smudges on the window. "His mink won't come off."

Vince laughed. "No, but I received three different voice mails with specific instructions about our celebrity passenger: one from Casey Carter about his transport, one from Warden Ben Franklin about the contents of his suitcase, and one from Danielle Eason about the dog's designer eyewear and snack preference—venison chews." Vince reached in his suit pocket and presented Woody with a pair of black plastic-frame sunglasses.

Woody pulled out his own pair from the compartment next to the seat. "I have mine."

"Mrs. Eason requested these. She said you would know what they're for. We'll be taxiing to the runway in a few minutes. Once we get to cruising altitude, there's a nice lunch for you. Greens with sliced roast chicken and avocado, accompanied with a fresh lemon and olive oil dressing. Casey said you eat healthy."

Woody flashed a smile of approval, convinced a conspiracy had been hatched behind the scenes between Casey and Ben with Danny. He'd find a way to repay his friend. "What time will we land in Portland?"

"We're scheduled to land at three o'clock Pacific. About four and a half hours flight time. We cruise at a smooth 550 miles per hour. Perfect day for flying. The air is cold, and the engines are hot to go."

"And the arrangements once we get to Portland?"

"All set. A driver will be waiting. Time to buckle up." Vince glanced at Beauregard. "Both of you."

"Can you store this in a safe place?" Woody pulled his leather duffel from beneath the seat.

"Of course." Vince placed the bag in a side closet and took his place in the jump seat. He drummed his knees, as if thankful for the cushiest job in aviation.

Buckle up. He had four and half hours to anticipate Olivia's reaction when he showed up at her door with Beauregard. This spontaneous trip might finally win her over, but what he hadn't anticipated was the freedom inside his chest, like taking a plunge from an airplane without a parachute. But he had the safety of a tandem partner who had done all the heavy lifting.

Woody patted his seat. "C'mere, Bo."

The dog took a leap across the aisle and landed on Woody's lap.

He pulled Beauregard to his side and extended the seat belt as far as it would go. As Woody tightened his arm around the dog, the buckle finally clicked. From the jump seat, Vince grinned and shook his head. Woody lit up inside at what their image must look like.

The engines escalated to a roar as the plane taxied to the runway. The sleek aircraft gained speed, and within seconds the wings caught buoyancy. Beauregard buried his snout in the crook of Woody's neck at the forward force. Unsure of who was holding who, Woody tilted his head and closed his eyes. Puffs of the dog's breath on his skin radiated gooseflesh down his arms.

Lift-off.

A *thump* stored the wheels as the jet soared at a forty-five degree angle.

When the plane leveled, Woody reached for the controls and eased back the seat to nearly a flat position. He pulled the release on the buckle, and as he did so, Beauregard freed himself with a vigorous body shake and collapsed like scaffolding across Woody's chest. They both let out a groan of relief and settled in.

Chapter 38

Waxworks

Olivia's abduction came on Saturday morning—more like an intervention. Out of nowhere, Danny and Lauren had chipped in to surprise her with a tune-up at the salon. By two thirty, after being soaked, clipped, exfoliated, polished, and waxed, Olivia goose-walked her shiny persimmon-colored toes up the steps to the house in yellow disposable flip-flops, her matching fingernails splayed. The luxurious experience had ended with the torture of multiple waxings. Her crotch burned like a barn fire. The skin on her legs stung. Even her eyebrows and upper lip pulsed from the trauma. The consolation? She'd forced Lauren to get a pedicure. Her sister's toenails resembled a parade of pink Chiclets led by a chunk of Double Bubble.

"I can't get my keys out," Olivia said and elbowed her purse. "I'll ruin my nails."

"My bandage," Lauren said and rocked on her heels in pink spongy thongs.

"Use the other hand."

"My turn to go through *your* purse." Lauren plucked out the keys with her left hand. "Figures they'd be right on top." She held the ring toward Danny to open the front door.

"My nails aren't ready either," Danny said, and swished her hands to prove the point. "Hurry. Ryan's coming here in half an hour. He's at the grocery store."

Olivia spotted her sisters eyeing each other. "What's the occasion?"

Still flapping, Danny inspected the sky. "It's a beautiful fall day, and you've been sequestered with Palermo's manuscript, cooking for one. Ryan wants to barbecue, and you have a better grill."

One-handed, Lauren sighed and struggled to insert the key.

Wincing as she scuffed into the house, Olivia rubbed the small of her back on her way to the kitchen. "I think there's salad in the fridge."

"What's the matter?" Lauren said. "You're walking like you've got a Pilates ball between your thighs."

"The massage chair aggravated my bruise. And the bikini wax didn't help."

"What bruise?" Lauren quickened her heel-steps behind Olivia.

"The one on my butt. I fell on the stairs after I found the ointment for your cut. That's what I get for being in a hurry to save *your* butt."

Lauren glanced at Danny, not an expression of concern but more like panic. "Pull down your pants. Let me check."

"I can't . . . my nails." Olivia leaned over the kitchen island and rested her elbows on the granite. "You do it."

One leg at a time, Lauren pulled down Olivia's yoga pants until they pooled around her ankles. She gasped. "Danny, check this out. We've got to do something."

Olivia knitted her stinging eyebrows. The statement sounded odd. "I'm the one who's black and blue, not you."

Like a feather, Danny ran her finger over Olivia's tailbone. "Ooooh. It's all purplely and mustardy yellow. Not good."

"Definitely not good," Lauren said. "It's the color of one of those mutant heads of cauliflower at the organic store. Danny, go up to Liv's bathroom and get some makeup to hide this."

Olivia stared at the pattern in the stone as Danny raced up stairs. "It'll be fine." As her words trailed behind her sister, Olivia turned her head to Lauren. "Why did you make me get that bikini wax? Feels like I rode home on a cheese grater."

Drawers opened and slammed upstairs. Tubes and bottles clattered.

Lauren snickered. "You're free to be the real you."

"You didn't get one."

"Scratchy is the real me."

Danny bounded back down the stairs and slid to a halt in the kitchen, triumphant. "Zit cover-up." She studied the label. "Wait. Says it covers under-eye circles."

"Perfect," Lauren said. "Slather that baby on."

The tube let out a burp of distress. "Reminds me of a certain sister who made a certain TV appearance." Danny smirked and rubbed the cream in small circles.

"What's even funnier is the view from here. Too bad the cameras aren't rolling now."

Olivia closed her eyes and moaned. "Careful. That's a bad spot. And nobody's ever going to see this view but you guys."

No response.

Olivia had to admit the smooth rub did wonders for her mood.

"Looks like you sat in a bowl of cream of pumpkin soup," Lauren said. "More around the edges, Danny."

"I just changed the sheets this morning," Olivia said. "They'll get dirty."

"They're clean for tonight. You'll be washing your sheets soon enough."

A car door slammed outside. Lauren dashed to the peephole, another unusual occurrence. "Pull up your pants. Ryan's here."

Danny let out a breath of relief and checked her watch. "And so's dinner."

Olivia glanced at the clock on the stove: 2:45 p.m. She adjusted the waist of her pants, being careful not to abrade her nails. Scuffing to the refrigerator, she pulled out a two bags of butter lettuce and inspected their freshness date. "It's a bit early to think about dinner."

Ryan came through the door in jeans and a hunter-green sweat-shirt that read: *Keep Portland Weird. Cops are doing their part.* He placed an oversize canvas tote on the counter and dispensed the contents. Ryan's dark wavy hair framing bright eyes suggested Irish mischief.

"I got chili-mint chicken kabobs, corn on the cob, and hummus," he said. "Here's to eating healthy, right?"

Danny widened her eyes and shook her head.

Ryan paused and held a corn cob like a nightstick. "What?" His gaze shot to Olivia. "I mean—your sister thinks I'm getting a paunch."

Olivia caught a conspiratorial glance between Danny and Ryan.

Throwing her arms up, Lauren walked away. "Ryan . . . My hand to God, I'm going to give you a bruise to match Liv's."

"What are you three up to?" Olivia narrowed her eyes. "You all look like you've been caught shoplifting."

"Nothing," Danny said. "We're trying to cheer you up. You're being a grump."

"I know I get grumpy after a wax." Ryan laughed.

Olivia squeezed her thighs to ease the sting. Then she rubbed her eyebrows.

~ · ~ · ~

The sensation of the jet's decent caused Woody to stir. Twilight sleep held two doors: a return to the abyss of deep slumber or a step toward the light of cognition with flashes of the past and future. The future held more promise. Warmth on his chest countered the cold dampness rimming the neck of his shirt. He opened one eye. Beauregard's head lay on his shoulder, his mouth half open and his upper lip pulled back. A string of drool enlarged the wet spot. Sound asleep. With two fingers, Woody pulled a sticky venison chew from his lap and reached for his glasses. He held his wrist to the window. Focus came with a bonus: 2:45 p.m.

Woody ran his finger down the length of Beauregard's long nose. "Hey, you. Almost time."

The dog offered a jaw-breaking yawn as Woody raised the seat. Within a squint and a blink, Beauregard went on full alert for instructions.

From the galley, Vince tilted his head into the cabin and pointed. "Mount Hood is a stone's throw out your window." His head retreated to become only a voice. "We'll be landing in fifteen minutes, Mr. Rainey."

Fifteen minutes. Olivia's within an hour. Woody dabbed his shirt with a cocktail napkin, a reminder of his need to freshen up for the big moment. Easing from the seat, Woody held up his hand. "Stay. I'll be right back."

Beauregard spread out to fill the warm gap and pressed his nose against the window. The top of the snow-capped mountain floated by with the dog's gaze scaling its peak.

"Hey, Vinny," Woody said and rubbed his chin. "You wouldn't happen to have anything that could help me rejoin the human race? Toothbrush? Shave cream? Soap?"

Vince nodded and handed Woody a Dopp kit, filled with more amenities than he needed.

One step in front of the restroom mirror confirmed what he'd feared: stubble, crow's feet, and a flattened crown of his head. Not quite the fresh start he had in mind. Woody balanced his glasses on the edge of the sink and stuck his whole head under a warm stream of water. The tiny razor posed a challenge for his long fingers but did the job. No nicks. For the first time in his life, he had no plan, no strategy beyond Olivia answering the door. The rest came down to trust. He reached for a towel and dried his hair until his scalp tingled. He studied his face for a second time. Not bad for a free man chained to a helluva story.

The toothbrush picked up speed as the plane descended in earnest. He spit, rinsed, and ran the travel comb through his damp hair. As Woody emerged from the restroom, Beauregard wagged his tail and turned a circle, the pads of his paws squeaking on the leather upholstery.

"Why don't you log the last few minutes in your own seat?"

Bo didn't go.

"Move over then."

Woody wedged himself into the seat, allowing the dog to retain his position at the window. He pulled the belt around them both as the airport came into view. The Columbia River sparkled on one side; spectacular homes graced the forested hills on the other. He'd never been to Oregon, but according to insiders, the Columbia River held top marks as the windsurfing capital. Maybe he'd give it a try. The jet slowed its trajectory to allow an F14 to take off and clear the airspace. Beauregard barked at the fighter jet zooming by in the distance. The Gulfstream resumed its speed and Woody tightened his grip on the dog. Vince nodded from the jump seat.

The wheels hit their mark on the tarmac, and Woody watched them drift outside the lines that guided the jet's taxi to the private aircraft section of the Portland International Airport. An image of the antique oil painting depicting Revere's midnight ride gave Woody courage beneath the adrenalin. Even though he shouldn't, Woody released the buckle as the plane slowed to a stop. Beauregard stood in the aisle and leaned against Woody's legs, waiting for the clamp of his leash.

After Vince handed Woody his overcoat and deployed the staircase, he carried both duffel bags to the open trunk of a waiting black stretch limousine. A town car would have sufficed. The driver closed the trunk and waited at the open back door, appearing to be an Italian linebacker squeezed into a too-tight black suit.

Beauregard glided into the seat as if to avoid the paparazzi. Woody turned and shook Vince's hand. "The best plane ride I've ever had. Thanks a million."

"Good luck, Mr. Rainey. Go get the girl." With that, Vince raised two thumbs, as if signaling Woody that he'd been cleared for his own takeoff. Woody slipped into the car and dipped his head in response. The hulk of a driver shut the limo door.

The leather crunched when the driver joined them in the car and struggled to make a half-turn in the front seat.

"I'm Dommie. Hear you got a plan."

"No, actually, I don't . . . beyond just showing up," Woody said. "Who told you that?"

"Got a call for this job from Ben Franklin, who got a call from a gal named Danny; then she called Casey. We got you covered."

Woody's ribs tightened, beginning to understand the depth of his benevolent conspiracy. It now had a life of its own. Vince had been in on it too. "So . . . how do you know Ben?"

The roll under Dommie's chin inflated and deflated with the nod of his massive head. "Ride's not long enough to dump that story. Suppose we'd better stop at one-a them pet relief areas before we leave the airport."

"Probably a good idea," Woody said, chuckling at the correlation between statements. "Bo's had a long ride."

"Sure he has. I know I can't get off a plane without takin' a wiz." Dommie glanced in the mirror. His eyes betrayed a story.

Woody cracked the window and took in the crisp, clean air and crystal-blue sky. Oregon might hold a story, too. He checked Beauregard's leash as Dommie pulled the limo into a cell phone waiting area rimmed with old-growth Douglas firs.

"I'll walk the dog," Dommie said and retrieved a roll of plastic bags from the glove compartment. "Damn, he's a biggun."

Woody opened the car door. "I'll join you. I need to stretch my legs." With his hands buried in the pockets of his overcoat, Woody strolled next to Dommie as they followed Beauregard to a shaded area beneath the trees. Tiny pine cones and dried needles covered the ground like Christmas mulch. The fresh, sweet scent held the promise of something new.

"Warden Franklin's quite the guy," Woody said, cracking the cap on Dommie's story.

"Known Ben for twenty years . . . Spent eight of 'em living in his house."

Woody pulled a few pine needles from a low-hanging branch and took a whiff. Fresh, like a new start. "Allenwood Prison? You were young. What are you? Mid-forties?"

"Used to be a cab driver in Philly. Worked for Palermo's organization. Delivered more people dead than alive, so to speak."

"Palermo's quite the character. My conversation with him was quite pleasant."

"You wouldn't say that if you worked for him."

"I'm sure not."

"I'm outta that life now because of Ben. Moved out here with my wife, to the land of trees and water. Nettie stuck around when I did my time. Visited me every Friday at eleven o'clock on the button—no exceptions. I counted 'em. Over four hundred." Dommie turned his gaze from Beauregard's sniff of the well-doused tree. "Nettie's a keeper, even when she gets noisy."

"Sounds like quite a woman." Woody tried to hide his smirk. "I think I found a keeper too . . . if she'll have me."

"You got that snooty Yankee accent, but you seem like a decent guy, the outdoorsy type. Dames go for lady-killers who talk funny. You staying?"

"Not sure." Woody's gaze scaled the seventy-foot fir. "The trees are amazing, though, and so is the woman."

Dommie ripped off a plastic bag. "Get her while you can, *mio amico*. What are you gonna say when she opens the door? Can't flub the first line."

"I've been rehearsing. How about this: 'I've missed you and couldn't wait to see you'."

Dommie squeezed his eyes and turned with a grimace. He stuck his hand in the empty bag. "Lame. Kick it up a notch." With a grunt, he stooped to clean up after Beauregard and tossed the bag in a receptacle. "I know all about you, Rainey. You're a smarty-pants lawyer like that Atticus Fitch . . . Finch . . . from . . . " He snapped his fingers.

Woody chuckled. "*To Kill a Mockingbird.*" That original edition had been in his mother's collection too.

Beauregard's gaze shot to Dommie. Believing the finger snap to be an instruction, the dog trotted to the driver's side. Woody listened, curious as to where the conversation was headed. No one had ever described him with such candor.

"Right . . . But you gotta make a grand entrance in an uppity jet, lookin' like one of those alien chasers in . . . " Dommie snapped his fingers again. Beauregard now appeared confused.

"*Men in Black*?" Woody laughed at the image. He glanced at the dog and put a finger to his lips.

"Right . . . in your long black coat and black sunglasses and all that silvery hair, and you're gonna stand at a dame's front door and say, 'I *missed* you'?" Dommie shook his head and let out a high-pitched, arching whistle. "You got the whole package, man." The dog stopped and cocked his head at Woody in frustration. Dommie swung his thick arm. "C'mon, Mr. Bo Regard. We got twenty minutes to come up with a better line for Agent Double-Oh Yankee."

The car glided around the ramp to Highway 205 south. Beauregard gazed out the darkened window, taking in the rolling slopes of evergreens dotted with fiery red maples along the Willamette River. A stacked logging truck rolled by, and the dog stared in amazement. From his reverent expression, Beauregard was trying to figure out how to wrap his mouth around a thirty-foot play stick. Woody patted the dog's back.

Dommie checked the side mirror and moved to the exit lane. "Hey, how old is this gal?"

"Late-fifties," Woody said.

"Good figure?"

"I happen to think so, but she's self-conscious."

"Hmmm . . . complications. Soften up that day-old bread with honey; maybe tell her she's got a nice butt." Dommie nodded at his profound insight into damedom. "The older ones like that, even if they don't got a great ass."

Woody burst out laughing. The tightness in his chest eased. "How about 'you're the most beautiful creature in the whole world, *and* you have a great ass'."

Beauregard whipped his head around and gazed at Woody with doughy eyes. His tail thumped the seat.

"Not you." Woody ruffled the dog's head. "But, yes, you're beautiful too."

"You're getting warmer," Dommie said. "Better get your game on. Five minutes to showtime."

Woody rummaged in his breast pocket for the second pair of black sunglasses. "We can't pull into the dooryard until exactly four o'clock. If we're early, drive around the block."

Dommie snorted. "What the hell's a *dooryard?*"

"A Double-Oh Yankee driveway."

Chapter 39

Showtime

Olivia sensed six eyes boring into her back as she rinsed the salad. Suspicion made her turn. From the kitchen island, three faces were, indeed, watching her spray the butter lettuce with rapt attention. Danny kept glancing at the digital clock on the microwave. So did Lauren, but Olivia figured it might be because the time was getting dangerously close to turning the spigot on her wine box. A weird sensation rippled in her stomach. The air crackled with electricity, as if the house might blow should any one of them light a match.

"I'll help you with that, Liv," Lauren said. "Go upstairs and brush. There's something stuck in your front teeth, like spinach." She elbowed Danny's arm. "Help Liv rinse the salad."

Danny scraped the floor with the counter chair and rushed to take the faucet sprayer from Olivia. "And put some lipstick on."

"It's just you guys," Olivia said. "I'm not out to impress anyone here." Olivia studied her younger sister's brown eyes, their lashes obscenely long. They pleaded for her to not ask a question. She wiped her hands on a kitchen towel. "Shuck the corn."

Ryan stood and opened the door to the refrigerator. "Too soon to start the grill. I'm having a beer." He twisted the cap, took a pull, and held up the bottle. "I think you're beautiful. Don't change a thing."

The comment became Olivia's cue to take action. "That's what all men say when they think you look terrible." She pulled out the clip and fluffed her wild hair. "Sorry, but I haven't been wearing makeup for the last two weeks. Palermo's blind. I don't need to get gussied up for our video calls."

Lauren pointed to the front hall. "Danny and I fixed one end; you go fix the other."

As Olivia limped up the stairs, she became even more convinced her sisters were trying to snooker her. And Ryan was in on it too, whatever *it* was. She inspected her face in the bathroom mirror and agreed with the consensus that she needed a spruce-up. Baring her teeth, nothing showed. She hadn't eaten anything with spinach. Why would Lauren say she had something stuck in her front tooth? After a brushing, she checked again. All clear. At least her eyebrows had calmed down, but her upper lip still had the shadow of a pink arch. A few sweeps of the mascara wand and a glaze of soft peach on her lips restored Olivia to her old self.

The long bong of the doorbell reverberated through the house, erupting a string of barks from Pogo. Olivia straightened and threw the lipstick tube in the drawer. She stepped to the landing. Freesia raced up the stairs and stopped at her feet, then stuck her head through the balustrades. Below, Pogo sat at the front door and whined.

"Can one of you get that?" she called out.

A mad scramble downstairs didn't elicit a response. Lauren and Danny raced to the bottom of the stairs with their cell phones. Ryan leaned an elbow on the banister and raised his eyes to the upstairs landing, offering Olivia a full-of-himself smirk.

"You get it, Liv," Danny said.

"This is your house," Lauren said. "What if it's the God people?"

Ryan shrugged and swept his hand toward the front door.

Olivia huffed down the stairs in her bare feet, being careful not to slip. "You guys are useless."

Peering through the peephole, Olivia sucked in a breath. Her throat tightened at the fish-eyed image of Woody shifting from foot to foot. At his side sat Beauregard in his official Pogo Trust vest. "Are you kidding me?" Her gaze made the rounds. They'd all known.

"Open the damn door." Lauren's eyes turned shiny as she fumbled with the camera on her phone.

"Open it, Liv," Danny said and started to whimper.

Ryan held up his phone and pointed for Danny to do the same.

As Olivia swung open the door, three flashes caught Woody's wide smile behind black sunglasses; Beauregard's long nose supported his own pair. Woody stood in a black overcoat with the unhinged leather leash looped over his arm. With his smile frozen, he reached out his hand until it rested on Beauregard's head.

From the side of his mouth, Woody said, "Say it, Big Guy."

Ruh . . . Ruh . . . Ruh

Pogo's tail thumped the front door as he went nose to nose with Beauregard. Woody removed the dog's glasses. "Bo Go!"

Pogo ran back to Danny's side. Beauregard gazed at Danny, then shifted his eyes to Olivia. Beauregard recognized her. An inordinate amount of cooing at the dog had accompanied her candid conversations with Palermo on the video monitor. She knelt and wrapped her arms around the dog. If only she'd had four arms. She released from Beauregard and took a step over the threshold.

"Wait, wait," Woody said and pumped his hands. "I had a different opening line all prepared. That was a last-minute change."

Grasping Olivia's shoulders, Woody positioned her back into the house and returned to his place on the welcome mat. Trying to suppress the golf ball forming in her throat, she leaned against the doorway. Beauregard leaned against her legs. Tears released the fresh mascara with a swipe under her wet lashes.

Woody took off his sunglasses. "I'm pretty sure I love you. There. I couldn't wait to tell you that. You're a family package deal—I get it—and after having that dog glued to me for the past six hours, I love him almost as much as I love you. And I couldn't have come without the dog because you love him too." He inhaled. "So if you—"

"I'm pretty sure too," Olivia said and stroked Beauregard's ears. The rest of Woody's words had scaled her emotional reserve and raced by, uncaptured.

Lauren started to blubber. Beauregard and Pogo scrambled up the stairs to Freesia. After a hiss and a swipe to establish who was boss, both dogs sat next to the cat with their heads protruding through the rails.

Ryan stepped forward and extended his hand. "Ryan Eason, Danny's husband. Boy, are you a welcome addition. I need an ally. These women are driving me crazy. Get in here, or I'll arrest you for breaking and entering a heart."

As Woody returned the gesture and stepped through the doorway, Olivia ran her hand under his coat, the heat of his damp white T-shirt warming her fingers. The remembered aroma of starch and tropical laundry soap had changed to *eau de dog kennel*. It didn't matter.

Woody released one arm to stick up his thumb to the driver, who pulled the bags out of the trunk of the limo.

"I did good?" Woody's breath warmed her hair.

"You did great." Olivia glanced up to check on Freesia and the dogs, still perched on the upstairs landing. The cat's cheeks puffed as her eyes raised to the ceiling above the front door. Olivia turned and pointed. The black spider raced across the plaster. "There he is!"

Woody's gaze followed the trajectory of Olivia's finger. "I'm on it. I need a stepladder. Somebody get an empty water glass and a stiff piece of paper."

Lauren raced to the kitchen. Danny dashed past her to the mud-room that led to the garage. Olivia kept her eyes locked on the un-suspecting spider. The china in the dining room rattled as Lauren appeared with a wine glass and a postcard reminder for Olivia's next teeth cleaning. Danny banged the ladder through the doorway. Ryan leaned against the banister, enjoying the show.

"Get behind it, Woody," Lauren said, "in case it goes backward."

"Make him run into the glass," Olivia said. "Get in front of it."

"Put it near the crack," Danny said. "That's his hidey hole."

Still in his black overcoat, Woody climbed up the ladder and placed the mouth of the glass over the spider. He slipped the postcard beneath it and descended.

"Well . . . that's another way to go," Lauren said.

"Out of the way." Woody stepped outside, shook the glass, and freed the spider to its new home in the front garden.

Every muscle in Olivia's body relaxed. Her eyes met Ryan's; his face beamed with amusement, then turned thoughtful. Their complicated history flashed between them. He'd been so tenacious in finding Adam's killer, and equally as gentle in breaking the news to her. Ryan's was the last face to melt away when she'd fainted, and his was the first face to clarify when she'd regained consciousness. That bond felt even more significant today.

"I would've done that for you, Liv," Ryan said and nodded toward Woody, "but I'm not on hero duty. He is."

The driver lumbered up the front steps and dropped Woody's and Beauregard's duffel bags in the entryway. "Name's Dommie," he said and nodded in sequence to the assemblage. "I take it this is a one-way trip?"

"So far," Woody said. He pulled Olivia back into his arms and lowered his lips to her ear. "At least long enough of a trip for a change of sheets."

Woody's breath tingled every nerve, making Olivia's arm hair stand on end, since she had no other body hair left. Catching her sister's eye, Lauren started to laugh.

Dommie winked at Woody. "Call me if things go south, Yankee." He leaned around Olivia to inspect her backside. "But you got nothin' to worry about."

Chapter 40
Spiderless

The atmosphere calmed considerably when Olivia stepped outside to give Woody a tour of the garden. She led him to the secluded world of her backyard for a private conversation. Pogo pranced across the lawn, competing with Beauregard for his driftwood stick. Purple asters popped against the gold maple leaves in the late-day sun, but an evening chill would descend before nightfall, maybe even a frost. Hickory-laced smoke filtered through the branches of the cedar tree in the corner of the yard. Ryan had started the grill.

"You know, you and I don't know that much about each other," Woody said.

Olivia chuckled. "Let's start with the quirky stuff. Get it out of the way."

"I make all kinds of noises in my sleep." He paused. "Or so I've been told."

"Me too. Because I snore," Olivia said, "at least that's what Lauren says. Adam never mentioned it, so I think that's one of those gifts of getting older."

Woody tossed Pogo's stick and threw her a sideways glance that buckled her knees. "She's right. You do."

"And as you've discovered, I hate spiders. You'll need to fly back to Portland if I find one."

Pogo dropped the stick in front of Beauregard and barked. "Keep it corralled for six hours, so I can catch a plane—unless I'm already here."

She smirked as Pogo took off running, an invitation for Beauregard to chase. "I don't eat pork or veal, and I'm allergic to curry, penicillin, and fleas."

"Duly noted." Woody nodded for emphasis and scratched his neck. "I don't eat shrimp or crab. Hives. All seafood must be hot, *never* cold."

"I don't work out as much as I should. I'm pudgy."

"Huggable."

"I like to cook at home, so I know what's in my food."

Woody dipped his head in agreement. "I can stir and flip like a pro." He smacked his wet hands of pine needles. "Pet peeves?"

"Hmmm . . . When the books I lend out come back dog-eared."

"Or don't come back at all, right?" He toed a pine cone and scooted it to the edge of the pathway. "I fume when people don't park within the lines of a parking space."

"A therapist would have a field day with that one."

"Probably so."

Olivia thought she could use a couple of lengthy spill sessions of her own. She picked a strand of her dark hair from Woody's white T-shirt. "I'm a neatnik."

He nodded. "Me too. Fresh towels and sheets on Friday are a religion." Woody's gaze scaled the cedar tree. "But we may need to do them sooner."

From the side view, hints of aqua reflected in his irises. The frame of dark lashes made the color glow in the fading sun. "*Never* more than one change of sheets when company comes," she said.

Woody turned to give her the full effect of his eye color. "Or they've overstayed their welcome, right?"

"You're not company." The speed of her pulse doubled. Only one subject could slow it down. "What about Della?"

"Her stuff or her crime? Her ashes are on the mantle in my office."

"Her crime."

"I found the note and the letters my father wrote to her."

Olivia gasped. "Woody . . . Did you read them?"

"No. I thought it might be something we could do together when you come back with me to scatter Mom's ashes at Indigo Lake. Afterward, maybe we can go down to Boston and snoop around."

The way he said it, the trip was a *fait accompli*. The thought of reading the letters, though, tempted her to run inside and purchase the plane tickets. Hunting down his father's family held even more of a lure. "You think there's more to Della's story? My mother's story?"

"I do." Woody lifted her fingers to his lips as if he might eat them.

Olivia's chest burned with those two words, ones that to him surely meant something different. She couldn't have written this situation in a million years, but her mother did, much more eloquently over sixty years ago. And here she was—planning to go to Indigo Lake with a scrumptious man who might change her future.

"There's talk about Ellen's book being made into a movie," she said.

Woody released her hand and scratched his chin. Wheels were turning, but she couldn't discern in which direction. "It's possible that if we dig deeper into the story, we might want to change the ending. You should negotiate to write the script."

"That's a Hollywood insider's game, Woody."

"Not if you make it a requirement for optioning the rights. Want me to have a discussion with your agent? Put it to bed, so to speak? I'm a good negotiator."

"I want a front row seat for that discussion." At this moment, Olivia believed that Woody's Yankee charm would reduce Karen's New York edge to school-girl giggles.

"Speaking of bed," Woody said, "I believe you like to sleep on the left side."

"I made an exception that night with you, only because I didn't know what I was doing." Olivia had an image of Woody roundtabling with all parties: Freesia having to relinquish her position as *Top Cat* to take the middle spot; Beauregard happy to sprawl across the foot.

"Objection. You were quite accomplished." He shook his finger. "And the matter of the bed position should've been entered into evidence earlier. We need a judge's ruling, or at least arbitration by an objective third party on that particular point."

"Lauren can decide. She has an opinion and a gun." She pointed to Pogo barreling toward them for another round of throw and retrieve, with Beauregard hot on his heels. "Here comes double trouble, Counselor."

Pogo sat and dropped the stick, his eyes pleading Woody for more. Beauregard offered a whine-talk combo.

Pogo! Bo! Leave them alone. Danny's voice skipped across the lawn to echo in the trees. Beauregard snatched the stick and bolted to the side patio. Olivia caught a glimpse of her younger sister's head retreating from the corner of the house.

"Now I want to see where you write," Woody said and squeezed her shoulders.

Olivia led him to the back patio and threw open the double French doors.

"*Voilà.* The den."

Woody slipped off his loafers and stepped inside with a dreamy expression; awe, envy, or sadness, she couldn't discern. Olivia was somewhat embarrassed by the stuffed shelves of first editions that lined the room, given Woody's association of old books with his mother. Her desk, littered with notes for Palermo's manuscript, lay in shambles. Two ginger leather club chairs faced each other in the center of the room, flanked by side tables with green-shaded lamps. Woody reached over and clicked one on. The den glowed in warm light, distinguishing the oldest books by the glint of their gold-embossed lettering.

Olivia kicked off her sandals and shifted in the doorway for the verdict. Woody nodded and thrummed his fingers over the spines of her collection. They lingered over the Steuben apple tucked into its own space next to *Indigo to Black*.

"You were right. It's exactly the same. I kept Della's apple because of you," he said and pulled out *Tex-Mex Nights*. "I haven't read your romance books."

"You probably wouldn't like them." Olivia stepped to the shelf dedicated to her earlier novels. "*Tex-Mex Nights* and *South of the Borderline* are my two last romances. No more." She shrugged and handed him one with an oil-muscled Latin man on the cover. "They paid for my kitchen." Internally, she added that they had gotten her through Adam's death.

"Writing these books kept you company." Woody threw her that side glance of his, the one that gave her a head rush.

Self-conscious, Olivia pointed to the desk. "I'm focused on the mob memoirs now."

Woody put on his glasses and gazed at her through the lenses. "Palermo helped to make this trip happen. I convinced him to release Beauregard and take another dog. He was quite the gentleman."

"Did you get to meet him in person?"

"No time. We talked over the phone."

"I'll introduce you on our next call. It's next week. I'm sure you'll still be here. Palermo will know your voice, make no mistake."

Woody straightened. "Where'd you put my coat?"

"In the hall closet."

"There's something I'm supposed to give you from Ben. It's in the breast pocket. And then I'm going to tell you some of my own news."

Olivia studied the features of his face. His dark brows knitted; iridescent-blue eyes drew her in for more, but she didn't want any news that might spoil the mood.

"I think the grill's ready," she said.

"It's fine. Ryan's got dinner under control."

Olivia dashed to the front hall closet and slid Woody's cashmere coat from its hanger. She buried her face in the collar and closed her eyes, allowing herself an adolescent moment. Squishing the breast pocket, she felt the lumpy contents that invited her to pry, but she resisted. She had no plan for any of this. Self-conscious, she carried the overcoat like a royal robe to the den. Woody was sitting in one of the leather chairs.

"Here it is," she said.

Laughter outside. Barks. The bang of Pogo's knobby ball against the side of the house.

Woody placed a copy of *Tex-Mex Nights* on the side table. He reached for the coat and rummaged in the pocket. A thick envelope extended in her direction.

Olivia tore the flap and glanced at Woody. His eyes held no information. She believed he truly didn't know what the envelope contained. Six flash drives cascaded from the envelope and bounced on the Oriental carpet. She left them scattered at her feet as she pulled out the white slip of paper.

Jiggly scrawl sloped downhill in overlapping letters, almost like a Spirograph drawing. Olivia stepped to her desk and searched for an extra pair of reading glasses. Woody stopped her and held out his tortoiseshell ones. She slipped them on, more comfortable in them than she anticipated, and pictured herself a lawyer, her head swimming with wisdom, principles, and convictions. She struggled to make out the words of Palermo's writing as she read the note aloud:

"'Every man wishes . . . for a queen to hold his story. You, Olivia, have . . . good hands. Take care of . . . my General B.'"

For one so ruthless, Palermo's words were eloquent and heartfelt. She raised her eyes from the note. "He knew. He knew all along that Beauregard wasn't Pogo."

"Yes, he did," Woody said.

"General *B* is for Beauregard . . ."

Woody's face from behind his own lenses added depth to his

features. He'd been studying hers too. She broke the electricity and lowered her magnified gaze to the carpet with new eyes. Her freshly polished toes corralled the flash drives into a regimented gathering. "I'll bet these hold all the offline recordings of Palermo, maybe Tullio, Rizzo, and Leonetti too."

"He's dying. He wanted to make sure you had what you needed." Woody smoothed the sides of his hair, distracted. "Is my bag still by the front door?"

With a vacant nod, Olivia stared at the note from a lawyer's perspective. Woody dashed from the den. Palermo's impending death would speed forward the writing of his memoir, but without the same sense of urgency. Everything the don had to say was now sitting at her feet.

Zip *of the duffel.* Clink *of ice in a glass.* Whoosh *of water in the kitchen sink.*

Woody returned with four books in hand. "Catherine sent the rest to an auction house in New York," he said. "They'll be sold next month." He presented the hardbound books like confidential files, their pedigree wafting to her in an instant. "I held these back from Della's collection because I think they hold a piece of you—and some of me—in the pages."

Olivia's fingers trembled as she exchanged Palermo's words for the books, to be given a new life in her library. She studied the spines and raised her eyes, incredulous. "Della had these sitting in her house . . . all those years? *Little Women? The Big Sleep? A Study in Scarlet? Five Weeks in a Balloon?* These are worth a fortune."

"All first editions, like you described. The last one's special. Catherine thinks the others will bring in over half a million." With two fingers, Woody slipped his glasses from Olivia's face and studied Palermo's note as if it were a binding legal contract. He set the paper next to the glass-shaded lamp. He sat and gestured to the second chair across from him.

Olivia sat with the books on her lap. When he took both her hands in his, the cartilage in her knees turned to gel.

"And every queen needs a king to protect the story she writes," he said and squeezed her fingers. "But I think you've still got some issues about Adam to work out, Liv."

A glimpse of the world through Woody's glasses had proved what she'd long denied: she had been selfish in the process of mourning Adam. Grief had become too comfortable, too exclusive, too lonely.

"I know. Hearing you say it, proves your point. You have some issues about Della too."

"I'm filing a continuance on that subject." He twisted the thick gold band on her ring finger, confirming its symbolism for infinity. "We have to do something about this. I'm a pretty competitive guy, but I don't stand a chance against a legend with a perfect win record"—he raised his eyes—"and a dedicated fan base."

After an uncomfortable silence, Woody took the books from her and placed the stack next to Palermo's note.

Olivia's lips went dry with the truth of his words. "I'll bet Asher won over Della's heart in those letters."

"You won mine in phone calls. But there's one major difference."

"Continue," she whispered.

"Unlike my father, I *can*, Liv. I showed up. I'm here."

Olivia set her hands on Woody's cheeks and pulled him forward. His lips were warm and alive. Real. Then her eyes widened in panic as Woody's hands moved down her sides. When he pressed the small of her back, she winced and gritted her teeth.

"Owww . . ."

Woody pulled away. "What's the matter?"

Without elaborating, Olivia stood and turned around. She lowered the waist of her pants and waited for his reaction.

The tip of Woody's forefinger lingered in its trace of the ragged purple, yellow, and fake cover-up outline on her tailbone.

"Who did this to you?"

"Lauren and Danny. They put all that stuff on."

"No. The bruise."

"It wasn't the mob, if that's what you're thinking. I slipped on the stairs when Lauren cut her hand."

After a suggestive pause, Woody burst out laughing. He wheezed to catch his breath and relaxed back in the club chair.

"Uh-oh," Lauren called out. "He found it." A collective roar of hysterics erupted from the kitchen, followed by a double dose of barks echoing through the house.

Olivia raised her eyes to the ceiling. "Not funny, you guys!" Turning to Woody, she could only offer him an embarrassed grin. "The price of saving sisters."

Pogo and Beauregard stopped short in the den doorway, their faces drooping like jilted beaus. Two jealous pouts volleyed from Woody to Olivia.

"I warned you we were a package deal," she said and pulled up her pants.

Woody held out his arms. "C'mere."

Slipping onto his lap, Olivia nuzzled Woody's neck. Within two strides and a jump, Pogo and Beauregard stretched over her knees to lick Woody's face.

Author's Note

So many of *Indigo Lake*'s locations in New Hampshire are real, and they hold my childhood in their palms. The aroma inside the Yum Yum Shop in downtown Wolfeboro is a bakery that can only be appreciated with a deep inhale when you open the door. Black's Gift Shop still holds court on Main Street and deserves a long browse.

The Wolfeboro Inn and Wolfe's Tavern are excellent choices for making a stay in Wolfeboro special. In the sixties and seventies I spent summers on Lake Winnipesaukee at Camp Kehonka and swam in Mirror Lake. My grandfather would throw down the top on his butter-yellow Impala convertible and, with my hair in a tangle, short the curves of Route 109A to Wolfeboro for an ice cream at the Dockside.

Indigo Lake is a fictional lake in the book. And while the structure of the old general store in Tuftenboro still stands, there is no Alten's Books at that location. Wishful thinking. Baxter Fields is the fictional name for a real neighborhood of homes built on a portion of my grandparents' farm in Tuftenboro. The original home still stands intact. The tiny one-room schoolhouse sits down the road. It has been lovingly restored.

A trip to the Mob Museum in Las Vegas supplied a wealth of inspiration for the fictional character of Nicky Palermo. He became an amalgam of colorful scoundrels, one of which is still languishing in prison. The real stories are chilling and thrilling for a writer in search of juicy details beyond the placards.

My research of therapy-dog programs in prisons revealed a gap that I sought to fill in fiction. While inmates are used for the training of dogs to assist the disabled outside the prison walls, I found few internal programs that support the inmates themselves as they age. Pogo and Beauregard had to swoop in to fix to that *faux* "paw" in fiction.

The Dushane sisters will be back in the final book of the trilogy, *Indigo Legacy* . . . stay tuned!

About the Author

Courtney Pierce lives in Milwaukie, Oregon, with her husband and bossy cat. She became transformed by the magic of fiction from a theater seat, observing what made audiences laugh, cry, or walk out the door. Following a twenty-year career as an executive in the Broadway entertainment industry, she published a trilogy of literary magical realism, *Stitches, Brushes,* and *Riffs*. The first two books of her latest trilogy series, *The Executrix* and *Indigo Lake*, follow the middle-age antics of the Dushane sisters. She has also published two short stories: *1313 Huidekoper Place*, for the 2013 NIWA Short Story Anthology *Thirteen Tales of Speculative Fiction*, and *The Nest*, for the Windtree Press anthology *The Gift of Christmas*. As a monthly contributor to *Romancing the Genres*, her blog articles showcase life as a baby boomer.

Courtney is a member of Willamette Writers, Pacific Northwest Writers Association, Sisters in Crime, and is on the board of the Northwest Independent Writers Association. Her books are published under Windtree Press, an indie author collective.

Follow Courtney's books at her website: **courtney-pierce.com**

Facebook: https://www.facebook.com/courtney.pierce.7505
Twitter: @CourtneyPDX
Windtreepress.com

Also by Courtney Pierce

Fiction

Indigo Lake
The Executrix
(The Dushane Sisters Trilogy)

Riffs
Brushes
Stitches
(The Stitches Trilogy)

Short Stories

1313 Huidekoper Place
(2013 NIWA Anthology of Speculative Fiction)

The Nest
*(The Gift of Christmas Anthology–*Windtree Press*)*

39732908R00185

Made in the USA
Middletown, DE
24 January 2017